SANDCASTLES, TALL SHIPS AND VANITIES

A Novel

WILLIAM HITE

ISBN 978-1-64258-944-3 (paperback)
ISBN 978-1-64258-945-0 (digital)

Christian Faith Publishing, Inc.
832 Park Avenue
Meadville, PA 16335
www.christianfaithpublishing.com

Printed in the United States of America

There is a vanity which is done upon the earth; that there be just *men*, unto whom it happeneth according to the work of the wicked; again, there be wicked *men*, to whom it happeneth according to the work of the righteous: I said that this also *is* vanity.

—Ecclesiastes 8:14, KJV

Book 1

Please, Not Another Shooting War

Two Families

And when Joshua heard the noise of the people as they shouted, he said unto Moses, *There is* a noise of war in the camp.

—Exodus 32:17, KJV

Chapter 1

The Worsham Family

Mary Alice Worsham
January 1762
Near Williamsburg, Virginia

"January. Midafternoon. Bitter cold. Wind howling." Mary Alice Worsham, a young woman in her mid-twenties, all the while complaining to herself, opened the front door of her home. "Who would come calling on such a day?" A draft of cold air pushed its way into the foyer. "Well now, two uniformed British gentlemen. And standing on my front porch. A pair of Royal Navy officers, a commodore and captain. My. My. My."

Sure enough, she thought, *I reckon this: I fairly ken these British uniforms. Navy blue now, is it? What would ye be but the bloody navy, eh?*

The two men smiled briefly in the cold, making shuffling sounds with their icy boots. Each man pulled the corner of his hat. Smiles faded to terse seriousness.

Mary Alice's thoughts came quickly, a jumble in her mind. *The little one is cute—even handsome. Yes. He is handsome. And a captain to boot—Captain "Cute."* She felt a warm rush of attraction for him. Strength and physical magnetism are in this good-looking captain. *Damn, I like him. The other one, the commodore—well, a bit too much girth about his middle—probably huff and puff in the bed too.*

7

"Gentlemen … will you come inside?" She spoke hurriedly, pausing only to tender a warm smile. "It's quite cold here on the front stoop." *And you'll be freezing your bollocks off right about now,* she almost blurted aloud. *Well, my dearest Mary Alice,* she thought— as if she were having a conversation with herself. *You must be a Tory. A Virginia "patriot" would say "balls," not "bollocks." But the important thing—is the captain married? He wears no wedding band. What harm would it do now for a nice widow like myself to have a gentleman friend? God. I could do worse!*

"Har-harrumph. Please excuse our uninvited intrusion, milady," responded the portly commodore, as if he had heard her thoughts. "Ah—what a stately farm manor you have—and facing the James River too." He turned toward the river as if to emphasize his statement.

All the manors face the river. Well—

"Harrumph." He cleared his throat again. "I'm Commodore Nigel Cornwallis-Phipps. And this gentleman here with me is Captain Philip Pocock—a good man himself."

She nodded, politely returning the gesture. "Welcome to Worsham Manor."

"I've a sealed letter for you from King George himself." Again, it was Commodore Cornwallis-Phipps doing all the talking. "And I have a verbal message from First Lord of the Admiralty, George Grenville. You are Mistress Mary Alice Moore, are you not? Sister of the late Midshipman Richard Moore …"

He paused, catching his breath.

"Of His Majesty's Navy?" Cornwallis-Phipps pulled his kerchief from his sleeve and rubbed his nose. "A brave young lad if ever there was one—that one."

She nodded yes for the commodore and thought, *Pink cheeks and fog breath. What's the "king's letter" all about?* "Come inside before you catch your death in this icy wind," she said. "I'll have my housekeeper fetch some tea. Give us your hats and coats. You'll be warmer for it, I promise. You brought a message to me from His Majesty?"

Shortly her guests stood in the foyer with the door closed against the cold.

She squinted as if she caught a glimmer—a stark memory—from her past and said, "Aye. I am Mary Alice Moore." There was a catch in her voice, almost a tremor. She continued, "Presently, Nigel—"

She stopped abruptly in midsentence, gazing for a moment into Commodore Cornwallis-Phipps's eyes. Then, rubbing her hands together, she began anew.

"May I call you Nigel?"

Cornwallis-Phipps nodded his approval. "Certainly, milady."

"As I was saying, Nigel. My name was Moore. Now it's Worsham." She pulled a sash that rang the housekeeper's call bell. "Wait a moment. Allow us to hang your hats and greatcoats. And stand on that runner to kick the ice off your boots—makes it easier to tidy up."

A rustling in the foyer announced the entrance of a young woman.

Mary Alice turned to greet her. "Miss June." She gestured toward the woman. "Gentlemen, meet my housekeeper. This is June Hopkins ... herself a Tory, I promise you. And Miss June is single, if that means anything to either of you."

These are troubled times, Mary Alice thought. *We are colonial Americans. Of course we—I—do love Mother England and certainly think the colonies should belong to the Crown. That makes us Tories. But not everyone hereabout is loyal to the king. We Tories must be especially mindful of that—such as when one forms new relationships with people, especially with men. Yes, these peculiar Virginia Yanks ...*

Strange. There is a sort of "Yankee mystique" developing hereabout. These Virginia people are British in origin for the most part. Well, they could be from practically any country—even France, for that matter. But then they become "Yanks" in a fortnight or so. Something grows on them. Sure, some were actually born in Virginia, but it's all the same. From wherever they hail, a brief glance or three at their reflections in a looking glass and they say, "Well, I'm going to the Americas," or "I'm going to the colonies." And here they be. These Yanks detest strong government—really resent it. They are frustrated with taxes, laws, and rules imposed by England—that sort of thing. They might even resort to violence at some point in time. If they do, Virginia surely will be the lynchpin. And here I be.

Yanks—funny, they call themselves "patriots," don't call themselves "Yanks." I think Yanks actually worship freedom—as if freedom were a goddess or something. Go it on your own, without the Crown, and there be too many chances to make mistakes. What would happen if there were no Royal Navy—or army—to call upon for help?

God save the king.

"June, our guests are Royal Navy officers. I want you to meet Captain Pocock and Commodore Cornwallis-Phipps."

June gave a curtsy—all ruffles, muslin, and lace. Again, the guests tugged one corner of their hats before handing them over, first the coats then the hats—officers to the very end.

"Bring tea and biscuits, missy, please. We'll be in the parlor." Mary Alice continued her story, leading the way toward the sunny side of her home: "So Moore was my maiden name when I lived in Halifax—the Halifax in Nova Scotia, that is. I married a Virginian. He passed away. I'm a widow now."

Mary Alice shrugged her shoulders then told them why. "In 1760, General Sir Jeffrey Amherst was commander in chief of British North America. My husband, Brigadier Charles Worsham, himself on the general's staff, helped England secure Canada. After the Montreal victory, Charles retired his commission and came home to half pay and our farm. That year he caught a fever and died—God love him." She took a deep breath. "I believe in my heart 'twas the rigors of war did him in. He was a tired man when I got him back … tired … wasted."

I couldn't even get a rise out of him, she thought.

Nigel slapped his tunic with the palm of his right hand. "We are sorry to hear of it, milady. Your family has given much, to be sure. Brigadier Worsham, what? God, what a family."

Mary Alice smiled, addressed Captain Pocock, "And your name is Philip. Shall I call you Philip?" *He would not like Shorty, I'll wager.*

"At your pleasure, milady."

"Then I shall. And a bonnie name 'tis for a gentleman."

"I say, milady. Were your ancestors, Scots?" Nigel asked. "My sainted mother, rest her soul, was a Scot. She was, as you say, 'bonnie.'" *And a bit plump round the middle, I'd fancy.*

"It's my blond hair gives me away," she said, a blush on her cheeks. *Gives me away, indeed. Perhaps I can be had, but I am not cheap.* "English they were, Nigel. English—descended from Vikings. From fair Nordic raiders, to be sure." Mary Alice smiled as she watched their expressions.

* * * * *

In the parlor, Pocock and Cornwallis-Phipps warmed hands and backsides in front of the fireplace for a few moments. Mary Alice seated herself in a comfortable Windsor chair and waited until Cornwallis-Phipps stepped away from the fire.

"Here gentlemen," she said, gesturing toward an upholstered settee. "It's time to take a load off your feet. Come rest a spell."

"Do you know the circumstances surrounding your brother's death, milady?" said Cornwallis-Phipps as he and Pocock seated themselves.

"Perhaps you have information I do not know," Mary Alice said. "Please tell the story again." Her cheeks blushed warmly. *Oh, Captain Pocock is an attractive man.* She focused her attention on Cornwallis-Phipps with difficulty.

"Aye, your brother died bravely," said Cornwallis-Phipps. "You see, he gave his life to protect our Admiral Rodney who was with Fox and Anson, part of a squadron headed for the first battle off Cape Finisterre. In that battle there were many prizes and much glory to gain by some. Of course, Rodney was not an admiral in those days. However, his time was coming. Your brother saw to that."

Cornwallis-Phipps paused for a moment to look around the room. Three young boys stood near the parlor door, eavesdropping.

"Milady, could we speak with you in private?"

"Gentlemen, these are my three sons," Mary Alice informed them. "The two oldest are Samuel and John. The youngest is Matt." She stood briefly, directing her attention to the boys who gathered in a group near the doorway. "Boys, would you go outside to play? Put on your hats and coats, mittens, scarves, and overboots. It certainly is cold today. I'll call you back inside after a bit." *Oh dear. Just look at the disappointment in their faces.*

* * * * *

As the boys left the house, June brought a silver hostess tray into the room then served sweet nutmeg biscuits, raisin teacakes, and steaming tea to all.

Cornwallis-Phipps leaned forward. "Let's see now," he said. "Where was I?" He hesitated a moment, staring at the burning logs in the fireplace, munching a teacake, then continued. "I am directed by the Admiralty to inform you of your late brother's great bravery and distinctive service to the Crown. It was the battle off Cape Finisterre in May of 1747. Your brother was midshipman with Rodney on the *Eagle*. They were in a squadron with Commodore Fox and Admiral Anson chasing a French merchantman prize. Rodney's ship soon fell in with the French man-of-war, the *Neptune*. In the furious battle that followed, with her wheel shot away, *Neptune* drifted clear.

"As the ships separated, a mast fell over onto *Eagle*. A crazed French marine hacked away at Neptune's rigging, cut a rope from the broken spars, and swung across to *Eagle*, his cutlass aimed directly for Rodney's gut."

Cornwallis-Phipps stopped, shifted uncomfortably.

"Your brother," he continued, "who was on the quarterdeck, pushed Rodney aside and took the full thrust of the Frenchman's cutlass himself. He died protecting Rodney's life. And in a way, he died protecting *Britannia* … the British Empire—kingdom, whatever."

"That was fifteen years ago," Mary Alice pointed out.

"I don't know, of course, why Rodney waited so long before contacting you, milady," said Cornwallis-Phipps. "He undoubtedly looked for the proper opportunity, duty first, that sort of thing. I imagine the man was quite busy. One cannot post such a letter as your letter from the king. Such a letter is delivered *in person*. I'm certain you understand. Could be it was fifteen years before he returned to Virginia. I do not know. He was detained in Halifax—as you just stated, *the Halifax in Nova Scotia*—in 1758 with his entire ship … the *Dublin* … sick, too sick to join Admiral Boscawen in the assault on the French-Canadian fortress at Louisbourg. Evil spirits, bad air in the sailor's quarters, or some such damn thing. While he was there, he did find out about your brother's family … about you, your sons here in the Virginia colony. At that time, as you well know, George II was still our beloved king."

Cornwallis-Phipps gave an odd look to no one in particular and rubbed his nose. After a short pause, he continued. "Rodney notified his interest, his sponsors, one of whom is George Grenville, concerning a request to repay your brother's endowment of noble sacrifice in some manner. Powerful man with political influence, that one. Very powerful man." Cornwallis-Phipps pursed his lips.

"By the by, milady—Rodney unquestionably was a 'king's letter boy' himself. Today he is rear admiral of the blue. You may know, rumor has it that King George II was Rodney's godfather. The sealed letter from George III is as such an introduction for one of your sons. Perhaps the letter is testimony to the truth of the godfather matter. I don't know. I mean, the letter probably 'speaks words,' and without making so much as a blasted sound. '*Res Ipsa Loquitur*.' Latin—*the thing speaks for itself*—what? At any rate … *mute*. And George III fulfilled Rodney's wishes, now, wouldn't ye say?" He picked at his nose with his thumb.

"May I see the letter?" Mary Alice asked. *So many Georges*, she thought but said nothing.

"Certainly, milady. Here." Cornwallis-Phipps reached for the pocket inside his tunic. "It bears the king's Great Seal," he said, passing the letter to her.

A king's letter, is it? Mary Alice examined the letter for a few moments, turning it over in her hands. *The king's Great Seal is impressive. No doubt it is a general "To Whom It May Concern" letter. I will not open it. There is no need. Perhaps one of my sons will want to invoke this letter—will see the need. Young Matt would be my guess. Such fearlessness and steadfastness in that one. Him holding burlap pokes while his brothers caught rattlesnakes with forked sticks and put them in it. The boys traded live snakes—which the Indians ate—for beautiful hand-made Indian moccasins made from various animal skins.* A shiver ran down to her backside. God. She dropped the letter to her lap and looked at the smaller of the two men.

"Tell me, Commodore," she said. "What of your captain here? Has he nothing to say?" *Captain Cute—you better watch yourself because I want you.*

Captain Pocock answered her. "Well, yes, milady, I'm really along for the ride."

"And because he loves the Navy." This time it was Cornwallis-Phipps who spoke. "But I think he's bloody well sick of the ride. The roads hereabout shake the bones and bruise one's backside mercilessly."

Mary Alice nodded, her brow furrowing with sympathy. "Can you gentlemen stay the night?"

"The captain might want to," Cornwallis-Phipps responded. "If I hadn't business this evening in Williamsburg myself, I might. I must meet with the colonial governor on a matter. And there is the business of the twelve soldiers with the coach—not to mention the coachman. I could stop tomorrow and recover Captain Pocock, if he's a mind to stay the night here, that is. There's a lady I could see in Williamsburg under those conditions."

"You mean, if the captain stays and you go on ahead?" said Mary Alice. "All are welcome to stay if you want, though some would have to sleep in the barn. What about you, Captain? Will you stay the night with me?" She winked at Philip.

Cornwallis-Phipps straightened his coat and cleared his throat. "Harrumph. Won't let me smoke my cigar in the landau anyway. Says it's a fire hazard or some such damn thing."

"And George Grenville?" Mary Alice inquired.

"He asked me to extend to you his condolences along with his warmest, best wishes, milady," said Cornwallis-Phipps, looking at the floor and rubbing his nose.

"I will stay the night, Mary Alice," said Pocock, "if you will call me Philip."

"Very well, Philip. Have someone fetch your things from the coach. You visit with me this evening. We can think of something to pass the time, certainly.

"For now, rest yourselves a bit and be ready for the evening meal in about two hours. Then go about your merry way—or stay if that pleases you."

* * * * *

Mary Alice passed round the various serving bowls and platters of food for second helpings.

"What with your social calendar so full, Commodore, you should eat heartily."

Pocock raised his eyebrows. "Milady," he asked, "where in heaven's name did you acquire Indian corn—maize—of this delicate quality in the middle of winter? Why, it's cold enough outside to freeze the ears off a prime billy goat. This corn seemingly was cut from the cob this very day, was it not?"

Do you really want to talk about corn, you rascal? Mary Alice thought, all the while smiling. "Philip, the settlers we call Pennsylvania Dutch put away Indian corn for the winter. It's dried in some fashion, I believe. It's cut as you say, but in the summer when vegetables are in season. Many times through the winter we enjoy the product of their different methods of food preservation. Peddlers carry these goods across the colonies." *Good lord, Mary Alice,* she heard her conscience complaining. *Do you have to be so damned technical, so boring?*

"Indeed? What—or rather *who* are the Pennsylvania Dutch?" Pocock asked. "German immigrants, I presume?"

Commodore Cornwallis-Phipps seemed content to listen as he enjoyed the dinner.

Oh, you are the cute one, Philip, she thought. *I can see the tip of your tongue when you make the* th *sound. You have no idea how attractive you are, do you?* "Yes. German, Swiss, as well as actual Dutch. Undoubtedly, by now, those Pennsylvania Dutch communities consider themselves Yanks, same as most others do. Or worse … patriots!" Mary Alice spoke the word with scorn, even hatred, in her voice. "Immigrant customs survive, witness the food preservation skills. However, ethnic nationality, most likely, is lost in the shuffle. Why, anybody can be a bloody patriot. No lineage required."

"And a wonderful beef pot roast 'tis." This time it was the commodore speaking. "Tell me, that is preserved as well?"

"No, this is a working plantation, one of several along the *James*. We share such things, at a reasonable cost, that is. One plantation will butcher pork, another beef. We've our very own cooperative and a butcher's wagon that comes round on Tuesdays. Sure, an occasional shopping trip to Williamsburg can be productive as well. We keep a full larder."

"An equitable arrangement that," Cornwallis-Phipps said, wiping gravy from his mouth. "A country butcher shop on wheels, rather handy, I should say."

* * * *

Later, with the meal finished and the last butter-and-honey biscuit washed down with warm buttermilk, the boys left the table to tend to chores. Commodore Cornwallis-Phipps and his entourage left to continue their trip to Williamsburg.

Mary Alice addressed Philip, a keen look in her eyes. "Tell me, Captain, how is it you never married?" *You wear no ring. Surely you're not married.*

"Milady—"

"Call me Mary Alice, Philip."

"Yes. Well, I never married because there is no room in my Navy life for a family. Perhaps someday marriage and a family will come to pass."

"Tell me, then, of your gunnery drills at sea. The broadside, tell me about that."

"Nothing much to say there, Mary Alice. The drill is for speed and efficiency, that sort of thing, thoroughness, accuracy and such, as well as repetitiveness."

"The old British Navy's virtuous standard, one gives one's all, and one stands by to come about and do it again if need be," she replied, smiling.

"Aye."

"And your limp. You have a slight yet noticeable limp. Were you injured in a battle at sea?"

"Oh no. I have gout, my dear. Most assuredly, gout is aggravated by the rum ration we drink at sea. It's nothing more than a bloody nuisance. You know of the rum ration, do you not? We mix a *tot* of rum with our drinking water, and the whole affair goes better. Rum drives the devils out—undoubtedly."

He paused for a moment, pensively.

"Gout?" He continued. "Well, some acquire it as a badge of service, something like that."

Mary Alice looked across the table at Philip. "And you came along with Cornwallis-Phipps simply for love of the Navy, is that so? Tell me, did the Admiralty send you to chaperon the commodore?"

"The commodore, dear lady, arranged for the carriage. This is his trip. Cornwallis-Phipps is an old friend. I am on holiday and about to be reassigned to a splendid warship—captain of the line. Cornwallis-Phipps invited me. I simply accompanied him. Seemed an entertaining thing to do."

"You could be carousing with the girls in Baltimore, or perhaps Williamsburg."

"No, my lady. I'm a captain. It's expected I behave myself better than that."

"By whom?"

"By myself." He paused for a moment. He continued, again with a pensive look on his face, "And by my benefactors, my *interest*."

Well, I am interested in you, Captain Cute. I am, indeed. She smiled and said, "My house servants are preparing a warm bath in the guest bedroom for you, Philip. It's quite cold in that bedroom, colder still in mine. The boys will be asleep by nine o'clock. Come to my room at that time." She paused. "Come straightaway to my bed. We'll keep each other warm through the night. I want to see at least one British broadside, if you please."

Philip, clearly at a loss for words, hesitated a moment, then smiled and left the room to obey.

Through the night, wind howled outside, pushing the cold through the shuttered windows and deep inside the house. Mary Alice and her new lover, at play in the front bedroom, noticed the chilling drafts not at all. They were warm, and it was warm for Philip as he pushed inside his newfound friend. He showed her three of his best broadsides before morning arrived, and it became time to return to the guest room. She helped him into his nightshirt, slapped him on the backside, and sent him on his way.

There would not be any more children. Something had happened to her insides when she delivered Matt.

Mary Alice lay quietly in her bed after Philip left the room. She could still feel him inside her.

"Don't you let anyone call you Shorty, Philip," she had said to him, laughing. "You're long and strong on that account—firm and bonnie."

"Aye, Mary," he answered, laughing back. "You being the one that knows, and all."

No doubt, she thought, *Philip will be tired when Cornwallis-Phipps comes to fetch him late by the light of day. Oh, but it was worth it. And I will see that one again.*

Chapter 2

Empty Nest

Mary Alice Worsham
Spring, 1770
Yorktown, Virginia

MARY ALICE STOOD ON THE pier beside the York River estuary not far from Yorktown. A British Navy longboat alongside the pier rocked in the wavelets. She threw a small pouch of silver coins to the older seaman in charge—the coxswain. In addition to him, two able-bodied seamen stood by as oarsmen and two Marine guards.

"It's time," she mouthed the words softly. "Spring. Just look at the wildflowers. Time for my boys to seek their fortunes." *Even Matt finally ... finally finished his English boarding school. God ... that boy has persistence.*

The coxswain caught the coin pouch bribe with both hands. "Aye, missy," he stated with his best Cockney accent. "She's a fast sloop-o'-war, that one. Named *Persistence*, sure enough."

Well held, lad. I reckon you couldn't drop such a pouch, eh? Is that an omen, that persistence echo.

The coxswain pointed to the anchored British ship in the estuary. "Me captain's a good man, 'e is. An' your boys'll be wi' Captain Pocock's grand man-o'-war in no time. Somewhere ..." He waved vaguely to the east. "There, off the coast of Virginia 'e is. Part of England, that. A grand warship to be sure."

He doesn't know the name of the bloody warship. Well, I don't either. "What's your name, sailor?"

"Why, it's Ben, missy—just plain Ben, 'tis."

"Very well, Ben. I shall write to my friend, Captain Pocock. I will tell him how helpful you are. Thank you, Ben. Thank you, indeed."

"Don't you worry none, missy. Good job your friends are so well placed." Ben threw the small pouch back to Mary Alice. "I won't be needing that," he announced with pride. "Me captain, God love 'im, put old Ben in charge of this 'ere excursion. That's enough for me. Time to go it is, missy." He saluted her, with a wide smile on his face.

"Give me a kiss, lads," she responded, reaching for her sons, almost crying. She turned her attention to Matthew, "The Runt." He was going off to the Navy. He had just turned thirteen. *By God, you are the runt of the litter. I don't think you've grown taller in the last five years. Perhaps a little. You stand so proud, so straight.* "Come here, Runt," she said, reaching for him. "I want to tell you something."

She paused, looking directly at him, tears streaming down her cheeks.

"You know, many is the laddie who's died in a sea battle, don't you? Your own Uncle Richard Moore, my older brother, died at Finisterre. And if that battle had been lost, we might be speaking French here today, or worse. Who knows? Freedom as we know it cannot exist without men and women willing to give their best, even their lives, to protect the rest of us, Mother England, that sort of thing. I reckon you know why the flag has red in it, don't you?"

"Aye," said Runt. "It's for the blood, Mum."

"Never forget the blue is navy blue. There'd likely be no British flag at all without the Navy. His Majesty's Navy, lad."

Runt seemed to accept that and grinned. "I've seen a flag with a rattlesnake on it, Mum."

Mary Alice ignored his comment, preoccupied. *Well,* she thought, *with that small frame and pointed nose, Runt ... maybe—just maybe—I'd swear Philip Pocock's your father. Only I met him that first time ... and you all but five years old. Curious, that. But oh, what a time it was ...*

Matthew—Runt—with your special qualifications—bravery, persistence—you could be an admiral someday. After all, you're a "king's letter boy." You never know. You never know—schoolbook learning is not that damned important, anyway. There are other important gifts. Outstanding yet rare character traits count for more—qualities you possess in fair measure.

The sailors pushed the longboat from the dock in the direction of the waiting British ship. All onboard turned and waved—even the Marines. The oarsmen set about their duty. And the boat left.

Mary Alice smiled and threw a goodbye kiss to her boys.

As a special favor, Captain Pocock would see that her two oldest sons, Samuel and John, went on to Bermuda. Then he would take Runt with him to the New York Station, so the boy could begin his naval career. Matthew would be the Navy man George III had been looking for when he sent the sealed letter in deference to Admiral Rodney.

This is a hell of a note, she thought. *My youngest will be at risk against these so-called Yanks. My boys will be with the Crown from here on in. There's funds in English banks to begin anew somewhere else—even funds for Runt. And you know, dear God,* she prayed, *John plans to start a British shipping company in Bermuda. Samuel wants the same in Antig'a. Please, God. Be with them all in everything they do.*

Perhaps ... perhaps, she thought, *I will just keep my mouth shut and be a bloody Yank. And I will keep out of this damned war.*

Must we always surrender our fairest lads to the sea? Dear God. Always, war is nearby. With my boys off to see the world, it's time for me to see more of Philip Pocock. I need to find that man. I surely do.

"Damn good idea." Having spoken silently to herself, she smiled and answered herself right out loud.

Rattlesnake flag, indeed. Well, Admiral Runt Worsham ...

Mary Alice turned, pointing her chin toward the waiting ship, and sniffed arrogantly. *You're not afraid of rattlesnakes now ... are you, my admiral? Please, God. Not another damned shooting war. We see the casualties of the last one hobbling about on our streets now, don't we? The wounded ones lucky enough to come home at all, that is. Some with legs shot off by cannonballs or worse.*

Grabbing her skirts, she left for Worsham Manor.

Chapter 3

Videau Family

Jean-Paul Videau
March 1780
Charles Town in the Carolinas

JEAN-PAUL VIDEAU STEADIED HIS HORSE, waiting for his friends to create a diversion. If everything went well, maybe, just maybe, the road out of Charles Town might not be carefully guarded and he could ride quickly out of town.

"This damned bloody siege business," he grumbled to himself through clenched teeth. He waited, waited …

It all had begun March 29, 1780, when a large military force under British General Sir Henry Clinton crossed the Ashley River south of Charles Town and approached the Carolina port city. As the month of April began, British military drums thundered—a steady, staccato, rolling sound of side drums calling the "Redcoats" to action. It was the sound of war. Artillery made ready to do battle. Suddenly, Charles Town was under siege.

On May 12, after a terrible forty-two days, the American Army under General Benjamin Lincoln surrendered to Lord Clinton, a spectacle few believed would occur. American soldiers laid down their precious long arms. Dearer still, they also laid down Charles Town with its very fine port, the South Carolina colony's "Holy City."

Suddenly, Videau heard cannon and musket fire off to his left.

It's time …

Videau barely made his escape from Charles Town, fleeing just ahead of British Lieutenant Colonel Banastre Tarleton. It was quite warm that night as Videau crossed the Santee River at Lenud's Ferry on the road toward Georgetown. Tarleton and his horse soldiers, green-coated dragoons they were, mistook the fleeing Videau for their archenemy Francis Marion.

Many people mistook Videau for Marion. Both men were small and dark-skinned. Short, dark, and handsome. Marion was hiding near Charles Town with a broken ankle. People called Marion "The Swamp Fox" and with good reason. A military genius, Marion had adopted the irregular, wild fighting tactics of the American Indians. Spanish people already had a term for Marion and his special raiders, *guerrillas*, a word based upon Spanish for war: *guerra*.

Videau planned to join The Swamp Fox's already legendary band of ragged bandits—guerrillas, whatever they were. Marion needed Videau's funds, his military knowledge.

L'argent est le nerf de la guerre, Videau thought. *Money is the sinews of war.*

Videau was French, from a well-to-do family with only a shadow remaining of its medieval feudal wealth. He'd left France with whatever funds he could salvage from his inheritance and moved to Martinique. Time and circumstance had brought him to Charles Town.

Videau was a smuggler's smuggler. Yes, he was a pirate when it came to raiding British merchant vessels sailing the waters of the Atlantic and the Caribbean. French merchantmen, on the other hand, got the Videau "permit" to pass unmolested. Business was especially good near the Carolinas. Videau loved his work.

The memory of bursting shells and the incessant roar of artillery remained fresh in Videau's mind as he kicked his heels sharply into his horse's flanks.

"*Merde*! Oh shit!" he said, almost in a whisper. He did not really care for the translation of that particular French word. Somehow it seemed guttural nonsense. He felt above that sort of thing and prayed God would keep Francis Marion safe. Yet the

French epithet rolled off his tongue easily, as if the word were a prayer.

Videau—as did many around Charles Town—usually thought or prayed in French, though recently he had begun to adopt English as his language. And this was invaluable, for *Anglais* helped him to converse with the Carolinians. Sometimes in excitement, his thoughts came in a jumble of both languages.

Like tonight …

The Creole girls in Martinique had found him very handsome and called Jean-Paul Videau *Beau*, although some called him *Beauregard, (good-looking, or beautiful glance)*. It was a name that stuck, a name that fit. He was the comely, olive-skinned lover of many Creole girls.

"Ugh," said Videau as his horse jumped a small stream. He was riding his stallion, *Mioche*, which from the French and freely translated means "brat" or "nipper." The horse was an especially strong and dependable mount, young and a bit spirited. Mioche "nipped" stable handlers and riders in their buttocks with his teeth at every opportunity. Nevertheless, he could run-run-run with the wind, and Videau loved this horse. He understood the animal's irascible attitude, its strength of character.

Videau married a Carolina farm girl related to Francis Marion named Esther DuBois. She spoke fluent French and English and had recently produced a son. The baby had Beau's olive skin, black hair, and dark eyes and was very tiny. Esther had named him Charles Dubois but called him Little Beau. The child would undoubtedly be slight in stature, as had been the lot of the Videau family in France. But definitely, the baby would be a handsome lad.

"C'est bien le fils de son père," she would say. "Just like his father."

In France, while a very young man and at his family's insistence, the elder Beau had studied military tactics and business matters in military boarding school. In Charles Town, he had become quite wealthy, pursuing trade with his European friends in the islands, especially the free port at Saint Eustatius, the one called "Statia" by shippers in the Carolinas. But British General Sir Clinton had ended all that. Unless Beau's ships operated from the coves along the coast, a very risky business, they were out of the trade business for now. British navigation acts had helped to make Beau rich. Beau's trade program was restrictive like theirs but in reverse: his "navigation acts" tended to benefit everyone except England, and they especially benefited himself.

When the British made it illegal to ship goods to one of their so-called enemies, what they really accomplished was to eliminate much of Beau's competition. All Beau had to do was keep ahead of the British warships. He traded to make a profit—not to line the pockets of faraway Englishmen.

After sunset but before moonrise, darkness had fallen. In a hurry, Beau wanted to join his family in Saint John's Parish, but first, there was the matter of escaping from Tarleton. He had come this way, toward Georgetown, as a diversion, because he'd hoped to escape in the darkness and not lead them to Marion, or to his own home and Esther. He wasn't certain why Tarleton had singled him out to be chased so doggedly. After all, the English considered him little more than a pirate, someone akin to Stede Bonnet.

They hung Stede Bonnet. However, they never chased after Bonnet like this—not that I know of, anyway.

Damn this darkness, he thought, barely able to see the road by starlight. His mind raced ahead along the road to Georgetown and beyond to where Cypress trees made the water run black, where many perils lay hidden, to the place called Little Peedee swamp. It was easy for his mind to race away to dreams and safety, to Waccamaw, to Socastee Swamp, to anywhere but here.

Beau knew the darkness along this road concealed him, just as the swift black water of the Little Peedee River concealed whatever lay hidden there. He shuddered. People said the black water cloaked drowned souls that had disappeared. He needed to be unnoticed right now, and the darkness would have to be his shield.

The only thing is, he thought, *the serpents, the cottonmouths, and diamondbacks came out sometimes of a hot evening, after a very hot day. Funny thing about that. I possess a special sense about danger, about serpents in particular. I can tell whether they are near. And they are here.*

The threat of death hovered all round. Behind him, however, death remained a certainty.

The moon had begun to rise.

Suddenly, his intuition told him to draw back on the reins. He did so, pulling his horse to a halt in the middle of the almost black roadway.

Mioche suddenly wheeled full circle in the road, nearly unseating his master.

Ahead Beau saw the serpent. It slithered in the ruts of the sandy roadway. Behind, he heard the horses of the Green Horse Dragoons—Tarleton's green-coated men. Beau could not wait for the serpent to clear the way. Kicking Mioche with his boot heels, Videau squeezed his eyes shut. Mioche bolted forward. Then perhaps he smelled the snake or saw it slithering in the darkness, because he reared up on his hind legs, snorting, whinnying, his hooves flailing in the night air. Beau tried to calm Mioche, to silence him, but it was of no use. The horse refused to budge. Beau turned to see flashes of light behind him and heard shots fired. In only a matter of heartbeats, a sound like a swarm of hornets fell on his ears, and a barrage of lead balls tore into his body.

"Quel dommage! Est-ce que c'était vraiment nécessaire?" he cried, falling from his horse. "What a pity." Beau fell hard to his back on the sandy road. He could no longer breathe. *Was all that really necessary?* The thoughts caught him speechless. He mouthed, "Damn you, Tarleton—"

"That's him—that's Marion!" he heard a soldier cry. "You've hit him, lads. We have him now!"

As Beau lay helpless, he realized he would not be joining Francis Marion after all. The Swamp Fox would have to fight whatever battles lay ahead without him. Tarleton's Dragoons had won. The blackness seemed to be pouring down on him. He thought again of the Little Peedee River and of the lost souls hidden there.

And now, gasping for breath, there seemed a steady current about him. As his life faded away, he was suddenly glad his family was safe. *My dear wife and son ... Esther ... Little Beau.* A rush of inner stillness calmed him. And then a torrent of darkness covered him. An intensifying feeling of light and of warmth entered the stillness within him.

And the rush of passing ...

Book 2

A Farewell to Naïveté

Therefore remove sorrow from thy heart and put away evil from thy flesh: for childhood and youth *are* vanity.

—Ecclesiastes 11:10, KJV

Chapter 4

The Premonition

About forty-six years have passed.

Amanda Worsham
April 1826
Bermuda

ON THE BEACH, MORNING SUNLIGHT glimmered on wet, pink sand.
The light hurt Amanda Worsham's eyes. As wave rivulets returned
to the sea, each momentarily reflected many bright images of the
sun. She looked again, fascinated, as she observed brilliant dancing
flashes of light awash in each subsiding wave, as if bronze pieces
of the sun itself were scattered there. Warm splashes of sunlight
reminded her of fireworks she'd once seen dazzling against a night
sky at White Point in Charleston, South Carolina. The old British
colonial "Charles Town" had become South Carolina's Charleston, a
proud city steeped in Southern traditions. Yet there remained an aura
of British aristocracy about Charleston. The natives spoke with an
odd mixture of "American," Elizabethan English, Cockney, German,
Dutch, Portuguese, French, Spanish, Gullah, Afrikkans, Geechee,
what might pass for the actual language as spoken by the stiff-upper-
lip English aristocracy, and a few other dialects not fit to mention.

    Odd, Amanda thought, *some think Gullah and Geechee are the
same. Maybe. But I think Geechee is Gullah the way it sounds coming*

out of some of the whites around Charleston and Moncks Corner—an amalgam of everything the sailors contributed over the centuries. Gullah would be somewhat of a warm language around the port of Charleston— warm as in showing or feeling kindness and friendliness. Gullah rolls off the people's tongues. It would change over time but more slowly. Geechee sounds harsh, grating, and abrupt. Whites …

Terrible news is coming. What the—

The thought burst like a vivid flash in Amanda's mind. It hurt to think such a thought and not know the meaning of it. *Heavens. What a vacation. We need to hurry up and leave for England. We don't need this particular stopover—this very peculiar stopover. I just know it. Someone will be hurt here, one of us, and soon.* Images of South Carolina flashed in her mind: rivers, pest-ridden black waters, sandy lands in the "low country" …

She couldn't shake the notion that something awful was about to happen.

Amanda's thoughts drifted toward her father, a well-to-do gentleman of ambitious social means. Joseph Worsham was proud of his rice plantation on the Waccamaw River north of Georgetown, a venture he and his longtime friend, Beau Videau, had pooled their resources toward and bought several years ago. Joseph liked to talk about "his" plantation in specific terms and about fishing in South Carolina in general.

He considered himself English—a member of the gentry, a fisherman, and a sportsman. *Well, maybe he is,* Amanda thought. Yet Joseph would always be a colonial. *Surely he knows that. No person who thinks himself "English" would ever give him more recognition than that. Father … just another British colonial. Whatever I know about this social status business, I care even less.*

Now his father, Samuel Worsham, hailed from the old British Virginia colony. He too was colonial in origin.

Joseph, born and raised on the island of Antig'a, was the son of a first-generation shipping magnate. Does being born in a British colony a landed gentry member make? Certainly not. He keeps modest estate houses in Charleston, Liverpool, and Manchester. It is the way of the wealthy. A British accent—well, he has cultivated a fine one. To his ears and to mine, his speech is perfect, on a par with Mother's. Perhaps too perfect. But is Joseph Worsham English? Father should realize that he never would be English. Why, those hidebound stuffed shirts in class-conscious Mother England would never allow that. Father is such a child in that manner—trying to be English. Joseph Worsham has a many-faceted persona, to be sure. Care? Who does? Not even I care one whit whether or not Joseph is English or British.

Facets ... facets? What an odd idiom, that.

Anyway, there's coldness about Father, at least toward me. What am I? Some stinking lower class in his mind?

Amanda frequently experienced a sinking feeling. She often discussed this feeling—whatever it was—with Frances but never made inroads toward understanding her situation.

Still, there is something about the way Joseph relates to me. I know he loves me. He certainly seems genuinely interested in my well-being. First he was "Da." Then he became "Father," and my father he was—is.

Well ...

He holds something back, some part of his affection and for reasons I don't understand. I'm not a son, is that it? Is he disappointed in me about that? I was born in Charleston. Am I a Yank? Is that it? Guess I will never be an English socialite, if that matters. Oh well, some things I simply will never understand. That is one of them.

Mother, dear Mother. Now you ... you might just qualify as upper class, as landed gentry. Indeed, you could be, or could have been, an English socialite. Maybe you were. I don't know. You're from Manchester, born in England as they say of the landed gentry—no peerage, of course. That seems so important, to be at the very least part of the landed gentry, and to possess a fair amount of brashness. Such nonsense makes a person "somebody" in this crazy British life.

And people of England think Americans rude!

Well, your family has the money—and has had it for generations. Frances Anne Courtney, that's you, isn't it, Mother? Let no one call you "Fanny," though. Amanda shook her head in disgust. *Oh well, what does it matter? Father could buy them all and run every one of them off.*

Amanda smiled, remembering her father's talk yesterday in Saint George's, a talk with the "horseman." The man, Emm

Pembroke, was a self-proclaimed many-talented factor and expediter. Horses were scarce on Bermuda, and there was no proper livery service. Well, there was *something* there—a barn maybe. One rented horses with difficulty here. From Pembroke, Joseph had hired a wicker carriage with horses, plus a riding horse and a pack mule.

Amanda had hardly listened to the remainder of that conversation because it had concerned fishing in Carolina and Bermuda. When Joseph began to brag to Pembroke about two Negro slaves he owned, she'd turned away.

There are many things to be proud of, Father. But not your diddly-dad-blamed slaves.

Amanda, born in Charleston, considered England to be her family's "home," and the Almighty had placed Bermuda along the way from Charleston to Liverpool. After all, one followed the trade winds from Europe to Charleston and then followed the Prevailing Westerlies back to England. Tall ships leaving Charleston for Liverpool either stopped in Bermuda or whisked right past at a considerable clip.

Amanda lost interest in her memories. *Ah,* she thought. *Joseph Worsham is a fair and handsome man. I don't resemble him at all. Oh well, someday I shall raise a family, and when I do, I hope to find me a man like Joseph. Maybe I can bear a child and call him Joseph. But one thing about Father surely is true,* she thought. *He treats me as if I were a boy. He reads Robert Burns' works to me—teaches me business things. Perhaps he believes male viewpoint poetry such as Burns' is beneficial to a young lady's upbringing. For my guidance and development? Heavens. And why business? Oh well.*

Amanda acknowledged Robert Burns's work as important because it muddled together pathos, hard lessons, truth, beauty, and poetry. However, Burns roiled with the male viewpoint. She believed herself to be the equal of any boy—or any man, for that matter. Yet Burns did have his moments. Now and again, strength and beauty in Burns's poems rang out clearly—the clanging of clear bells across Scotland. One such poem, a dirge—"Man Was Made to Mourn"— suddenly invaded her thoughts.

Many and sharp the num'rous ills
Inwoven with our frame!
More pointed still we make ourselves
Regret, remorse, and shame!
And Man, whose heav'n-erected face
The smiles of love adorn,
Man's inhumanity to man
Makes countless thousands mourn!

Remembering such extraordinary verse by the Scot some called the Bard of Ayrshire came easily to Amanda. She suspected Burns composed that dirge on a saloon bar top.

Nevertheless, the man cut a mean phrase now and again, did he not? Her thoughts brought sharp pains to her chest, a cramping shortness of breath. *Slavery is the most awful curse of all mankind. And slavery is what that verse is all about. Once again, it is mankind's curse upon himself that drives its shaft into his heart. It's certainly biblical, that. Romans had slaves. Hebrews, too, had slaves. Slaves ...*

Curse the Ancient Romans for their slaves! Curse the Ancient Greeks, Egyptians, Celts, and all the rest. I take that back—I don't know about the Hebrews ... God's chosen.

Nowadays, British own slaves. Americans own slaves. Others own slaves. Even freed slaves own slaves. Curse them too. Why must it be so? Well, Mother says it is because slavery is economic lubrication. Slavery underlies everything in our "free" economy. Makes it all work.

A freed slave understands only what he has learned from the "school of hard knocks." Slaves get no book learning, not even marketing or some decent trade experience. Mother told me long ago about the economics of slavery, things even Father does not know. Have to change that ... somehow. Someday.

My Lord, I think Mother is smarter than Father. Surely she is. But what can she do? What can anybody do? Cannot simply free a slave. How would Moses live? How could he support Sally? Something must happen about the support community for freemen of color. Moses needs the wherewithal to make a living. I don't think it's all that easy for a freeman of color to live in Charleston. He and Sally are probably better off now, here with Father, although I certainly know much about that. Have to educate myself. Bermuda seems to be a better place in many ways than Charleston.

The sound of each wave hurrying up the beach echoed comfortably in the background of her thoughts. First, as a wave began to break, the sound was a soft roar. Then, as the foamy water made one last push toward the dry sand, the sound became a smooth, crackling hiss. Before each wave spent itself, a new breaking wave took its place. The taste of salty spray lingered on her lips, and the cool fresh air was clean and fragrant in its own special way.

Amanda looked along the beach known as Horseshoe Cove because of the way it curved around the shoreline. She was looking for Joseph, who was away horseback riding. He loved to ride, and so did Amanda.

She pictured Joseph reining in his mount and looking seaward, as if there were some evil, perhaps a ship, waiting out there for him. She wondered about that. *Someday I will ask. Father must have his very own devils.*

Amanda shivered, remembering the old stories of wild boar on the island.

Wild boar can be dreadful if encountered in the bush. But there are worse perils, I suppose. Some say there've not been wild boars here for ... forever. I don't believe that.

Something in the brush. What is that?

Chapter 5

Uncontrolled Fear

Joseph Worsham
April 1826
Bermuda

ON THE TRAIL BEHIND THE beach, Joseph rode effortlessly, decisively. He was looking for a high place. When he found it, he coaxed his horse up to the sandy top where a man on horseback could see farther out to sea. In his youth, he had learned his riding skills while exploring Antig'a's hidden coves and beaches.

My people, thought Joseph, *the British, call the island Antig'a, a corruption of the original Spanish name. And the English-speaking people rarely get these continental sounds just so, now, do they? At any rate, early on England claimed the island.*

Those carefree Antig'a days spent wandering, exploring, helped Joseph to dream and to expand his goals.

Joseph, the firstborn, was the only one of the Worsham children still living. The others had all died before the age of five. But Joseph had his father's keen sense of commerce, and as a young boy, he had planned to expand shipping routes to the Americas once he'd reached his majority and had inherited the business.

Joseph halted the horse and turned seaward, finding the morning beautiful. Except for sunlight reflecting off the waves, his view was clear. Despite recent financial success, he felt something gravely amiss, something tugging at his consciousness. Well, there was the matter of those people who always seemed to be following him, a group trying to lure him into their wicked business.

But why now? It has been almost twenty-one years since I left Liverpool and the white slave business.

Joseph saw with relief that there was no ship on the horizon. He was safe. No clandestine harbinger of death had followed him to Bermuda. The horse shook its head, sidestepping in an equestrian morning dance.

"Whoa, buddy."

Am I really safe? Dark terror stalked him. *My family must not find out about this,* he thought. *This fear would appear irrational. I am not neurotic, and I must not appear so. I must be careful. No one must know …*

Those awful people … Why won't they leave me alone? Do they even know where I am? Why won't they just carry on with their lives and leave me to mine?

Joseph was furious with himself that he was so very foolish and selfish in his youth. *God, please forgive me if You exist at all!* He thinks, silently to himself. He hears, feels no answer to his prayer.

A sinking feeling overcame him as he remembered the early days in Liverpool where he'd spent far too much time drinking gin and enjoying the carnal pleasures. He really did not want to think about that. He recalled those bad times with difficulty.

"All right, buddy," he said to the horse and started back toward the sandy beach, trying to put his dismal thoughts out of his mind.

However, he could not. He thought them again … and yet again. He simply could not shake the thoughts away.

In those days, he grimaced, *I remained in a drunken state for weeks at a time. I was selfish, self-centered, and mostly, pretty damn bad. Maybe I should have simply realized that one day my father's shipping business would be mine and gone to a monastery or something.*

But no. I just had to leave my home in Antig'a and go to Liverpool.

His mind took him to the darkness of a Liverpool tavern, to early 1805 …

Chapter 6

Unspeakable Memories

Joseph Worsham
1805 (Flashback)
Liverpool

"Sir Gay," said the bearded man, breaking into a stutter, voice and hands trembling, "When you g-going to talk to Warner D-D? Warner D-D ... 'Awke?" He shook his head and finished wheezing. There was a twitch in his right cheek, and his mouth always hung ajar so he could breathe. Some long-ago injury had damaged his nose. Most of his teeth were gone.

Old Timer's ruddy skin and deeply wrinkled face reminded Joseph of an old saddlebag. He had a look in his blue eyes of far too many glances toward the sun. Old Timer was quite old now, too old for the press gangs, too old to man the cannon, and too old to captain the foretop, as had been his calling. Press gangs were after younger men, especially dandies with big mouths full of high-sounding talk. Such a gang had almost caught Joseph the week before.

"Name's Joseph, Old Timer," Joseph slurred, his speech heavy with drink. "What business is it of yours, anyway? And there's no damn *D* in Warner Hawke's name. You know better."

"On the Admiralty's ship *B-Britannia* ye'd be, lad. That's where ye'd b-be."

Old Timer stopped to sneeze, spraying Joseph with spittle.

"Press gangs on the prowl, d-drunk dandies none the wiser, that's what. On *B-Britannia* tonight, ye'd be if Warner had turned his b-back. Ye know that, don't ye?" Old Timer looked at Joseph with disgust. "'Awke sent his men to save ye, d-didn't he now? Ye'd be the one called Sir Gay, right enough. We all know that, d-don't we?" He closed his eyes and belched. "B-Bloody *D-D* stands for D-De'il—Old 'Orny himself, that's what. Ye live long enough and ye'll know about that, Sir Gay. And you …" Old Timer pointed his finger at Joseph, his hands trembling, spilling his drink. "Ye with your fine garments but with no b-bloody peerage. When did the Crown knight ye now? Eh?"

Old Timer turned away but continued talking to himself. "She came in for provisions and for men, she d-did—the fine ship *B-Britannia*. Many rue the d-day they took to the b-bottle. And men what love her will climb high in her rigging, they will. Oh yes, they will …"

Joseph stopped listening. He knew "De'il" and "Old Horny" were names that some used for Satan, which said something about the depths of wickedness in Warner Hawke. Everyone knew it.

"Damn it all to hell," he said, pulling sharply on the reins, bringing the horse to a sudden stop. The horse made no sound but dug at the sandy soil with its front hooves. Joseph dismounted, stood silent steadying the horse by its disheveled mane.

Joseph's vision of a dark tavern in Liverpool faded.

Hawke was a mysterious figure in the underworld—his business, white slavery. It was an awful business Joseph knew well, having been inducted to serve an apprenticeship under Hawke. Joseph covered his face with his hands, made a small moaning sound, and remembered more about Hawke's way of doing business.

"How could I have been so stupid?" he spoke into his hands. Then he made a praying gesture with his hands but said nothing for several long moments. He only shook his head.

"I was Hawke's protégé," he finally said, looking to his horse. "That was how I learned about Hawke's awful business. Hawke ran his sinful empire from East London. The man required skillful agents, and I was one of them."

In his mind flashed images of young girls' faces, all jumbled together. Yet those images focused clearly enough to cause shortness of breath. Joseph knew the depravity of how he had recruited them.

He pulled hard on the reins. The horse snorted and stumbled to a stop. Girls with families in America and with the wanderlust, as some said, were easy targets. Some girls wanted to travel to America—Boston, New York, or Philadelphia—and could easily be snared under the guise of obtaining smart, well-paying jobs in the New World.

Handsome men like Joseph recruited the girls, men who promised passage to America in return for honest work. It was the appeal of the adventure in the New World, coupled with the appeal of the recruiter that wooed the girls.

So an adventurous nature, naïveté, and a desire to visit the New World made the first part of the ruse work. Joseph's green eyes and handsome looks were also powerful lures. But the second part of the dirty business—the second part had made a drunkard of him.

The girls were immature, maybe not so pretty, but always they were deserving of much better than what they received at the end of their voyage. Rough people met them and took them to hotel rooms and locked the doors. Each was visited one at a time by many men who raped and beat them until their spirits broke. The girls became enslaved by shame and by the horror of what had happened to them. Worse, pregnancy occurred frequently. When it did, the 24-karat-gold abortion tool, a monstrous curved instrument with a slender, sharp point at its end—a long bird's beak—had to be administered. It was the tool of an awful business, and one with which Joseph wanted no part.

In his thoughts, he looked through dirty windowpanes toward the sea. Mesmerized, his mind choked with Warner Hawke images; he stopped giving the horse the necessary knee-and-hand instructions. The horse slowed to a halt at the crest of a sharp drop to the sandy beach.

Joseph brought his thoughts abruptly to the present. Visions of the Liverpool tavern faded. Fighting to forget Sir Gay, he gazed toward the sea, as if a ship were waiting off in the distance.

"Damn you, Hawke," he cursed. "Damn you to the hell of your making."

He tugged the reins and headed for a wooded grove behind the beach. No ship bobbed in the distance. No Warner Hawke disciple lurked nearby.

Sir Gay, indeed, he thought. But he always had the special fear in his heart for what might happen one day. Whacking his boot into the horse's flanks, he put it all behind him.

As Joseph rode toward his family, he thought briefly of historic events—the recent decade or so—happier times, indeed. He let his thoughts run back to a time when it was hard to leave Charleston, harder still to remain.

In his mind he was there …

Chapter 7

Good Memories

Joseph Worsham
1813 (Flashback)
Charleston

THE YEAR WAS 1813. SPANISH moss majestically draped the live oak trees. At that time, Joseph had been three years on his own. In many ways, he was a ship adrift, open to any random suggestion, and often open to the wrong ideas. Even he agreed it was time for his life to change.

A few years beforehand, during 1810, he'd inherited his father's shipping business. Later, in the spring of 1813, he moved to Charleston, built a home, and married Frances. *Met her on that trip to England*, he thought, *shivering. Crime rate in London was bloody awful.*

My mind is full of useless shit. It keeps me all upset—vexed, wide-eyed, and wild. Got to think of more cheerful things.

Met her in London. That was a wonderful turn of events. Damn good thing I took that trip after my Charleston home was ready …

In his recollection, Joseph was standing on the wooden sidewalk in front of Saint Michael's Church in Charleston. His mind's eye allowed him to look up and down the street, even so much as to see what the ladies were wearing. Steps led down to the street itself, and posts and fences stood tall where one could tether a saddled horse or perhaps carriage horses. Granite mounting blocks were scattered here and there. It comforted him to realize that his wife, Frances, was far and away the most beautiful woman in town. At that moment, she was around the corner and down the street at their place near White Point, a modest yet attractive home.

Frances Courtney. I always liked the sound of that name. Someday I will name a merchant ship after her—could be pretty damn soon too. We shall see.

Joseph paused with that Charleston reflection in his mind.

Frances was a Courtney, of the Manchester and Liverpool Courtneys at that. Damn hide-bound bunch, if you ask me. Probably ought to name that ship Frances Worsham. 'Twould serve them right.

No. The Frances Courtney it would be. There was a time when he could think of no one else, no one at all. In his heart, he longed for those days.

Some members of the Courtney family objected to the marriage. However, Frances was carrying his child. He was confident of that. And this new war with England was brewing, which would be a problem. The economics of shipping came to naught during such times—unless one was a pirate, or a smuggler.

Yanks, thought Joseph. *Why not leave Mother England alone for good and all? No … the shipping lines simply had to shut down because of the blockade. Why, ships flying the proud, new British Union Jack were fair game to these Johnny-come-lately Yanks. For that reason, it was good to have the British Navy help ease one's British-flagged ship into the Charleston harbor. Still, it was a bother, wasn't it?*

Damn. There's no escaping Carolina until the war ends. The British blockade, he thought, wincing. *Whoever is here right now gets stuck here. That's all there is to that. What if I need to send to England for something? Well, the truth is, it's not that easy to get to Carolina from England. I cannot afford to risk one of my own ships. Why, that's the reason I hired passage for my bride and for myself. Had to. Forget about using my own merchantmen. Booked passage on a British sailing vessel out of Bermuda, I did. Even so, one must deal with the British blockade. British merchantman or no, they board all the ships. That bit of business is certainly something to avoid, if possible. A bloody hailstorm of papers, proving who you are and trying to prove who you are not. That part is really tricky ...*

Yes, Lord. Returning to Charleston from England with my new wife in tow was memorable. It was lucky—damn lucky—that my late Uncle Matt was once an admiral in the British Navy. The captain of that blockade ship, the one that challenged us, must have been bored because he came aboard with the boarding party. The man remembered Uncle Matt, thought highly of him. Mac was his name, Macalister, Macdonald ... Mac something. However, I do remember most of what he said ...

"Yes," the captain whispered. A deep scar arced across his throat. "Your Admiral Worsham was a godsend to the Crown. A colonial Virginian he was and fearless, absolutely fearless. Maybe you know that. When I knew him, he was captain of my ship. I was midshipman. And that was 1798.

"I remember Admiral Worsham standing on the quarterdeck as our ship fell in broadside with a bloody French man-o-war on Abukir Bay. A cannonball struck right below the gunwales, sending a shower of oak splinters and shrapnel everywhere. Splinters took his right eye. Chunks of broken oak took off his left leg below the knee. Napoleon's fleet, that was. And England has many heroes, to be sure. Most are dead now, as you well know. Many heroes, yet precious few remain of that one's caliber.

"Admiral Worsham lived long enough after that bloody sea battle with Old Boney's fleet to die with our beloved Lord Nelson in yet another one, this time the 1805 Trafalgar affair. His ship was totally demasted. Blasted to kingdom come by the French cannon. Yet he stood on his quarterdeck to the very end—peg leg and all. The ship we salvaged, but we lost our much-admired and respected admiral, your uncle, as you say, God rest his soul. He was a good man ... a damn good man."

Joseph continued with his special memories.

Captain Mac-whatever allowed us to return to Charleston, allowed our ship to pass the blockade. Frances was surely impressed. I remember being proud about that.

With the decline in shipping, maritime commerce in and out of Charleston fairly stopped in 1813. There were few alternate methods of shipping. The stage line from Charleston to Wilmington was rough, too rough for anything but mule skinners, corduroy roads, mudholes, boulders, dangerous fords, ferry boats, rickety make-do bridges, and the like. Yet it was one way one could ship cargo, rough-and-tumble-tough cargo—hardly transportation for people.

Money provided another problem. Mostly, Joseph banked his money away off in England; he kept very little of it in the Carolinas. He'd brought a small chest of gold along with his return to Charleston, and this arrangement proved convenient most of the time. However, with the war on against Mother England, the money he'd left behind there proved nearly inaccessible. Maybe he could slip away and run to the Leeward Islands.

But what of my wife Frances? he thought. *I can't take risks now with my family. Frances is with child. Good God, man! You must care for your dear wife now, and not just manage your damn maritime shipping business.*

Yes, Frances was with child. But frailty was not part of her character. She would go wherever he went. She wanted to see all of Charleston, to meet all the people and to dance. Frances endeared herself to many because of her love of life and her striking beauty.

Charleston was a queer place, socially structured, much like England. Both were keen to pleasures of affluence.

Joseph and Frances had the proper British accent that afforded a certain degree of social acceptance. Nevertheless, many Carolinians bore a grudge against the Crown and abhorred any reminder of royalty government. For that reason, some of Charleston's social pillars refused favor toward the disadvantaged English couple new to the town. Joseph and Frances probably were the wealthiest people in Charleston, yet they got no respect.

Who did the bastards think they were?

In his memory, Frances danced and Joseph thought of a gracious swan turning on a pool sparkling with reflected sunlight. He heard her voice call to him across the years …

* * * * *

"Oh, Joseph. Come and dance with me," she called, her voice all bubbly with punch made of wine and precious Madeira. "Oh, I do love this punch. Wouldn't it be wonderful if we could add orange and lime from the islands? But no. There just has to be a war with England."

Frances twirled around, slowed, and said, "You mustn't leave every dance for Beau, love." She waited for Joseph with outstretched arms. He turned to place his glass on a tray then ran to her.

Joseph loved Frances very much but wanted her to have the freedom he thought she needed. He wanted to dance with her, but the thing was, he was not good at dancing. Some sea chantey or raucous dance, maybe, but not …

"Silly," she said. "You handsome, silly man. I'll teach you to dance. Hold me. I love you so much."

He put his arm around her.

"I know," she said, a giggle in her voice. "You think you'll embarrass me with your fancy footwork. Think nothing of it, love. I want my dance always to be with you … from this moment on. I just told Beau to find Leonora and dance with her. It's time he grew up and accepted his responsibilities, don't you think?"

Joseph took her at her word and began to dance as though the music were a sea chantey. He held one hand to his waist and danced round her, the other arm above his head in a cavalier gesture.

She laughed and put her arms around him. "Slow down, love. We might miss something warm and wonderful."

Joseph stopped dancing to kiss her, and her response pleased him …

So it was with Joseph and Frances. Love and mutual acceptance filled their lives, and there was no substitute for the love they felt for each other.

On January 6, 1814, Amanda was born in Charleston. They named her after Frances's great-aunt, a nun in the Church of England. Joseph was happy he had married so well.

* * * * *

The soft images of the party faded, replaced by the bright morning sunshine of Bermuda. In a moment, he rode the horse briskly along the wet pink sand on the beach, heading toward his family and Horseshoe Cove. Images of long ago faded into the sea mists. Safe for now, he enjoyed the sound of the horse's hooves pounding the wet sand.

I wonder what Warner Hawke is doing right now. Good God— will it never end? I guess I thought he would just go away if I didn't think about him.

Chapter 8

What's Hawke Up To?

Warner Hawke
April 1826
London

THAT SAME DAY BUT INSIDE a warehouse in London's East End, huge framed mirrors covered walls above garish chair rails. This was the hidden office of Warner Hawke. Six patent whale-oil table lamps burned brightly, even at midday. The mirrors served to concentrate the light, reflecting it into dark corners. For security, trapdoors had been strategically placed in the floor, and hidden passages meandered behind the walls. Hawke had hired many guards; however, who could trust guards?

Hawke liked his office that way: bright. He preferred lamps to natural sunlight, as the fickle glare of sunlight blinded him, confused him. One could not control whimsical clouds and sunlight. He glanced toward his reflection in a mirror and carefully positioned a silver lock of hair. A green patch covered the blind right eye. The fetid mixture of cologne and Hawke's body odor hovered about, as he eyed the redundant specter of himself in the brightness of the place.

Nervously, he checked the room, aware and ever on guard. Here culminated most of the world's white slave trade. Assassins came often to kill men in his business, and Hawke was afraid. Hidden right in front of society, white slavery was a disgusting business, operating as a defiant mechanism fueled by lust. Yet it surely was greased by the naïveté and greed of human beings. Not that Hawke, one of the greedy lords of white slavery, was naive. No. However, his was not the keenest mind about. Hawke's steadfast depravity proved to be a solitary strength in itself. He certainly understood the useful but rotten and sinful aspects of society—and perhaps not much else.

Naïveté arrived easily to society by many paths. Yet mostly it came from fashionable well-to-do people. Hawke scoffed at society's foolishness, at its laws, social mores, and the like. If honest men abandoned a trade because it was against the law or because it was socially distasteful, like as not that business became fertile territory for Hawke. Smuggling was always good. Empires stumbled and faltered upon less and he knew it.

"That's right, simpletons," he murmured to himself. "Make white slavery illegal. Decide it's really distasteful so I can make more and more money at it."

First came Admiral Lord Nelson's crushing victory against French and Spanish Navy forces off Trafalgar in 1805. And with that victory came a grand absence of French and Spanish warships in the sea lanes. Then in 1815, Sir Arthur Wellesley, First Duke of Wellington, defeated Napoleon at Waterloo. In silent testimony to these monumental events, British trade grew worldwide. British investment was quick to realize the advantage. The empire grew.

Hawke drew a quick breath through his nostrils, his lips held tightly together. Suddenly he spun about, his hand reaching for a slender object, a dart, beneath his jacket. In a brassy blur against the lamplight, the dart left Hawke's hand, its point jabbing inside a small circle drawn carefully into the door facing about eye level, head high. The circle sported many dart holes, its face recessed about a quarter inch from long-term, habitual target practice. Hawke had not missed his mark in years. Because of this fetish of his, this target practice, visitors were always careful to announce their presence as they approached the doorway, sometimes whistling, sometimes coughing. Some actually sang out loud. One man carried a cowbell.

Hawke's dart was no gaming plaything. Rather, it most certainly was a lethal weapon in his hands.

There was the matter of Sir Gay, a man who, long ago, had betrayed Hawke's trust. Whispers carried recent news of him ... rumors of his whereabouts within the past five years. Vengeance festered in Hawke's thoughts and produced old, almost-forgotten images that took him backward in time ...

* * * * *

A year after Nelson's naval forces won at Trafalgar, Sir Gay had worked his way into Hawke's inner circle. He did not remember the date exactly. *Was it 1806?* Then Gay slipped away to venture on his own because he'd inherited his father's shipping company somewhere in the Leeward Islands. Therein lies the problem: nobody deserted Warner Hawke.

Napoleon's war nagged at everyone's mind. Times were bad. Even Hawke's business suffered for a while. No sea travels, no white slave trade.

Hawke remembered more: he and everyone else had thought Sir Gay dead, cut to shreds by a cannonball fired from a French man-of-war. His shipping business reverted to a man named Moore out of Manchester. *Yes. That was it.*

Then a recent rumor surfaced. Sir Gay was alive, living in Charleston, living among those North American fools that populated the place.

"Well," said Hawke, when he'd heard the news, "many devils are."

* * * * *

Hawke abruptly surrendered his mental images of the past. Such things tired him anyway. He had plans to formulate and decided to send Semmes, the "bomb thrower," to fetch Sir Gay. The relatively unknown Semmes had recently associated himself with Hawke following an accident with a homemade bomb. Semmes had tried to make a name for himself as a paid assassin, but an arrangement made in The Duchy of Warsaw with a certain French military attaché backfired—literally. The only thing that saved Semmes' miserable life was the bomb's poor quality. The bloody thing did not fully detonate.

And that ill-conceived affair of Semmes was a plan to assassinate with a bomb the hated but otherwise rightful heir to a piece of valuable property.

Well, thought Hawke, *Semmes lost an eye, an arm, and the job for his trouble. But could Semmes bring Sir Gay to this very room? It is worth trying. Sure. Semmes is expendable anyway.*

Hawke's best enforcer was Grewno, the "Jungle Cock." Rumors had it that Grewno was somewhere rotting in chains, captured by the British Navy, probably aboard a Bermuda prison ship.

Too bad, thought Hawke.

He smiled, mentally picturing the Admiralty attempting to frighten the truth from Grewno, the man who *never* told the truth or acknowledged anything of his family history. One could only guess his country of origin. Apparently, his given name was Ru Gnojec, a name slurred to "Grewno" in Cockney—those Londoners born within earshot of Sir Christopher Wren's Saint Mary Le Bow church bells in The East End.

To make matters worse, Grewno could speak practically any language or dialect. Just as his namesake, the common and verbal Amazon tropical parrot, he could mimic in speech whatever sounds he heard.

But does he understand all that nonsense? Who can say?

Grewno came to Hawke as a boy-slave, part of a cargo of human goods purchased from a Siamese prince. Hawke had taken pleasure often with him, yet over time, Hawke's Jungle Cock grew into the best and most effective enforcer in the white slavery trade.

Grewno has no morals, thought Hawke, *no morals or conscience at all. Just my sort of man.*

Hawke grinned at his reflection in one of the mirrors. No one knew him as "Jungle Cock" but Hawke. The two had become lovers.

What does the Admiralty want with a man like Grewno? thought Hawke, suddenly quite angry.

He looked down at the palm of his left hand. There he saw something that he and Grewno shared. Each man had a fat cobra tattooed on their left hand, with coils on the ball of the thumb and head up in a striking pose. The snake was visible only when the palm faced the viewer. Moreover, the image could be hidden simply by closing the left hand carefully or by placing the left-hand palm down on a table. Grewno often hid his tattoo with a glove, as did Hawke.

I wonder what the Admiralty thinks of such a magnificent mark, he thought. Hawke smiled wickedly at his reflection in the mirror. *Why did we do that? Tattoo our thumbs?* He grinned maliciously. *Well … well, who can say?*

"I'll have you back, my Jungle Cock … I will," he said, tears streaming from his good eye. He was not amused.

Chapter 9

And Now, A Sandcastle

Amanda Worsham
April 1826
Bermuda

MEANWHILE, ON THE BERMUDA BEACH, Amanda watched her four-year-old sister, Sarah Jean, dig quietly in the wet pink sand. The girls were playing at the water's edge, while the rest of the party lounged up the beach on dry sand, under a green-and-white-striped awning.

Amanda, nine years older than her sister, reflected, *We celebrated her birthday gala in Charleston before we left on this damn trip. Children do not know when their birthdays are. So we celebrate when we can. Did our parents do that for me?*

"Sand fleas and billy goat lips," she whispered, something she often said instead of swearing.

I'll just bet they did not. Well, I think I am very lucky to even have a birthday at all. Mother could have lost me somewhere along the way. She lost other babies, didn't she?

My sister is tall, she favors Joseph, and at the rate she is growing, soon she will be every bit as tall as I am. Humph. And that is because I take after my mother. And she is slight in stature—tiny, some would say. But my sister resembles Joseph, doesn't she now?

Sarah Jean sang a verse from a French nursery rhyme. "La-la-la, la. La-la-la." She repeated the little ditty quietly.

Sarah Jean, born May of 1822 at the family estate near Manchester, lived there for almost two years as Frances recovered from weakness brought on by childbirth. All the while Frances was away, Amanda spent her time eyeing Charleston's young men. Today on the beach, Amanda and Sarah Jean wore similar play clothes, a sundress and a hat to keep the sun off their fair skin. Amanda wore a local hat made of Bermuda palmetto; Sarah Jean, a sunbonnet.

An uppity four-year-old if ever there was one, thought Amanda. *Oh, sand fleas and billy goat lips.*

Yesterday, before leaving Saint George's port on the ship to Hamilton, Joseph had purchased both his little girls a small bucket from a street pushcart vendor. The cart man said such buckets were *piggins*, made in Bermuda of local cedar wood. Instead of a handle of rope or otherwise, a piggin had one lone stave sticking out about four inches above the rest. Amanda said to the pushcart man that the little Bermuda piggin smelled like a freshly cut pencil—not at all like her mother's cedar chest in Charleston. Father enjoyed very much hearing his daughters squeal in laughter at such a funny name for a bucket. His broad smile gave him away.

For most of the morning, Amanda ran barefoot through the edge of the surf. Most times she was happy, yet on occasion she felt a cold chill run down her back beneath her sundress, sensing something was wrong—but what?

She sometimes felt as if she knew what was about to happen before it actually did, but she never seemed to know exactly what would happen or when. However, this time a great fear rose in her about a premonition she could not shake.

"Try to put that kind of thing out of your mind," Frances had often said to her. "Ignorance of the future is a blessing, Amanda. It really is. Surely the Lord doesn't intend for us to put faith in premonitions as you do."

On the morning the family arrived in Saint George's, in a Worsham-Moore Company merchant vessel, Amanda awoke from a frightening dream that left her with the same feeling she was experiencing today. Unfortunately, she could not remember the dream. She could only remember the fear it gave her. Like it or not, the cause of her uneasiness was something in Bermuda.

She ran to where Sarah Jean was playing in the sand. "Hey," she said. "Would you like to make a sandcastle?"

"Oh yes," said Sarah Jean.

Amanda held her piggin by its long stave. Walking to the sea, she scooped up a bit of sand and water from a receding wave and carried it back to where Sarah Jean knelt digging. Pouring the wet sand carefully on the beach, she started building a sandcastle.

Oh, where is Father? she thought.

Amanda surveyed the beach both ways, trying to see him, and then she looked back to the business at hand, the sandcastle.

"We need a moat," she told Sarah Jean and started to dig a narrow trench with her hands. She hoped she could catch part of the next wave in the moat, thus making it easier to pour high towers on the sandcastle without having to run down the beach for the water. She smiled as a wave crested and finished its run up the beach, leaving seawater in the moat.

"Manda," said Sarah Jean, "I don't like it when you dig up my side like that." Sarah Jean sat beside the sandcastle, her clothes now thoroughly wet at the bottom.

"But, Sarah Jean," Amanda said. "Look at what you can do."

Amanda scooped from the moat with her bucket and poured a little of the wet sand into a spire to make a corner tower stand taller. She loved the way the beach looked: pink because bits of ground pink coral mingled with the beige sand.

Oh, Father, why didn't you take me riding with you? she thought.

"I can do that too," Sarah Jean said in a cheerful voice as she poured another tower onto the sandcastle.

Just then, Amanda heard a bird cry overhead and looked skyward in time to see two seagulls, Bermuda longtails Joseph had once informed them about, flying in a straight line over the beach. She could see the long feathers that trailed behind each bird. The sound the seabirds made was neither sad nor mournful, as sometimes was the sound of seagulls in Carolina.

The longtails appeared to cry, "I'm here, I'm here." It was a good sound. She wondered what they were saying or if they were talking to each other at all.

Amanda, who loved reading, remembered something she had read. A large part of her studies included various religious texts, so she was proficient in ancient Hebrew, Latin, and Greek. She remembered something Jesus said—something from the book of Matthew, the New Testament.

> And every one that heareth these sayings of
> mine and doeth them not, shall be likened unto a
> foolish man which built his house upon the sand:
> And the rain descended and the floods came
> and the winds blew and beat upon that house;
> and it fell: and great was the fall of it.
> —Matthew 7:26–27, KJV

Amanda shook her head. *Oh, the foolish man who built his house on a sandy place,* she thought. *That is the Southern Plantations for you, now, isn't it? Where will I be when all that grand cascade of catastrophes arrives? I reckon it surely will come. I will probably be in Charleston—right in the middle of it—and feel all the fury. Damn. I'll bet it is going to hurt too. Oh well … foolish people lead foolish lives, don't they? Maybe when I grow up things will be different.*

She turned away and looked toward the awning where her mother sat on a small folding chair. Sally sat near helping by holding long loops of yarn between her hands while Frances rolled the yarn into a ball.

Sally always helps Mother with whatever needs to be done.

The sound of a horse galloping toward them rose from the brush area behind the beach.

"Da," squealed Sarah Jean, running toward Joseph, not thinking of the danger from the tired horse.

Oh, Lord, please help Sarah Jean. Amanda quickly stood, horrified. She could do nothing to help her sister. Sarah Jean alone seemed unaware of the danger. Everyone else stood mute, petrified.

Chapter 10

Moses

Amanda Worsham
April 1826
Bermuda

MOSES—OH, MOSES, AMANDA THOUGHT. *THANK goodness, you are with us today. Moses, you are a blessing in this life.*

Moses Ward's strong brown hand reached out and caught Sarah Jean before anyone could say "Look out!" or anything else. Moses, a young Negro who'd come with them from Carolina, had been quietly watching the girls.

Joseph jumped to the ground, handed the horse's reins to Moses, and then grasped Sarah Jean in his arms.

"Oh, my sweet little girl," he crooned, visibly shaken by what had happened. "Thank goodness you're safe. And thank you, Moses."

"Yes, sir, Mist' Worsham."

Moses was proud of himself, and it showed. He had probably just saved Sarah Jean's life.

Fantastic. Father had insisted on bringing you to Bermuda, Moses. That certainly was a good job too. What if you hadn't been there just now?

Years ago, Joseph acquired both Moses and Sally as slaves when he became part owner of the rice plantation. Sally, the best housemaid in Charleston, was Moses's wife. Joseph wanted them to stay together, so when the family left for Bermuda and Sally was to help

58

with the two girls, Moses came along as well. He was here as Sally's husband, as the family's helper, and as the man who saved Sarah Jean's life today.

Amanda was very pleased that Sarah Jean was safe. She looked at Moses and was happy for him too. She liked Moses. She felt a bit jealous because of the attention Sarah Jean was getting, but she didn't want to admit that, even to herself. After all, Sarah Jean had come very close to falling under that horse's tired hooves.

Amanda glanced toward the dancing sunlight off the waves and thought briefly about a time four years previous when a Worsham family celebration had taken place in Charleston. She thought about something that happened in response to the ship's mail about a girl-child named Sarah Jean having been born—born in Manchester, England, in March. March the second of 1822.

My baby sister's birthday ...

In an instant, Amanda's thoughts fled the Bermuda beach. Her mind's eye danced its way across sunlit seas toward her home in Charleston.

Bright sounds of laughter greeted her through the warm colors of her memory. It was a birth-celebration party. A new Worsham girl-child had been born in England. The ship's mail, along with Amanda's red party dress, had arrived at the house near Charleston's White Point just this week. She could see it all in her mind's eye as well as if she were standing there ...

A group of young, strong, neighborhood boys moved the heavy joggling board off the front porch where it was kept to protect it from the elements. It weighed at least two hundred pounds and featured rocking stands on each end that raised it up about four feet. The main part, the joggling part, was a one-piece wooden plank fashioned of American chestnut: two by fifteen or sixteen inches wide and fifteen feet long. It was traditionally painted Charleston green. Some were whatever color the porch was. However, most of the children played "drop the handkerchief." All the young boys loved to run. Any running game was fine.

Amanda sat sullenly on the front steps with Moses. The boys had mocked her.

"You're afraid to go under the big magnolia tree with us, Manda. You're afraid. You're a sissy."

She was not certain which boy had spoken. Maybe there was one boy with whom she would have done that under-the-tree business. Maybe. However, they had some nerve to say such a thing.

If only my mother were here in Charleston and not spending so much time in England, she thought. It was so dark under the magnolia tree. The lower limbs ran almost across the ground.

Moreover, the girls had teased her about the red dress.

"Only Manda would wear such a rag," she heard them whisper. When they all began to giggle, Amanda ran back to the safety of the porch and to Moses.

Sand fleas and billy goat lips, she thought.

"Oh, Miss Manda," Moses said. "I hear the boys taunt you 'bout that ol' magnolia tree. I know you don' like that. They's plenty times those boys tried to get you under that tree, and I walk up and speak for you. It'd be different." He leaned forward to rub his ankles. "Dad-gum ol' red-bugs. Different if they was a billy goat in ol' Marse Fanderhoss' yard when he plant that magnolia tree."

"Whatever do you mean? Vanderhorst?"

"Yes'm. Marse Fanderhoss, he plant most everything round here. I hear folks talk 'bout him. An' a billy goat will eat everything that sprouts out the bottom of a tree—if he can get to the tree 'fore it grows up tall."

Moses stood and stretched to his full height. He was a tall, muscular man, his skin color a light brown. There was a sparkle in his eyes.

"A billy goat will prune a tree better than Moses ever could, don't you know?"

"Please, do me a favor and stop saying that word."

"What word, Miss Manda?"

"*Marse*. It means 'master.' And I don't like it."

* * * * *

Amanda shook her head and brought her thoughts abruptly back to the present and the pink Bermuda beach. She thought about the pink sand and the sandcastle. Sandcastles reminded her of Southern plantations where slaves did all the work.

Plantations are large estate farms without moral foundation. They are sandy places along the southern coastline or sandy places along some river or mud flat. Frances had told her all about it. Textile products worldwide—products made from cotton—cotton produced by Southern plantations, thought Amanda. *Low-priced cotton means higher prof-its—and rice ... well! Slavery makes the difference. It's an awful business built of misery. Now, rice is making money. Yet it depends so very much on slave labor ...*

* * * * *

Amanda shifted her view to Moses as he walked the horse slowly back to the brush area where he had the two horses and the mule tied off. He was singing to himself and to the animals. She could hear the strong bass of his voice.

Moses wants to be a carpenter.

"Amanda," Joseph called. "Come here and tell me about this sandcastle." He had Sarah Jean on his hip with his arm around her. Joseph lowered Sarah Jean to the beach and squatted beside the sandcastle, hands on his knees. "If your mother's right, this planta-tion-sandcastle—if that's what it is—will soon be washed away," he said. "Rice plantation, is it? All such plantations fall away to ruin, to hear Frances tell it."

Amanda walked up to Joseph. She could almost look directly into his eyes because of the way he crouched before their sandcastle.

Sarah Jean is a big child, yet I am tiny compared to her. Mother is like that. But does that explain it all? Father is tall and a very handsome man. What does it all mean? One thing is for certain: I love Joseph. He looks so dapper and wears his clothes so well. I especially love the green flash of his eyes. Father. Yes, Joseph, that's you. All these things made her think of the way he looked when he would lean over her to kiss her good night, before he blew out the lamp.

What Amanda really wanted was to find herself a man, a hus-band, similar to Joseph in every possible way: tall, handsome, talented, virile—yes, she wanted that too. She believed such attributes would make her life what it should really be.

"I like the way you pour a sandcastle, Amanda," Joseph said. "You made a moat, didn't you? Just like the ones we used to make on the beaches near our rice plantation. You formed the middle part with your hands and then poured a bucket of sandy seawater on the corners. That always makes a pretty spire, tall and graceful. I like that."

"This one is pink." *Rice plantation-sandcastles, indeed,* she thought, but said nothing.

"Pour a sandcastle," he said, and that's precisely what he meant: tall spires. "Cannot form them with your hands. Pouring sand-water slurry from the piggin forms a spire."

"Da," said Sarah Jean. "Will the sandcastle last if we make it way up on the beach where the waves can't reach it?"

"No, child," said Joseph. "The sea will always take a sandcastle. I mean, the beaches belong to the sea, they are part of the sea. You just can't make a sandcastle strong enough to stand up to the sea. When the tide comes in, it will disappear."

"Not even way up there?" Amanda asked, mocking her sister, pointing toward Frances.

"No. Not even up there." Joseph smiled, outwardly pleased that his daughters were playing so well together. He reached to put an arm around each girl. "The sea is relentless in its power," he told them. "It just never stops wearing away at the shoreline … wearing away the clods from the shore."

"And Europe is the less," said Amanda, smiling.

"You know that verse, child?"

"Yes, Father."

"I think it's not so much a verse about the sea wearing away at the shore, though," he said, still smiling.

"Whatever does it mean then?" Amanda asked.

"Did Miss Alice read that poem with you?"

Amanda nodded. Alice Kemble, her governess, had spent winter a year ago with the family in Charleston. She had left in spring to go back to school in Massachusetts.

"I think it just means that every person in the world is important to God. You know that an Anglican clergyman wrote it, don't you?"

"Yes," said Amanda.

"Well, Amanda, he wasn't Methodist. Still pretty good, though, wouldn't you say?

"Da, can I have a biscuit … a cookie?" Sarah Jean asked.

"You don't need to be eating between meals, little one. Anyway, your mother has packed us a good lunch."

"Bread, cheese, and some dried fruit," said Amanda. "Not exactly a proper lunch."

"And cookies. I want some cookies. Please, Da?"

On the beach, Amanda saw a figure walking toward them, a redheaded boy. The boy sort of lumbered along, in no particular hurry, it would seem.

Dear God, she thought. *Now what?*

Chapter 11

A Redheaded Boy

Frances Worsham
April 1826
Bermuda

WHAT? WHO IS THAT? THOUGHT Frances, looking up from her knitting. *On the beach, a young man—a boy, really. He certainly has red hair. He's ambling along, dragging something awkward—a cutlass?* She hadn't been paying close attention to the sandcastle project, to the beach scene. *Goodness. I thought we would be alone for this outing. Well, Joseph is there with the girls. He will take care of this.*

The redheaded boy raised his hand and called out, "Sir? Oh, sir …"

When the young man got closer, Frances could see that he had many freckles to go along with his bright-red hair. She guessed he was fourteen or fifteen years old, and his clothes were those of a landsman, a hard worker, perhaps a farmer. She drew in a quick breath. He was wearing an old odd-looking, curved sword.

Sure, it's a cutlass.

Frances stood up and went over to stand beside Joseph.

Joseph placed one hand on each of his daughter's shoulders and answered the boy, who was now quite close to them.

"Yes? What can I do for you?"

The young man answered, anxiously, "I don't want to alarm you, sir." He stopped to catch his breath. "But I saw you riding back there just now and I wanted to tell you about the escaped convict loose round here. If it was me, sir, I wouldn't ride off and leave the rest of me party alone. The ladies, I mean—"

"What sort of convict?" Joseph asked, his brow furrowing.

Both girls remained silent, snuggling close to Frances.

"One of the British convicts that are here to work the roads and fortifications."

"Did he escape near here? Or was he working someplace else?"

"Right here it was, sir, and two days ago."

"Is that why you're carrying the cutlass?"

"Aye, sir. This old blade has been in me family over a hundred years. A regular heirloom, it is. Me great-great-grandfather took it off a pirate near the island of Jamaica. But that was a long time ago."

"So you live round here?"

"No, sir. Well, I don't live too far away."

"Why are you here alone?"

"I'm the whale watcher for this week, sir."

"Yes, I know about that. You're watching to see if a whale gets trapped by the reef."

"Aye, sir. That's right. It's a change from me farming chores. And if we find one, well, that would be quite a different harvest now, wouldn't it, sir?"

The young man appeared to be nervous.

"Me name is Harry Smith, sir. I live in Warwick Parish. And I really think you should stay here with your party," he stammered.

"I am Joseph Worsham, this is my wife, Frances, and these are my two daughters, Amanda and Sarah Jean. I appreciate your concern indeed, lad. Would you care to join us for lunch, or perhaps some tea and biscuits, or cookies, as they call them in America?"

"No, sir. I think I'd best be going on."

"Very well, Harry Smith. As you wish. Thank you for your candor. I think you had best look to yourself as well."

"Thank you. And, sir, I certainly will be doing just that. Actually, when I have me lunch me mother packed, it'll be well nigh time to start for home."

Harry Smith turned and started up the beach, looking off to his right to the sea. Then he stopped, turned again, and said, "Are you from Saint George's, sir?"

"No. We're from the Carolinas."

"I've heard there's a Worsham family in Saint George's."

"My uncle John Worsham lives there. Our family has been here in Bermuda since before the American War of Independence—the War …" Joseph shifted his weight on his feet and finished the statement quietly, almost under his breath. "Of Insurrection."

"Yes, sir. Well, I wish you good fortune." He looked to his left over his shoulder as he walked away. After several paces, he stopped and turned to face the small party again. "Sir," he called out. "I wouldn't be long after dark."

"We won't. Thank you."

After a time, he was gone.

My. What a nice young man, thought Frances. *Amanda should start looking about now—looking for her own young man. But that will happen soon enough, I fear. She is an attractive girl … She certainly is. Beau told me she was a repeat of myself. When I was her age, I didn't think I was especially attractive. But now.* She squeezed Joseph's arm. *Maybe so, maybe so.*

Chapter 12

Could a Sand Crab Save a Sandcastle?

Amanda Worsham
April 1826
Bermuda

"Da? Do you think if we leave our sandcastle here?" Sarah Jean pointed toward the stately pink structure. "A sand crab would move in and save it?"

Sarah Jean can ask the dumbest questions. Amanda shook her head.

"Well, I don't think there are many sand crabs right here, little one. You mean the crabs with a big claw that's orange and a small one that's not? Here people call those little fellows red land crabs."

"Yes, Da. Like the wee ones we see in the marsh down the way at home. You know ... that live by the ocean. Do they have those here in Bermuda?"

"Do you mean on our beach at White Point in Charleston? Yes. I think so. Fiddler crabs, you know—there would be nothing any old fiddler crab could do to save your sandcastle."

Amanda wondered if Harry Smith walked home every evening. She was worried about him. She said a prayer for them all, which included Harry Smith.

Joseph left the girls to walk toward his wife while Amanda and Sarah Jean played quietly with the sandcastle.

Amanda turned her head to look toward her parents.

Mother is from Manchester, England. She is a Courtney and has the black hair and lavender-blue eyes to prove it. She has the Courtney money too. Father met her while in London attending a theatrical play, something like that. They married after a short courtship.

The Courtneys spent a great deal of free time in London and not very much time at home—or in Manchester, for that matter. Frances told Joseph it was her father's business interests, banking—whatever—that kept them in London so much. Maybe business is first but boredom is second. London is more interesting than Manchester, but that is changing.

The Worsham family keeps an estate near Manchester today, which after Joseph's father died, became his mother's home. Joseph elected not to live with her. He, too, had many financial interests and lived in a London townhouse. His well-known shipping firm, Worsham-Moore Limited, has offices in London, Liverpool, and Charleston.

Amanda liked her uncle Howard Moore, but it always seemed odd to her that Uncle Howard was younger than Joseph. *They don't look as if they are related at all. Howard is Father's mother's brother. She was a Moore, Christine-Alice Moore Worsham. I mean, Howard is Father's uncle—he's my great-uncle.*

Amanda pondered that for a moment.

When Howard was born …

Amanda stopped amusing herself with the sandcastle.

Let me get this straight … about the family history. Maybe I need a stick to write this all down in the sand …

Very well now, when the three brothers Worsham left home in 1770, they were all Tories and had to leave Virginia before they were conscripted into the Yankee militia.

Now, Mary Alice Worsham, their mother, was maybe thirty-five at the time. Or maybe twenty-five? She was a Moore—or rather, had been a Moore. At least I think she was. I call her Grandmère. She was my great-grandmother. But Mary Alice was also a widow woman and stayed behind in Virginia to chase all the local men. She was a Tory, right enough. Still, she stayed with her Virginia farm. I wonder how she managed that. If she were alive today, Grandmère would be over eighty or maybe ninety. So she was seventeen or so when Grandfather John was born. John was eighteen when he left home. Whew. This family's history makes me dizzy.

Very well, dizzy it is—Grandfather John Worsham, Joseph's father, Grandmère's son—lived on the island of Antig'a. And Joseph was born there in 1773. Yep. He was born before the thirteen British colonies became the United States. This year—right now—is 1826, and Father, our very own Joseph Worsham, is about fifty-three years old.

Oh dear, all this is so boring. Where is Uncle Howard Moore—make that Great-Uncle Howard—in all this? Gracious!

Now Mother, Frances Courtney Worsham, is about forty, although they never speak of age when we celebrate a birthday. Hmm.

Father is an old man, isn't he? And Mother's having real trouble with this pregnancy. At forty, no wonder. She's an old woman herself.

"Manda, I need go potty."

"Very well. Shall we walk over to Mother and Sally?"

As wet as you are right now, Sarah Jean, who would believe you hadn't just wet yourself?

Amanda took her sister's hand.

* * * * *

"Mother, you seem to be quite busy. Could you spare a moment to explain to me about the Worsham side of the family?"

"What do you wish to know, Amanda?"

"How is it that Uncle Howard is Father's uncle—but he's the same age or younger than Father? That really seems strange to me."

"Howard Moore is Grandmère's brother—a very young brother. When Howard was born, she was fifteen."

"She was a *coquette?*"

"Amanda!"

"I'm sorry I said that, Mother. I overheard you and Father talking about her. I don't really know what that word means. Well, I've read. What is a coquette, anyway?"

"A Jezebel."

"As in the wife of Ahab?"

"Well, Grandmère certainly wasn't really wicked," Frances explained, "unless chasing after men is considered wicked. She was a healthy woman, that's all. Ahab's wife, on the other hand, really was quite wicked. She arranged the death of many. The Lord's prophets, I think. Angered the Lord, and wild dogs ate her at the edge of town. Gobbled her up, I guess. Grandmère, on the other hand, simply needed men, right up until she died with a fever. In her seventies and still sniffing after men, she was a beauty, that one.

"Let's see, it was the year you were born that she died, 1814. We were in Charleston, so couldn't go to the memorial service. There was that awful war, you know." Frances shook her head. "Yes. Man-hungry, that one was. But we must not speak ill of the dead. We need to leave that sort of thing for the Lord in heaven."

"She hated anything remotely French, isn't that so?" Amanda asked. "And nobody, but nobody, called her *Grandmère* to her face. Though everyone did behind her back. Beautiful and a real bitch. That is what I think. Shamelessly chasing after the men folk? She caught them, took them to bed—"

"Amanda, just don't you worry about it. Grandmère is simply no concern of yours. So many people of French descent in Charleston. So many French words in our language. It's no wonder you call her *Grandmère*. Some of your friends were second-generation French—little Beau for example. The boy's name is Charles—still he is called Beau—Little Beau. Well, he a darling little boy! You undoubtedly picked up that word *Grandmère* in Charleston. Now it almost seems as if it were a joke. A rather sharp, cruel one at that. No. She would hate—did hate—being called *Grandmère*. She was English, not French."

No concern of mine? She was my grandmother. "But her blood runs in my veins."

Frances interrupted with, "Amanda. I must talk to you about that. Not now, but maybe later. We shall see."

Oh dear, what is that all about?

"And lest we forget, Grandmère's youngest, the boy Matthew, 'Runt' as she called him, turned out well. An admiral in the Royal Navy, he was."

70

She's changed the subject. Damn, my mother doesn't want to talk about it.

"Matt was your great-uncle," she continued. "How old would he be if he were alive today? Well, he was thirteen when he left home in 1770, so that would make him sixty-nine today, would it not? Matt died in that grand battle off Cape Trafalgar. He was forty-eight and a hero. I just don't know much about that. He was with Lord Nelson, fought Napoleon's fleet. And her husband, Brigadier Charles Worsham, died fighting the French in Canada."

"But tell me about Uncle Howard." *I can change the subject too.*

"Now, Amanda, I've told you all about that before. You're not paying attention. Although the Worsham lineage is confusing, to say the least. Listen, Uncle Howard, Grandmère's very much younger brother—about the same age as Joseph—came along late in great-grandmother, your great-great-grandmother Moore's life. Yes, she was over forty at the time. As I said, maybe forty-three."

Pay attention, Amanda, she thought. *You might get lost in these blasted great-greats any minute.*

"But your *Grandmère*, the *coquette* as you say, was the second child. The first child, the one who was killed by the French in yet another battle at sea, near Cape Finisterre which is off the Spanish mainland, now that would be Richard Moore. Well ... Great-Grandmother Moore must have been about twelve when she had Richard.

Good God, thought Amanda, wincing at the thought of it. *Twelve! Yet there was something more.*

Beware the Cape ...

The thought both stunned and scared Amanda.

What does that mean? Cape Finisterre, er, Trafalgar, was long ago. I don't understand. Yet I must remember, for it will be important someday, I just know that too.

"Howard lives in Manchester with his wife, Margaret, your beloved Aunt Meg, and with Joseph's mum. Now there is a woman whose name hardly ever comes up in conversation. Meredith-Elizabeth Worsham."

"Miz Eee," said Amanda. "Wasn't she a Forsythe?" *She certainly wasn't a Moore. They just don't mention her name. It never comes up in casual conversation—at least not around me. Yet Miz Eee certainly is my grandmother too. She's the family secret, a secret they call senile dementia. It is a form of madness, something worse than just senility. She doesn't know where she is, who she is, or anything. She is not just a simpleton. She simply isn't there anymore.*

"She's a Forsythe. I remember when she was normal. I mean it. They always called her Elizabeth. I have no idea where the name Meredith came from. What's more, Joseph is ashamed of her, I think. His very own mother." Frances shook her head. "Well, we all have our faults. It's a good job Aunt Meg lives with Miz Eee. Aunt Meg dotes over her, takes good care of her, waits on her hand and foot, as they say. But listen to me, child, do not concern yourself about Joseph's family. If you are simply interested, that's one thing. But if you're worried about having some of their blood in your veins, forget about it. That is no concern of yours—or mine, for that matter. Almighty God has served you better, I think."

Mother, what in the hell are you talking about? Goodness. I should clean up the language I use in my secret thoughts. Sand fleas and billy goat lips! I shall have to talk further with Mother about this ... at a better time.

Amanda decided to think about Joseph, anyway. She said some parting words to her mother, turned, and started walking back down the beach toward the sandcastle.

I am proud of Joseph and his success, she thought, walking along. *He and his father before him stood at the brink, as it were. And they turned every venture, new or old, into a moneymaker. Father could live at his pleasure wherever was best. On average, we have visited the family in England as guests on our own ships every two years. Certainly, many cannot afford such a luxury as that.*

Amanda ran to the edge of the surf and stood looking at the sea as it frothed and surged over the reef offshore. *Joseph told me the reef had always protected Bermuda from invaders. It was a barrier of sorts, a wall against unfriendly vessels.* She curled her toes and felt the water wash away the sand beneath them, leaving packed sand under the wide part of each foot. It was an odd sort of feeling.

Sarah Jean ran to Amanda and held her hand while the waves poured across their feet.

"Oh, Manda, the water is such a pretty color, all blue and green."

"Yes. Blue green, that's what it is. There is pink sand underneath, and the water's so clear. I think the color we see is called turquoise blue. Look at the rocks over there. They all have a pattern, a sort of wood-grain look. The lines come up like this." She made an angle with her thumb and forefinger.

"What's the green stuff on some of them?" Sarah Jean asked.

"It looks like moss to me. Come on. I'll race you to that jumble of rocks."

As Amanda and Sarah Jean played together, the time passed quickly. Soon the sun was high in the sky.

"Children, it is time to come in out of the sun," Frances called.

Amanda, Sarah Jean, and Moses walked to the awning and sat on the sand in the shade.

Joseph cast a scrutinizing glance at the horses. "Moses, have you seen to the animals?"

"Yes, sir, Mist' Worsham."

"Joseph, the horses are fine," Frances said. "These poor people need to eat. We all need to hide from the sun at midday. Sally, serve Mister Worsham and me and our little ones, and then serve yourselves. Something has come up, and I think we should start back as soon as we rest from our meal. I have a surprise for you. I brought some limes from Hamilton and Sally has made limeade for us."

"I could do with some tea myself." Joseph wore a pensive look.

"Well, Joseph, perhaps we should light the Limoges *veilleuse* teapot I purchased yesterday while you were so busy. I believe it has a *veiled,* protected, floating wick, a spirit burner, and we can have our tea now if it is not too windy. Sally, please see to it. I know you can figure out how to work the wick."

"Misses Worsham, do you want your tea with dinner?"

"Well, yes, Sally. But I would hardly call this picnic dinner."

"Yes'm."

"Mother, will we leave early because of that convict?" Amanda asked.

"Mum, what's a convict?" asked Sarah Jean.

"I'll tell you what," Frances replied. "Moses, get the trunk for these girls so we can put them in dry clothes."

Mother is trying to change the subject, thought Amanda. *That's twice she has done that today. Surprise, indeed.*

* * * * *

Moses hefted the travel trunk to his shoulder and brought it to Frances, who had him drop it on the sand. He then brought water from a cask resting in the shade under the carriage.

Joseph picked up Amanda and then Sarah Jean, placed them on top of the trunk, and started to brush off sand from their legs.

Sally brought a pan of soapy water and began washing Sarah Jean's feet.

"Miss Manda," she said, "I'll wash you off in just a minute."

"Joseph, why don't you organize things with Moses so we can start back?" said Frances. "I think I'm about ready to leave this place. I'll help Sally dress these two."

Amanda could see the worry on her mother's face. She looked at Joseph and realized he was worried too. Then she wondered if the thing that she had been fretful over was about to happen.

Sarah Jean jumped down as soon as Sally finished tying her shoes and ran to where Moses was loading the carriage and tying items to the mule's pack harness. Amanda stayed to help Frances. When the tea was ready, they sat on blankets for the noon meal.

Some time after the awning had been dismantled and the last item tied to the pack mule, they were ready for the trip back to Hamilton.

"Father, may I double up with you?" Amanda asked. "That horse any good?"

"Amanda, you ride the horse, good or no. I'll ride in the carriage with your mother."

"Splendid," Amanda replied. *Well,* she thought, *he trusts me with a strange horse.*

Moses held the saddle and stirrup steady while Amanda mounted the horse.

"Moses, you drive the carriage," said Joseph.

Amanda turned her thoughts to her mother. *Frances is a very attractive woman. No wonder Joseph married her. She brought the security and love into his life that was needed so very badly. Money is not everything. She'd heard Joseph say that often enough. Still, money can buy the kind of lifestyle that the Worsham family enjoys.*

Frances was with child, about four months, and her regular clothes would no longer fit. Frances wanted more than anything to raise a small family and to bear a son, Joseph Jr. Everyone knew that and prayed for it.

Amanda hoped this baby would live. There had been a miscarriage two years ago, and there had been others before that. Sarah Jean was four years old. Yet it had been difficult for Frances to have any more children.

Amanda made a clicking sound and brought her feet smartly against the horse's flanks.

Moses snapped the reins over the carriage horses. They started toward Hamilton.

Chapter 13

Frances's Thoughts

Frances Worsham
April 1826
Bermuda

THE WICKER CARRIAGE ROCKED STEADILY on the rough path behind the beach. Frances unfolded her kerchief, rubbed her nose, and caught a whiff of the lime she had squeezed into its folds earlier. The lime juice had been on her fingers then, and she had wiped her hands with it. She tucked the kerchief away, and as the carriage steadied along a smoother path, she grasped Joseph's hand inside both of hers. His hand seemed so large to her. He was telling her all about his horseback ride up between the sand dunes and about the escaped convict. She looked directly into his green eyes, not hearing a word he was saying.

It was not that she was ignoring him. Frances often looked at Joseph with a flurry of her own thoughts racing above his spoken words. She knew what he was saying, yet she felt uneasiness within her abdomen, as if the unborn baby were fitful. She smiled at Joseph, remembering an earlier time when he'd tried to explain away the British Admiralty's blockade of the sea lanes and of the Charleston harbor. His small family had been trapped during the second awful war with Mother England. And because of it, Amanda had been born in Charleston. There had been no way to return to the family estate in Manchester until the war ended.

Oh, these Yanks, indeed. That was what she'd thought during that war. But now she considered herself one of them. Not simply a Yank, but an American. For one thing, Methodism was more acceptable to the Americans than to the English, although that might be different today than it had been during her grandfather's time. Frances and her children were all Methodists. Joseph did not know what faith he was, or indeed if he even had one.

Old Man Courtney, Frances' grandfather, came back out of India a wealthy man. He'd served with Clive. But some Anglican stuffed-shirt English called Courtney a nabob. That nabob business was a derogatory term. It meant new-rich colonials from India, a takeoff from Hindi: "nawab," or provincial Muslim rulers out of Northern India.

Oh well. He was Grandfather to me, or Grandpère, and he'd turned a modest fortune into a banking empire. First, a bank in Manchester, and then several banks across England, even in London.

They might look at Grandfather and think, perhaps Old Man Courtney is British but he certainly is not "English." His wealth made them nervous, and they always seemed to exclude him from their social calendars, or so the story was told. And despite everything else, he upped and married a Methodist. God, was that so unforgivable? Who do these Church of England people think they are, anyway? But that was long ago. Could it be that they no longer think that way? After all, during the eighteenth century, many Methodists moved to Savannah in the Georgia colony. Did the Tories accept them? Well, probably not.

So much hullabaloo about liturgy.

Today Frances was simply changing her allegiance. Funny how time can do that sort of thing to a person. It did not seem fitting, somehow, to have the English royalty as the conscience of a church. But what do I know?

Right now, Frances was trying to put behind her wayward thoughts about Beau. There seemed to be no way to escape Beau's presence. *Always he is nearby. He lives near Charleston. He travels as he sees fit. We travel to England. He might show up in London, Manchester, or Liverpool. He is almost part of the family. Sometimes I fear he is following me. Oh well …*

* * * * *

"And another thing," said Joseph, interrupting Frances's train of thought.

She began to pay attention to him.

"There's no reason for us to tarry hereabout anymore. Perhaps we should return to the ship tomorrow and go on to Liverpool. The sooner I get you to Manchester, the better things will be."

Now, thought Frances, *he is speaking of my female problems. It was a repeat of the experience with Sarah Jean. Almost every day the baby seems to want to come. But the timing is all wrong. The baby is not strong enough to make it on its own. Not yet …*

"Yes," said Frances, answering Joseph. "While there's still time it would be best for the baby. You know, I wish all my pregnancies were like my prenatal time with Amanda. She was such a strong child before birth. And she is strong today. Sarah Jean is tall like you, Joseph. However, she was so difficult to bring into the world. Amanda is tiny. And she was so easy. I really don't understand."

In Frances's heart, she understood. She'd lied to Joseph. There was something Frances would never tell him.

There is no good reason for him to know. Moreover, as for Miss Amanda—I never will tell anybody, much less Amanda.

Amanda is small, dark, intelligent, self-sufficient, and very damn cute, just like her father. Dear me. Dear me. Dear me.

Her biggest fear was that Joseph would find out her secret. Frances was not ashamed of her past, only afraid it would reach out and harm her oldest child, Amanda.

Chapter 14

Amanda's Thoughts

Amanda Worsham
April 1826
Bermuda

Sand dunes, brush, and small trees lined the path from the beach to the narrow road, and wildflowers bloomed everywhere. Ahead, Amanda could see the large cedars for which Bermuda was well known.

This is a beautiful place, she thought. She glanced toward the carriage.

Father and Mother are holding hands and talking. Sally has Sarah Jean beside her on the seat.

She certainly thought Joseph had done well by Moses and Sally. Some people who owned slaves didn't treat them as fairly and justly as he did. A slave's basic human needs were sometimes ignored, such as the need to live with one's family.

Why not be good to them? It was only fair. Anyway, if he didn't own Moses and Sally, they wouldn't be here in Bermuda and they might not otherwise have ever seen this beautiful place. Still, the thought of slavery was a pained thought. She hated slavery as much as did her mother, who had a tendency to say a great deal about it.

Amanda's mother had a special friend, an old suitor, Charles DuBois Videau. Frances affectionately called him Beau. Almost everyone else did as well. Beau's father had been one of the Charleston patriots killed during the Great War with England by the British raider Colonel Banastre Tarleton.

Beau was a loyal Southerner who lived on a country estate near Charleston with his family and about a hundred slaves. He had married well, to Leonora Pinckney Allston, a Charleston debutante. The marriage produced a son named Charles II, whom practically everyone called Charlie.

Now, Frances had met Beau some years before, when Beau visited England to have a ship rebuilt in a Liverpool shipyard. Beau was a single man then, a man unattached—at least that is what he avowed. All the girls considered him a good catch. After Beau tried unsuccessfully to convince Frances to marry him, he returned to Charleston alone at the end of summer. All the while Leonora Allston was alone in Charleston, pregnant with Beau's son, Charlie.

Needless to say, Leonora, as a single young lady, must have been quite upset about carrying Beau's child. Everyone knew about the pregnancy, but people did not say impolite things about Beau or his family behind his back. He was a hero. He was wealthy. Those things mattered to people in Charleston.

That story fascinated Amanda because she really loved both England and the United States. She thought well and often of Beau and his family—particularly about Charlie. He was so adorable to her. Yet her feelings for Charlie were hampered by something she really did not understand. It was almost as if she was forbidden to love him. *But why?* There had been no real instruction about that. It was simply a feeling. But it hurt.

If Charlie Videau had ever asked, she thought, *and we were alone, I might have gone under the magnolia tree with him, if ever I would have done so with anyone.*

He was always provoking her, not cruelly, but always laughing, teasing. And he might have done … might have taken her under the magnolia tree. That trait of Charlie's infuriated her. He never did anything that would be considered exciting, only devilish, teasing things.

Amanda's thoughts returned to the present. Frances had met and married Joseph three weeks after Beau returned to Charleston.

Oh, Beau was fiercely pro slavery. Amanda had heard him say, "To control the slaves, they must be kept ignorant and dependent."

Beau saw slavery as an absolute necessity and the lawful right of every free, white landowner. He did not spend much time worrying about the feelings of a slave, the rights of a slave. Any enemy of slavery, any abolitionist, was his personal enemy, someone in league with the devil. When Beau came to visit, the conversation would likely involve slavery, specifically the expected end of it.

Joseph did not just tolerate Beau; Joseph was his friend and, further, a friend of his family. The two shared many of the same interests, and both were in the cotton trade. However, he and Joseph did not really agree about slavery. Joseph thought slavery was just another economic force in the world. Beau would probably fight to preserve slavery. Moreover, although Frances hated slavery, she seemed to have quite a fondness for her "Beau."

There was something about Beau Videau … something Amanda just could not put her finger on. And oh, Charlie Videau, he had his own place in Amanda's heart.

When the Worsham family was in Liverpool or Manchester, Beau sometimes came to call. He often traveled to England during the "sickly" season, when temperatures in Charleston soared unbearably and people were likely to become ill. Also during that season, Joseph took his family away, either to the northern United States, to Canada, or to England, leasing his vacant Charleston house for the season, usually to a planter from the swampy areas.

During these visits Amanda had learned of William Wilberforce and his movement to end slavery in the British Empire. To Frances, Wilberforce was a hero. To Joseph, the man was a meddling philanthropist with no real knowledge of the economic forces at play in the world. According to Beau, Wilberforce was an idiot. Amanda knew their opinions because she had heard the men express them. Certainly, much disagreement churned within Frances on that point.

Beau usually traveled to England alone. Leonora rarely left Charleston, even in the sickly season, because she detested travel. She moved into town where the sea breezes made for a better situation.

Either Beau rented a vacant Charleston home for her, or she stayed with her family, the Allstons.

And the slaves—well, that was another thing altogether. When Frances went to England to deliver Sarah Jean, Joseph purchased a portion of Sand Hills plantation, a rice plantation located in All Saint's Parish along the Waccamaw River. Into that venture, he brought his sense of fair play, his sensitivity, and his money. The Worsham family holdings were many in the Carolinas, but the rice plantation was the only one involving slavery. Joseph had good feelings toward the slaves he owned, but he did not intend to set them free.

But what of Negro human dignity? thought Amanda. *Where is the fair play in that situation?*

"Amanda," Joseph called. The carriage came to a halt before continuing around a fallen cedar tree. "Why don't you ride behind the carriage instead of out in front? That way I can see you better."

"Yes, Father."

She pulled back on the horse's reins while the carriage went ahead. As she did so, she noticed the pack mule follow along behind her horse. Moses had told her it was because the horse was a mare and the mule reckoned the mare—any mare would do—to be its mother. Anyway, there was no need to tie the mule to the carriage, or to lead the mule, because it always followed the mare.

The path followed close to the so-called tribe road that led to the other side of the island. The way was dark and in shadows because of the large cedar trees.

Amanda felt the cold chill again. She heard a noise in the brush ahead of the carriage.

"Father, are there any wild boar here? Are there any in Bermuda, I mean?"

Joseph answered with a bit of sarcasm in his voice, "I think that is just an old wives' tale. Could be that Robin Hood's descendants live here in Bermuda. Any wild boar would wind up on their roasting spit over an open fire. Don't you think so?"

"Indeed. Steal from the rich and give to the poor. Isn't that right?" *Father is pulling my leg.*

"Hardly. There were no bloody rich when Robin Hood was about—rich people, rich ordinary citizens, I mean. Robin was stealing back from the *government*. The government, the king, and the church, had all the money. Too much taxation. And the boar population is long dead, I think."

Amanda heard a sound ahead of the carriage.

That sound … a wild boar?

Chapter 15

That's Not Harry Smith

Amanda Worsham
Mid-April 1826
Bermuda

Suddenly, a man jumped in front of the horses, cutlass raised above his head, both hands clenching the grip. The man screamed something unintelligible, and then he swung the cutlass in an arc toward the horses as they reared.

Damn. That's not Harry Smith. The thought burst into Amanda's mind. *Jesus. Beware the ides of April. That realization was a bit late in coming.*

Hooves flailed in the air. Horses whinnied, fighting the bridles, trying to get away, yet the bridles held.

One of the horses screamed—an unbending, high-pitched, snorting sound.

God. I've never heard that sound before. The horse must be hurt.

Moses stood, pulled back on the reins, and tried to control the horses. One was indeed hurt, and it stumbled. Both horses struggled to keep their footing.

All at once, the carriage careened over on its side.

Amanda's horse reared and turned. She couldn't see. Was anyone hurt? She heard voices cry out, heard her mother screaming, then silence but for the grunts of the horses.

When Amanda got the mare under control, she turned to look. The man had Sarah Jean, cutlass in one hand, dragging her with the other, pulling her by her pinafore away from the carriage. Amanda saw the scene before her in an instant, as if the man were playing out a role in some dreadful, bizarre drama. He had a wild and crazed look in his eyes. His face, covered over by his shirt, wrapped about his head, across his face and around his neck, enabling her to see only his eyes and nose. He lifted Sarah Jean and held her with his left arm, dangling the cutlass against his side.

The cutlass is in his right hand. What? Is he left-handed? He will drop her for sure.

What? Bare-chested, dark-skinned—not Negro, not tanned from the sun, but dark—hurting my family, hurting my sister. Who the hell does he think he is?

"Da," screamed Sarah Jean. "Help me, Da."

Amanda looked frantically for Joseph. *Where is he? He is under the carriage.*

Amanda could see only his legs and feet, so she couldn't tell whether he was hurt or not.

How can this horrible man be stopped? She didn't know what to do, but she had to try to do something. She wasn't afraid for herself, only tired of waiting.

She kicked her heels against the mare's flanks and slapped its backside. *Let's go, horse. Oh, Lord, help me save Sarah Jean.* The horse leaped toward the man.

The man grabbed her horse by the reins, letting go of Sarah Jean and looking as if he were about to attack Amanda with the cutlass he held in his right hand.

I thought you were left-handed, she thought, wincing. *Damn … damn … damn.*

"*¡Bruja chiquita!*" yelled the man. "*¡Consiga de ese caballo!*"

He had a thick, strange accent, but Amanda understood what he'd said. *Called me a witch, a little witch, in Spanish,* she thought. *Little witch, indeed.*

The man's pronunciation sounded strange to her and not at all like the inflection in her beautiful governess Alice Kemble's voice.

He must be the convict, she thought. *A criminal.* She watched in horror, unable to move. *The desperate madman is about to kill me.*

Amanda heard a gunshot, then heard the ball whiz past her ear.

The man dropped the cutlass and fell, wounded in the right shoulder. He clutched his shoulder with his left hand as blood seeped through his fingers. She had never before seen a person hurt in such a manner.

She tried but couldn't close her eyes. Somehow, she just had to look.

Maybe you will be left-handed now. You ... you son of a bitch, you.

A British soldier ran out of the shadows and kicked the cutlass away, then rolled the man over to inspect him. As soon as he was certain of the wound and that the desperate man no longer posed a threat to anyone, he turned to grab Amanda's horse.

"Are you all right, lass?" he panted.

Amanda was speechless. The soldier helped her dismount.

"Forgive me, lass," he said. "Please, I'm worried about you, I say. That is, I'm Private Nigel Wiggins, Royal Engineers. 'Ave ye been injured?"

Chapter 16

Grewno in Bermuda?

Joseph Worsham
April 1826
Bermuda

THE SHOCK OF FALLING TO the ground dazed Joseph. He felt a great weight pressing upon his chest, and for a moment, he did not know where he was … or how he got there. Something squeezed him tightly against the ground. He couldn't breathe.

Slowly, he drew a painful breath, making a hissing sound between his teeth. The action blurred his vision, and the following breathless moment seemed to stretch forever. Filled with scrambled thoughts, strange flashes of light, and the taste of dirt in his mouth, he thought of what people said: "Your entire life will pass before your eyes in the last moment of your life."

A rock pressed hard against his back. Shifting his weight, he looked to the sides of the carriage and saw red-coated men.

What's happened? Who are these people? Soldiers?

Then he remembered. *I recognized that wild, berserk man who caused this horror—the man with the sword.*

Joseph shuddered. He saw in his mind's eye a dark face wearing an unwavering sneer.

Grewno! But it couldn't be true. People had warned of an escaped convict. Had someone captured Grewno? Was Grewno a convict? And if he is, what is he doing in Bermuda? He tried to speak, but only a groan escaped through his teeth.

A group of British soldiers surrounded the carriage. It began to move, gently, and a painful rocking motion compressed Joseph's chest as they lifted the carriage away.

The brick-red color of their uniforms filled his thoughts. Regulars. These men are regulars. For the first time in his life, he was happy to see the British Army within an arm's length. These images moved before his eyes: polished leather, shiny buckles, stout leggings. These were youthful and healthy military men. Course conversation and curses filled his ears.

Damn comforting.

Chapter 17

What about Mother?

Amanda Worsham
April 1826
Bermuda

AMANDA WATCHED AS SEVERAL SOLDIERS righted the carriage and pulled Joseph from where it had pinned him under the side of a seat. Other soldiers began freeing the horses until both stood on their feet. One was limping badly.

After a few moments of difficulty, Joseph stood, looking bewildered. His head was injured, and he held his bleeding forehead with one hand. He looked toward Frances, who lay unconscious on the ground, then stumbled to her side.

Was Frances dazed? Hurt?

Amanda thought of the unborn baby.

"Frances ... Frances!" Joseph screamed, kneeling beside his wife.

Amanda stood beside Joseph.

Moses put Sarah Jean down beside them. "Sweet Jesus," he said. "Is Misses Worsham hurt bad?"

Sarah Jean put her head on her mother's arm and lay beside her, sobbing uncontrollably. "Mum. Oh, Mum. Please wake up," she said repeatedly. She rolled over and tried to hug her mother.

Joseph put his head against Frances's chest to listen for her heartbeat. When he seemed satisfied that she was alive, he looked to the group of soldiers.

"Which of you is in charge?" he asked.

Amanda studied the soldiers. Two of them were tending the horses. The young officer approached Joseph.

"I am in charge of these men," said the officer. "Lieutenant Hawkins, sir—at your service."

Hawkins stood up straight, shuffled his feet, and saluted Joseph.

The man looked tired, but Amanda thought his uniform was striking.

They still wear the scarlet, she thought.

The man straightened his coat and set his palmetto hat at just the right angle. She thought he was cute.

"What the hell? Who is that man … that scoundrel? That imbecile?" demanded Joseph.

"He's an escaped convict, sir. My man Foxworth was able to get a clear shot when the young lady here ran her horse toward the blighter." He pointed toward Amanda. "And a lucky, fair shot it was, too, I must say. We were a long ways off."

Joseph nodded. "Thank you, Lieutenant. I am Joseph Worsham, and these are my daughters. My wife has been hurt. Can't tell if she's fainted or what."

Joseph's voice sounded calm. He is getting his strength back.

"By your leave, sir," said Hawkins.

He removed his coat, knelt on the bare ground, rolled the coat into a pillow, and put it under Frances's head.

How dashing. Such impulsive chivalry, thought Amanda. *Royal Engineers.* She liked British soldiers very much. *Hawkins and his men are the cream of the crop.*

"I'm sorry we didn't catch up with him in time," said Hawkins. "The man's dangerous, sir. We've been looking for him for two days."

"Yes," Joseph replied, scooping the sobbing Sarah Jean into his arms. Holding his daughter close, he told the soldier, "A young man told us about this convict."

"Harry Smith, sir?"

"Yes. Do you know him?"

"I met him today, sir. The convict attacked young Smith, took his water bottle and his cutlass."

"Is Smith still alive?"

"Young Smith is a stout lad. He has a nasty bump on his noggin, but he's none the worse for the wear."

Amanda knelt down and rubbed her mother's cheek with her lace kerchief, attempting to remove the dirt from her mother's skin. She stopped trying to rub it off when she thought it might hurt, though her mother still lay unconscious.

How beautiful she is. The thought overwhelmed Amanda. *Will I be that pretty when I grow up?* A tear rolled down her cheek.

Sally sat on the ground. Settling the child in her lap, she began to rock back and forth, as if Sarah Jean were a little baby and they were sitting in a rocking chair. Joseph dropped down heavily beside Frances and put his head in his hands. Soon Sarah Jean fell asleep in Sally's lap.

Moses, who had been standing behind her, unnoticed, for some time, placed his hand on Amanda's shoulder. Amanda reached up and squeezed his hand. His presence and Sally's meant a great deal to her.

After Moses spread a blanket on the ground for the two girls, Sally carefully put Sarah Jean down on the blanket so the little girl did not awaken. Amanda stretched out beside her sister to rest for a while.

Joseph still sat silently beside Frances.

Amanda wondered if they would ever go back to that simple life again in Charleston. It seemed so far removed from this place. It was difficult to stop worrying about her mother, but somehow Amanda managed to fall asleep.

* * * * *

Starlight ... deep shadows ... glimpses of dreams across the way ... Charleston—shiny, deep-green magnolia leaves with burnished, yellow-gold undersides ... Bermuda: Redcoats ... Redcoats. Charlie Videau—oh, Charlie Videau ...

Amanda awoke from a fitful sleep. "What? Oh. Damn," she said.

Sally reached over and patted her on the back. The gesture comforted Amanda. Moses and Sally were like that.

But Mother needs medical attention, she thought, horrified. *This place is so remote—even for Bermuda. What will happen to Mother? How will we attend to her? Oh dear …*

Preparations began in the small military encampment for the evening meal, and the noise had awakened Amanda. *What is all the commotion?* She looked off through the trees. The sun lit up the late afternoon sky with a beautiful sunset as soldiers ate their field rations, offering some to the Worsham group.

Amanda told Moses and Sally to stop what they were doing and eat. Sally brought a cookie to Sarah Jean and some leftover limeade from the carriage supplies that had not been damaged.

Joseph must have been asleep too. But now he stood and straightened his coat.

"Lord," he winched. "My ribs! Sore but maybe not broken," he mumbled quietly to himself. He turned to face Hawkins and finished brushing the dust from his sleeves. "Do you know of any medical help near this place?" he asked.

Amanda felt some anxiety lift away. Her father was alive, and now he was in charge again. Her brief nap had helped her to regain some of her own strength.

"Our military encampment is nearby, sir."

"Is there a doctor … a physician?"

"Yes, sir."

"She mustn't be moved. I really think she has fainted, but there's no way to be sure."

"I quite agree, sir."

"Tell me—Lieutenant Hawkes, is it?"

"Hawkins, sir."

"Yes. Why was this man sent here, to Bermuda? What did he do to become a convict? I mean, is he an Englishman?"

"I believe that happened when a pirate vessel sank off the coast of Africa, sir."

"A pirate," Joseph said, obviously startled by that turn of events. "I am led to believe the Admiralty, and indeed the Crown, *hangs* pirates," he said, squinting his eyes.

"Indeed, sir," said Hawkins. "But this one was found in the brig when the pirate ship was taken. The man damn near drowned before they got him out of the cage."

"The brig, you say?"

"Yes, sir. He would have been set free, but he attacked an officer when they were trying to question him. His English is sometimes limited to curse words. But not only that, he pulled out a *dirk* and went for the officer at the table, or so I am told."

"Well, there's no doubt he's a dangerous man," said Joseph.

"No, sir," Hawkins agreed.

"How long has he been here working on the roads? Smith told us about that."

"He was one of three hundred convicts on the HMS *Antelope*."

"When did he arrive? That was the prison ship, was it not?"

"Yes, sir. Two years ago, sir, in '24."

"Loaded with convicts?"

"Yes, sir."

"Hawkins, what are you doing here yourself? I mean, what is your regiment?"

"I … we are but a small detachment of the King's Engineers."

"Here because of the construction?" Joseph asked.

"Aye, sir."

Amanda stood quietly, as was her nature, and studied the convict. Apparently he was not badly hurt. The soldiers had fashioned a bandage for the man's wound and had shackled the good arm to the carriage with a short length of chain. Both legs were shackled, and the wounded arm, the right arm, was cradled in a sling. Two soldiers stood guard.

"Lieutenant, can you please send someone to your camp for the physician?" Joseph asked.

"Aye, and I'll have a someone fetch a wagon to transport your party, sir."

Joseph walked over to Amanda and hugged her. "I'm so glad you are safe," he said. Then he picked up Sarah Jean.

"Little one, how are you?"

"Is Mum going to be all right?" Sarah Jean asked, wide-eyed.

"I don't know." He hugged her and kissed her.

"I'm all right," Sarah Jean added. "But I'm afraid, Da. What about the awful man?"

"Mister Worsham," said Hawkins. "You've a cut on your head that needs attending to if it pleases you, sir. I would like to see to it. Moreover, the lady should have a blanket put over her. I have sent two of my men to the camp. They should be back soon."

"Thank you," said Joseph, turning to look around.

Then he said, "Moses?"

"Yes, sir, Mist' Worsham."

"Go to the carriage and find something to use as a pillow. The lieutenant will be needing his tunic … his coat. There is a chill at sundown."

"Yes, sir."

When Moses came back, he carried blankets and a pillow. The pack mule was still with the riding horse, and Moses had unpacked things he thought they might need.

Joseph stood quietly while Hawkins put a dressing on his head, girls watching.

Moses brought over the folding chair and other items that could serve as chairs.

Sally gently covered Frances with a blanket and replaced the red uniform coat with a pillow, then she returned the red coat to Hawkins.

Bowing her head politely, she murmured, "Thank you, sir." Then she brought warm wraps for the two girls.

When she finished taking care of her charges, she sat beside Frances. Moses sat with her and put his arm around her, hugging her and pulling a blanket tight around them.

Amanda noticed that neither had wraps. She was glad there was an extra blanket.

Hawkins finished donning his red tunic, then sat on a folding chair to talk with Joseph.

"Young Smith tells me you're from the Carolinas, sir."

"That's right. We live in South Carolina, in Charleston. But my family has been in Saint George's for a time. My brother still lives there. I came from Antig'a, or Antigua, as the Spanish say."

"Are you British?" Hawkins asked.

"I am. My family is British. My father, Samuel Worsham, was born in Virginia back when it was a colony. Frances, my wife, is from Manchester."

"I have seen tall ships in the bay at Saint George's belonging to Worsham-Moore and flying the British red ensign. Are they yours?"

"Yes, mine and my uncle's."

Joseph briefly rubbed his fingers over his mouth.

Was he thinking about what had been said? Amanda thought.

"I say. You know nothing about that convict, really?" Joseph asked. "Nothing of where he comes from?"

"He speaks Spanish, French … English. His accent is obscure. Certainly, he is of strong pirate stock. But he has not said where he hails from. Nobody really knows, sir. No one's bothered to find out."

"How old do you think he is?"

"I reckon him to be about thirty," said Hawkins.

"Tell me. What is the convict's name?"

"We don't know for certain. He gives a name that sounds like Grew-No, something like that. Anyway, they call him Dirk Grewno. That's what the Welch ship's officer put on his papers, sir. That and 'ethnic origin unknown.'"

"You're certain no one knows where he comes from?"

"He hasn't answered that question. The Barbary Coast, Madagascar, Corsica, Sumatra, or somewhere along the way … who knows? Just a guess. I don't think it's important to him."

"So he's a blasted pirate," Joseph said and paused for a moment, kicking sand with his right foot. "Is he rather *daft* as well?"

"No, sir. Well, could be. But he has another reputation."

"Which is?"

"He is accused of making advances to prisoners for lewd and unnatural purposes, especially the young ones, if you know what I mean."

"You mean he's a ho—"

Hawkins interrupted Joseph. "A blinking molly, sir," he whispered, a sheepish look on his face.

"Dear Lord."

Amanda turned away. She did not want to listen to this anymore.

Chapter 18

No Peace for This Family?

Joseph Worsham
April 1826
Bermuda

JOSEPH SUDDENLY FELT ILL. HE feared the man called Grewno.

Oh, God, he thought. *Is there no peace? Grewno!*

That name haunted him. It was part and parcel of very personal white slavery memories. He remembered Grewno as Ru Gnojec. Grewno was an assumed name, but it was the same man. Joseph knew it.

Hawkins has spoken with Grewno. He knows all about me! He just said Grewno's a "blinking molly"—that's polari—*a queer word. Does he realize I understand such things? Does he know my checkered past?*

"Blast," he muttered under his breath.

He tried not to show his fear. Inside, he knew real trouble waited for him ahead. Ru Gnojec was a murderer, one of the wicked enforcers of the white slavers.

"What drives a man to do such abominable things?" he said to Hawkins.

"I can't honestly say, sir. But he seems to hate any form of order or decency, any rules." Joseph looked Hawkins in the eyes. Was he smirking?

"Is he North African or Mediterranean or—?"

Again, Hawkins interrupted Joseph. "I really don't think he is. We know those people. For the most part, they have strong religious convictions. I believe it's safe to say Grewno has none."

"He had his shirt tied about his head and face. What sort of crazy people do that? Some nomadic religious wild man or other?"

"Maybe he's imitating someone from his past—some fierce warrior. Or maybe he wants to show off. I really don't know. Religious people, nomadic or no, wouldn't take their bloody shirts off to expose themselves, now, would they?"

"Probably not. Anyway, you may be right. From what I've read, the nomadic people have strong religious beliefs. What is this Grewno, a bloody barbarian?" Joseph managed a slight but nervous laugh. *God*, he thought, *what is Grewno doing here?*

"The man is only interested in himself. He doesn't appear to speak Farsi or any of that Arabic lingo. He speaks only Spanish, French, English, and something that sounds unintelligible. And he is like a bloody parrot. He can mock anybody, any accent as good as you please. And that maniacal laugh of his ..." Hawkins shook his head and shivered.

Joseph knew he would speak to Grewno at some time—privately. He decided to wait for just the proper moment. For the first time, he really studied the convict. It was Ru Gnojec.

He might recognize me. Oh, God, is there no end to this terrible business?

Chapter 19

Grewno Up Close

Amanda Worsham
April 1826
Bermuda

AMANDA FOUND THE CONVICT SUBJECT at once boring yet fascinating. She realized she had best leave this alone. But she wanted to see for herself, so she made her way over to where the convict was chained to the carriage wheel. As she neared the man whose name was a curse word to her, "the Grewno," his eyes followed her.

What kind of surname is Grewno, anyway? And perhaps this awful person is actually French and named Groulx with "no" a sort of tagalong suffix. Grew-no ...

Quebec's remote Groulx Mountains. Alice Kemble had spoken of those, hadn't she?

Grew no what? Who knows? I've heard him speak English, Spanish, as well as French. But his olive skin—

He must be French. Anyway, could be he is thirsty, she thought.

Amanda went back for a moment and returned with a cup of water. What was wrong with the strange man, now French in her mind, that he would do such a desperate thing—to jump out in front of the horses—to cause such pain to people and horses? The chain from the iron cuff on his right wrist was just long enough for him to sit on the ground. She looked at him, at his face, at his body. Then she noticed his hand.

His hand—what was that on his hand? She looked again. *A tattoo. A large, horrible-looking tattoo.* A snake had been drawn on his left thumb. She shivered as she surveyed the man and his awful tattoo, noticing that her reaction amused him. She drew nearer and held out the cup so he could drink.

"Lass!" a voice cried out of the darkness. "Lass! No, lass …" It was Private Wiggins, the soldier that had helped her down from the horse right after the convict Grewno was shot.

"Stay back from that man, lass. He's crazy, that one. Anyway, I just gave him a wash to swill the dust down."

As if on cue, Grewno spat at her and laughed—a wicked, high, loud, and wavering laugh.

Horrified, Amanda dropped the cup and ran back to Joseph, leaving Grewno to himself.

Joseph put an arm around her and gave her a strong, comforting hug.

"You can't save the world, Amanda," he said with love and compassion in his voice. "I think the scoundrel is well," he said. "The musket ball's been removed from his shoulder. Maybe the ball was pretty well spent by the time it hit him, anyway. Just leave him be, Amanda."

Amanda looked up at Joseph with love in her heart. He was a good man, this Joseph Worsham. She was glad he was her father.

"You know, Amanda," he said, "it was a good thing you did today—something I don't know if I could've done."

"Whatever do you mean?"

"When you kicked the horse with your heels and made straight for that man."

"It was the only thing I could think of to do."

"You changed the way the whole business would have unfolded."

"Oh?"

"You were tired of waiting, weren't you? I see that in you sometimes. In that way you're like your mother." He gave her another hug.

"I didn't see what you did myself," he said. "Hawkins told me about it just now."

* * * * *

In a quiet moment, Joseph closed his eyes and tried to make sense of the situation. When he thought it safe to visit the prisoner, he approached Grewno in the darkness, from the wagon side, his mind filled with frantic, alarming thoughts. What to say to Grewno … how to approach him … what will Grewno's reaction be? He stood in the darkness for a time. Grewno sat with his back toward the firelight and had not noticed Joseph in the darkness.

"Ru," said Joseph. "I know who you are."

"Sir Gay, I presume?" said Grewno with a heavy Cockney accent. "I saw you earlier. I thought you were dead."

"What're you doing here, Ru? What're you about?"

"I've been here for two long years. They caught me, you know. A bit of bad luck that was. But you think I'm here to catch you, don't you, Sir Gay? For truth, everyone thought you were killed at sea."

"Why the hell do you insist on calling me Sir Gay?" said Joseph. "You bloody well know my proper name."

"Too much talk," said Grewno, turning his head to face Joseph. "Too many people to tell the tale and remember names. No harm done if they remember Sir Gay now, is it?" Grewno chuckled to himself. His whole body shook. "But I remember, don't I?" His accent changed to that of a Frenchman. "Hawke wants you, lad," he said in the new affection.

"Why won't Warner Hawke leave me alone?" Joseph asked. "Can I not change my mind about your dirty business and get about my life?"

"You know too much," Grewno replied. "Sure you do. And you know it too, don't you, Joseph?" An evil light shone in his eyes, and he'd returned to his Cockney voice. "Ye be so prim and proper, Sir Gay. But what good does it do ye? Eh?"

"I left Hawke's dirty business."

"Well, we never really quit looking for you," said Grewno in a normal English voice. "You hurt Hawke's feelings. Don't you know that, mate?"

"Ru … Grewno … why is it they found you in the brig on a pirate ship? You really are a devil, aren't you?"

Grewno fell silent for a moment. "You know you can't ever really leave Hawke, don't you?"

"I've not said a damn word about Hawke to anyone. If I had done, he'd be out of business now, wouldn't he?"

"Sir Gay," said Grewno. "Two pretty girls you have, isn't it?"

"Leave them out of this."

"You go right back now to Liverpool to Hawke and I will."

"I'll never go back to that awful business. Never."

Joseph knew in his heart this man called Grewno would have to be dealt with in some manner, and soon. But how? If Joseph told Hawkins about Grewno and the white slavery business, that might keep Grewno in the prison ship for some time. However, telling Hawkins would present enormous risk because then everyone would find out.

"The best thing," Joseph began, but he then stopped for a moment and shook his head as if he knew his plan would not work. After a moment, he continued, "The best thing here and now is to tell Hawkins about you and who you really are."

"I wouldn't do that, Joseph. Really, I would not."

"I'll be the judge of that."

Uneasiness swelled inside Joseph. Immediately, he wanted to run away from this threatening, awful man, yet he had to admit, it would feel good to kill him. He knew he should ignore Grewno. After all, who among the people here today would believe a word of this "Sir Gay" white slavery story? Still …

"Don't forget the girls, Joseph," said Grewno, laughing in his high, wicked way.

"Damn you, Ru—you and Warner Hawke." Joseph could no longer control himself. In an instant, he found his hands wrapped around Grewno's throat. How good it felt to choke the life out of him.

"Get this bloody bastard off me," screamed Grewno, suddenly twisting free from Joseph's grip. "'E's mad!"

The British guard heard the commotion and yanked Joseph back from the prisoner, then struck Grewno full across the mouth with the butt of his musket.

"What in Hades is this blighter up to now?" the soldier panted. "Best to keep a distance from this one."

Grewno fell silent, cowering down in the flickering orange light of the fire. Only his eyes spoke of the hatred he harbored about the incident.

Suddenly, Joseph knew there would be no talk about white slavery from Grewno. The reason? Each could expose the other to criminal charges. Moreover, those charges might be quite serious. The authorities might even want to hang both of them.

In time, Joseph thought, *I'll have to talk to Warner Hawks about this. Right now, Grewno poses no real threat.*

Suddenly, a stir of excitement rippled through the camp. Sally stood up and waved to Joseph.

"Mist' Joe, come quick! Come quick! Misses Worsham just called yo' name. She's awake."

Hawkins jumped up as Joseph ran to see about Frances.

Chapter 20

Colin and Miss Tilly Stuart

Amanda Worsham
April 1826
Bermuda

AMANDA TOOK SARAH JEAN BY her hand as they ran toward the torch-lit place where her mother rested on the ground. Hearing a commotion behind her, she turned just in time to see three British officers on horseback and a wagon carrying a man and woman come rumbling through the trees toward the small camp.

Oh, it must be the doctor, she thought. *Thank goodness. They got back so fast.*

In about a quarter hour, the doctor called for the Worsham family. Joseph, nervous and fidgety, put Sarah Jean into Sally's arms and ran over to see the doctor.

Amanda watched and listened: Colonel Pakenham, the doctor, and the other two newly arrived officers wore Hawkins's same bright uniform. All the others, the regulars, Joseph had called them, were wearing dull red uniforms. They seemed so concerned and polite. Although some regulars were a bit coarse, she liked them all.

The couple that arrived with the doctor, Matilda and Colin Stuart, had a farm nearby. The Stuarts had just served tea to the three British officers when Hawkins' two soldiers passed by, recognized the horses, and stopped. Precious time had been saved because of this fortunate event.

After about five minutes, Joseph called for Sally.

"Well, I just gonna go talk to dem horses," Moses said. He got up, started singing a quiet little song to himself, and crossed to where the two carriage horses were standing, hobbled.

God bless you, Moses, thought Amanda. *You have a special understanding, a gift with animals. I think you have that with people too. But I'm worried sick about Mother, and I know you are too. Why can't I see her?*

* * * * *

Matilda Stuart came over to talk with the two girls. She stood in front of them, her hands on her hips.

"I want you to call me Miss Tilly," she said. "Your mother is resting now. Frances will feel better when she has rested. She took a nasty blow to her head and face, but I think she'll come out of it in time."

Sarah Jean started to cry.

Amanda felt that familiar cold chill again as she sat on the ground to try to comfort Sarah Jean.

"Oh, love. Your mum is going to be all right. She just hurts from the fall," Miss Tilly tried to comfort Sarah Jean.

"What about the baby?" Amanda asked.

"You know about that … about the bairn?" Miss Tilly lowered her arms against her sides, a friendly but sad expression on her face. "Well, the colonel says the bairn is doing well for now, but nobody can be sure about those things. In any case, I am taking all of you to Stuart Manor. That is what we call our farmhouse near here. You'll be comfortable there while I see to your mother. The colonel will see her every day too. Now don't you worry, girls."

Amanda couldn't help it. She started to cry.

Miss Tilly knelt on the ground and put her arms around both girls.

"Here now, we must thank God that things went as well as they did. Dear Lord, we just want to thank You for seeing to it that these two girls are all right. We ask for special grace for the recovery of Frances over there. Thank you for bringing them all to me at a time when I could help them. Bless this family with Your loving kindness."

She squeezed the girls with a strong hug and said, "Amen." Then she took out a handkerchief and wiped the tears from their cheeks, after which she kissed them.

When Joseph returned, he found the blanket chest, stood the two girls in front of him, and sat on it to talk with his daughters.

Hawkins came over to listen, appearing to be very concerned.

"I guess Miss Tilly has told you Frances is resting," Joseph said. "I talked to Frances some while she was awake. She recognized me, but she doesn't remember what happened. It's just as well, I guess."

"Yes, that is a blessing," said Miss Tilly. She stood and gestured for her husband, who was helping the soldiers.

"What we must do now is take care of her," Joseph said. "Miss Tilly has offered her home to us, and I have accepted. This is a time to take friendship and kind gestures when they're offered. We're a long way from home. I know Frances would rather continue on to England as we planned, but she cannot stand the trip right now."

"We are honored to be of help," said Colin Stuart, who had just walked up.

Colonel Pakenham called for Hawkins. They'd taken the screen down, and soldiers began helping to lift Frances into the back of the Stuart wagon.

In a few minutes, Hawkins returned to tell them the carriage would be ready as soon as two of the officers' horses could be rigged into harness. The British soldiers, except Colonel Pakenham, would march to camp. The rented carriage horses needed attention from the regimental veterinarian, but for now, they were walking slowly beside Moses.

Grewno seemed fit enough to walk, and Hawkins said it would do him good to do so.

Very quickly, the carriage was ready, and Colonel Pakenham and Hawkins walked away to talk privately.

Joseph picked up Sarah Jean and turned to speak to the Stuarts.

"I want to thank you for your kindness," Joseph said. "It is certainly appreciated. I will remember this night and how you helped us for the rest of my life."

"You're welcome," Colin replied. "Say, I'll drive the wagon. You see to your wife. Tilly can take the girls in the carriage with the colonel."

Miss Tilly nodded her head in agreement.

"I'll be in the back here with Frances then," Joseph said.

He put Sarah Jean down and turned toward Amanda. "Sally and Moses can sit on the tailgate. I think the colonel would be pleased if you two girls went with him in the carriage," he said.

In a few minutes, Colonel Pakenham joined Joseph. "Worsham," he said, "may I drive your carriage? These regimental horses might be a bit difficult in harness."

"Indeed, you may, Colonel. But please tell me what to do if Frances wakes again."

"There's just room there for you to be beside her in the back, isn't there? Right. Just talk to her and try to keep her calm. There is precious little anyone can do for her now, I am afraid. I have given her a sedative. She probably will sleep the whole way to the Stuart place."

Joseph stopped to speak with Amanda. "Do you remember back on the beach when we were talking about the John Donne poem?"

"Yes, Father."

"I told you I think the poem means all people are important to God."

"Yes, that is what I think too."

"There is more."

"More?"

"I think the minister was reminding us we need other people. What happened here today has made that point clear. No matter how independent we think we are, there's still that basic need of ours to be reckoned with. Chance sometimes finds us laid bare."

"Yes, sir."

"Maybe sometimes we all need other people, whether we think so or not."

Amanda thought the Worsham family didn't need Grewno very much at all. However, she knew what Joseph meant. She kept her thoughts to herself.

In about an hour they arrived at Stuart Manor and soon found themselves before a warm fire, ablaze in the Stuarts' hearth, the smell of burning cedar filling the air.

Frances had slept the entire way.

Chapter 21

Agnes Phillips

Amanda Worsham
April 1826
Bermuda1341

FRANCES'S ROOM WAS ON THE second floor where clean, fragrant air drifted through the open window and the sound of birds and the fragrance of flowers brought a healing quality. Every morning a small, multicolored clutch of flowers was lovingly cut from the garden and placed in a vase at her bedside. Because of the nuisance of mosquitos in Bermuda, the Stuarts hung mosquito netting around all their beds.

The unborn baby was alive. She could feel it move and kick.

For the first week, Frances slept more than she was awake. Gradually, her strength returned. But each try at getting out of bed, each try for a return to normal life, induced labor pains.

Everyone agreed that Frances might best serve herself and the baby if she stayed in bed, so Sally and Miss Tilly took turns tending to her.

Amanda spent as much time with her mother as she could. Colonel Pakenham limited the visitation for the two girls to an hour in the mornings and an hour in the evening at bedtime to say prayers.

Time passed quickly, and Amanda got to know the Stuarts very well. It had been three weeks since the incident with the convict. Already, April had slipped into May.

Miss Tilly employed a widow cook named Agnes Phillips—an attractive thin, tall, black-haired woman in her midforties who came by every morning to prepare the meals for the day. Amanda enjoyed visiting with her and learning something about cooking from watching and asking questions.

Evening meals at the Stuarts usually consisted of leftovers. Agnes left food from the noonday meal in serving dishes on the dinner table, sitting upon a clean tablecloth and covered with a second clean tablecloth to keep insects away. In addition, this method kept bad air, evil spirits, and whatever else might be floating about in the dining room, from the food. Such was sanitary food handling for the modern times in which they lived. Agnes threw some uneaten food away at the end of the day, some the next day after using her best judgment. As long as the weather remained cool and comfortable, it would be so. When the hot, summer afternoons came, the evening meal would become the main one. Everyone in the house took an afternoon nap during the heat of the day. Amanda wondered if maybe during those nap times Agnes would go home and come back later in the afternoon.

Why not? There would be no need for her to stay here. She could have a life of her own …

The girls helped with chores, played in the garden, and time passed gently. Sometimes Colin took Amanda with him on walks through the fields. At these times, Sarah Jean either took a nap or stayed in the house to play. She had little interest in the workings of Stuart Farm. Amanda thought Sarah Jean was simply too young to enjoy such things.

Chapter 22

Colin Stuart

Amanda Worsham
May 1826
Bermuda

It was bright and beautiful, a lazy type of day—a day when Amanda wanted to run outside and play.

Gazing at the sky from the porch, she thought, *If I could fly, I would fly up there and play hide-and-seek with the tufts of bright white clouds scattered across that glorious azure sky.*

However, she could not fly, and her mother remained quite ill upstairs. But she kept trying to help her mind escape from the harsh reality of what was happening all round her anyway.

Mother doesn't seem able to get out of bed for very long. It's almost as bad as the time she spent in Manchester with the Courtneys—Frances's relations—when Sarah Jean was born. Father seems in a sort of trance and is practically inaccessible to me. Sarah Jean is becoming a very spoiled brat, and there is little beyond reading to pass the time, once the chores are done.

But Amanda used the time well and continued with her studies in the Stuart library: the Bible, in Greek and Latin, as well as history. Oh, but this morning is special.

Fresh in Amanda's mind, whispers of a dream she had last night floated through her thoughts.

What was the dream about? Who was that young man? Was he a courier for some government? He was so mysterious. Why couldn't she see the man's face? She remembered only that he was young and quite good-looking, a dashing man she found fun to be with.

Yet he had no face that she could distinctly remember. *Oh, but he was handsome.* Of that, she was certain.

Yes, this is a special morning. There is hope in my heart about this strange courier. Just who is this young man? Where is he? How long must I wait for him? I am certain that he is real and exists somewhere. He is preparing himself to come for me. Oh my.

Several weeks passed. Amanda went for a brisk long walk across Stuart Farm with Colin. They paused in a field of sweet potatoes.

Colin turned to her and said, "Amanda, I have always heard we are but tenants to the land, even though we own it. I think it is not so much what we own as what we do with it that matters. I think your father understands. We have discussed this farm several times."

"Father has told me nearly the same thing, Mister Stuart. I am impressed with what you and Miss Tilly are doing with this land."

"Your father wants to buy a place hereabout. I offered to sell him this farm."

"But then, what would you do?"

Colin, with a wistful look in his eyes, knelt to inspect a sweet potato plant. "Well, I don't know. Maybe move into Saint George's and rest for a spell," he said then stood up.

"I think you would miss the farm." Amanda sighed.

"It's just a thought, lass."

"Well, I'm certainly glad you haven't sold out before now."

"It isn't so easy to sell property here. Anyway, I enjoy working the land. No Scot would admit he does not need the money. Still …"

With that, they walked back toward Stuart Manor. From the open field, Amanda could see the house. Colin had told her that the roof made of white limestone had been constructed to catch rainwater. The wooden-framed, two-story house painted white with gray trim on shutters and corner moldings had space enough underneath for another short level. It reminded Amanda of houses in Antig'a …

where Joseph was born, where he still owned property and visited from time to time.

Those are servants' quarters beneath the house, but until now, no one ever used them, thought Amanda. *These days Moses and Sally live there and help with whatever is needed. Moses is a good jack-of-all-trades and takes over routine chores in that respect. He is by trade a carpenter, but there is little real need for that now. His other skills, being yardman and babysitter, have not come into much use in Bermuda. Miss Tilly works constantly in the garden. Hardly ever needs any help with that.*

As they approached the house, Amanda heard a happy, bubbling sound of laughter and saw Moses and Sally emerge from the door that led to their quarters. They were holding hands. Amanda wondered as she watched them enjoying each other why there were no Ward children.

Amanda blushed and felt a little embarrassed as she walked the rest of the way to the front porch. She said nothing to Colin of her thoughts. She was afraid he could either sense them or see the redness of her face.

Amanda heard Sarah Jean crying and hurried to see about her. She found her sitting on the bed with her doll in her lap. Sarah Jean was all right, just lonely. These were stressful times for them all, especially the youngest Worsham. Already the month of June, Amanda wished they could continue with the trip to England, but that was impossible now. They would have to wait until the baby came.

Chapter 23

Blasted Mosquitoes, Anyway!

Joseph Worsham
June 1826
Bermuda

Joseph awakened suddenly. At five o'clock in the morning, the hard, uncomfortable chair that had been his bed for the night made his body sore. He stood up stiffly and rubbed his eyes.

Damn that chair, he thought, working his arms and legs, trying to get the blood moving again.

He made his way to the bedside table and turned the lamp up slightly, wanting to check on Frances. He found her sleeping peacefully, her skin color good but pale.

He was beginning to think maybe she would recover before it came time for the baby to arrive. He stood beside the bed for a moment, trying to sense her needs.

I don't think she requires anything right now, he thought. *And maybe it is too early for me to be up and about. I don't know. Damn that Grewno bastard.*

He checked the mosquito netting. Sometimes Frances pulled it open for fresh air, but this morning it was in place over her bed.

Blasted mosquitoes, anyway! In the evening they swarm all over us. Good job we remembered the mosquito netting last night. They were eating poor Frances alive. Oh well—harmless, I guess.

When he considered the prospect of trying to sleep on the chair again, he decided to stay up and get ready for the trip to town with Colin. So he went to the room across the hall, freshened up, and dressed himself for the day.

After finishing up, he walked downstairs to the front porch where he stopped for a moment to take a deep breath. The morning air was cool and clear to his senses.

Joseph thought it was about time for things to get better. His little family had been with the Stuarts for two months now, a long time to endure such an abnormal life. The Stuarts were really good people—but he knew they must be getting tired of all this commotion in their home.

It was still quite dark, but a light shone from the kitchen, and he could see the glow from the lamp reflected on the shiny leaves of the holly bushes growing against the garden wall. The hollies had come from Philadelphia. Colin had gotten the plants from a friend of his, a ship's captain, and was always talking about something he was growing … in the yard or on the farm.

Joseph walked down the steps and around the house to see what was going on in the kitchen. He found Agnes Phillips there kneading bread dough. When he knocked and walked in, she smiled at him the way he had seen Miss Tilly smile at the colonel.

"Good morning, sir," she greeted, turning the dough into an oblong ball and beating it on the countertop with her fist.

It is good to be liked, Joseph thought. "Good morning."

Agnes, a very pretty woman, had black hair and dark eyes, but she was so thin he wondered if she ate properly. Even as he thought it, he realized that she ate as well as any of them here at Stuart Manor. She was the cook, after all. Anyway, the way she was pounding the bread dough, she seemed to have plenty of strength.

I wonder what it would be like to go home and crawl in the bed with her? he thought. *I will bet she would be good in the bed, a lean, strong woman like that.*

The idea had flashed in his mind almost in the same instant, as had the first thought about her. Suddenly, he blushed with embarrassment.

My dear, sweet Frances so ill upstairs and me having such a notion. Anyway, Agnes is a bit thin. Maybe too thin to have any real fun with? Well, I guess I cannot help it, he thought. *It has been a long time. I wonder if she finds me attractive.*

At those times when he would look at himself in a mirror, he found his reflection to be acceptable—not especially handsome, but acceptable. He had never understood the attraction women felt for him, yet he had sensed it since he was but a small boy. Something about him brought out the more basic instincts in whatever female he was near.

He could see, or thought he could see, Agnes was no exception. He watched her as she pounded the bread dough. As she hit the table with her hands, her breasts jiggled.

"Would you care for a bit of breakfast, sir?"

"Aye. Perhaps a cup of tea and a biscuit?" Joseph smiled at her and took a chair beside the table.

"I've already cooked a proper breakfast, sir … well, most of it. Here are some sausages." She uncovered a pan to show him the sausages. "And it won't take but a minute to cook you the rest … whatever you want. And there's biscuits in the oven. Biscuits and marmalade, maybe?"

She turned to search the pantry. "Why, I've a fresh jar from London," she said. "Well, fresh as can be, with us so far away and everything."

Joseph looked up at her and smiled. "Marmalade," he said.

Agnes poured him some tea and brought biscuits and sausages for him, along with the jar of marmalade. She had a clean, well-scrubbed smell about her.

He thought again about her in a lustful way.

"Do you think you might want some eggs?" she asked.

He smiled again. Agnes was definitely arousing him. "No," he said. "This will do, Agnes. Thank you, though." He had recovered from his twinge of guilt feelings. He looked at Agnes and blushed, wondering if she could see it. *Somehow, she knows,* he thought. *Anyway, she is not really arousing me. It is my fault. My fantasies are the problem.*

There came the sound of someone walking across the porch and over to the kitchen door. He turned in time to see Colin entering the room.

"Good morning to you, Colin," Agnes said. She bowed her head slightly and executed a little curtsy. It looked to be a playful flourish rather than an obligatory action.

That is a cute woman, Joseph thought.

Colin smiled. "Aye, good morning, Agnes. Good morning to you, Joseph."

"Yes, I think it's a good morning," Joseph replied. "You've a happy face, Colin. It's good to see you. It always is."

"'Tis going to be a good one today, indeed," said Colin. "I can just feel it. Would you have any eggs ready, Agnes? Woke up with a fierce hunger this morning, I did."

Agnes nodded. "Only take a moment."

"You know how I like them," said Colin. "Joseph, I heard you stirring about. You couldn't sleep, could you? Worried about your sweet lady, is it?"

"Yes, I reckon so."

Colin took a seat across the table, and they sat quietly as Agnes waited on them.

The breakfast was excellent. Joseph thought Colin was very fortunate to have such a cook and housekeeper. He had put aside his secret thoughts and feelings about Agnes, trading them for better, more socially acceptable thoughts.

After breakfast, he and Colin went to the barn, made the wagon ready, and started for Hamilton.

Chapter 24

Sue the Military, Indeed

Joseph Worsham
June 1826
Bermuda

THE TRIP INTO HAMILTON PROVED slow and uneventful, and as soon as the party reached the edge of town, they stopped at the black-smith's shop. Several days after the trip to Horseshoe Cove, Joseph had returned the animals and the carriage to the blacksmith. It was something the Saint George's factor had arranged. He thought maybe they belonged to the smith but had not asked.

Colin had told him that only one or two hundred horses were kept on the islands, more or less.

"Not that anyone's counting horses, you understand, but they are dear."

Joseph had seen several wagons pulled by donkeys and some by mules while he had been in Bermuda. He listened while Colin talked to the smith about the weather and about farming. Every now and again they would glance his way.

When they finished talking, Joseph asked the blacksmith about the three horses he had used for the beach outing. That day, all the horses had been shaken quite a bit, and one of the carriage horses had received a cut on the right foreleg. An injured horse could be a nervous, temperamental creature.

Colonel Pakenham had kept the two carriage horses at the military camp until they were calmed enough and the cut had healed enough to bring them back.

Joseph wondered about the pack mule he had rented, but he said nothing. *That old mule just kept quiet and did its job. Any mule can hold its own. Mules were ornery … but trustworthy.*

The blacksmith told them, "The horses are recovering well, and both carriage horses are back in service. Sorry to say, though, the other horse is in the back, lame."

They then talked, briefly, about the convict and the things that had happened to the Worsham family. Joseph made the smith happy and paid extra for the lame horse. Goodbyes were said, and Joseph and Colin walked toward the wagon while the smith turned to continue his fiery task with bellows and charcoal.

Colin drove the wagon to the center of town and stopped beside the water trough. When the horse had drunk its fill, Colin maneuvered the wagon slowly on toward a wooden fence where a horse could be tethered for an hour or so in the shade.

"I'm going to see about the ship's mail," he told Joseph and began walking toward the wharf and the post office on Front Street.

Joseph took off in the direction of the constable's office. As he left the wagon, he noticed a man wearing a dark suit and a top hat step out of a shadow behind a tree to follow him.

Must have been watching us all along, thought Joseph.

"I say, sir," the man called. "Could you stop for a moment? Like to have a word with you, I would."

When Joseph turned around, the man tipped his hat, and Joseph saw that one eye was covered with a patch.

"Couldn't help overhearing your conversation with the blacksmith," the man said. "About the escaped convict, the misadventure, as it were. I was in the back of the establishment seeing to my 'orse."

Joseph's eyes narrowed. "Well, how may I help you? I mean, what business is it of yours?"

"Quite. I say, what is your name, sir?"

"Worsham … Joseph Worsham," Joseph replied warily.

"It was you what suffered distress at the hands of the escaped convict, was it not?"

"Yes, it was my family right enough. However, you haven't answered my question. What business is that of yours? I was on my way to the constable's office on the matter."

The man pulled out a kerchief from his right sleeve and wiped his forehead in a nervous way with his left hand.

"I'm sorry to approach you in such a manner, sir. Really, I am." He took off his hat and held it between his right arm and his waistcoat.

Well, that is odd, thought Joseph. *What is the matter with his right hand?*

The man nodded and wiped the headband of his hat with the kerchief.

"My name is Franklin Semmes," he said. "I'm solicitor in Saint George's. 'Ave a proper office there, I do. I've come to Hamilton today on business. The events involving your family are common knowledge in Saint George's."

Semmes put his top hat back on but held the handkerchief in his hand.

"I say, your accent is very British," said Semmes. "I thought the people involved in that unfortunate business were all Yanks from the Carolinas, as it were. Someone in shipping … to England from Charleston. Something like that."

"I'm English." Joseph put his hands on his hips. "You haven't told me what business you have with me."

"An expert in certain legal matters, I am. You need such an individual, I think. What plans 'ave you formulated to punish the wretched man, the perpetrator, as it were? If I may be of service to you?" Again, he took off his hat and turned the brim up between the thumb and forefinger of his left hand, his right hand shoved inside the crown.

As it were? As it were? What kind of nervous talk is this?

Joseph didn't care for this man or for his nervous left-handed mannerisms. "In what way do you believe you can help me?"

Semmes turned his head to one side and cut his good eye over toward Joseph. "Perhaps you would be wanting to press charges against the military for letting the scoundrel escape in the first place," he said. "Or maybe against the bloke for what 'e did to you. If that be the case, I have certain friends in proper places what could be of help to you. It could be justice might best be served if the man were to be transported, as they say. We sends the likes of him to New South Wales these days."

Semmes raised his eyebrows and rolled his one eye around, seeming to study the ground.

Joseph decided to discuss this man Semmes with the constable. He did not know whether Semmes was competent or if he could be trusted. Perhaps the constable would know. He seemed harmless enough, but there was something Joseph did not like about him. The man had a sniveling way that disgusted him.

What in the hell does he have to be nervous and upset about?

"I don't really have time to visit your office in Hamilton as yet." Joseph thought for a moment. "And I do not wish to discuss this further with you today. I must give the matter of legal assistance careful thought. Do you have a business card, a calling card you can give me?"

Semmes tucked the handkerchief into his right sleeve, reached inside his jacket, and pulled out a card. He turned it over to examine it briefly then handed it to Joseph.

"I'll be there at whatever time you specify, I will."

Joseph tucked the card into his breast pocket. "I'll send you a message should I wish to consult you," he said.

"Right. Well, 'ave yourself a good day, Mister Worsham, sir." He popped his hat back on, pulled the brim as a gesture, bowed slightly, and turned to walk away.

"Good day to you, Semmes."

Joseph wondered why this man from Saint George's, especially a man supposedly of letters, had not mentioned John Worsham, a well-known shipper. He watched as the man walked into the side street from which he came and disappeared.

Sue the military, indeed.

Suddenly, Joseph heard a man running, breathing hard.

Lord, what now? Wherever I am, there also is drama.

The man held a knife in his hand, heading straight toward Joseph.

Then, just as suddenly, a pistol exploded from the alleyway across the street, the ball striking a large oak tree nearby. The man turned away from Joseph, ran down the street, and into the morning sunlight.

A moment later, Semmes appeared from the shadows, carrying a pistol. Had he fired the shot?

"Oh, Worsham," he said, "Lucky it is for you I turned in time to see that one. Must have been a robber … no doubt after your pocket gold? *Gorblimey!*"

God blight you, indeed, thought Joseph, turning and hurrying toward the constable's office, leaving Semmes standing in the street. He had a bad feeling about Semmes and about the shot he had fired. Was this business somehow connected with Warner Hawke? Both men wore an eye patch.

Was that reason enough to associate them?

Joseph could have saved the trip. The constable wasn't there. He wrote a note to the gentleman, slipped it under the door, and started toward the wharf. Semmes was nowhere in sight.

"Hawke be damned," said Joseph to the empty street.

After locating Colin, they headed for the tearoom. Colin paused by the front door to leave his cigar on a low wall at the edge of the stone steps.

"You about ready to head back?" he asked.

"Well, maybe. Let us talk about that inside, shall we?" Joseph opened the door for Colin to enter.

They took a table near the front window, ordered tea, and talked for a few minutes. Joseph told Colin about the meeting with Semmes and the absent constable.

Colin said, smiling and waving at someone he saw outside, "I say. There's Miss Agnes and her carriage. Didn't expect to see her in town today. She could've come with us."

Joseph turned to look at Agnes. He had never seen her away from Stuart Manor. *She certainly is pretty,* he thought. "Don't suppose I could interest you in staying to see the constable, could I?" he asked Colin, waving at Agnes.

Agnes halted her carriage and waited while Joseph and Colin paid for their tea. Colin arranged for the waiter to follow him out with a tinderbox.

"Why, Miss Agnes," said Colin, stooping to retrieve his cigar. "What brings you to town?"

The waiter had a flame glowing in the tinderbox. Colin paused to light the cigar.

"I've a bit of shopping to do," she said. "And yourself?"

"Joseph wanted to see about the horses, the ones involved in the accident, you know. I need to stop by the feed and seed merchant—ordered a new plow from Massachusetts. Joseph wants to stay and see the constable. I'd just as lief go back and see to my crops, if I can."

"Maybe Joseph would like to stay and go back with me?" said Agnes. She looked sternly at Joseph. "What about it?" she said.

Joseph wondered what the stern look meant. He rubbed his lips with his thumb and forefinger. "Why, yes, I would like that," he said. "Are you sure it would be no bother?"

"Och, no," said Agnes. She had a sparkle in her eyes and was almost laughing. "Colin," she added, "you don't really need that cigar, now, do you?" She reached out, and Colin gave it to her, whereby she promptly placed it between her own lips. She satisfied herself that it was lit, then reached over to Joseph for him to grasp and steady himself for the climb to the seat. Then she slid to the other side to make room for him. Agnes seemed to enjoy the cigar.

"How about you, Colin? You need a ride somewhere?" Agnes asked.

"No. I enjoy walking. See you both later." Colin backed away from the carriage and waved while it pulled away.

"You going marketing with me, Joseph?" Agnes asked. "I've some lady's shopping to do. Want a new summer hat, I do. And what about you? Want anything from the haberdashery or the general store?"

"No, but I'll go along with you, Agnes. Maybe the constable will return soon. In the meantime, perhaps I can get to know you better."

While Agnes went shopping for her hat elsewhere, Joseph tried on several items of clothing in the haberdashery. He purchased three shirts and a half dozen collars to match, a loose-fitting summer jacket, and a cap that he thought was becoming. When he finished with his shopping, he gathered his parcels of new clothing and went to find Agnes.

He found her in the general store. She had apparently finished smoking the cigar since it was missing.

Agnes knew the storeowner, who was a friend of the constable. She checked with him to see whether he knew anything about the closed office. As it turned out, the constable was ill with a fever. He wasn't expected to return for a week or more.

Nothing further to keep them in town, they left for Stuart Farm. On the way, Joseph did his best to appear nonchalant and not too interested in Agnes. But as the carriage pulled into the Stuart's yard, he sensed that Agnes knew the struggle he was under … the struggle to behave himself. She smiled and told him he must visit her home sometime.

"Whenever you can," she said. "And bring your sweet little girls," she added. "Maybe the visit will do you good."

"Where is your home, Agnes?"

"Back at the crossroads, it's a little house off to one side. You can't see it from here or from the road. I usually just walk the distance, but I bring the carriage when it's raining."

It's not raining today, he thought.

Studying him briefly, she smiled again and said, "Colin tells me you are a wealthy man. I must say, it just doesn't show, either on yourself or the rest of your family. I've not ever seen more unassuming people. Think that's a tribute to your true worth as a human being."

"Thank you, Agnes. That's very kind of you to say."

"I like you, Joseph Worsham. Take care …"

Clicking her tongue, she brought the reins down smartly on the horse's rear. She laughed as she drove the carriage away, leaving him standing in the Stuart's yard, feeling both relieved and ashamed of himself.

He thought, watching her drive away, that he'd came close to ruining everything, probably for both of them, assuming she was interested in him in that way.

It's hard sometimes, he thought. *Mighty damn hard. Anyway, I'm always thinking about more than I can get.*

Chapter 25

Impromptu Conference

Nobody knows this Semmes character but Father.

Amanda Worsham
June 1826
Bermuda

IT RAINED ALL DAY. ABOUT noon the weather cleared somewhat, the sun came out, and birds sang in the trees around Stuart Manor. At two o'clock, Colonel Pakenham and Hawkins arrived in a carriage to check on Frances. Amanda met them at the door, but they brushed her aside. Hawkins said they wanted to speak with Joseph, so she went upstairs to call him and then followed Joseph back down to the foyer. The four men—Colin, Joseph, and the two officers—entered the parlor to have an impromptu conference.

Amanda stood in the doorway to listen.

"Worsham, I'm not going to mince words with you," said the colonel, his voice gruff. "Frances should be a damn sight better by now. It's the bairn ... too much of a strain on her. We could take the baby, could induce a miscarriage, and give your wife a chance to get well. Think on it and let me know. She's taken a turn for the worse. Today she awoke with the fevers. We are well into the sickly season—in another week, it will be July. You have that sickly business in Charleston, eh? It may mean nothing. Or ..."

"I'll speak to Frances," Joseph assured him. "But I know what the answer will be. She has wanted this child too long. No, Colonel, my Frances is adamant on that point, and I agree. It is never best to kill a fellow human being, especially one as wee, slight, and faint as that one."

The colonel cleared his throat. "I …" he began but stopped. Then he rubbed his chin. "Joseph, there's another matter. This Grewno person. We figure the best thing would be to just hang the bastard. He has caused too much trouble. He's a bad sort, that one. Could be the law would see it that way … especially if you file charges. The people here about are afraid of him now. Nobody wants him to go back to the prison ship."

"A bit harsh, don't you think?" Joseph countered.

"But," said Colin, "what if Frances dies?"

"Grewno might have dealt a fatal blow to any one of your party, sir," Hawkins added. "He certainly had no thought for your safety and well-being when he jumped in front of the carriage."

"There must be some alternative to hanging Grewno," Joseph objected. "What of the military rules he has broken? I mean … would you do that … ?"

Joseph hesitated for a moment, and Amanda wondered what he was thinking. He looked intensely troubled all of a sudden, almost as if a demon were chasing him.

"I mean," Joseph continued, "is he that much at odds with the Crown for crimes because of his escape? Is it such a serious crime to run away from one's situation as a prisoner? Hanging is out of the question, I think."

"If every blighter that deserted his post was hanged, his Britannic Majesty's forces would be decimated," said Hawkins. "Several good floggings might be more direct and to the point."

"Father," Amanda interrupted. She'd been trying to catch his glance. "Why not just send him to the penal colony? The place beyond the seas, the place beneath England on the globe, the continent in the South Seas?"

"Beneath England, indeed," said Colonel Pakenham. "The lass has a flair for geography and words. What?"

"Hobart Town," said Hawkins. "That's transportation today. Bloody good idea, if you ask me."

Amanda took note of the fact that Joseph's breathing had relaxed somewhat. *Maybe that really is the answer: transportation. I think Father agrees.*

"The lass may be on to something," said the colonel. "She's a good one, right enough. But really, Worsham, children should be seen and not heard."

Why, you self-righteous ninny, thought Amanda. *Children, indeed. Thank God you're not my father.*

Amanda looked away. It was difficult for her not to express her thoughts as the inner voice welled up inside. Swallowing her fury, she thought better of it. Instead, she blinked her eyes, smiled, and looked toward Joseph.

"Well, Colonel," said Joseph, "I'm certain some children should keep their mouths shut, but my Amanda has a clear head. I listen to her. And so, I think, should you."

"You mean about the penal colony?"

"Why, I've been approached by an attorney-at-law about that," said Joseph. "His name is Franklin Semmes … a one-eyed man. He tells me his office is in Saint George's. Perhaps you know him."

"I can't say I do."

Nobody knows this Semmes character but Father, thought Amanda. *Well, the military probably would not either then.*

The colonel shifted his weight in the chair. "Look here, Worsham, this is a military matter. You don't need a solicitor." He drew a cigar from inside his tunic.

"And Hawkins," he added, "the man's *been* flogged. Still, he continues his crimes."

"Now, Colonel, you know Tilly wouldn't like that," said Colin, pointing to the cigar.

Amanda smiled and squinted her eyes as the colonel put the cigar away.

"Right," he said, shifting his weight again. "What is the world coming to? So many people minding the king's business," he said, almost under his breath.

"If you'll pardon me, sir," said Joseph, "the man Grewno has made this *our* business."

"Why such interest in sending that one to Hobart Town down under?" the colonel asked.

Amanda turned and climbed the stairs toward her mother's bedroom, leaving the discussion to the men.

Hobart Town, Sullivan Cove, wherever Mother England's penal colonies are located, is a boring subject. The Americans took away the colonial penal colonies—that convenient banishment place—from the English. Many fine men fell into bad straits with England and wound up deported to such places. Many Irishmen were deported—not all political prisoners—men, women ... even children were actual criminals. But surely, our blasted Grewno is such.

One patriot said—or wrote—that perhaps they, the colonies, should send back to England a boatload of rattlesnakes in kind to return the favor.

* * * * *

Miss Tilly sat in a chair beside the bed, knitting a sweater of soft Irish wool.

She looked up and spoke as soon as Amanda stepped through the doorway.

"I hoped it was you, lass. Come in. We were just talking about you. How is the meeting downstairs going?"

"They want to punish that awful man, Grewno."

"Where is Grewno now?" Miss Tilly asked.

"I don't know where he is, but wherever that is, I hope he can't get out."

Frances frowned. "What does your father say?" A pillow propped her up in the bed. She looked so frail, but her black hair had been neatly combed into a prim and proper coif, and she wore a pretty nightgown.

How very prissy, thought Amanda. "Colonel Pakenham said he and Hawkins want the authorities to transport Grewno, or hang him and be done with it. A military hanging."

"Doesn't the Lord tell us vengeance is His?" said Frances. "Hasn't the death penalty been eliminated now for many crimes in England? And what is the need for this … this transportation?"

"Transportation, is it?" Miss Tilly frowned, peering over her knitting. "Like as not, Old Pakenham wants to protect the world from the likes of Grewno. Maybe Grewno is daft. Maybe he has lace on his drawers, as Hawkins tells it. But transportation. Well, maybe that is too good for Grewno. I wonder. We just don't know much about that one. Talk in town is he's too dangerous to stay in the prison barge."

She stopped to count the stitches that had fallen out of count because of the excitement. "Criminals are not hanged today," she said. "Now there's transportation because there aren't enough prisons to go round."

She glanced up now and then, peering over her glasses at whomever she was addressing.

"Well," she said, "Old Pakenham may sound rough, but inside beats the heart of a real … well, a kind person. Christopher has devoted his life, up to this minute, to service to the Crown and to his fellow man. The colonel's name is Christopher. Did you know that?"

Amanda remembered what had been said about the baby Frances carried. She decided not to say anything about it.

"Why is Pakenham posted *here* as physician and not at some easier post?" asked Frances. "Surely a man of his station could secure a post in England during his declining years. Perhaps in Bath. That would be capital."

"Christopher Pakenham has interest enough to place himself at his pleasure, but he chooses to be stationed here with us. We have a problem with yellow fever in Bermuda, and that is his specialty. He served in the fevered areas of the Leeward Islands, Cape Town, and India. Somehow, he seems to have a resistance to it. Bermuda is most fortunate he's chosen to serve here. And anyway, I think what he has in mind is to retire and go on half pay in Bermuda." She put the knitting down for a moment then sat straight up in the chair.

Amanda could see that Miss Tilly liked Pakenham.

"Did you know the yellow jack, or *fièvre vil jaune,* I believe the French call it, served once as an ally to the British and the Americans as well? Some call it 'epidemic' fever or 'prevailing' fever.

"Napoleon's brother-in-law, General Charles LeClerc, along with some twenty thousand of his frog troops, died of the disease on the island of Saint Domingue, right before the time of the American's Louisiana Purchase. Did you know that? Ravages of the fever thwarted Napoleon's plans of a North American empire." She resumed her knitting.

"Mother," said Amanda, "Father said he has already contacted someone who offered to check into sending Grewno to New South Wales."

Frances nodded. "We have discussed it," she acknowledged.

"Can't you just send him?"

"Certainly not, Amanda. Such things are arranged by the authorities."

"But you can't be sure he will be transported."

"No, that's true," Frances sighed.

"Christopher would help, if there is a problem," Miss Tilly offered.

"How long would his sentence be?" Amanda asked.

"I have heard such things come in multiples of seven years, lass," Miss Tilly answered. "Say, why don't you visit with your mother while I go and ask Agnes to bake some of her tea biscuits."

She tucked her knitting away in the bag beside her chair and stood up.

"Would you see if Sarah Jean is ready to get up?" Frances asked Amanda. "I think she's sleeping too much."

Miss Tilly smiled warmly and gestured to Amanda. "Lass, Frances wants to talk to you. Why don't you stay and talk? Come on now, just you visit with your sweet mum for a bit. I'll go and check on Sarah Jean on my way to the kitchen."

Amanda moved closer, then reached out and held her mother's hand. "Thank you, Miss Tilly."

Miss Tilly left the room.

Chapter 26

My Dear, Sweet "Frog"

Frances Worsham
July 1826
Bermuda

FRANCES FELT FAINT, DIZZY. NOTHING she'd eaten today had agreed with her. She sat upon the side of the bed, rubbing her swollen belly.

The baby will be coming soon ... ready or not. So it is July Fourth—the day all Yanks should be celebrating. I certainly do not feel up to it today. Just as well—hardly any Yanks here about now, are there? Haven't felt well since I asked Tilly to take the mosquito netting away. When was that? God. I believe it has been a week. Time passes so frantically anymore. Turned out so awfully hot, didn't it? That's what's the matter. I cannot breathe ... not a breath of fresh air. Bad air, that's the problem. And I feel awful. I vomited blood during the night. It's worse than the vapors, isn't it? Something ... something more than a blow to the head ...

She looked at her oldest daughter asleep in the chair, the sweetheart she had named Amanda.

I took that name from the Courtney family, from a sainted lady who gave up worldly pursuits to become a Church of England nun. Oh well. No Methodists there, either. Church of England, Methodist, what does it really matter? Much to do about nothing—foolish to stir up controversy when really none exists. No control by the Crown over Methodists, that's what it's really all about. If they cannot control a thing, it's considered bad. Royal decree, that sort of thing ...

There was no hiding some things, but Frances had successfully kept a secret from all of her family. She'd heard Tilly use the word *frog*.

That word was a British slang term for a Frenchman. Frog ... damn, she thought. *If they only knew. My dear, sweet Frog.* That word brought images gushing from the depths of her memories.

"Oh, Mother, what is it?" Amanda stretched, awakening. "Is there anything I can do for you?"

"My firstborn, my sweet Amanda. Whatever happens, I want you to know that I love you."

Frances held out her arms and beckoned for Amanda to come closer.

"Frog" was a pet name Frances called Beau. But mostly, that was long ago. Beau was of French descent. Everyone knew that. But not many knew the real story about Beau.

Frog, indeed, she thought.

Amanda stood beside the bed.

Sally, who had been sitting quietly in the chair beside the window watching, stood and brushed a wrinkle from her dress. "Miss Frances, may I be excused for a few minutes?"

Snuggling up to her mother, Amanda sat on the bed.

"Certainly, Sally. You've been so quiet I hardly knew you were there." Frances gently lifted Amanda's chin so she could look into her daughter's eyes. "I need to discuss some things with my oldest now."

Sally left the room, singing softly.

"My little lady, you must be strong," she said. "The truth is, I've had no warning of impending doom, no grave prophecy of death. Still, there is this feeling—"

"Oh, Mother, you feel it too?"

"Feel it? Yes, I think I do."

"That something is very wrong?" Amanda probed.

"Are you worried about the baby, love?"

"Something more. But about the baby too."

"This child is not as strong as you, Amanda. That's for certain. But sometimes I feel him move. It's a boy, you know."

"No, I didn't know." Amanda frowned, puzzled.

"Oh, I just know. And Pakenham, I know all about what he wants to do too."

"What are you talking about?"

"Pakenham wants to induce a miscarriage. I'll not stand for it. He told me his thoughts first off. The nerve of that pompous ass."

Amanda managed a weak smile. She understood well about Pakenham. Her expression betrayed her.

Frances relaxed on the bed and put her hands on her stomach. "When the subject comes up," she said, "I want you to know about it too. There'll be none of that nonsense. This child and I will make it together or not at all. That's God's business."

"Yes, Mother. I know, and so does Father."

"You are always so strong," said Frances. "It seems to be your nature. I won't have to worry about you if I should … Well, no matter. I think I worry most about your father and this unborn child. You girls will be lonely without me, but you are attractive, and in time someone will come along in each of your lives to relieve the loneliness."

Frances looked away toward the window.

"God knows your father has plenty of money," she said after a moment. "That will certainly help." She sighed.

"But I worry about your father, should something happen to me. He loves me dearly, but he would be so lonely. I would want him to remarry, as soon as possible, and not be lonely. I have discussed it with him, of course."

"And there is the other business," she said, wrinkling her brow. "He loves to look at pretty young ladies. And he is such a beautiful man. Really, he is. You must know that, Amanda. But he wouldn't like for me to say that. He would blush if I even said he was handsome. But he is certainly a most desirable man. Joseph needs love and vivacity about him, just as a flower needs sunlight."

Frances looked past her chest at her stomach. "I cannot offer him much at present, I'm afraid."

"Oh, Mother, he loves you very much. You know he does. There could never be any other woman in his life."

"You can never be certain, my love. And should something happen to me, I want Joseph to remarry." She paused for a moment and pulled Amanda close to her again. "So I have made arrangements for the two of you."

Frances wore a stern look, as if she had something important to express. She had postponed the *Frog* business for now, perhaps for good and all. If it came to it, Beau could tell them their secret. It would be his responsibility.

"I made the arrangements long ago," she said, "when each of you girls were born. You have what many would deem to be a fortune, just waiting for time and circumstance to bring about your need."

"Oh, Mother! Please don't say things like that. God can make you well. And I have prayed for you so much. I know that He will help."

"My dear," Frances soothed, "I have the faith. It is because I do that I am not afraid for myself. It will be because God has called me home that I will go. You know I am Methodist. I have lived my life for our Lord as well as I could. But I'm not afraid, not for myself. It's the wonder of it that ties my stomach in knots. The not knowing when or what."

"What are we to do, Mother?" Amanda wiped her nose with her kerchief. "What would you have me do?"

Frances took the kerchief and patted the tears from Amanda's cheeks.

It is time to tell her, she thought. The unspoken thought turned her expression into one of pain, almost a pout. *I cannot do it.*

Frances held her daughter's gaze. "I was about to tell you of the accounts you and Sarah Jean own in Manchester. If either of you needs funds, I mean. Otherwise, your father has quite enough money. It is only the realization that he could remarry and you might lose the independence I want you to have that troubles me for you. Just contact my family's bank in Liverpool or London. Whoever is the trust officer will know all about it. There is no need for you to worry. If you need your very own wealth, it will always be there."

A bit overwhelmed, Amanda simply nodded.

"It seems curious to me, ironic. God knows I didn't marry your father for his money. I had more of my own money than I, or anyone, could need. Since the fever took my brother Harry, I was your grandfather's only heir. In his will, he left a lifetime bequeath to Mother. The rest he left in trust for me and my son—should I ever have one.

"And if that weren't enough, your father invested my dowry and increased the sum all the more, which he insisted was mine. In his hands, that dowry has grown to noble proportions. He has never, to my knowledge, made a bad investment. Somehow, he knows what the world needs at the moment. He has told me investing well is something anyone can do."

Frances huffed through her nose and shook her head.

"He just looks to the needs of whatever he is about. If he doesn't know what those needs are right away, pretty soon somebody will tell him. According to your father, all that is necessary to execute a sound investment is to listen and look."

Amanda smiled. "If it were so easy, Mother, everyone would be wealthy."

"At the very least," said Frances, rushing on, "I need not worry about my little girls. Now, help me with my robe, would you? No, help me put on something pretty. I want to look attractive for your father and for my girls."

She stood beside the bed with an air of determination as Amanda picked out her prettiest bed jacket. It surely was large enough, having been tailored during her Sarah Jean pregnancy.

"Mother, you are always *very attractive*," Amanda commented.

"Someday all the slaves will be free and women everywhere will take possession of their natural rights. Someday … but not today. Society treats women as if we were children, as if we were property, as if we could not possibly do the rightful thing if we were allowed to have a hand in world affairs.

"Someday the entire world will be a fair and proper place for all its people, all its children. But for now, I'm just glad to be alive."

Frances turned toward Amanda, her hands pressed together in a prayerful manner.

"Oh, Amanda, I do want to talk to you about Moses and Sally while Sally is still out of the room. It will only take a moment. And if I have the strength, I must tell you something else." She sat down on the side of the bed.

"You know I have long wanted those two to be free. Your father has agreed. No longer does he argue he owns only the right to their labor ... that the slave is still free to live." She paused to take a deep breath. "Or that slavery in his hands is a sort of indentured labor agreement, or that aside from the labor thing, the person is still free. They just cannot quit and leave." She shook her head.

"There is something about that slavery situation he won't talk about, something he's never shared with me. 'You know,' he has said, 'some things are worse than slavery.' But I can't imagine what that might be. You see, your father believes that it's enough to be thoughtful and benevolent to slaves. Freedom is out of the question. It's as if the investment he has made in these slaves hasn't yet come to fruition."

She looked up as if she were looking toward God.

"Well, no more," she said. "Joseph has agreed to see both Moses and Sally free by the time slavery is forbidden in the British Empire. And that day is coming, Amanda. Everywhere, people are talking about it. All civilized people will abolish slavery soon, I feel certain. The God-given grace of William Wilberforce will prevail. You do know Wilberforce always worked to bring about freedom for England's slaves?"

"Yes, Mother. I've heard you speak of him before. I admire the man. Tell me more about him and his group of friends, *The Saints.*"

"I really want you to know this, so pay attention. I met him just once. He attended an antislavery celebration in London, and I was there. I've learned to love the man.

"Wilberforce was a close friend of William Pitt the Younger, and both men were educated at Cambridge. Beginning in 1787, Wilberforce and his group of friends in the House of Commons— Thomas Clarkson, Granville Sharp, Henry Thornton, Charles Grant, Edward James Eliot, Zachary Macaulay, and James Stephen— caused quite a stir with their antislavery ideas and legislation. So far,

Wilberforce's efforts have lasted some thirty-nine years. The man is silver-tongued and a tireless sponsor of antislavery legislation. He's a well-deserved hero of mine, and he certainly should be one of yours. You are right, Amanda, those men were known as *The Saints* when they began their efforts—an aptly named group if there ever was one. Think of it, Wilberforce has fought against slavery for the better part of forty years—a long, uphill battle. Economics, you know.

"The slave trade—but not slavery itself—is now outlawed throughout the British Empire. That Empire, Mother England, has taken it upon itself to eliminate what we call slave trade. Ships hauling slaves from Africa, that kind of 'slave trade.' It is still lawful to own a slave that has been 'grandfathered in,' so to speak. That means British warships are patrolling the high-seas trade routes right now, intercepting and seizing rogue nations' slave ships and freeing the slaves at the nearest port. British plantations are allowed to keep their existing slaves for now, but they aren't allowed to import any more slaves from Africa, or anywhere else. Curious. *The sea lanes belong to England.* Imagine that. For now, anyway. God bless the spirit of Lord Nelson.

"Slavery itself will be outlawed next, and they all will be set free, I just know it. If not, I fear the wrath of God will rain upon nations that flaunt such wickedness."

She shifted her weight against the side of the bed.

"Your father has agreed to see that Moses and Sally are schooled before they are turned loose. On this point, we agree. It is very important they attain the means to survive. They are to be paid for their labor, from this day forward, as though they were free. And he will see them set up in some business or trade, so they can be certain to survive. I told him a piece of land might be appropriate too."

Frances straightened. "Well, I took him at his word. I have purchased Moses and Sally for you," she said. "Today, I sent to England for the papers certifying the transfer of that ownership to you. They belong to you. I believe they'll have the best chance if you are their owner."

"Me … a slave owner?" Amanda covered her heart with her hands.

"Yes, you. Joseph will make certain it works out … and God will too."

"But I'm hardly able to be my own master, let alone be the master of two other human beings. Mother, I'm only twelve years old!"

"For now, they are slaves," she said, ignoring Amanda. "We owe them the chance at a normal life. They can't afford to wait for emancipation in Charleston. It may be a long time coming. And Sarah Jean will still be but a child when all this happens. But enough of that. There is something more."

Frances stared beyond her swollen stomach toward the floor.

"I've written a letter to Beau. I must tell you about that now. Anyway, you're almost thirteen, Amanda."

Chapter 27

Frances Tries to Tell Amanda

Something about Beau.

Amanda Worsham
July 1826
Bermuda

"Something about Moses and Sally?"

Amanda knew Frances was referring to Beau Videau. Yet her heart felt as if it hung in her throat, and she could not say such a thing.

"No, my dear. About you … and about Beau."

Damn. Such a sinking feeling. "Whatever have I to do with Beau Videau?" Amanda asked. *Well, here it comes—time to put a brave little face on this.* She was not positive about it, but maybe, just maybe, Frances was about to admit to her that Joseph was not her real father. *Something I desperately need to know …*

"There is something about him I must tell. I've watched you mature with wonder and always with pride, Amanda. And Joseph loves you very much. That is the problem. Your father really loves you …"

She shakes her head slowly. Is she really saying "no" with her involuntary gestures?

"You and Joseph have a wonderful relationship. I don't want to harm that."

Amanda hugged her mother. "Don't tell me, whatever it is, Mother. Maybe I don't need to know."

"And," continued Frances, "I've heard you telling everybody Charlie Videau was your sweetheart. He was lovable and tiny, like his father."

"Mother, that was long ago. I haven't said that in years—just years and years."

"Yes," said Frances. "But you must be made aware of something about that now. Truths that only I can relate to you, Amanda. And Joseph … Joseph must never know. You mustn't tell him, either."

An urgent expression crossed Frances's face as her eyes caught Amanda's. Perhaps a twinge of regret, a feeling of futility and sadness?

"I hadn't planned to tell you, my darling. Up until now, there was no need. Maybe there would never be a perfect time. This illness—whatever it is—it surely is a thief of time. I must do this now, for as bad as I feel, I cannot take a chance—oh, Amanda, I might not be around to see to it later." Frances looked across the room and bit her lip. "It's about Charlie."

Amanda took her mother's hands in her own. Frances would not look directly into her eyes.

"Charlie Videau is spiteful and mean," Amanda declared. "And he can be so very hateful. He is just spoiled—that's what."

Stricken, Frances looked away. After a long moment, she managed, "Perhaps I can tell you tomorrow, my darling. Let it rest for now. Only know this: you must not marry Charlie Videau."

"But for heaven's sake, why ever not?"

"Tomorrow, my sweet. Come now, say your prayers and kiss me good night. And please send Sally to me to help me change back into my nightgown. I can't do any more today. I am so tired." She turned her head away.

Chapter 28

Amanda Frees Moses
and Sally, Sort Of

Amanda Worsham
July 1826
Bermuda

FOLLOWING AFTERNOON TEA, PAKENHAM AND Hawkins returned to
their military encampment. Agnes went home, and Frances had been
asleep at least an hour. Joseph stood with Colin on the porch, and
Amanda strode out into the dark front yard, looking for Moses.

Frances had told everyone: "I will carry this child no matter
what comes."

Now Amanda looked up at the stars. *I am grateful, dear God, to
stand and view Your magnificence.*

She made her way to the corner of the house by the back porch
steps, thinking that Moses would be working there on a cedar crib for
the new baby. The glow from his lantern illuminated the area, and
she heard the sound of his voice, a song he was singing to himself.

Amanda couldn't hear the words but caught the melody. She
had heard him sing the song before. Each time he sang it, the words
were different, but the melody was always the same. A love poem
especially for God. As she drew nearer, the words became clear. The
pounding of his chisel struck in time with the words:

Come by here, Lord. Come by here.
Come by here, Lord. Come by here.
Baby's a-comin, Lord. Come by here.
Oh, Lord. Come by here.
Miss Frances needs You. Come by here.
Miss Frances needs You. Come by here.
And she needs You, Lord. Come by here.
Oh, Lord. Come by here.
Baby needs you, Lord. Come by here.
Baby needs you, Lord. Come by here.
And we needs You, Lord. Come by here.
So bad. Come by here.
Don't You know, Lord? Don't You know?
Oh, Lord. Come by here …

He stopped to inspect his work.

As she drew nearer, Amanda could see Moses shaping a piece of wood with a mallet and hand chisel under just enough light to see what he was doing. Moses began his little song again:

And Lord …
Come by here, Lord. Come by here.
Come by here, Lord. Come by here …

"Moses," Amanda called. "You need a better light."

The singing and pounding stopped. Moses searched for her in the darkness.

"Miss Manda," he said, happily. "What you doin' out here in the dark?"

"I came to talk with you, Moses. Have you got a minute?"

"Yes'm. 'Course I do." He put away the woodworking tools. "Miss Frances any better?" he asked.

"Not much."

Moses looked down at his shoes and shook his head. "It just ain't right," he said. "It just ain't right."

"Moses, I have something to ask you."

"What is it, Miss Manda?"

Amanda reached out and placed her hand on Moses's sleeve. "Would you like to go to school?" she asked. "Would you like to learn to read … and to write?"

Suddenly afraid, he shook his head. "That's 'gainst the law. I can't do that. You know I can't do nothin' like that, Miss Manda. Why, they would whip ol' Moses."

"You and Sally have been reading Bible lessons with Mother for the last few years," she reasoned.

"But that's different, Miss Manda. It's against the Charleston law to teach some things to a slave, but I don't reckon it against the law just to talk about the Bible. Neither one of us can read about Jesus, but we can talk about Him. Yo' mama gave us a Bible, and we look at it a lot."

Well, maybe that was different somehow, she thought.

"How old are you, Moses?" Amanda looked at the grown man before her, and she knew the Bible reading just wasn't enough.

"I don't know for sure. You see, my mama had me up in the Socastee Swamp by the Waccamaw River. I mean, I was born out in that swamp. She was a runaway, don't you know? And I was with old Moss Moonie, the crazy woman, for a long time. She make her livin' sellin' things she find in the swamp. Potions and the like …"

Moses scratched the side of his head and looked at Amanda, clearly puzzled, as if he wondered what this conversation was about.

"My mama done run away from the plantation and the rice fields and that overseer Bills," he said, continuing. "She still runnin', 'far as I know. Last anybody heard 'bout her, she was up in the Wahee Neck by the Peedee River."

"Tell me about old Moss Moonie," said Amanda. "Is she a Negro? Is she a free woman?"

"You don't know her? Well, she free and she ain't white, if that's what you mean. She what y'all call mulatto, or crow o'tan. She ain't as black as I am. She sort of light-skinned. She not red-boned, like they say, but she got those black spots on her face. People say those spots the mark of the devil. I don't know. I just think people afraid of ol' Moss Moonie. People sometimes say bad things about something they don't know much 'bout."

"Moses, some people don't know much about anything. You know that. But they do love to talk about somebody else."

"Some of 'em don't know much 'bout spots, anyway."

"She was the only mother you ever knew, wasn't she, Moses?"

"Yes'm, Miss Manda."

"You love her?"

"I reckon I do."

"You with her long enough to get to know her, learn anything from her?"

"She taught me lots o' little songs and stuff. And she told me 'bout Jesus—I mean, for the first time. Do you know, she taught me how to work with a piece of wood, to make somethin' out of it?" He smiled, sort of chuckled to himself, and hooked his thumbs in his pockets. "Was ol' Moss Moonie who say that the Lord put somethin' in the wood He want Moses to find and let out."

"Like a baby crib?"

"Yes'm."

Amanda was trying to guess how many years Moses lived with Moss Moonie.

"You were just a little boy, and Moss Moonie knew many things. I think she liked you too. Why did she give you to Mister Bills? Do you know that?"

"Well, he come and told her I was his property." Moses looked from side to side, clearly nervous. "An' he said he owned my mama outright and so I was his too. It was a lie, 'cause yo' daddy come along years later and got me with his part of the rice fields. Ol' Bills just work for that place, don't you know? But he threatened Moss Moonie, and she was afraid. She didn't want to give me away. I know it. I remember she cried and cried."

"And he took you, anyway?"

"Yes'm."

"Do you know about how long you stayed with her?"

"For … five Christmases, I reckon."

"It wouldn't be right not to see her again, would it?"

"No, ma'am."

"And Sally, what of her family?"

"Sally got folks in Waccamaw Neck and Charleston too. She sho' does. Johnsons, don't you know?"

"Well, what we should figure out now is how to visit those places and see those people."

"Yes'm." Moses put his finger against his lips. He looked as if he wanted to say something, but he didn't. Then he smiled and said, "Moss Moonie kin rub a wart off, don't you know?"

He's changing the subject, isn't he? "Well, that may be true, but tell me more about when you were a little boy."

Moses sat on the step behind him, then he rubbed his hands together as if in deep thought. His lips curved into a strained smile.

"So ol' Moss Moonie took me to raise, an' raise me she did." With his head down, he spoke the words slowly, deliberately. "She give me the name Moses, 'cause she found me floating in a boat in that swamp, where my mama left me."

His smile faded.

"And after a time, she give me to that man Bills, the overseer at the plantation yo' daddy bought. And I don't know how long old Moss Moonie had me 'fore all that."

He suddenly looked at Amanda and smiled a bright, happy smile again. "She the only person kin cure a snakebite, don't you know?"

It was obvious he either didn't know any more about himself, or just didn't want to talk about it. Maybe he had told her everything he knew.

"What name do they have on your plantation records, Moses?"

"My mama was a Ward, don't you know?"

"Moses Ward?"

"Yes'm."

"Do you know who your daddy was?"

"I reckon my mama she know, but I don't know. I sho' don't. I guess it don't matter much."

Father said you served about twenty years at Sand Hills plantation."

"Yes'm."

"So I think you're about twenty-four or twenty-five years old, Moses," she said.

"Yes'm."

Moses didn't appear to like the conversation much. Amanda remembered Joseph had once told her that some people thought the overseer Bills was Moses's father.

"What if you were free, Moses?" Amanda asked carefully.

Startled, Moses seemed to reel a bit. "Free? What you mean, Miss Manda?"

Amanda paused and watched his face. *He is puzzled. And rightly so*, she thought.

"How you goin' do that?" he asked, just as carefully. "Mister Joe owns old Moses—and Sally too. I mean, whenever I look up at them stars, I long to be free, but—"

"It's something I'm considering, Moses—for you and Sally. But I want you to learn to read and write before I just turn you loose in the world," Amanda said before he could say more. "This afternoon, Joseph gave the two of you to me—in a roundabout way, that is. It was what Mother asked him to do. She believes slavery won't last much longer in the British Empire, and she wants me to see that you learn a trade so when that time comes, you'll be able to take care of yourself."

"Free! Great Lord a' mighty. Free ..." He jumped up and gave a happy dance.

Amanda said, sharing his happiness, "I want to help you all I can. Maybe I could help you learn a trade and then set you up in a business."

"Oh, sweet Jesus!" he cried, his eyes flying wide open.

"Do you want to go back to Charleston?" she asked.

"Miss Manda, when I'm in Charleston, I walk up and down the road, and if I'm free or if I ain't, the truth is, I'm just another nigger and ever'body knows it." He shook his head. "But when I'm here, I'm somebody."

Nigger! Amanda cringed at that word. *Words like that are so degrading and hurtful*, she thought. *People who spit that word out showed no respect for their fellow human beings. Negro is bad enough. Why must people identify everyone according to some status or other? Today I met a man whose skin was dark brown. He's a friend of mine. Why not just call him friend?*

"Moses, please don't ever use that awful word around me again," she said. "I hate it. God did not make that word."

"But God make the white folks, and they say the word."

"Well, I will have none of it. It is a trashy, despicable word. It is intended to be hurtful—to degrade a person at the very least. You certainly are somebody," she said. "You are a dear human being, and a good one, I might add. I don't know a better man than you—and that includes every man in my family. Moses, I hear slaves sometimes use that word when they talk about each other … behind another one's back. You know what I mean?"

Amanda stood up as straight and as tall as she could.

"You're darker than I am," she said, "but God made both of us. I don't know why we're different in the way we look, but I do know it doesn't matter … not to me, not to my mother, and certainly not to God. If you are in the company of people who dwell negatively on such things, you are in the company of fools. I have heard Mother say that many times."

"Miss Frances is a sainted woman, Miss Manda. An' you a mighty good person yo'self. But the truth is, I ain't got the right color to my skin. It must be God favors the white folks. If it don't matter to Him, why then do He make us look so different? An' don't the Bible say don't ever call somebody a fool, Miss Manda?"

"Don't worry about the fools, Moses. Color is important only when you're matching the clothes you wear. I think a great deal of you and of Sally."

"Miss Manda, I'm worried 'bout that baby. Miss Frances don't look too good herself. An' in the last few days, she got a bad color to her skin to boot."

Though relieved that the tone of the conversation had changed, she felt suddenly afraid for her mother and the baby, just as Moses was.

"You noticed," she said.

"Yes'm. I see her three days ago, and she look pretty good. An' when she walk down to the porch, I see her. She got a sick look about her. An' it ain't 'cause she got a baby. I don't believe it is."

"Mother's had trouble with this one, that's for sure."

"The baby?"

"Yes."

"You know, Miss Manda, sometime' it's hard for folks to get a baby. God knows that be so."

Amanda was reminded that Moses and Sally had no children.

"I prays and I prays. But it don't do no good."

"You mean for a baby?"

"Yes'm and for yo' mama too."

"Moses, do you want children?"

"Well, yes'm. But it ain't the way God wants things. It just can't be. Not yet, anyways. You know, I don't really want to talk about it, but my Sally like that … She can't have no baby. Don't know why … don' know …"

Moses looked straight into Amanda's eyes.

"Boys, men, use her on the plantation, don't you know? But yo daddy put a stop to all that."

"Would you not want to go back to Waccamaw again … ever?" she asked, changing the conversation again.

Dear God, sounds like Sally is safer now than she was before Father took over. What a horrible thing to just be used by a bunch of ne'er-do-wells. Did Little Beau do that? I best not ask—don't really want to know.

"I reckon I would, sometime or other. Might want to see somebody back there again. I'd ask ol' Moss Moonie if she ever hear tell 'bout my mama again, if I could."

"But for now you want to stay here?"

"Wherever you be, Miss Manda, that's the place I wants to be. Me and Sally. An' if yo' daddy give us to you, it must be God loves us a whole bunch."

Very well. Staying here in Bermuda would be good for Moses and Sally. And I'm going to see about that. Don't really want to go on to Manchester, anyway.

149

Moses looked very serious all at once. "Miss Manda, You 'member when yo' daddy told you that they wouldn't be no way a fiddler crab could save that sandcastle you and Miss Sarah Jean made?"

Amanda's thoughts flashed back to that time on the beach with Joseph and Sarah Jean. "Well, yes," she said. "I didn't know you were there right then, Moses. I thought you were over with the horses or something. And anyway, you certainly have a good memory. What about that?"

"Well, he say the fiddler crab had one big, orange claw."

She nodded.

"Well, you know, the white folks see what they call an uppity Nigger like that, don't you know?"

"Whatever do you mean?"

"Well, God give the crab the orange claw, and the crab, he don't know for sure what to do with it. So he dance around with it and put on a show."

"And you see that in some of your people?"

"Maybe so." Moses reached out and took her hand in his. "If I be free and go to school and ever'thing like that ..." He shook his head. "Could be they see ol' Moses like that."

"Uppity, you mean?"

"Yes'm."

Amanda was surprised that Moses had such insight into what many saw as a serious social problem. At least, they surely got upset about it in Charleston.

"Moses, I'm but a little girl," she said. "I'm afraid what is needed here to solve these problems is a grown woman."

"You growing. You sho' is."

"But let's not worry about that right now," she said. "All right, Moses?"

"Yes'm, Miss Manda. Only thing I'm worried 'bout just now is yo' Mama."

"Well, I'm worried too, Moses. But that's all I wanted to talk about right now. I need to go see Mother again for a while. It will be time for prayers soon. Thank you for visiting with me."

Amanda turned and started toward the front porch.

"Miss Manda, you sho' is welcome."

"Good night, Moses."

"Yes'm. Good night, Miss Manda."

Amanda went back inside, thinking she must be one of the world's youngest slave owners. She didn't like the feeling very much. But she was beginning to see Moses in a different light. It would certainly be a shame not to educate such a smart mind.

She remembered she had heard Beau and even Joseph say, "That uppity so-and-so!" in some conversations with his business associates. *The bad old* N-*word.*

She refused even to think of that awful word. Instead, she returned to the front porch where she had left Joseph and Colin. They seemed to be having a good conversation, and Colin was enjoying a cigar.

He never smokes around a lady.

Amanda thought Colin to be a true gentleman, just like Joseph.

A fleeting remembrance of her mother struggling to say something about Beau Videau ran through her mind.

Is Charlie Videau my brother? Was Frances indiscreet with Beau? Surely not … Beau just can't be my father.

Chapter 29

The Bairn's A-Comin'

Amanda Worsham
July 1826
Bermuda

A CRY ECHOED FROM UPSTAIRS from Miss Tilly.

"Colin! Joseph! Come quickly," she screamed. "I think the bairn's a-comin'."

Colin set his cigar on the stone steps; then he and Joseph ran into the house and up the stairs.

Joseph burst through the door first. "Tilly, what is it?"

"Where's Colin?"

Colin rushed into the room with Amanda following right behind.

Miss Tilly grabbed Colin by the forearms. Shaking him, she said, "Listen, have Moses saddle one of the horses, then you ride like the wind to fetch Christopher Pakenham. Tell him the bairn is a-comin'. She is so weak with the fever again, she doesn't know me anymore. I just don't like it. I don't like it at all. By all that's holy, she has taken a turn for the worse—racked with tremors, burning up with fever, vomiting old blood—fresh blood too. It's awful"

Miss Tilly pushed Colin toward the door. "Get cracking, Colin. Time's a-wasting!"

Dear Lord, please help my mother! Amanda pleaded. She needed to go to see about Sarah Jean. If Sarah Jean were asleep, so much the better. If not, well, it would be rough for a time for all of them anyway.

Odd, she thought. *God must have prepared me for this.* She knew, finally, that the birth was about to happen.

In a few minutes she heard the horse leaving at a gallop. God and horse willing, Colin was riding like the wind, just as Miss Tilly had instructed him to do.

Amanda found Sarah Jean asleep where she had been playing with a toy Moses had made for her. Carefully she scooped her sister up and laid her on the bed. Kneeling beside the bed, she said her prayers, asking God to spare her mother's life and the baby's as well.

After a time, Colonel Pakenham arrived. Amanda heard him jump from the horse and yell for Moses. He must have ridden the same horse that Colin took, she thought. And when he came inside, he sent Joseph away, just as he had done at the time of the Grewno incident.

In a few moments, Joseph entered the bedroom to be with his girls. He found Amanda still kneeling beside the bed.

"How is Mother?" she whispered.

Joseph had tears in his eyes; it was difficult for him to speak. "She is in God's hands now," he said.

"What about the baby?"

"It's too early for the baby. I haven't counted the weeks, but it's not full term—not by a long shot. I don't see how the baby can survive."

Miss Tilly entered the room and in a hushed voice said, "Thought I'd find you here, Joseph. Come down to the parlor. I want to talk with the two of you. It's best we leave the little one to her sleep."

They descended the stairs, quiet and subdued. As they entered the parlor, Miss Tilly motioned for them to sit.

They took a seat on the settee, and Joseph put his arms around Amanda. Miss Tilly stood before them and began to speak.

"The fever, lad … it's the yellow jack fever. It will take Frances and the bairn before this night is out. I know it will. Prepare yourselves. There's not a thing Christopher can do to save them. All we can do is pray. He told me to tell you now."

She held out her arms for Amanda to come to her. "Come here to Tilly, lass. Come here so your father can go to be with his sweet Frances now, before it's too late."

Joseph rushed from the room. That night both Frances and the baby died. As Amanda longed for sleep that evening, she remembered the Burns poem: "Death and Doctor Hornbook." Forming the words in her mind, a shiver racked her body:

> But just as he began to tell,
> The auld kirk-hammer strak the bell
> Some wee short hour ayont the twal',
> Which rais'd us baith:
> I took the way that pleas'd mysel',
> And sae did Death.

Chapter 30

Is Beau Videau My Father?

Amanda Worsham
August 1826
Bermuda

AMANDA THOUGHT BRIEFLY OF BEAU Videau as a way of changing the subject in her thoughts—a way to give herself some respite.

What was Mother trying to tell me about him? The thirteenth of July—wouldn't that be the ides of July if one were to reckon such a thing? Well. The fifteenth, anyway. Thirteenth ... fifteenth. It doesn't make a lick of difference. This isn't Rome. Oh, Shakespeare—please leave my wretched mind alone!

For a moment she thought she'd grasped the truth:

Beau is my father—my actual blood father. Mother never said it, but what of all the things she did say? She even told me once not to be concerned about the mental illness that runs in Joseph's line—about it not having any bearing on me. What about that? And there was so much that Mother didn't say.

Suddenly, Joseph squeezed her tightly in a bear hug. "I'm so sorry about your mother, Amanda." Releasing her, he backed away to sit on the porch railing.

Dear God. It's been a little more than a week since Mother's death. I think he's looking forward to leaving me here in Bermuda while he goes on to England. He's taking Sarah Jean. He's also commissioned the undertaker in Hamilton to pickle poor Mother for the trip. Just like Lord Nelson. The lead-lined coffin will be ready tomorrow afternoon. Then it will be time for him to leave.

The picture in her mind's eye caused a shiver.

It takes a good deal more than mating to make a real "father." What of the years of loving and caring that Joseph Worsham has given me? I refuse to accept the notion that anyone but Joseph is my "real" father. He has earned the respect and the benefit of the doubt ... and then some. A part of Amanda always reached out for Joseph to clutch him to her heart. She would never let go of Joseph Worsham—birth father or no. *Now that I no longer have a mother, I should hang on to whatever father I have left. Beau Videau is my father? Well, I could do worse. And could be I have two fathers. Hmm ...*

"You remind me of Frances, my child," Joseph said. "When I look at you I see her, the way she looked that day in London when I first met her. She was very beautiful. You favor her. It is uncanny, that. Amanda, you'll certainly be a heartbreaker. Don't settle for anything but the best."

Joseph wore a faraway look in his eyes as he spoke. "Of course, I wanted a son—a male heir. I suppose every man does. But that wasn't to be. But little girls are special too. I have learned that. Perhaps you will be the one to carry on when I am gone, you and the lucky man you will marry."

Amanda thought, *Father must be thinking of Charlie Videau.*

She believed in her heart that he often did think of Charlie. Joseph knew—and Amanda knew—that Charlie had promised to marry her at the earliest opportunity.

God. Charlie calls me sissy. I never knew that was an omen. My God. "Someday I'll marry you, sissy," he would say, laughing. He has already come to Joseph and asked for my hand, the way any Southern gentleman would. It's odd, though. Joseph didn't tell Mother about that, only me. Mother would've had a fit. Yet I can't bring myself to say aloud what I am thinking. Maybe Joseph knows Beau is my birth father. Maybe so. But what if he doesn't? And anyway, Joseph needn't worry about that right now. I would never marry that boy. Dear God. What if Charlie Videau really is my half brother? Damn ... damn ... damn.

Amanda blushed. *Oh, dear. Father will see me blushing. I just know it. Joseph Worsham is nobody's fool—or is he? I think he's leading up to something—to tell me something. What?* She gazed quizzically into his beautiful green eyes, mesmerized.

"Would you want us—what is left of this family—to have a homeplace in Bermuda so that we could visit here from time to time?" Joseph asked after a long pause. "We could visit while on holiday."

Whew ... the relief she felt nearly overwhelmed her.

"Oh, Father," Amanda cried. She could hardly contain her emotion. *He didn't see my blush. I don't think he knows what Mother was hiding from us all, that business about Beau Videau being my father. Oh, dear God ...*

Amanda backed against the porch railing and clapped her hands. Of course, she didn't wish to return to Charleston just yet, but she welcomed this change in his Bermuda plans very much.

I just don't want to go on to England, or worse, to return to Charleston right now.

"If you would like that," said Joseph, "I'll buy this place—this farm and house from Colin, and as much land as I can buy around it too. Moses can begin to build a guest cottage and perhaps a second as well. There's no telling what our family will grow into tomorrow, is there? Moses and Sally will be here with you, anyway. What do you think?"

"What about the Stuarts?"

"Well," Joseph replied, rubbing his chin, "I've discussed this with Colin on several occasions. All he wants is to be free to travel if the mood strikes him, or to work the land, if that's what he decides to do. He could be the overseer—that would be appropriate. He could do as he wishes. I think Colin would enjoy that life. You could be his alternate overseer. You were born to supervise, I think."

"Yes, it's a good way to live, to travel. We do some of that, too, don't we? The traveling, I mean."

"I suppose in some ways that is so, Amanda. But the truth is, I never really stop working. I have business to attend to, affairs to see about, no matter where I happen to be. The money works, too, on its own. But you simply cannot leave money or property to itself, if you know what I mean."

"Yes, I think I do. It's not what you own that counts but what you do with it that really matters."

"Yes, that's it. Money can gather dust in a bank vault, or money can put people to work. Not everyone is born to manage others, to supervise. Good people need jobs, and supervisors are needed too. Money can create that sort of thing. Never forget that, Amanda. Investment makes the world go round."

"Love does that, too, Father," she smiled.

Joseph leaned toward her with his hands on the porch railing. "Well, I can take care of purchasing this property in England," he said, as though he were thinking aloud. "There's no need to do the paperwork here, right now, I mean. If I leave Colin in charge as overseer, we can all go to England. You can come in any event, if you want to. It's entirely up to you. Colin and Miss Tilly can continue to live in this house as long as they wish. Colin can run the farm—for a share. It will all work out."

Joseph went inside, ostensibly, to make the plans. Amanda stayed on the porch for a time and then went inside to be with her sister.

I am not going to England right now. The thought made things final. She realized that she would miss Sarah Jean terribly very soon.

Amanda had long ago begun to miss Charlie Videau in a very permanent way. She had no idea what she would do about that in the coming days, but here in Bermuda—right now—she would remain. *At least Charlie isn't here.*

During the next week, Joseph bought Stuart Farm, including the house and all the animals. He and Colin shook hands on it. The arrangement called for Colin to be overseer and for Moses to begin construction of two small vacation cottages around the same central garden. The financial arrangements would transpire through the banks in Liverpool and Manchester. Building materials probably would ship from Liverpool, whatever was not available locally. Colin could handle all that.

Chapter 31

Misadventure, Indeed

Joseph Worsham
August 1826
Bermuda

THE MAN NAMED SEMMES VISITED Stuart Manor before Joseph left for Saint George's with the coffin. Joseph talked with him on the front porch.

Amanda detested Semmes the moment she first met him. Apparently, the feeling was mutual. Semmes didn't stay very long.

"Very well, Semmes, what is it this time?" Joseph asked, barely masking his impatience.

"Mister Worsham, sir. If you please, I really do wish you would allow me to deal with the convict, the perpetrator as it were."

"Semmes, I wash my hands of the matter. The perpetrator, as you say, is in the hands of the authorities now. I must leave quite soon for England. After that, I must attend to some business in Massachusetts."

"Right."

"Good day to you, Semmes. I really am busy now. Submit any expenses to Colin Stuart."

Semmes turned to leave, and Joseph returned to the hallway.

"Oh, sir," Semmes called as he started down the steps, "I almost forgot."

Joseph returned to the porch.

"Do you know anyone who might benefit from knowing an excellent factor—or agent—in the New England area? I've a friend in Boston, a business associate, you understand, who's been very successful in working out new avenues of trade for shippers such as yourself. Very successful, indeed, as it were."

"I've arranged for trusted factors, thank you."

"Well," Semmes continued, "I just received a letter from Gill Fletcher, a factor I know in Boston. That be your destination, eh? I thought I would ask while I was here, you understand." Semmes reached inside his coat and pulled out a card. "This is Fletcher's business card," he said. "You think of anyone can use his services, I'd be much obliged."

Joseph took the card. "Thank you. I'll keep Fletcher in mind."

Amanda followed Semmes from the porch to the front gate. She watched as Moses untied Semmes's carriage horse and handed him the reins. Semmes took them in his left hand.

To Amanda, Semmes was offensive and abrupt as he climbed into his carriage to leave. He said vulgar things under his breath as though Amanda couldn't hear. And he called Moses "boy." Then he hit the poor horse fiercely with his crop as the carriage left the drive.

Joseph didn't see or hear any of this because he had already gone inside the house. And Amanda didn't tell him. She preferred to put the likes of Semmes from her mind and hoped never to meet him again. Semmes had referred to the Grewno incident as "the misadventure."

Misadventure, indeed, she thought. *Like as not, Semmes had a hand in that affair as well.* The thought caused a chill to run its course through Amanda's small frame. *Is that a premonition? My Lord, how do I sift truth from fiction here?*

* * * * *

Four days later, Pakenham stopped by to say that it was his understanding the Crown had shipped Grewno in chains on a British warship to Tenerife in the Canary Islands. There, he would be transferred to a man-of-war bound for Van Diemen's Land. That is what all concerned parties believed was the case.

Grewno has been transported, thought Amanda. *That's the meaning of Pakenham's statement. Van Diemen's Land is part of colonial New South Wales, an island penal colony somewhere ... Botany Bay? Anyway, somewhere near Port Jackson or Sidney, something like that. It is the acceptable thing, to banish capital offenders overseas forever—well, to banish them for a long time. That's how Grewno got to Bermuda in the first place.*

What caused all this? Why, that damned prison ship—

Within the week, Joseph and Sarah Jean were ready to leave for England.

* * * * *

On the dock at Saint George's, Amanda stood with the Stuarts and waved goodbye. She thought, as she watched Joseph board the ship, that there was much work yet to be done and a long way to travel by all. Now they would be making their way without Frances. She thought briefly of her uncle John Worsham who lived in Saint George's.

Uncle John is too feeble to leave his home. He cannot tolerate visitors, either.

Amanda's great-uncle, her grandfather's brother, never had any children. He and his wife Catherine had lived in Bermuda with their housekeepers until Catherine died. Now John is alone—except for his faithful housekeeper who takes care of him. Joseph and Sarah Jean had said their goodbyes to Uncle John earlier in the day. In effect, Amanda had said goodbye too.

I just have a feeling about it, she thought. *I make Uncle John nervous. The dear old man cannot care for himself, let alone a twelve-year-old great-niece from the Carolinas.*

Chapter 32

Manchester, England

Joseph Worsham
October 1826
Manchester

On a fog-shrouded hill near Manchester on the Worsham family estate, Joseph watched the lead-lined walnut coffin being lowered into the open grave. Of course, it was a Methodist funeral service. He stood quietly in the mist for a few moments thinking about everything that had happened. Soon, it began to rain—slowly at first, then in earnest.

Damn. Joseph had said his goodbyes long before. *These Courtneys.* The notion that Frances should be buried on the Worsham estate had almost caused blows to be struck between him and the Courtneys. He would miss Frances, and the salt from his tears flowed freely with the raindrops. *But by damn, Frances was a Worsham when she died. She was mine. She was a Worsham …*

He studied the people gathered at the graveside. The Courtneys were all there—what was left of the family. Clearly they blamed him for Frances's death. Was it not always that way? The in-laws blame the husband for whatever ills befall their beloved daughter.

Yes, thought Joseph, his mind racing. *It's all my fault.* He knew Sarah Jean would be safer with family in Manchester. *Aunt Meg really loves Sarah Jean. Perhaps it is due to the strong Worsham family resem-*

blance, something Amanda never shared. Amanda is a Courtney. Well, she does look like Frances. Or is she a Videau? My God. I just don't know.

The only real success Joseph had known was in the building of his financial empire. Other than that, he considered himself a social failure. He had really tried with Frances, but he had ultimately failed. Beau forever lurked in the background. Frances seemingly had tried to tell him often something about Beau and about Amanda, but never quite made a success of it. Joseph believed in his heart that Amanda was not his child, that she was Beau's little girl. Her actual conception must have happened before Frances married Joseph. He'd always had strong suspicions, yet never … never had those suspicions caused him to waver in his love for Amanda.

Always … I have been her father. A child cannot help the conditions under which it is born. A child is a gift from God. I have done my duty by her … will continue to do so.

Joseph shook his head. *Damn,* he thought. *Surely God is punishing me for the evil things I did as a young man in Liverpool.*

"Mister Worsham," came a voice from behind him. His driver approached, carrying an umbrella.

"Yes, Robert? What is it?"

"Please. May I hold this brolly for you, sir?"

"Yes, Thank you. I'm through here. Take me to the very best place to purchase gifts for Christmas, Robert. We have a bit of time for shopping, don't you think?"

"Right away, sir. If we hurry, I think we do."

Good. Robert knows I'm a colonial man. He didn't point out Christmas is two months away.

✶ ✶ ✶ ✶ ✶

Before departing Manchester, Joseph purchased one of the new, fascinating toys known as kaleidoscopes—a Christmas present for Amanda. He had the shopkeeper provide a mix of semiprecious stones inside that were mostly blue and white in color. Amanda loved new things, and blue was special to her. Joseph was certain she would enjoy the toy. While in Manchester, he had showered Sarah Jean with gifts. He realized that she was thoroughly spoiled and that her manners were atrocious.

Oh well. Aunt Meg—and maybe sometimes the Courtneys too— were in charge now.

For a moment, he pitied Aunt Meg for the stress the Courtneys probably would cause her.

For now he had business to attend to in London.

＊ ＊ ＊ ＊

On the way to Liverpool, Joseph composed his thoughts in the carriage and later inside the stagecoach.

This should be a simple case of what money can do.

Over the past week, he had recruited the services of men, men loyal only to money, he felt he could "trust" with a somewhat wicked arrangement. He believed most men could be bought outright. Perhaps that was because he at one time in his life had been so compromised.

He was looking forward to a surprise visit to Warner Hawke at the man's hideaway in London's East End. Joseph's mind buzzed with the planning of it.

He caught the stagecoach to London.

Chapter 33

A Business Deal, Hawke

Joseph Worsham
January 1827
London

With perfect timing, Joseph picked an exceptionally bright day to carry out his plan. No clouds would diminish the glare of sunlight. He knew that if the doors and shutters of Hawke's warehouse were thrown open to the bright daylight at just the proper moment, the glare would confuse Hawke … what with the man's intolerance for bright light, oil lamps, all those mirrors, and the like.

Hawke's noon meal was about to be delivered when Joseph and his group of rough men arrived. It had been so easy. All it had taken was Joseph's money and a keen bit of planning. By bribing off Hawke's guards and replacing them with new guards loyal to the Worsham money, Joseph's safety was practically assured. All that remained to be cautious about was the Hawke Dart.

With his ruffians carefully, quietly in place, Joseph gave the signal, and his men threw open the warehouse shutters. Along with the explosion of light, Joseph rushed into the hidden room, the office of the white slave empire.

"Well, Hawke," Joseph announced, ever mindful where he placed his head in the doorframe, "aren't you the sly and cunning one? You think you're safe here at all times, isn't that so?"

Obviously surprised, Hawke spun around on his swivel stool to face the intruder's voice. As he recognized Joseph Worsham's face, he turned ashen. Struggling for composure, he finally said, "I've looked for you for quite some time, Sir Gay."

"Yes ... reckon you have."

"Don't stand there. Come in and sit awhile."

"I want you to leave me and my family alone, Hawke."

"I've not bothered a hair on the head of any of your lot."

Joseph shook his head. "I keep a sharp eye out for your men, your enforcers, everywhere I travel, Hawke. I've come to put an end to all that trouble. I won't stand your dogging me all the time. Not anymore."

Hawke nervously fondled the opening of his coat, flipping the lace on his shirt from side to side. "What have you in mind?"

"A business deal. A partnership, nothing more." Joseph detested the name Sir Gay, but it did serve a useful purpose at the moment.

"A man of your word you are," said Hawke, grinning. "But what is it now? What is it, this ... this business deal?"

"You want to expand your business in the Americas. I have the ships to facilitate that. You need me, Hawke."

"Should I trust you with so much of my business's potential? The Americas ... could very well garner someday an annual growth of 20, 30 percent. I think I would like that. In time I could do everything myself. Why should I risk an association with you?"

"You have little to lose on this venture, Hawke. Just warrant the arrangement. All will be well. If you do not ..." Joseph paused. "If you do not take me up on my proposition," he continued, "I will end your business dealings permanently."

"Think you've that much muscle, do you, Joseph? Perhaps you could do so—perhaps not. I favor not. Who are you to wield such power? Before you came along, the Crown tried, you know."

"Perhaps. Financial strength—or power—is what I have, Hawke. I have done well. But you ask if you should risk it? To answer, I offer this: how do you suppose I managed to breach your defenses today?"

"The guards?"

"Right you are."

"Their faces kept changing over the last months, new men, as it were. That's how you did it?"

"One method … one of many, Hawke. All it takes is money. You should know that."

"Very well, Sir Gay. You have your deal. Want my contract on it?"

"Hell, no. No papers … just your bloody handshake … your warrant." Joseph stepped toward Hawke, right hand extended.

The bastard's too stupid to know this is a trick.

Hawke slid off the stool, proffering his right hand.

Yeah. Look at you … you dolt.

Joseph grabbed Hawke's hand and pulled it toward him. As he did so, the left hand slipped beneath Hawke's coat to claim the dart.

"Now we can shake hands, Hawke," said Joseph with a wide smile on his face. "I only trust those whom I can control."

Like stepping on the head of a snake. You have to be quick. Now what?

Hawke slapped Joseph on the shoulder. "Good man, Sir Gay. Good man. As I said, the deal's right by me. Make your arrangements with my accountants. Here … now you can shake my hand, right?" Hawke again extended his hand.

Joseph raised his right arm briefly … a prearranged signal. Then he shook Hawke's hand. This was his warrant, Hawke's warrant.

How will I keep such a wicked promise?

A number of men crowded into the room—men loyal to Joseph—men whose "loyalty" had been quickly negotiated, quietly purchased for a great deal of money, and whose formidable appearance was their greatest asset.

Why do I actually trust such men as these? Joseph trembled with both fear and excitement.

Hawke looked nervously about the room, obviously afraid for his life.

Damn, that was easy. Joseph trembled still. "You are right to fear me, Hawke," said Joseph, gritting his teeth. "I came here to kill you." *Would I have gone through with it? Hell, I doubt it. But I—my family—we must be free of this man and his horrible business, the white slavery business. How could I ever have done such? God forgive me …*

"So you came to kill me? Well now. You'd best not have done that, Gay."

"And why not, pray tell? Anyway, only in retrospect have I threatened you."

"Because if you'd killed me, you wouldn't have left this warehouse alive yourself, that's why." Hawke stood shaking. Again he stated, "That's why, Gay." Then he mumbled something unintelligible.

What's the bastard saying to himself now? "I believe you're wrong, Hawke. I think there'd be a celebration amongst your men—a jockeying for power the likes of which would amaze even you."

"My men are loyal," Hawk blustered.

"They only fear you."

"Fear has its usefulness, to be sure."

"If I were to kill you," Joseph answered, "I would simply walk away from all this, leaving your minions to squabble amongst themselves. Whatever. Enough of this small talk. I have business arrangements to make, new trading territories … partnerships to forge."

The handshake quelled the fear in Joseph's heart. But the need to look over his shoulder? He could only hope for the best.

Further, he hoped for the safety of his family. He detested Hawke and Hawke's business. But what was he to do? So much remained at risk.

Will I ever really be free of Hawke … free of my past?

Book 3

A New State of Affairs

These men *are* peaceable with us; therefore let them dwell in the land and trade therein; for the land, behold, *it is* large enough for them; let us take their daughters to us for wives and let us give them our daughters.

—Genesis 34:21, KJV

Chapter 34

I Need a Fresh Start

Joseph Worsham
December 1827
Bermuda

WHEN JOSEPH RETURNED TO BERMUDA in late December, mostly to visit Amanda, he stayed but a fortnight before leaving for Boston. He was eager to take care of his new business dealings and begin his new life.

Pleased that Amanda was doing so well, he approved of the progress she had made and told her so. He was disappointed about one thing, though. The kaleidoscope noticeably failed to please her—not even a smile, only a small "thank you."

Perhaps it's the loss of her mother, Joseph thought. *Women are a difficult lot. Little girls are no better.*

Now, on to a fresh start.

Chapter 35

We All Need to Start Over

Amanda Worsham
January 1828
Bermuda

COLIN HIRED A GOVERNESS, A local girl, who was also an excellent teacher. Upon Amanda's insistence, the education of the two paid "servants" was to be considered. In Amanda's mind, slavery had come to an end.

A small group of children from nearby farms came to the improvised classroom in Stuart Manor, where they found the teaching first-class and *free*. Amanda saw to it that Moses and Sally learned many things. Since classes had already begun the previous fall, Moses and Sally had some catching up to do.

On January 6, 1828—Amanda's fourteenth birthday—Joseph arranged for a surprise party. Amanda knew it was her birthday, but she didn't know that so many people had been invited. Her friends from church, from the military, and from the surrounding area had all been sent invitations. So many people had been touched by Amanda and her family. Their wanting to help her celebrate comforted her in the very warmest way. Everyone brought thoughtful presents, tokens of love and acceptance, but the very best present of all came from her father. Joseph presented Moses with a business license and the architectural plans for the buildings that were to be constructed. This officially made Moses a contractor, and he could hire himself out as such. Joseph endorsed Amanda's plans. Moses and Sally were not indentured in any way, at least not to him. They belonged to Amanda, and he gave them the documents to prove it. As soon as slavery became illegal in the British Empire, they were to be *free*.

Joseph also gave Amanda a gold chain and Methodist cross—one that did not depict Jesus suffering on the cross. He had been resurrected and had gone on to heaven, leaving only His garment draped across the cross's face.

Oh, happy day, thank You, dear Lord, she prayed.

* * * * *

This time as Amanda waved goodbye to Joseph in Saint George's, she felt good about his departure, sending her prayers and thoughts with him. She believed Joseph would soon begin to find new happiness in many ways.

Dear God, may it be so, she prayed as the ship followed the pilot craft out of the harbor. *This family has suffered quite enough.*

I've essentially been thrust into womanhood without so much as even one sordid affair. Damn such rotten luck. I'm fourteen now. I've long since had my first period. I am a woman. Mother told me Great-Grandmother Moore was twelve when she had Richard Moore. Our ancestors married very young—they didn't live as long as we do. Lord, have mercy.

No good having family here in Bermuda …

Must remember—Uncle John can't even care for himself, let alone a fourteen-year-old great-niece from the Carolinas. I might as well be alone as far as kinfolks are concerned. But then again, I do have friends.

Chapter 36

Trouble at the Graves
What the Hell Is a Dog Cutter?

Joseph Worsham
January 1828
At sea—en route to Boston

THE *ANNE BAYLISS* LABORED NIGH on gale-force winds as she tacked past Cape Cod and the fishing banks. She soon would come about with some relief toward the choppy, demanding passage leading to Massachusetts Bay. Joseph recalled that old nautical charts identified some of these places by the fishermen's catch commonly found there. For example—here Crab Bank, there Pollacks Bank, there Haddock Bank. Yet these things sometimes changed with each hurricane.

Fish swam wherever they bloody well pleased, he thought.

Joseph looked off into the distance, remembering how Cape Cod appeared on the charts.

It reminds me of the cobra tattooed on Grewno's thumb. Warner Hawke also has one of those. I wonder what it means? Birds of a feather, or some such damn thing.

Joseph shivered as he crossed toward the stern of the ship, remembering Grewno and his disgusting tattoo. A dampness—a coldness—swept Joseph's soul. But it was not due to the brusque, quite cold weather. He wanted to get out of the full force of the

174

depressing elements. His ship's captain, Captain Bob Mathison, had said that the wind would subside and that it would change direction.

Very well, the storm seemed to be dying. Yet enough bad weather remained to make entrance into the Boston harbor difficult.

It was late January and nearly three o'clock in the evening. The weather had been mostly good for the passage; however, you bloody well took your chances when you went to sea during the hurricane season.

"Sail-ho, Captain Bob," a voice called from high in the ship's rigging. "There, toward the Cape."

"Aye, Red-Jack, lad," Captain Bob returned, cupping his hands to his mouth. "What do you make of her?" Captain Bob paused, looked upward, and pointed toward the foremast. "My man Red-Jack's up there, Joseph, on the foretop. A redheaded son of a bitch if there ever was one. He's my Red-Jack, he is—eyes like a red-tailed hawk. Good man, that. Has to hide his bloody skin from the sun— uses a canvas jacket and wide-rim straw hat. A real Jack Tar, by God. Been with me the longest, has Red-Jack."

Joseph couldn't see the man. The lower sails stood in the way.

"It's the dog cutter again," Red-Jack shouted. "She's off the larboard bow, slinking through the mist. Can barely make her out."

"No flag, Red-Jack?" Captain Bob yelled back. "Any chance she's one of their revenue cutters out here to scout us for revenue?"

"No, sir! There's no bloody flag. I think she's a pirate, I do."

"Keep up with her, Jack, lad."

"Bob," said Joseph, "by larboard, did he mean the *loading* side of the ship ... the port side? I don't see a damn thing."

"Red Jack is old-school—really old-school. Port side, loading side, larboard side, left side—it's all the same thing."

Captain Bob put his finger on his nose and turned a puzzled look toward the sky. "She's ahead of us too," he said, almost to himself. He looked upward again. "And check your rigging, Jack, lad. I'm looking for a sea change soon. Pretty damn soon, I'll say."

"Aye, Captain Bob. She's no bloody revenue cutter, that one." Red-Jack's voice trailed faintly above the wind whistling through the rigging.

"Bob, what the hell is a 'dog cutter'?" Joseph asked.

"At sea we see many things, Joseph. If you're a man-of-war, well, there be no worries, but anything else—a merchantman, for example, of which we are, those who don't mind their company at sea might just fall prey to pirates. That cutter, or any such vessel slinking about in the mists and following you at a distance, watching your every move at sea, is a dog cutter. The vessel's dogging us, don't you see?" He grinned. "Maybe that term isn't in the *Encyclopedia Britannica*, but you'll find it in my ship's log.

"That vessel is a fast cutter. You know what a cutter is, I think? Similar in many ways to the Yank privateer, *Rattlesnake*, the one that pestered our shipping during the bloody war we fell in with about 1812. The damned Yank can be a bloody pain in the arse sometimes."

"Very well, Bob. You take care of the dog cutter, and I'll not worry about it." Joseph returned to his thoughts. He didn't know much about Red-Jack, but he did know most of these seamen were special in one way or another. It was good to have such men working in one's business. He understood that part of it very well.

Soon, maybe a half hour, the wind shifted and diminished.

"There's my sea wind, change I've been looking for," yelled Captain Bob. "Look lively, men. That dog cutter will jump way ahead of us now. She can change round to take better advantage of the wind. Unlock the arms locker," Captain Bob ordered to a group of sailors who'd come out to watch. "Load both deck cannon," he added, pulling his cap down hard. "You know what to load. You men see to the rigging. She must be gale-rigged now for this part of it."

The captain looked aloft. "Do you still see her, Red-Jack?" he called.

"No, sir, Captain Bob. She's gone—the mists."

The crew worked aloft to change the sails.

The ship rounded Cape Cod and picked up speed toward the place known as The Graves, a place along the way toward Little Brewster Island lighthouse. Then she headed on toward a rendezvous with the steam tug and the harbor at Boston.

Joseph heard again the forlorn whistling of the wind in the rigging and the taut rippling sound it made against the wet sails. Shivering, he pulled his coat tight about him.

The Graves—what's that about? Walking back to his cabin, he thought, *dog cutter? What does it all mean? Why not put on more sail if speed is needed? Bob has the men rolling and tying some of the canvas. Well, surely he knows what he is doing, doesn't he?*

It had been a lonely trip from Bermuda. On many other occasions, Joseph had spent long days at sea, but this time Frances was neither near at hand, nor was she waiting at the end of his voyage. Frances was dead, and the realization of it chilled him. He reflected on the trip to England he had just completed and about his companion, his sweet child Sarah Jean. She was as fragile as he.

Maybe I should have brought the girls along with me, he thought. *No. They would have been lost without Frances. It is best for Sarah Jean to be with her Aunt Meg at the Worsham family's estate near Manchester. And Amanda seemed happy to be with the Stuarts in Bermuda.*

He took off his coat and shoes and stretched out on his bunk. The notion of loneliness did not sit well with him. He tried to think about something good, perhaps the business he had planned in Boston. Surely, he could think of something more suitable for taking a restful nap.

And what about the pirate? To hell with the damned pirate, anyway.

Joseph daydreamed of the time he'd spent alone with Miss Agnes. The next moment found his mind chasing down the road toward her cottage.

Soon, as he closed his eyes and began to relax, he drifted back again to the warmth of that Bermuda afternoon as he remembered ...

Chapter 37

An Amorous Afternoon with Agnes

Joseph Worsham
January 1828
At sea—a *daydream* en route to Boston

JOSEPH SAW AGNES'S COTTAGE IN the distance and thought her place suited her. It was pretty and svelte—the way he'd always pictured her in his mind's eye: a white cake-icing roof and lightly colored walls. Her place, a small, Bermuda-style cottage—not at all like Stuart Manor—was painted pale yellow, a warm smile against the cedar growth behind in the cottage garden.

Joseph called out as he rode in, dismounted, then walked onto the front porch. He found the door open.

"Is that you, Joseph?" Agnes called from inside the cottage. "Come on inside."

Joseph hesitated.

"Please, come in."

As he walked through the doorway, Agnes was not in the front room. The aroma of a cigar permeated the house.

"Are you entertaining?" he asked, placing his hat on the rack beside the door.

"I'm back here, Joseph." Agnes's voice came from the next room. "Come on in here."

"Is Sarah Jean here, Agnes? I was hoping she would ride back with me."

"Tilly came and took her about an hour ago."

Joseph entered the room where Agnes had invited him, shocked to find himself in her bedroom and Agnes in her bathtub. She held a lit cigar in one hand, a book in the other.

"Oh, forgive me. I had no idea you were in your bath." Joseph started to leave.

"There's many a lady who would welcome such a handsome man as yourself into her boudoir, Joseph. Please don't leave. Come here."

Agnes set aside the book and cigar then beckoned him with a crooked finger.

"Here. You can help me out of the tub. Just you look the other way."

"Surely you don't mean for me to stay, Agnes. Why, I'm embarrassed." It was a lie, and he thought she knew.

"Fetch me that towel and robe, Joseph." She pointed across the room to a chair beside her bed. "And give me your hand. Just look the other way while I step out. I've fallen, stepping from this tub. It really is dangerous, you know."

Joseph brought Agnes the towel and robe. He obliged her and put out his hand, turning his head as she stepped from the tub.

In a moment she said, "You can turn around now. The old lady's got her robe on, and it's safe to look."

She smiled as he turned to face her. "You look beautiful with your hair down, Agnes," Joseph said. "You should wear it so more often." That was certainly the truth. Agnes was very pretty.

"What? Old lady Agnes?" She smiled again and reached out to grasp his hands. As she did so, the robe fell open.

"There ... now I've gone and done it," she said. She looked down at his shoes. "You needn't be alarmed, Joseph. You don't have to be here, you know, but this could be such a fortunate event for both of us. You did say you wanted to get to know me better."

Joseph put his arms around her. "I'm not afraid if you're not." Strangely, he felt no guilt ... only lust.

Agnes blushed and tilted her head to kiss him.

Removing the robe the rest of the way, she led him, still holding his hand, to her bed. "Come along, Joseph. I want to get to know you better too."

He took off his clothes as she watched him from the bed, her curvaceous body concealed by the linen sheet.

He was very excited, and it was beginning to show.

"Please come here, Joseph. Please."

He crawled into Agnes's bed at her express invitation and spent an hour or so getting to know her better.

Joseph was a master at prolonging his climax, and at just the right moment, he would interrupt the natural flow of things to complete the finale outside. It was something he had learned with years of practice … the times when pregnancy had meant health risks.

Certainly, he would do the same here and now. To do less would leave him with guilt feelings that would be difficult to reconcile.

He made the wet track on the bedsheet between her legs, well after she'd relaxed her grip on his body. He thought she was very happy with his performance because of the look on her face. She looked exhausted.

He got out of the bed and began to dress, remaining silent until he finished. Agnes still lay naked on her back across the bed.

"Tell me, Agnes," he said, tugging his right earlobe. "Did you do that for my benefit? Did you do that to help me?"

He was thinking of something he had heard in a broker's office: *A sorrow cannot grow where ye tend your lust.*

"Joseph, I think we both benefited from that. Don't you?"

"Yes." He was certain he had done so. "Tell me," he said, "I remember the time when I rode back from Hamilton in your carriage. You wore a rather fierce expression when you looked at me. What did that mean?"

"A fierce look, you say?"

"That's right."

"Well, I don't know for certain why that would be. But I do remember I had a premonition. Maybe that was it."

"A premonition … indeed?"

"Aye. A premonition of that spot you left on the bed between my legs just now. *Noblesse oblige*—you perform as a true nobleman. I reckoned it would be you coming along sooner or later. It had me excited some that day. I'm sorry if I caused you any grief."

"I see."

"I say, Joseph. You sure do know how to please a woman."

He had begun the rest of his life that day in Bermuda with Agnes. His mind danced from one thought to another as he began to drift off to sleep in his cabin aboard the *Anne Bayliss*.

Chapter 38

Tea with Captain Bob

Joseph Worsham
January 1828
At sea—en route to Boston

A KNOCK SOUNDED AT THE door. "Mister Joe?" It was George, the cabin boy.

"Oh yes. What is it, lad? Come in."

"Captain Bob would have ye join him for tea. In his cabin, sir."

George stepped into the room, holding on to the doorway with one hand, his cap behind his back in the other.

Well, now, thought Joseph. *Bob Mathison, my man from Bristol, loves his afternoon tea. He's a pretty good ship's captain too.*

Joseph stood, straightened his collar, and ran his fingers through his hair.

Maybe I need to be with someone right now, and the company would do me good. Loneliness is a rotten bedfellow. He grimaced at his reflection in the mirror beside the cabin door as the thought struck him. He thought again of Agnes and her lithe, firm curves.

"Run along, George," he said. "Tell Captain Bob I'll be pleased to join him straightaway."

Joseph put on his coat and stood looking for a minute at his image in the mirror. *Come on, snap out of it,* he thought.

Satisfied that he looked as put together as he could, he slipped out into the hallway and then followed George's lead to the captain's cabin.

Captain Bob met him at the doorway. His was easily the finest and most spacious part of the ship, occupying most of the stern.

"Come in, Mister Worsham," Captain Bob invited. "I worry about you."

Joseph extended his hand. "I guess I've not been too happy on this trip, Bob. And please, call me Joseph."

"Yes, Joseph. We've had happier crossings." Captain Bob firmly shook Joseph's hand. "Maybe next time you can bring the two lasses?" he said. "I get on right well with them. And Miss Amanda is one to ask questions. Old Bob has to work just to stay ahead."

Joseph smiled as he made his way over to the expanse of windows across the ship's stern to look out at seagulls in the wake of the *Anne Bayliss.*

Turning, he said, "Bob, I have business to attend to in Boston. While you wait for the factor to contact you about off-loading our cargo, I'll be going into town."

"Aye."

"With any luck at all, I'll be able to set up a new trade route to and from Liverpool with a more profitable trip down to Charleston. There must be something we can haul South that won't violate Yankee Corn Laws. We've been running in ballast too much from Boston to Charleston. If we haul directly into Charleston or Wilmington, the goods we sell hardly pay for the trip—not as they should. For example, I live in Charleston. I bank the bulk of my funds in Liverpool and London. Goods factored in Charleston take too long to sell—and it's difficult to get the right price. Southerners want to give us script, not hard currency. Makes me believe the best place to market goods is here, in Boston. Am I wrong in that?"

Captain Bob shrugged his shoulders.

"So we return to England with a load of cotton, which we purchase—barter—in Boston. Well, I need the cotton. My company's textile mills in Manchester can use all the cotton my ships can haul.

We're expanding. I have friends in Charleston who grow cotton. I buy it, store it, and ship it. I ship cotton out of Charleston."

Joseph picked at his front teeth with his thumb and forefinger. "But consider this," he continued. "We buy cotton in Boston, it's been hauled up from Charleston by somebody else. Do you see where I'm going with this, Bob?"

"Well, sir. You just tell us what we're to do, and that part of it will be easy."

Heavens, thought Joseph. *Bob's not much help with this. I'll have to find some factor with new ideas, sure enough.*

"Bob, what does that dog cutter's maneuvering mean? If you think it's following us, then why did it cut ahead? Could she be a revenue cutter after all?"

"That's no revenue cutter, no ship of State, Joseph. It's a pirate rig if ever I saw one. Been dogging us for a while, following in the mists. We'll be looking sharp till we're safe in Boston Harbor. We won't let that one catch us with our pants down—lacking for defensive strategy, that is. Heavy laden as we be, speed is a problem. Joseph, you try to haul trade goods from Boston to Charleston under the British Union Jack, and you'll run afoul of the Yanks for sure. You'd see revenue cutters then for a fact. You must be the lawful owner of a Yankee flag to haul Yankee coastal trade. Don't you know? It's their bloody corn laws."

"Do you have any idea why the dog cutter is following us? Are they just a nosy bunch of bastards?"

"We're a fat target, Joseph. A merchantman loaded with costly cargo. Expensive English goods, you know. If we dawdle, we'll stand to lose more than our cargo. That's a ship of thieves. Blackguards. Like I said before, bloody pirates, Joseph. The kind of bloody bastards we need to get rid of. Those people don't leave any witnesses about to spread tales after they do their evil deeds. You've heard about that sort of thing now, haven't you?"

"Should I load my traveling firearms, Bob?"

"No. Just you leave it to old Bob and to this fine Aberdeen-built ship. We're mindful for pirates. You'll see. We'll make harbor fit and on time."

Joseph smiled, felt better about it. *After all, Captain Bob is good at his job*, he thought. *But I'll load my damn pistols, anyway.*

"Say," said Bob, "why don't you sit yourself down and let George pour you some tea."

Their chairs rumbled as each took a place at the captain's table.

George appeared from the hallway. "Aye, sir?"

"Pour us some tea, lad. And fetch the tin of biscuits me Alice bakes special when I'm to home."

"Tea biscuits?" Joseph raised his eyebrows.

George returned so quickly he must have placed the tin in the passageway in advance, knowing his captain would ask.

"Aye." Bob opened the tin and offered it across the table.

The smell of spice biscuits reminded Joseph of Antig'a.

Tea cakes, biscuits … cookies, he thought. *Maybe now I'm a Yank myself.*

Joseph took one of the tea biscuits and could almost feel the warmth that Alice had put into it for her Captain Bob. It saddened him he couldn't have shared anything more of that sort of thing with Frances. But he had his memories.

George arrived with a teapot and poured the tea.

"So what do you think we can take on in Boston instead of ballast for a trip to Charleston or Wilmington?" Captain Bob asked.

"Well, I don't know. But I expect to find out from the new factor, a man recommended by a solicitor in Bermuda."

"Watch yourself, Joseph." Captain Bob rubbed his nose with the back of his hand. "You're apt to find a den of thieves when you seek out a solicitor's cohorts, especially if they're in some foreign port or other."

Joseph was surprised. "Why do you say that?"

"Sometimes they're smugglers, blackguards, or worse. Maybe that's the meaning of the pirate rig."

"You sound as if you have experience along those lines."

"When I made the India run three years ago, I was approached by just such a man in Liverpool … right before I left for the East."

"And?"

"He wanted me to bring him something special in the way of cargo from his friends in Calcutta."

"Did you accommodate him?"

"No, sir. I turned him down flat, I did."

"How did you know something was amiss in the deal?"

"Joseph, I was a midshipman for a time, back in the old days. And I guess I've seen all kinds. I mean—you can just tell."

Captain Bob pressed the lid back on the cookie tin and gave Joseph a narrow stare.

"It wasn't so much what that man allowed," said Captain Bob, beginning to grin, "but what he didn't say that tipped me. I just had an odd feeling about it. Sure, I might as well have taken his money and brought his special package back to Liverpool. I'm certain someone else did. He offered more than I thought the arrangement was worth. Some poor ship's captain probably made a fortune on that deal, and all the rummy had to do was smuggle a wee, small box past the authorities, you understand. I'll wager it contained counterfeit notes, bank drafts, or worse." Bob's eyes widened. "Hey, it might have been human cargo—young Indian girls. Girls for Liverpool's sporting houses. You understand. That could be it, not documents at all. Not a small box at all. Or maybe it was clandestine letters for some foreign authority or other … spies, something like that."

"Wants a package or letter delivered overseas?"

"Certainly. But this blighter had a peculiar smell about him. I don't know. I shudder to think of it, what he wanted me to carry to Liverpool. Something appalling, you can count on that."

"Right."

Joseph looked at Bob with newfound interest. *Does he already know about Warner Hawke? Should I tell Bob of the new plans with Hawke? No. That had best wait for a better time. Bob just might retire before too long, and there might be no need for such dark truths.*

"Bob," he said, feigning a smile. "As I've said, I hope to work out some way to make this run more profitable. But I'll have no part of anything that's illegal."

Odd that he said these things without any emotion to betray his lie. How could Bob understand that I might be compromising legitimate business to protect my family? There's no bloody way the man would understand. And neither do I, for that matter. I simply will not carry young girls into slavery, so that settles it. I'll have to figure out something else to keep my family safe. But what?

"There's precious little in the way of finished goods to be had down South," said Joseph, "even in New Orleans. Everything enters by ship or barge. The problem is, it's so much easier to sell the English goods up here in Boston. And we need to make enough in gold to take our profit back to England. That's a problem for any trader, isn't it? It seems to me, given the right set of circumstances, there'll be a way to work this out."

"I'm certain of it," Bob agreed.

Joseph sat listening to the captain for about a quarter hour longer, all the while feeling the twinge of heartache the loss of Frances had left in him. He enjoyed the company and the spice tea biscuits. But after a while he felt the need to be alone, perhaps to take a nap—another dream or two?

At that moment a cannon roared in the distance. As they ran to see, a second shot blasted through the air.

Joseph heard the whirring of the ball as it fell into the sea.

Chapter 39

Pirates

Joseph Worsham
January 1828
At sea—en route to Boston

"HEAVE TO, YOU MERCHANTMAN! HEAVE to," came the hoarse voice from the pirate rig, the so-called dog cutter. "Stand by to be boarded." A bearded man stood on the bowsprit holding a brass hailing trumpet.

A third shot fired, just missing the *Anne Bayliss*'s rigging. A dozen or so men with long muskets peered over the gunwales of the pirate vessel, awaiting orders from their captain.

"Well, pirate," said Captain Bob, "that was your last bloody chance to be civil." Watching through his ship's glass, he told Joseph, "I've seen that bearded swab drunk on his arse in front of a whore house in Rio. They're up to no good."

The pirate vessel headed toward the *Anne Bayliss*, closing at an angle to the port bow.

"Turn straight into her, lad," yelled Captain Bob to the helmsman. "Do your damnedest to ram her. Forget the bloody sails. We're gale-rigged. She can take it."

The captain turned to the group of sailors who had gathered nearby. "Man the deck cannon," he ordered. "Don't fire till ye see her veer away."

"Stand by for a ram!" Red-Jack shouted, issuing a warning to the pirate.

Slowly, the ships maneuvered into a collision course. *Anne Bayliss* leaned heavily as she lumbered through the turn. And in a few moments, the pirate veered away.

As the ships passed, one deck cannon thundered. Joseph looked but saw no cannonball hole appear in the pirate's sails. He thought the shot had missed. But the pirate was in trouble. The helmsman threw hands over his buttocks, and the ship sharply listed to starboard. As the sails shredded in the wind, the bearded man was nowhere to be seen. But the men armed with muskets began pulling off their shirts and cursing in chaos.

"We've come by the last of that one," Captain Bob chortled. "Thirty-two pounds of rock salt and nails in the backside will change their bloody minds. Never catch us now. And we'll have no cargo worth stealing on the way back out of here. We're safe for now."

Joseph returned to his cabin as Captain Bob made his preparations to take the *Anne Bayliss* into Boston. In a few moments, Joseph found himself stretched out on his bunk again, drifting off into a restless, troubled sleep. He couldn't usually remember his dreams once he was completely awake, but hey, he smiled because he could always remember Agnes.

Chapter 40

A Man Called Traveler

Joseph Worsham
January 1828
Boston Harbor

JOSEPH SLEPT.

At the sound of George knocking on his cabin door, his first waking thoughts were of his daughters. He knew, sadly, their loss ran as deeply as his, and in many ways probably more so. They had no fancy daydreams to cushion their fall.

He noticed right away that the ship's rocking motion had ceased. There came a second knock at the door.

"You missed the steam tug, sir," George announced after Joseph had called for him to enter. "And I've brought you some bottled medicinal water, if you care for that sort of thing. Captain Bob sent me ashore for a bottle, so I bought one for you—good for what ails ye an' all that. It's what they say."

"Well, thank you very much. You're a thoughtful lad, that's for sure. Take whatever I owe you from the change on the nightstand."

George did so and left the room. For a few moments, Joseph considered the bottle of water, turning it over in his hand. He thought better of it and placed the bottle on his bed.

"Don't really need a cathartic right now—if, indeed, that's what this is. Don't know …"

And so he ventured out of his cabin and onto the deck. While he had slept, the crew, with the help of a steam tug, had brought the *Anne Bayliss* in carefully to her berth at the long wharf in Boston Harbor. He had missed all the excitement. He breathed in the strangeness of the waterfront, at once sweet- and spice-laden, yet spoiled with the neglect and refuse of a busy seaport.

Just the sort of place I'm looking for, he thought.

"Lad," he called to the cabin boy who with a dust mop had followed him out, "tell Captain Bob I'm going into Boston now. When I know where I'll be staying, I'll send for my baggage."

"Aye, Mister Worsham. You need any help just now?"

"Not now, thanks."

Joseph made his way toward the wharf. *Pirates, indeed,* he thought. *We might need a bit more than a cathartic if those bastards are waiting on the way out.* He had seen a carriage parked alongside a tavern near wharf's end that might be a cab. He hurried toward the street.

Yes, it was a cab, and it appeared to be empty. He raised his arm and hailed the cabbie. As he reached the cab, he yanked open the door and hauled himself up. At that moment, he noticed a man already seated inside. The man said something in an unfamiliar language. The man spoke again, carefully and precisely, as if expecting a reply from Joseph.

Slavic? Perhaps Polish or Ukrainian? "I say," Joseph said, startled, "I can't understand you. Is that Russian? Do you speak English?"

Joseph scrambled back to the street, his breath coming in short gasps. "I'm sorry," he said, peering through the open cab door. "I didn't realize this cab was taken."

The man held an unlit pipe. The carriage smelled of a blended, aromatic pipe tobacco, as if the man had been puffing on the unlit pipe for some time.

"Beg your pardon," said the stranger in perfect English. "I took you for a Russian gentleman. This is, I'm afraid, the only cab about. Tell the driver where you wish to go. I'm in no hurry. We can share the ride."

"That's very kind," Joseph said, turning to address the driver. He showed the driver the card Semmes had given him. "Can you take me to this address?"

The driver nodded, and Joseph again climbed into the carriage.

"Well, to be sure," said the stranger as he tucked his pipe away to a vest pocket, "I'm in no particular hurry. Come on in and settle yourself. This isn't much of a day for a ride, but my appointments are flexible. You must go first to your destination. If you don't mind my asking, where are you bound?" He tugged at the rim of his hat. "We haven't been introduced. My name is Trevelyan. Augustus P. Trevelyan. And what, may I ask, is yours?"

The man spoke so quickly Joseph had to wait for a pause before he could speak.

Why the unlit pipe? Had the man been waiting in the cab for someone else when Joseph came off the ship? Was he afraid the pipe smoke would give him away?

The man paused, and Joseph cleared his throat to take advantage of the opportunity. "My name is Joseph Worsham," he said. "I am happy to make your acquaintance … Mister Trevelyan, is it?" He handed the card to Trevelyan. "This is my destination," he said, with a look of confidence.

Trevelyan studied the card, then smacked the card with the back of his fingers. "Is that your ship, sir? Damn. Why do you want to see this man? If you don't mind my saying so," said Trevelyan, "this man Fletcher, the name on the card, is a criminal with some notoriety here about. You simply don't look to be that sort yourself."

Trevelyan leaned forward in his seat and pulled his coattails straight behind him. A thin, tall man, he probably stood over six feet tall.

"And another thing," he said. "This address is in a rough part of Boston. If I were you, sir, I should think twice before I went to this neighborhood for any purpose … certainly not for business. Besides, it's sure to be getting dark soon."

He fidgeted in his seat before saying, "By damn it!" Then he shoved his hat down tight on his head and turned toward the window. After a time, he said, "I'm not keen on going there myself. Say,

Worsham, maybe we should go to my destination first. Then you can have the cab and be on your merry way."

Joseph said nothing for a moment, reflecting on Trevelyan's warning. Semmes had told him to see this person whose name was on the card. If he didn't, his plans would have to change. He looked at the card.

"Gilbert Fletcher," it stated in scroll print. "Esquire."

My business of setting up a new trade route for my Worsham-Moore shipping company isn't the sort of thing to entrust to a person operating from a bad part of town. This man Trevelyan says so.

"Worsham?"

"Yes?"

"I've taken this station. I'm here in this cab now, to meet a gentleman inbound on a British ship."

"Oh? What's his name?"

"Sergé Gnojec. He's a Russian gentleman, I believe. You have anyone by that description onboard your ship?"

"I'm afraid not," Joseph answered a bit too quickly.

Dear God, thought Joseph, beginning to shake all over. His mind raced. *Is there no end to this? They look for me here … in Boston? Obviously, someone gave the name to Trevelyan. The name was a mixture of "Sir Gay" and "Ru Gnojec." Who is this Trevelyan? Is he some representative of the American authorities? Did some Bermuda or Liverpool operative forward a tip to Trevelyan by fast steam packet?* Joseph fought for composure, reaching deep for strength to feign a calm that he did not possess.

This business, this knowing ahead of my arrival—the Sir Gay thing. It makes no bloody sense.

With effort, Joseph stated calmly, "Inbound, you said? Inbound from where?"

"The islands."

"My shipping company operates out of Liverpool. I live in Charleston."

Why did this man, Trevelyan, ask if Anne Bayliss *is my ship? Why did he not think me to be an ordinary paying traveler just arrived from some far away British port? How does he know my nom de guerre, "Sir*

Gay," the name from my youth? How does he know about Grewno? How does he know about me? I have been away from that hideous business for quite some time.

Plenty was unknown about this tall stranger, yet something about him Joseph liked. Maybe it was his abrupt manner. Or was it his frank honesty? Maybe it was the keen look in the man's eyes that belied his hurried words?

Joseph tucked the card away. "Mister Trevelyan," he said, "if what you say is true, and somehow I believe it is, you may have saved me from almost certain heartaches and trouble, neither of which I need right now."

Trevelyan nodded.

"And yes. The ship, the *Anne Bayliss*, is mine."

Trevelyan answered with a grunt.

Joseph signaled the cab driver. "Say, cabby, hold for a moment while I rethink my plans," he called.

The carriage eased to a halt.

"I say," said Joseph, eyeing Trevelyan.

"Yes, sir?"

"Can you recommend a good hotel?"

"Indeed."

"Well, tell the cabby where it is. If there's a place nearby to enjoy a good meal, I want to buy you dinner … if you have no other plans. I'd like to talk with you about this man Fletcher. And there may be other topics of discussion as well, if you're willing."

"Sounds like a capital idea. I'm traveling right now on business myself and was planning to dine at that restaurant later on. Yes, sir. I'm willing." He gave instructions to the cab driver and the carriage started off again.

Joseph leaned back in his seat. *So,* he thought, *this man Trevelyan is a traveler, a businessman, and he thinks I am too. Yet he seemed to know beforehand about the* Anne Bayliss. *Has he decided I'm a gentleman traveler, a ship owner, or what? And what kind of business brings him to the wharf right beside my ship?* He remained silent. *What of the "Sir Gay" business? Does he really know?*

"May I call you Joseph?" Trevelyan asked after a while.

"Please do."

For some odd reason, Joseph felt that he could trust Trevelyan. Yet suddenly he knew there was something more to the man than the conversation would suggest. He thought he would listen, with care, and maybe learn just what that something might be.

"Joseph, some of my friends will be joining me at the restaurant. I know they will be pleased to meet you."

Joseph nodded, then asked, "Say, what shall I call you? Augustus?"

"Call me Traveler. Everyone does, and with cause, I might add. Only my mother calls me Augustus."

"I don't want to intrude upon a meeting with your friends. Perhaps you can be my guest for dinner another time?"

Traveler appeared upset by this statement. It was hard enough to follow his hurried speech, but if anything, now his words became even more hurried.

"Please," said Traveler, "I guess I should not have told you so much about my plans. I want you to join us for dinner. Really, I do. If you don't, I will be offended. The meal is on me."

Traveler took off his hat to finger-straighten his hair. After putting the hat back on he took out the pipe. Again, he puffed on the unlit blend of tobacco.

In the confining carriage, Joseph welcomed the sudden silence. But soon, wanting to find out more about this man and his friends, he said, "Thank you for your kindness. I would be pleased to join you. Say, Traveler, where are you from?"

"I grew up in a slum right here in Boston. I was born in a corn shuck bed not far from the wharf where your ship is moored."

Joseph ignored the remark about the slum. The idea of being born in a corn shuck bed sounded most appalling to him.

"What is your occupation? I mean, do you always travel?"

Traveler put the pipe away. "Freelance writing," he said. "Newspaper articles, periodicals. Whatever I can find to write about. I travel the East Coast for the most part. I do visit Mexico, Europe, the Mediterranean, South America, and the Western territories on occasion, but mostly I am a free man, a poet errant, as it were."

Well, thought Joseph, *a poet errant, is it? A wandering poet on a mission … and what would this poet's mission be?* He saw humor in it rather than anything else.

"Do you visit Charleston?" Joseph asked, barely concealing his smile.

"Sometimes."

Joseph wondered if Traveler had seen his company sign in Charleston, the Worsham-Moore sign, but he didn't ask. Instead, he looked out the carriage window at the city.

Shops, business offices, and better parts of Boston were coming into view. The streets and sidewalks looked clean, and everywhere people in fashionable attire hurried about their business. Some were arriving or departing in carriages. Some scurried between shops. And some had gathered in small groups along the wooden sidewalks, talking to one another.

He saw pretty young ladies wearing pastel colors with folded parasols and lace ruffles, talking and laughing with their friends. Most hurried to their carriages because it was nigh time for the evening meal.

Oh, what have I gotten myself into? Joseph thought. *I should be with my girls in Bermuda.*

There …

Is that someone I know? Isn't that Semmes from Bermuda? Joseph turned to look as the cab passed. *I'm not sure. It was a one-eyed man. And what did the appearance of that pirate ship off Cape Cod mean? Did that business have something to do with Semmes?*

"Joseph?"

"Yes, Traveler?" *The name seems to fit him somehow.*

"Here is our hotel. Come on, I want to introduce you to the management."

"Right."

As Joseph climbed down from the carriage, the cab driver tipped his hat and said, "Would you be wanting me to fetch your luggage from the ship, sir?"

Joseph took his wallet from his inside coat pocket and handed the driver a silver Spanish coin he still carried from the exchange in Saint George's. For an instant, he'd exposed the gold in his purse.

"Yes, please do. Here, this is for you. Now please wait a moment so I can write a note to my captain. He won't release my things without it."

Joseph wrote a short note on some stationery he had in his coat pocket for just such a purpose, then handed it to the cab driver who accepted it with a smile.

"Thank you, sir," he said, tipping his hat. He clucked to the horse, and the carriage pulled away.

"Damn, Joseph," said Traveler when the driver was out of earshot. "Don't ever show that much gold to a cab driver here, or anywhere else, for that matter. Plan ahead, man. Have a small amount of coins ready to show when the fare is to be paid."

Joseph grinned. "Well, you certainly have a way about you, Traveler." He was beginning to like Traveler very much and felt certain that his trust was warranted. But he found it stressful to trust someone and then to hope that he never finds you out.

"I say, Joseph. I pride myself of having a sixth sense. I sense a sadness about you. Maybe it's none of my business. Maybe you'd rather not talk about it …"

Maybe he's figured me out, maybe he hasn't. I'll assume the latter and let it rest, for now. "I'm a widower. My wife had yellow fever and died in childbirth. The baby came too early because of the fever."

Joseph found he could talk about his wife's death more easily now. Though he was still hurt and felt the loss.

"I'm sorry to hear about your wife, Joseph. Did the baby survive? Do you have other children? How long has your wife been gone?"

"She passed away three months ago in Bermuda. And Little Joe didn't make it. He only lived for a few hours."

"Is that where you're from? Bermuda?"

"My family originated in the Virginia colony before the War of Independence, or Revolutionary War, whichever is your preference. I'm originally from the island of Antig'a."

"That explains the profoundly British accent."

They ascended the hotel's front steps, and Traveler held the door open for Joseph. A cool, clean scent greeted them from the lobby. Joseph caught the fragrance of a woman's perfume. Yes … and the memory of a fine Cuban cigar also pleasantly excited his senses. He was confidant things would go his way, yet the thought confronted him: *But what the hell will happen next?*

Chapter 41

Patience

Joseph Worsham
1828
Boston

AT THE DRY SINK IN his hotel room, Joseph poured water from the pitcher into the washbasin, splashed cool water on his face, used his towel, then assessed the room. The furniture pleased him. He glanced at the bed, checking for mosquito netting.

Yes, there it is, folded neatly and conveniently out of the way. Maybe I won't need the damn netting so late in the year, he thought. However, he was glad to see it. *Blasted mosquitoes, anyway. Why did God make mosquitoes in the first place? What else do mosquitoes do but suck the blood out of a person and make bloody nuisances of themselves? On days and nights when the weather is at its worst, when there's hardly a breath of fresh air to be had, one has to hang the damn netting.*

He combed his hair with his fingers. *I should've asked George to pack a few of my toiletry items before leaving the ship. But I didn't think of it. Oh, well. It won't be long till Traveler's man returns with a few things, toiletry items in particular. No problem at all.*

Earlier, as Joseph registered at the front desk, he met the hotel's manager and staff. They were polite and seemed well acquainted with Traveler.

Speaking of Traveler, he thought, *it's about time to meet in the hallway.* Joseph left the room, leaving the door ajar for the room keeper to clean the washbasin and leave freshwater.

Traveler stood waiting at the railing.

"I say," Joseph said, starting down the stairs, "I haven't seen anything of that cab driver. Have you?"

"No, he must have had some difficulty." Traveler did not appear concerned.

"I wonder if I should leave now … until your man shows, I mean."

"Why don't you leave him to me, Joseph?"

Traveler paused to speak with the man at the desk.

Outside, they crossed the street and walked past several storefronts. The corner business establishment appeared similar to a Virginia tavern, a French café, or an English pub—a place where people gathered to discuss business or maybe enjoy a meal.

Soon it will be dark.

A lamplighter climbed his ladder, lit the corner gas lamp, and watched them go by.

Odd? No. Lamplighters no doubt are bored silly as they go about the business of obliterating the evening shadows hereabout.

Joseph looked overhead at clouds illuminated by the setting sun. The sight gave him a warm, happy feeling. The day had turned out well after all. The rain had cleared away splendidly.

There's a most welcome warm freshness in the air. "Red skies at night, sailors delight." Is that how that goes?

"Hello, Traveler," a rather loud voice called from behind them on the street. "Coach coming up now—behind. Look lively."

Joseph turned, saw Traveler waving and smiling.

"Lester," said Traveler. "Do you have Miss Patience with you in the coach?"

"Indeed, Commander. She wants to discuss something with you."

The coach stopped. Lester set the brake and jumped down to the street. Opening the coach door, he helped an attractive buxom lady step down to join the group gathered in the street.

"Traveler," she said. "I'm sorry I cannot keep our dinner engagement. And who is this handsome gentleman with you tonight?"

"Allow me to introduce Joseph Worsham. He is from Charleston, has a delightful British accent, and wants to acquire ships, good Yankee ships, to bolster American trade for his shipping company."

"Joseph." Patience extended her hand. "I am Patience Hannah Caldwell. I am pleased to meet you. You certainly are an interesting character, aren't you? A British, Southern gentleman ..."

Joseph smiled, bowed in a gesture of civility, and said, "Heavenly days. Such a beautiful lady." *Such a line of blarney.* "It is my pleasure. I say, we are about to enter this club for dinner. Could you change your mind and join us? It would give us time to become acquainted."

"No, my dear. Something terribly important has come up and must be dealt with this very evening. I cannot change it, I'm afraid. There will be other times, other places—there will be a next time. And, Joseph, I see no wedding band on your finger. Are you a single man? Do you enjoy the company of a lady? Well, perhaps I overstep. It is my nature to do so, I'm afraid. Forgive me."

"Think nothing of it, Patience. I look forward to that next time."

Joseph again bowed, then helped Patience back into the coach. And in a moment the coach drove off.

Traveler made no comment, thought Joseph, beginning to be quite confused. They approached the club.

Traveler opened the club door, made a sweeping gesture with his hat, an obvious invitation for Joseph to enter.

Joseph surveyed the people seated inside, laughing, talking. Cigar smoke hung across the room in a blue haze. A dapper gentleman sporting a full mustache walked to the entrance to greet them. He recognized Traveler, took their coats and hats, and bid them welcome. Traveler removed an envelope from his vest pocket and handed it to the man.

Now, what is Traveler up to with that? What is this place?

Then Traveler excused himself and left Joseph standing alone in the club entranceway.

"Well, I'll be damned," said Joseph. "I may as well go ahead and have my dinner. I'm quite hungry. This place looks just fine to me."

And so he did.

Chapter 42

The Morning After

Joseph Worsham
September 1828
Boston

"Top of the morning to you, sir," Traveler called, knocking a second time.

Joseph, not quite dressed, opened the door, squinted, wrinkled his brow, and surveyed his guest standing in the hallway.

Traveler handed Joseph a letter sealed with navy blue wax.

"A letter, Traveler? From whom?"

"Bob Mathison, your captain. Good man himself."

"Do you know the content of this letter? I saw Bob just yesterday."

"Read the letter, Joseph. I'm going to arrange for breakfast. Scrambled eggs, bacon, toasted muffins, and so forth. That agreeable with you?"

"Of course. I will read this letter over breakfast. You will not escape discussing it with me. Off with you now. I'm not yet fully awake. I suspect you play some role in this. You certainly left in a fury last evening, didn't you?"

"Very well, Joseph. Later."

"I say, Traveler, did your driver, Tom Wilkins, bring my things during the night?"

"They're in my room. But there really isn't much, I'm afraid. Your captain sent only toilet items in a small bag with a change of clothes. Shall I bring them now?"

Damn. George must be psychic. Good lad, anyway. He packed the very things I need—I certainly didn't ask him to. Have to reward him somehow.

"Please. I wish to freshen up." Joseph left the door slightly ajar and went back to his washstand. *Jesus, these Yanks are strange.*

Traveler brought the duffel, then left to attend to his breakfast errand. Joseph shaved, washed, and put on fresh clothing. He wondered if it were time to remove himself from the Hawke white slave business before he dove too far in—before he got found out. He felt terrible, his misery due to the weight of guilt. His self-worth as a person had reached an all-time low. Although his personal wealth was outstanding, it gave him no solace.

Chapter 43

Captain Bob's Letter

Joseph Worsham
September 1828
Boston

"Now tell me, how are things on my ship? Everything under control? Bob says in his letter, 'Everything is under control, thanks to Traveler and his men.' Now Traveler, whatever does 'under control' mean?"

"All parties, including your ship, are in good shape, Joseph. We had somewhat of a scare. That's all."

"No. You explain this to me right now. What the hell is going on with my ship?"

Traveler pulled out the pipe again. It remained unlit, as usual.

"I might as well tell you," he said as he puffed intermittently on his pipe. "Our greatest concern is that Fletcher and his men will set up new avenues of smuggling. Too much gets by far too often as it is. This East Coast is the mother lode of smuggling in America."

Joseph felt as though he had known this was coming all along.

"As you well know," Traveler continued, "we have protective tariffs. What you may not know, however, is that Fletcher is right in the middle of the smuggling trade, which is quite lucrative, I might add. I'll tell you all about it over breakfast. What do you say?"

In about an hour, Traveler returned with the hotel porter and breakfast. The porter set up a folding table in Traveler's room near the bay window. Traveler waited for Joseph to prepare his cereal before he began any conversation. Joseph took a few moments to say grace.

"Very well. Tell me about my ship." Joseph placed the napkin in his lap then smiled when he looked up to see that Traveler had his napkin tucked under his chin.

"Joseph, I work for a separate part of the government—a part that is very interested in discouraging smuggling and ultimately putting smugglers out of business for keeps. Well, maybe not part of the government in any real sense. It is our country's tariffs and laws, our social mores, that sort of thing, which causes the problem. For one reason or other, it is always profitable—if risky—to bypass the law when importing foreign items. Yet no real government agency, as underfunded as they all be, will be doing anything about it, you see?"

"Gilbert Fletcher?"

"Yes. White slavery is his specialty. We have but to catch him red-handed. Yet what we really want is the lot of them."

Traveler paused to look directly into Joseph's eyes.

"I think you should know something else, Joseph." He carefully smoothed the napkin across his shirtfront and tucked the edges under his coat lapels as he spoke. "We knew you were coming," he said, busily slicing his steak.

"How in heaven's name did you know? I haven't known it myself very long."

"You engaged the services of a man named Semmes in Bermuda?"

"Yes," answered Joseph. "There was a problem. I needed a solicitor. Do you know about that also?"

"No. I only know what you told me. But Semmes wrote a letter to Fletcher concerning your business trip to Boston. Actually, he wrote three of them. In that way I became aware of your coming. We intercepted his mail. We want to know what he is up to, so to speak. I read the letters. They told me you were coming to meet Fletcher and the approximate date of your arrival. And here we all are. Of course, having a man on the steam tug helped. Otherwise, there would have been many ships to meet every day."

"As simple as that?"

"Yes, Joseph."

"Why are you telling me all this now?"

"I made a judgment call about you last evening. I suddenly realized you are a respectable gentleman. It is my job to suspect every possible contact Fletcher makes. But there's no reason I can see now to suspect you of any wrongdoing. Rather, I should be protecting you from the likes of Fletcher. I think you are an honest man and that you have been victimized. You don't need a troublemaker like Fletcher in your business, and certainly not in your life."

"You are an expert judge of character, aren't you? Being a gentleman yourself," Joseph said. "Your family name is Trevelyan? Isn't that an old British name?"

Joseph felt a chill. He remembered long-ago days in Liverpool … and London. God. Would it ever end? That was such a long time ago. At that moment he decided to refuse Hawke the use of his ships, no matter the cost. He was out of the wicked white slave business for good and all. It simply must end. But he feared that it could only end with his death. The cold shudder must be visible, he thought. He could hardly hide it. Hawke would know soon enough that he had betrayed him. Things would turn ugly, very ugly.

"No, Joseph," said Traveler, suddenly sad-faced. "Gentleness never came my way, with my mother being the only exception, God love her. I'm a whore's son. My mother's Welch, brought here under false pretenses by the white slavers. We never knew my father. Mother gave me the name of a British gentleman she serviced."

"I'm sorry." Joseph straightened his back, sat up taller in his chair, and eyed the man across the table from him. He believed the things Traveler was saying, and he thought it safe to make a judgment call himself. He would wait to express it, but he thought Traveler to be a good and honest man. "Thank you," he said and smiled. "Please tell me about my ship now." He knew he must never meet Traveler's mother. She might remember him.

Traveler put down his knife and fork.

"We were lucky," he said. "We arrived just as the trouble was starting. Today Fletcher and his men are all under the jail, as we say.

And the bastards are likely to stay there, I might add. That's about it, I'm afraid. Nothing exciting or romantic to report. Your man Semmes wanted to help Fletcher set up some new way to smuggle contraband past our revenue cutters. That is my best guess. Fletcher only looks to incite the murky shadows beneath whatever situation is at hand. I think Semmes thought he could take advantage of you … of your broken life … so to speak. And he thought you were easy pickings. Who can say? We operate under the assumption that Semmes and Fletcher are in the smuggling business together. We'd intercepted correspondence from Semmes in the past. But none of that concerns you."

Joseph accepted the explanation of the events from last evening and returned to his meal. *May God help me to make it so*, he thought.

After breakfast, the two men simply sat and talked.

Chapter 44

Sobrecargo

Joseph Worsham
September 1828
Boston

"I say, Joseph."

"Yes."

"I've been thinking," Traveler said. "Could be you need to work out a better deal than you have so far in Boston. Or perhaps what you really should be doing is looking elsewhere."

"Where? Do you have any suggestions?"

"Well, yes, I do."

Traveler rocked backward on the two rear legs of his chair. "I'll get to that in a moment," he said. "What cargo do you ship to and from England? Finished goods out of London, Bristol, or Liverpool, and cotton out of the South?"

"That about covers it," Joseph affirmed.

"What? From here to Charleston, then back to England?"

"Well, more or less. Whatever the factors can work out."

"In ballast to Charleston?"

"That and the goods we don't sell here."

"Cobblestones—and sometimes other dead weight?"

"I have been wondering myself about that, Traveler," Joseph said. "Could we haul stone storefronts, facades, and the like, something profitable that would be within the Yankee law?"

"How would you like to shorten your trip, add a trading leg from the North to Charleston, increase your profits, and sell all the cargo you can haul? And no more stone ballast, unless it is something you choose to haul?"

"I like the sound of that. What have you in mind?"

"Do you have ships in the China Trade?"

"I do."

"What do you haul from India to China?"

"Lead, tin, wool from England or here, and opium from India … same as almost everyone else."

"Why do you do that—the opium, I mean?"

"Because, the Chinese accept payment in opium for tea. We don't transact with British *specie*—you know, gold, silver—the coin of the realm—in China. The arrangement is really quite simple. And it works very well. Opium is grown in India on plantations controlled by the British. The best, the favored—*Benares*, or *Malwa*—comes from the poppies grown in the west central region of India. I think you know all this, don't you?"

"Of course. But, Joseph, I think you might consider trading with something else. I'm sure you do well with tea, but people who are opium users don't live long. And they wind up being nonproductive. Certainly, they're not a happy lot. It is my understanding that the Chinese are not happy about the arrangement."

"Opium is sold here, is it not?"

"Yes, it is. I have seen the result of its use in the frontier territories and right here in Boston. You must visit the opium dens on Pell and Mott Streets in New York sometime." He shook his head, as if in disgust or pity; Joseph couldn't tell which. "I think opium should be outlawed," he continued. "Cotton can be grown in India, Joseph. Cotton brings a good price. Cotton is used in China, for instance, and almost everywhere else. Cotton. Could cotton be your medium of exchange?"

"You were about to tell me how I should restructure my entire shipping trade," Joseph reminded him.

"Sell your ships, either here or when you return to England. Buy yourself a ticket back to New York, and build your ships here. In this country, I mean. Maybe right here in Boston. It is illegal because of our Navigation Acts to transport American goods to and from American ports, that is, port to port, unless your ships are of United States registry and have mostly American crews. It is the only way you can lawfully haul anything except ballast to the South from up here. And, Joseph, you must ship in and out of New York."

"Why New York? Why not Boston?"

"For the simple reason that New York is closer to Charleston, and it's a better market in which to sell your English goods. Soon major trade routes will be established that lead inland to the rest of this growing country, routes that begin in New York and make their way everywhere—even to Boston—although probably coastal traders rather than large ocean-going ships such as you will build will use them. Why, Dewitt Clinton's canal is open, and you can ship from Lake Erie to the Hudson River at Albany and on to New York, or from New York to the West. And with everybody using steam-powered machines to run their mills, soon the North will become a major supplier of the world's manufactured goods."

"There's no market in England for American manufactured goods, not much of one, anyway," Joseph commented. "Well, there's tobacco."

"No. But there will be in other parts of the world. Hire yourself a *sobrecargo* for each ship. Trade with the world. You could establish a coastal trade loop between New York and Wilmington or Charleston—or even New Orleans—to bring cotton up here for your English ships to pick up in New York. There's a market here for English goods. And there's a market in the South for Northern goods even, with growing resistance in the Carolinas."

"You mentioned a *sobrecargo*. What is that?"

"A shipping master, cargo master. The supercargo. Usually he's stationed onboard the ship. If the man is good with language and has a good business head to boot, all the world becomes your trading partner. New trade possibilities exist now in South America for fast, safe ships. Think of it."

Joseph pushed back from the table. He knew about the super-cargo business. *An old shipping practice. He just made it sound roman-tic by saying it in Spanish—I think that was Spanish.* Sobrecargo. *The Corn Laws and Navigation Acts in England make it a bit more complicated than Traveler makes it seem. And recent wars don't help much, either. In many ways, it would be like selling out of a bloody pushcart.* He thought immediately of the man in Saint George's with his cart filled with aromatic, pencil cedar buckets. *"Piggins,"* he had called them.

"Are you available for the job?" Joseph asked as he looked across the table at the tall, young man with the bright, new ideas.

Bang.

Traveler set the chair legs squarely on the floor.

"Is this a job offer?"

"Yes. And I am quite serious."

Traveler removed his napkin from under his chin, stood up, paced to the door and back to the table again, then sat back down.

"I cannot answer you today, Joseph. It will take at least a fort-night to decide. Maybe it will take a month. Can you wait that long?"

"Yes, certainly. I have an idea a few weeks or so here could be quite enjoyable, actually." He was thinking of Patience.

He wants time, he mused. *Very well, we can talk about this busi-ness startup now, but I'll give him all the damn time he needs. I like this traveling man. But as fast as he talks, I don't think he will need all that time. We discuss some details now—shake on it later.*

"By the by," he said, "I'll not be selling any of my ships right now. I can use them elsewhere. It may not be the thing to use English ships in these American waters for coastal trade, but I am proud of my ships, each and all. I do not need to free the capital, as it were. No problem."

"I meant no offense, man."

The Yankee shippers are so arrogant, thought Joseph. *All full of innovative ideas. Well, if there are shipping opportunities in South America, my British ships will do very well for that commerce. The American restrictions on coastal trade wouldn't apply there. Traveler can work it all out.*

Joseph made up his mind right then and there to finance whatever Traveler wanted to do. *Whatever he wants to try will be given a fair go of it. But he'll have to take care of all the details. I've other business to tend to. I'll trust my British office with the paperwork.*

"Your acceptance can wait," he continued, "but I'll put you in charge of whatever you can work out, I will trust you with everything, and I will pay you a generous broker's fee in addition to a salary. Say 5 percent. Your percentage will be based on the overall total. Is that agreeable?"

"Remember, Joseph, I cannot accept even this fairy-tale job offer without a due-diligence consideration on my part. But yes, positively. And the men that we must hire?"

"High range of whatever is fair." *Fairy tale, indeed. I predict that you will accept my offer, and together we will make this work very well.*

"And the ships?"

"Let the best yard build them. I'll see that you have whatever funds you need. Just don't bother me with every little detail. And, Traveler, when you make up your mind, tell me all about it. Please …"

"Certainly, my good man."

Why, thought Joseph, *maybe this could be a good chance to put Captain Bob on a trade route closer to home, perhaps the Mediterranean. Or maybe a run from Liverpool to the ports around the British islands and right back home again. He would love that. He would be in Bristol often. He has served me well. No business can operate profitably without good people like Captain Bob. Unhappy and bad employees can break the back of a good company. And in another direction, some of my friends in Manchester would like to see the East India Company's China monopoly broken for good and all. I could use any ships freed up here for that. There's plenty of need for a good Aberdeen-built ship in my business. It must be that Traveler knows very little of my affairs, else he might not have suggested I sell my ships. Anyway, surely he knows very little, if anything, about my textile interests in Manchester. I sorely need cotton from the South.*

"Joseph, you don't care who builds your ships?"

"Yes, I care. Make the shipbuilders only the best—as I said."

"Certainly."

Joseph drummed his fingers on the table, thinking Bermuda and … "Name the first ship the *Frances Courtney*," he instructed.

Traveler gave him a questioning look.

"My deceased wife," Joseph explained.

"Of course."

Joseph thought of the *Anne Bayliss*. "Say, Traveler, can we see about my ship now?"

"Tom will be here in about a half hour, Joseph. If you have anything more to do before we leave, there's just enough time to get ready."

I should have guessed that you would have it all planned. Joseph stood up, placed the napkin on the table, and started for the door. "I'll meet you here in twenty minutes," he said.

Chapter 45

Visit to the Anne Bayliss

Joseph Worsham
September 1828
Boston

JOSEPH AND TRAVELER ENJOYED A restful ride to the wharf. Traveler seemed reflective and talked little, much as he had been the night before in the few minutes before the ladies arrived. Joseph took advantage of the silence and gazed out the carriage window, viewing more of the city this trip. He saw young, pretty ladies in day dresses of cotton-lined muslin, some wearing smart Marie Stuart morning caps. Others hid from the sun under wide-brimmed hats or bonnets of various types.

A lumbering coal wagon with a team of huge horses that was delivering a load somewhere trudged along in the road in front of them. The carriage pulled around it.

Joseph heard the crack of the coal wagon driver's whip as it smacked out into the air above the horses, and the mumbling curses the driver mouthed as the carriage rolled past.

The character of the neighborhood changed as they neared the waterfront.

In a few minutes, the carriage made the turn at the wharf, and the *Anne Bayliss* came into view. *She appears right enough*, Joseph thought. When the carriage stopped, he and Traveler stepped down beside the ship.

"Mister Worsham," called George the cabin boy, as he worked at scrubbing grime from the deck. "Good morning. I'm glad to see you, sir. We had a bit of trouble here last night. It's a good job you missed it."

"Top of the morning to you, lad," Joseph replied. "Please tell Captain Bob I am here."

"Aye, sir. And good morning to you, Commander Trevelyan."

"Good morning, George. How's your head today? Better?"

"I'm better, sir. I'm all better. Thank you for taking me part last night. That blighter was set to split me noggin, he was. He got in a pretty good lick anyways."

George went looking for Captain Bob, and in a few minutes, Bob Mathison came to meet them.

"Do you know Commander Trevelyan?" Joseph asked the captain, stepping back so that the two officers could shake hands. "I take it you two gentlemen have already been introduced."

"Aye, Joseph," Captain Bob replied. "Had this gentleman not showed up when he did last night, the events might've turned out far differently. That's for sure."

Traveler pushed the brim of his hat back high on his forehead. Joseph thought it meant the man was pleased with himself.

"Captain Bob, please call me Traveler."

"Is that your pet name, lad?"

Traveler smiled. "It seems to suit me."

Joseph noticed how tall Traveler was compared to Captain Bob and how his top hat added measurably to his height.

"Why don't you two come to my cabin where you can sit and enjoy a cup of tea?" Captain Bob offered with a wide grin on his face.

The men followed Captain Bob to his cabin and, after they had shed their coats and hats, settled themselves at the captain's table.

"Now. Please tell me what happened," said Joseph, impatient to hear what mischief had transpired.

"Well, a man came here last night you don't ever want to invite to your ship again," began Captain Bob. "A group of blackguards and ne'er-do-wells accompanied him that would surely steal anything not lashed down. I knew when I first met the blighter what he was. I'm sorry to say it, but I believe I was right in me advice about him on our ride into Boston yesterday."

Traveler blinked. "Joseph, you knew about Fletcher before you got here?"

"No, I really didn't," Joseph said, once the news had settled in. "What Captain Bob is referring to is his advice about not engaging in business dealings with a solicitor's friends, especially in foreign ports. I had told Captain Bob about Semmes, the solicitor I met in Bermuda and Fletcher, whose name *was* on the card. That's all."

"Fletcher arrived in a coach full of his henchmen," Captain Bob continued. "He came up the gangplank cursing and calling your name, then pushed young George in the chest with his cane, spit tobacco juice on the deck, and bullied his way into this cabin."

"Good Lord," Joseph moaned, horrified.

"What was probably but three quarters of an hour seemed like an eternity while Fletcher and all his cohorts tarried here. Then Commander Trevelyan and his blokes showed up and threw them off ship."

Joseph swung his gaze toward Traveler. "So what happened when Traveler arrived?" he asked Captain Bob.

"Well, Boyd Hampton, whom I don't think you've met, came to ask if I was all right. One of them blackguards pulled a knife on him and was holding him down when Traveler arrived, and the fun really started. When Commander Traveler and his men came aboard, one of Fletcher's lookouts spotted them. Pretty soon, all scrambled on deck, and Boyd threw the pig-sticking one over the side. George, of all people, came running up with a belaying pin and went for Fletcher. Then, and I love this part, Traveler and the three men with him drew their firearms, some kind of official identification, told them they were under arrest for a federal offense, and hauled them all away. But before they were put to rest, and I'm sorry about this, Fletcher took the belaying pin from George and hit him across the head with it. Traveler knocked the bloke senseless for his trouble, and the next moment they were all gone."

Captain Bob turned to Traveler. "You don't waste any time, do you, lad?"

Traveler shook his head and smiled.

"How long will it be safe for us to remain in New York?" Joseph asked. "What of this man Fletcher and his henchmen?"

"I'll arrange for them to remain out of sight for a while," Traveler replied.

Joseph sighed, then turned to Bob Mathison. "I want you to contact our regular factor, Bob. See what arrangements you can make along those lines. I plan to stay here in Boston for at least two weeks, maybe longer. Perhaps you should continue the next leg of your trip to Charleston without me."

Captain Bob nodded.

"And, Bob …"

"Aye, Joseph?"

"Soon I will expand my shipping interests in the Americas—South America in particular. My ships will be away for longer periods. Would you rather stay closer to home?"

"No, sir," said Captain Bob. "Excuse me for saying so, Joseph, but that might be the top duty for any of us sea traders, I think. Wouldn't leave me out of it now, would ye? I mean, I'm not ready for the old sailor's home just yet."

Joseph chuckled. "Very well, then. I'll include you. You'll have a ship. I have some important new assignments for a few carefully chosen people. We shall speak more of this later."

He turned to address Traveler. "Sir, I'm quite serious about my offer. Do whatever you must to make up your mind. Meanwhile, how can I contact Patience Hannah?"

"You're invited to her townhouse this noon for lunch and conversation. I'm sorry I haven't told you about that as yet. I guess your job offer took me by surprise."

"Traveler may be coming to work for me in the shipping business," Joseph told Captain Bob. "There may be some changes made. When that is all finalized, I'll tell you everything about it."

"I'm certain you'll make the right decisions," Bob said. "As I have mentioned, you tell us what it is we must do, and the rest will be easy. For now, shall we enjoy a spot of tea?"

Joseph sat with Traveler and Captain Bob for another a half hour, discussing some of what had transpired. Then they left for the hotel. He wanted to freshen up for the appointment later that morning with Patience Hannah. All the while he thought about the dog cutter and his arrangement with Warner Hawke to provide passage for hapless young girls to the Americas. Concerned, he frowned. All his problems were related. He had only purchased time with that surprise visit to Hawke's office. What he knew for certain was that he could not kill Hawke. Rather, he must devise a plan of subterfuge— something that Hawke might believe and which might provide much-needed time for some serious thinking, something he should have done long ago.

He'd allegedly set up a business deal with Hawke, yet he'd come away with no real solution to his problems. Would tomorrow provide an opportunity for a better plan?

Chapter 46

Patience Will See You Now

Joseph Worsham
September 1828
Boston

THE CARRIAGE RIDE TO THE hotel proved uneventful. Joseph leaned back and enjoyed the ride. For now, he remained happy with events as they had happened and looked forward with eagerness to the visit with Patience Hannah in the early afternoon.

"I say, Traveler?"

"Yes, Joseph?"

"Will you and Mary be joining us?"

"Well, no. I've other business I must attend to this afternoon."

"I've been wondering. Does Mary work with you?"

Traveler nodded. "Yes. Mary is one of our best investigators—one of our best operatives."

"Then you're not really engaged?"

"Oh yes. I plan to marry her someday. I just don't have the kind of security right now it takes to be a family man."

"Well, if you throw in with me now, you may gain that security. But I must warn you, you won't spend much time at home."

"I believe that. But you know, I don't spend any time at home now. I live so much on the road I'm not sure where home is."

"What about Patience Hannah? Does she work for you as well?"

"No, sir. That lady is her own boss. And while I'm thinking about it, Joseph, I believe she likes you."

"Why do you say that?"

"Because I have known her for years. I met her about the same time I met Miss Mary. Patience simply doesn't have much to do with men. It's not that she doesn't like men … nothing like that. It's just that she doesn't trust men very much. She thinks they're all after her money."

"Money is fine, but is it enough for happiness? I hardly think so."

"Well, Joseph, I really wouldn't know. I have enough money to satisfy my modest desires, and I think that's all anyone really needs. Don't work all the time, anyway. I mean, I don't get paid all the time."

"You were saying that you think Patience likes me?" Joseph experienced a definite surge of eagerness. Somehow, the possibility that she liked him was paramount.

"Yes," said Traveler. "Never, as long as I have known her, has she asked me to arrange a visit with a gentleman the next day."

"The next day? Does she meet all the men you've under investigation? Is it always a meeting in that social club?"

"Well, no, it's only because she's with Mary so often that she meets anyone accompanying me. And I guess I do see her in that place more than any other. I don't run in her social circle, so to speak, but I think you do."

"How in heaven's name did Patience speak to you at all? I mean, you were gone when she left for home last night. I put her into the coach myself."

"She told Mary Haverty. And I saw Mary when I returned."

"Oh? Well. When do you sleep? You certainly do keep a busy schedule."

Traveler laughed. "Yes. Sometimes I'm rewarded by seeing the right things happen, and that offsets the bad parts of an affair."

"You are talking about the Fletcher business, aren't you?"

Traveler nodded. "Yes. With any luck at all, that one'll never bother you again. Maybe you'd be fine on your own, as they say. I don't really know. But there's a chance real pain might come your way because of Fletcher."

Joseph believed in his heart that he could trust Traveler. With his business, with his soon-to-be-built ships, even with his life. Why? Perhaps it was Traveler's timely appearance that had coincided with the need. Or was theirs a merger of convenience? After all, Joseph had new pastures in which to graze, didn't he? Yet he prayed there would be no more dealings with Fletcher. Not when he felt so out of control over his destiny.

Quickly his thoughts shifted to Patience, whom he suddenly felt as though he needed to visit. She had invited him for lunch. He wondered if the invitation was a good thing.

How could it not be? he reasoned.

Chapter 47

Lunch with Patience

Joseph Worsham
September 1828
Boston

AT ALMOST ELEVEN O'CLOCK, THE carriage drew to a stop in front of the hotel. Traveler told Tom Wilkins to park around the corner and wait.

Shortly after the two men returned to their rooms, Traveler left to take care of his business. On the way out, he stopped to tell Joseph that Lester would call for him around eleven thirty.

Joseph left the door open. *Traveler must have sent a note to Patience early today, maybe before breakfast. How else could he have arranged for a trip to her place this morning? As usual, he must have planned this well.*

At twenty minutes past the hour, a strong knock sounded at the door, and Joseph glanced up to see red hair and a green livery coat.

Lester, he thought. "Come in," he called.

"Good morning to you, sir," Lester greeted in a happy voice, cap in his hands.

Joseph wondered why Lester was squinting, thinking maybe the lad's eyes were bad.

"Miss Patience would like you to come to her home this noon."

"Yes. I've been expecting you. Your name is Lester, isn't it?"

"Sir."

Was that a 'yes, sir'? "Come on inside and take a seat. I'll be ready in a few minutes."

As Joseph struggled with his collar, Lester set his cap down on the chair beside the door and hurried over to help.

"Here. Let me help you, sir." In a moment, the job was done. "If you please, sir, we'd best to hurry. Miss Patience is expecting you in a half hour."

Joseph finished tying his tie. "Lester, how often do you call for her beaux?"

"In the three years I've been her coachman, this is the very first time. Honestly it is. You must be a favored person."

Lester, shifting his weight from one leg to the other, appeared to be embarrassed.

Joseph brushed his hair and studied his reflection in the mirror. Then, picking up the clothes brush, he whisked the lint from his shoulders, happy that he hadn't lost any hair. He'd heard people remark that he appeared young for his age. He was forty-eight.

"I'm the first, eh?"

"Many have held her hand for her to climb into me coach of an evening, but you're the only one what was invited to visit her Boston *pied-à-terre* the next day."

"You speak as if she has other dwellings, lad. *Pied-à-terre* is a French phrase for 'place in the township,' isn't it? 'Townhouse' is a fair translation, I think. A wealthy person's temporary retreat."

"Indeed she does, sir. *Pied-à-terre*, that's Miss Patience's word, in French, *foot on the ground*—I asked her—something she picked up in France. I've not seen but three of them: the cottage on Cape Cod south of Barnstable, the farm place south of here—well, that place is out in the sticks—and her original home in Philadelphia. She doesn't take me or her coach to the other place."

"Other place?"

"Portersville in Connecticut by Mystic Harbor. She doesn't need the coach there, I guess. She only has a biweekly housekeeper for that one, or so I'm told."

"How do you like working for her, Lester?"

"I like being Miss Patience's coachman. She's a good and kind lady. The only time she ever really scolded me was when she smelled rum on me breath. Odd, that bit of business. I've smelled it on hers, I have. But I had best not speak of that, eh?"

"Do you think you're fortunate to have this job?"

"If you don't mind me saying so, I'd say you're the lucky one. Are you British, sir?"

"Yes, but I have a home in Charleston. My paternal family home is in the Virginia colony."

"Oh?"

Joseph thought Lester a bit outspoken, but the lad seemed friendly enough.

"I say, Lester?"

"Sir?"

"Are you Irish?"

"Half. Me sainted mother was. And a beautiful lady she was too. Me father is just plain American."

"Is she gone, deceased … your mother, I mean?"

"A fever took her five years ago."

"I'm sorry to hear that, lad." *Well. Maybe Patience is sort of looking after you now. Damn good job I'll not be running into Lester's mum. She might have remembered me.* "Let's go, lad," he said as he finished donning his coat. With a twinge, he remembered that not all Irish immigrants came over under the Hawke false pretenses. Most actually came honestly, if you could call such a cramped and filthy passage honest. Sensitive on that point, he shuddered.

Joseph locked the door to the room, and they hurried down the stairs to the lobby, then out to the coach.

Lester helped Joseph step up into the coach and then climbed to his coachman's position. The doorman released the team. Lester took the reins and spoke softly to the horses as they pulled away. They executed a careful roundabout in the narrow street, and the coach hustled toward its destination.

In a few minutes they arrived at Patience's townhouse. Lester left Joseph at the entrance to the yard and then departed to stable the coach. He told Joseph that he had a lame horse and had taken the shortest, quickest way home on that account.

The difficult roundabout in the street …

Joseph hastened up the steps to the front door and knocked to announce his arrival. A very pretty girl dressed in the uniform of service quickly opened the door. She had olive skin and was, perhaps, twenty-five years old.

Must be the maid, he thought. *She certainly is pretty. God, I think all these women in Boston are pretty.*

"I am Joseph Worsham," he announced.

"Good day, Mister Worsham, sir." The girl bowed her head and executed a polite curtsy. "The mistress is expecting you in the parlor. My name is Helen. I'm the housemaid. If you please, sir, come this way."

He followed Helen along the hallway to the parlor, enjoying the view of Helen from the rear when he caught a whiff of perfume. It was a faint floral scent that seemed to be drifting through the hallway from the room ahead.

Patience must have purchased that elegant and appealing scent from one of the Paris parfumeries, he thought. Looking around, he noticed several pieces of French furniture and some French tapestries decorating the walls. *Wonder if she travels to Europe much.*

Patience met them at the parlor door, her arms outstretched in an open gesture of friendliness.

"Joseph," she greeted. "Don't you look happy today? And handsome, I might add."

Oh, Patience, you look bright and attractive yourself, he thought. He took her hand and bent to kiss it, noticing her full, feminine shapeliness as he did so. As he straightened, he caught a strong whiff of her perfume and something else. *Miss Patience has been drinking.*

Patience smiled and turned to Helen. "That will be all we require for the moment, Helen. Go and tell Cook to call us when our lunch is ready.

"Come and talk to me, Joseph. I want to hear all about what happened last evening. I gather you're involved in some of Traveler's government business."

Joseph sat with her on the couch and discussed events as they had been related to him. As she listened attentively, he wondered what she was thinking.

Why didn't she dine with me in that club last evening?

Freshly cut flowers graced the table behind the couch, and he wondered where they had come from. He was surprised to see such flowers in Boston in late September.

Maybe in Charleston or Bermuda, he thought. *But surely there had been a number of hard, killing frosts this far north. It would be difficult to keep delicate flowers growing in an ordinary cottage garden. That would require an orangery or greenhouse, wouldn't it?*

When he finished his account, she smiled and reached out to touch his hand. "Why are you in Boston, Joseph?" she asked.

"I'm here on business."

"Ah. Is it the shipping, the merchant vessels out of Liverpool you told us about last evening? Or is there another reason you're here?"

"It's the shipping. I have no other business connections here."

"You actually *are* married, are you not? I mean—you have a white circle on your ring finger. Where is your family?"

Joseph thought Patience was more than just a little interested. He smiled at her and felt relieved the conversation had progressed to this topic. No longer reluctant to talk about his wife's death, he was eager to speak with Patience about it, becoming more attracted to her as the moments passed by. The pain associated with Frances's death was fading.

He told her of his deceased wife and of his two little girls. Then he told her of his shipping business and how his involvement with Boston was perhaps declining. He told her about New York and Traveler's involvement. He told her also of his family having lived in the Virginia colony before the first war with England—the time when some of them moved to Bermuda and Antigua, pronouncing it correctly.

She listened attentively to his wandering chatter.

"Philadelphia could be important in your shipping plans, I would imagine," she said when he finished.

Instead of replying, he asked a question of his own, pointing to the vase of cut flowers. "Where do you manage to get such flowers in the fall?"

"I have a floral business here in Boston."

"Hothouses?"

Patience drew in a breath. "Tell me, Joseph, do you think you might need an office here? And yes, I have hothouses and greenhouses." Clearly she didn't want to talk about the details of her own business.

"No need. Business can be managed from Charleston—if I find the right people, that is."

Helen appeared at the parlor doorway and rang a small handbell. "Lunch is served now, Mistress Patience. Shall I continue with my duties?"

"Please, Helen. Go ahead and have your lunch with the others," Patience told the girl. "And tell Randolph to wait the table for us. We won't need you for a while."

"Yes, ma'am." She bowed slightly and left the room.

As they entered the dining room, an ashen-faced elderly man-servant with honey-colored skin came to help with Patience's chair and to serve the meal. Joseph wondered if he were a white man or colored, but it didn't matter.

"Thank you, Randolph," said Patience. "Our gentleman guest this noon is Mister Joseph Worsham. His family lived in Virginia in the old days, before the first war with England. Then they moved, or some of them moved, to the islands before the outbreak of hostilities."

Randolph bowed to Joseph and smiled, revealing several missing teeth. Joseph had the distinct impression he heard the word *"Tories!"* spoken under Randolph's breath as he began to serve the meal.

"Randolph knew Ben Franklin," Patience said. "Several strong lads used to carry Franklin about … gout, you know. Randolph was one of those in Philadelphia when Franklin attended the Constitutional Convention. He has been with me now for over eighteen years."

"Weren't all those stout lads prisoners?" Joseph asked.

"Some were there's no doubt of that. Randolph was not. Old Ben needed somebody he could trust."

"Yes," Randolph interjected through his gapped teeth.

Joseph smiled and nodded. *Eighteen years? Randolph must be in his middle sixties. God. Was her man Randolph ever stout enough to carry Ben Franklin about? Will I be that worn down when I am sixty? Wonder how old Patience is, anyway.* He wanted to ask, but instead he just answered her questions about himself. Her questions became more pointed as they talked, until he had told her just about everything about himself—almost everything, that is.

She did not ask any questions about his wealth. He liked that.

Patience set down her glass and smiled across the table at him.

"Joseph, I am over forty years old. I have everything a person could ask for. I do whatever I wish to do. But I spend far too much time alone. I am not ready to give up my freedom just to be with a man. I know for a fact that you are not here today, in Boston, I mean, simply to take advantage of me."

"No, Patience. I have no such plan in mind." He wondered if he were telling the truth. *What do I have in mind?* He thought of her shapely body and wondered if she could see the blush he was trying to hide. *Amanda would have seen through me in a moment*, he thought.

"So. Most of my needs are filled. And frankly," Patience added, "money matters bore me. Perhaps I'm too old for you. I don't know. But I believe you are a man of means, and I certainly do enjoy your company. You didn't ask very much about my financial situation. Anyway, that impressed me. I'd like to get to know you better. How long will you be in Boston?"

"Two or three weeks."

"You are sure you have no plans to keep an office here?"

A sense of urgency colored the way she phrased her question.

"No, I don't think so. It's too early to tell. Really, it is. But probably my main office will be in either Charleston or New York."

"Well, while you are here, what are your plans?"

"I've no plans save waiting to see if Traveler will throw in with me. His decision will determine whether or not I expand in this part of the country. What do you have in mind?"

Patience sat up straight in her chair and drew in her breath. "Hmm. What would you say to spending the time with me? I need to spend a few days at my cottage on the Cape before winter sets in. What do you say? Will you come with me? Maybe there will be a few autumn colors left in the trees."

Joseph folded his napkin and put it beside his plate. Rubbing his mouth with his fingers, he thought, *She's right. I want to get to know her too.* He focused on his plate and the napkin. *Too late. There would be no fall colors. That was just a ruse. But it worked.*

He looked up at her, and she smiled. *She certainly seems to be happy about it.*

"I would enjoy that very much," he said, suddenly very happy too. A warm, giddy feeling sprang into his chest. He liked Patience Hannah. He felt a little guilty when he thought about it, but he decided he liked her very much.

"Why don't you move in here for now?" she offered. "Until I can make the arrangements. I have several extra rooms."

"That's most kind of you," he said, smiling.

"I can send Lester for your things, or whatever you wish."

They rose from the table, and Patience reached to grasp his hands. "Joseph Worsham, I have a feeling about you. I think I'm safe and can be myself around you. Is that true?"

"Patience, please. Always be yourself … for you are a delightful person. As for me, don't ever drop your guard around me. You may not be safe at all. I fear I am attracted to you in a very profound way. What else can I say?"

"Perhaps you have said it all. Come. Let us make our plans." She held his hand and led him back to the parlor. "Shall I send Lester for your things now, or what?"

He took a place beside her on the love seat. "I think it will only take a few minutes to pack the things in my hotel room. The bulk of my luggage is still aboard my ship, the *Anne Bayliss*. So I have belongings to pick up there as well. Lester can take me to the hotel and help, if he will."

"Yes, I know Lester wants to help. He told me this morning he thought you are a lucky man. I think he likes you."

"I think it means he *thinks* you like me, Patience. Is there any truth to that rumor?"

She blushed. "Yes, I think I do."

"Say, Patience, would you care to go with us to the hotel?"

"Maybe that would be fun. I tell you what. Give me a few minutes to powder my nose."

"You're on. And, Patience, do you have any stationery I can use? I want to write a few letters to send to Bermuda and England while we're on the wharf. You know ... ship's mail and all that. I think that would be best. I can find some ship's captain bound that way, or Captain Bob can take them on his return voyage to England."

"Of course. I'll get the box of stationery for you."

Patience crossed to the open-front bureau and released the fold-down writing table. Joseph moved a chair to the bureau and seated himself as Patience handed him the stationery.

"You'll find whatever you need here with—or as you would say, in this secretary—Joseph. I'll go and get ready now."

Secretary? thought Joseph as she left the room. *She means this bureau ... this piece of furniture, doesn't she?*

Joseph wrote his letters, noticing the stationery emitted a faint odor of perfume, the same floral scent he had noticed earlier. He would write three letters: one to Amanda, one to Colin, and one to Aunt Meg in Manchester.

One never writes only one letter when the sea lanes are involved ... too much chance of just a single letter being lost. As he wrote, he found himself thinking quite often of Patience.

But in a few minutes he became totally engrossed in his writing.

* * * * *

Later, Helen entered the parlor to tell him that Patience would be a few minutes longer because she had decided to change her clothes.

Joseph finished the letters, lit the candle at the table, and sealed the letters with the wax and seal he'd found in the bureau. He thought it best for them to have a seal than not to have one, even if the seal bore the name *Patience*. He put the letters in his inside coat pocket, blew out the candle, and sat on the couch to wait for Patience.

I think I have just experienced a sea change of my own, he thought. *Oh boy ...*

Chapter 48

The Intruder

Joseph Worsham
September 1828
Boston

IN A QUARTER HOUR OR SO, the coach arrived at the hotel.

The doorman stepped into the street to help with the horses, opened the door, and helped Patience and Joseph step down to the sidewalk.

"Is there any luggage, sir?" he asked as he tipped his hat to Patience but smiled in an unflattering and condescending way. "Will the lady be staying long, sir?" His smirk gave away his salacious, unspoken thoughts.

Lester, who was standing to one side, saw the whole thing and jumped in front of the doorman.

"Why," he said, "what's the matter with you, Tim? Don't you know Miss Patience? She owns this bloody hotel, man. It may be you ought to learn yourself some manners, considering she probably owns the very coat on your back. Everybody knows Miss Patience."

Tim took a step backward. "I'm sorry, ma'am. If I have in some way offended you I, apologize. I certainly meant no such thing."

Patience sniffed. "You haven't been the doorman here long," she said. "Perhaps you should always think and act at your best, sir. It could be old Marsh Winkler made his selection too hastily from those who answered his newspaper advertisement. We may still have need of a good doorman. I don't know. I'll speak to Marsh about it."

The doorman was biting his fingernails as they walked inside. Lester stayed to speak with him.

Patience suddenly turned. "Lester," she called, "I want you to follow us upstairs and gather anything ready to bring down. Then Joseph will want to go to the wharf for the rest of his things."

The three made their way to the second level. When Joseph reached his room, he found the door slightly ajar.

Must be the room keeper, he thought. *I remember locking that door.* He gently pushed the door the rest of the way open.

A noise by the wardrobe across the room startled him. A man was bent there with his back to the door, rummaging through the drawers of the wardrobe.

"You won't find very much there, sir," Joseph announced, walking quietly toward the bed between them, now certain the man was an intruder.

The man spun around, then bounded across the bed toward Joseph with his arms outstretched, screaming at the top of his voice, "Out of my way … get out of my way, damn you!"

The intruder slammed into Joseph's chest with the full force of his momentum, shoved Lester aside, then scrambled down the stairs.

Joseph stumbled against Patience, who now stood behind him, and the two of them toppled over the chair beside the door.

"Who was that man?" Patience cried, trying to catch her breath.

Joseph helped Patience, who'd lost her hat in the scuffle, to regain her footing.

"Was that one of the room stewards? Is everyone in my hotel crazy, ill-mannered, and rude?"

"That man was a thief," Joseph concluded as he quickly retrieved her hat and handed it to her. "I'm certain of it."

Lester raced down the stairs after the intruder, Joseph following right behind.

As the man ran past the front desk and kicked open the front door, Joseph yelled, "Be careful, lad."

Suddenly a commotion rumbled in front of the hotel.

Lester, breathing heavily, threw the door open and yelled, "Stop that man! Tim, stop him!"

As Joseph reached the door, he saw Tim struggling to hold the intruder, but Tim was losing the battle. The two men suddenly fell off the sidewalk and beneath the coach, unsettling the horses. The horses sidestepped and reared, but the reins held.

The men rolled with the intruder on top, pummeling the doorman repeatedly in the face with his fists.

One frightened horse kicked with both hind legs, one hoof striking the intruder full in the side of his head. Tim rolled the other way, barely escaping a blow himself.

Lester grabbed the harness and tried to calm the horses, managing to steady them after a great deal of effort. Afterward, Joseph and Lester pulled the limp intruder by his feet from underneath the coach.

At first blood surged from the head wound, but then it curiously stopped.

"I think he's dead." Lester looked up at Joseph and shook his head. "I think Bessie's hooves blew the poor bastard's lamp out. Or bloody well kicked it over. He's done for."

After examining the man carefully, Joseph stood up. The cut ran deep. Joseph could see part of the man's skull protruding from the wound. There was no more bleeding because the man's heart had stopped beating.

"Tim, are you all right?" Joseph asked.

Tim sagged against the hitching post, holding his head in his hands.

"Yes, sir," Tim answered slowly. "I think so. What the hell was the matter with that man? He tried to steal your coach—that's what."

"We caught him rifling through the things in my room. Do you know him?"

"No," Tim shook his head. "I don't know that one." Blood trickled from his nose, and his eyes were red and beginning to swell.

"Say, shall I send someone for the constable?" Lester asked.

"There's no urgent need," Joseph answered. "That man's dead. Send for the coroner first, then send for the constable."

Joseph took out his pocket handkerchief and offered it to Tim. "I'm going to see about Patience."

As Joseph turned, Patience fainted, falling to the sidewalk. She hadn't said a word, but apparently she'd seen the whole affair. When Joseph reached her, she was breathing in short gasps, trying to regain her senses.

Joseph gently slapped her wrists then drew her to a sitting position so she could breathe easier. In a few moments she seemed able to focus her eyes.

"Oh, dear, I've done it again," she said, attempting to rise. "Forgive me. I feel such a fool when this happens. But it was good to open my eyes and look up at you, Joseph."

He helped her to stand and brush the dust off her clothes.

"Well, now what?" she said. "I heard you say the man is dead, killed by my carriage horse." She put her hands on her hips. "So I fainted," she said. "It was the least I could do."

"It's my guess this has something to do with Gilbert Fletcher," Joseph stated flatly. "But we'll not find out from this dead man, I'm afraid."

"Gilbert Fletcher? Who is Gilbert Fletcher?"

"You don't know? Thought the Boston newspapers would be filled with stories about that one—to hear Traveler tell it."

"Oh, Traveler, is it? So that's what this is about. No. We ordinary folk don't know much about Traveler's business, I must say. So secretive and so serious. Mister Red, White, and Blue that one."

* * * * *

Back upstairs in the hotel room, Joseph searched quickly through the drawers of the wardrobe to see if anything was missing. As he opened the last drawer, his breath caught in sudden fear. Inside the drawer beside his stockings lurked a huge black scorpion, very much alive and quite agitated. Dear God! The name Warner Hawke flashed in his mind. With the glass cigar ashtray, he smashed the scorpion. It writhed for a moment, and then it lay still.

God. The blasted thing must have come first-class from North Africa. Damn good job it wasn't a cobra. What the hell does that tattoo on Grewno's thumb mean, anyway? And yes, doesn't Fletcher have one on his hand as well?

Joseph looked about the room. He packed what remained of his things, still wondering if the intruder had stolen anything. Then he thought better of it. The would-be thief lay dead on the boardwalk out front.

So be it. He had plans to make with Patience Hannah.

* * * * *

Patience checked with Marsh Winkler as they departed, who could only offer his apologies concerning the matter. She said nothing about the doorman's rudeness, only that he needed to be relieved the rest of the day to tend to his bruises. Joseph assumed she was still mulling the matter of the man's employment status and would decide what to do about him later.

While they waited for the constable, Traveler arrived, apologizing for not being close by when he was needed. He had two men with him in the carriage, strangers to Joseph. Traveler recognized the dead man immediately and offered to take care of the matter and to deal with the authorities. The man had been one of the people working for Gilbert Fletcher, all right.

They gathered up the luggage from the room and left for the wharf, leaving Traveler to deal with the constable. Joseph was anxious to post his letters.

During the remainder of the afternoon, they visited the *Anne Bayliss* to retrieve the rest of Joseph's things. While there, Joseph found a trustworthy ship's captain to take his letters to Bermuda straightaway. Captain Bob took charge of the other letter himself, the one to Aunt Meg in Manchester. He would take it with him to Charleston and then on to England on his return trip.

Patience chartered a steamboat the next day to visit the cottage at Barnstable. It had been what the locals called an Indian summer, but in Boston the leaves had just about finished their show of color.

Admiring colorful fall foliage was not the reason for the trip, anyway. They had much to do and many plans to make in the limited time available between them.

Maybe Patience just wanted to visit her cottage.

And so did Joseph.

Chapter 49

The Butterfly

Amanda Worsham
November 1828
Bermuda

It was a beautiful Bermuda Saturday afternoon. A storm had blown in earlier in the week, and dark clouds and haze had hung about for several days, but this day was stunning with the sky a bright blue and the clouds all soft and wispy.

Amanda had just finished a light lunch and had gone upstairs to be alone in her mother's room. She stood looking out the window, trying to get her thoughts in order. So much had happened. Sometimes she felt lonesome, even if there were friends around her.

She heard the sound of horses and a wagon on the road in front of the house. The wagon stopped at the front gate before continuing to the barn.

Miss Tilly's voice rang out, "Amanda, it's a letter from your father. Come, lass."

Excited, Amanda dashed down the staircase. *A letter from Father.*

Miss Tilly met her on the front porch. She and Colin had made an early morning trip to Hamilton to do some shopping.

"Here, lass," she said, handing over the letter. "Colin always checks with the port authorities to see if there's any mail. Today there's this. And it's for you."

They sat in rocking chairs on the porch while Amanda studied the unopened letter.

"Colin got one too, love," said Miss Tilly with a smile on her face. "He'll be here in a minute, as soon as he finishes with the wagon. I'll wager he'll wait until he's read his letter before he puts the horses away."

Miss Tilly rocked back and forth, an expression of eagerness on her face.

Amanda turned the letter over several times in her hands.

"Come on, lass. Open the letter."

The word *Patience* greeted her, pressed into the red sealing wax. Amanda wondered what it meant. *Quite pretty, that.* Yet she had a definite feeling about the letter—not frightening, but strange.

She opened it.

The first page told her that Joseph was in Boston, he was well and happy, even though he'd experienced some bad turn of events. To that end, he had made a change in plans. There would be no office in Boston. Some gentleman named Traveler had saved Joseph from making a desperate mistake concerning that factor recommended by Semmes, the solicitor in Saint George's.

Semmes. Now there was a man Amanda detested. She'd only met him once, the time he'd come to meet with Joseph, but that was enough. He'd looked down his nose at her and said abrupt, crude things. She tried to put the loathsome man from her mind.

Amanda didn't finish. She let the letter and her arms fall to her lap and looked off toward the barn.

"What did he say, lass?" Miss Tilly sounded impatient. "Is it bad news?"

"Oh no. He's well and happy, as far as I can tell." Amanda turned to face Miss Tilly. "He said the man in Saint George's, the man named Semmes, is in league with smugglers in New England."

"Well, I never …" Miss Tilly sighed and ceased her rocking, gazing past the porch rail for a few moments. Then she looked back at Amanda. "Would you look at that, love?" she said, excitedly. "Why, you've a butterfly in your lap just resting on that letter. Say, now, it's a good omen if ever I saw one."

Amanda looked down at her lap. There was, indeed, a butterfly sitting on the letter, sweeping its wings up and down in slow, deliberate motions.

A monarch … no, a painted lady—unless I'm mistaken, she thought. It paused, turned, and moved its wings again. *Well, little Miss Painted Lady, how are you today? Is that a dance you're doing especially for me?* The notion of it being a *painted lady* suited her frame of mind, anyway.

She didn't speak out loud for fear of scaring it away.

Turn … lift … flex … wave, the butterfly made its rhythmic motions. And again, turn … lift … flex … wave.

Little butterfly, are you following some tiny dancing master I cannot see?

The butterfly seemed happy to be dancing in Amanda's lap.

She watched until it flew away. Lifting the letter to her nose, she detected a faint odor of a floral-scented perfume about it. She wondered if that were the reason for the butterfly's visit.

"Oh, look at it flutter away," Miss Tilly said. "Why, that must be the last one of the season. I hadn't noticed it fluttering about before I saw it on your lap."

A breeze stirred just then, and Miss Tilly stopped rocking to rub her eye. "I got a bit of dust in my eye, lass, but it's all better know. There I was, watching your butterfly, and the breeze came up and blew something in my eye."

Amanda smiled. She had a good feeling about the butterfly. But it was almost as if she knew what the rest of the letter would say, and she didn't want to read it.

Miss Tilly had a happy look on her face, so maybe her eye was clear. Or was she crying? Was that a tear in her eye?

"I think Father has met someone special, Miss Tilly. I really do. Here, smell this letter. I think her name is Patience."

"Did the letter say that?"

"Not yet. But I believe it will."

"You always seem to know things ahead of time. Well, the seal did have *Patience* pressed in it, didn't it?"

"Yes, but there's something else."

"What?"

"Oh, I don't know. Something I feel when I'm reading the letter."

"Well, get ye started, love. Read the letter out loud. Old Tilly wants to know how he's doing."

Amanda hesitated for a moment longer because she really didn't want to read the rest of the letter just now. Finally, she opened it and read the pages through before she told Miss Tilly more of what was written inside.

"Her name is Patience, as we thought," Amanda said after a moment of silence. "She lives in Boston, but she has other property in various places. She sounds like a good match for Father."

Why does he have to do this so soon? The unspoken thought burned inside her head as bitterness welled up inside her.

Her displeasure must have shown because Miss Tilly said, "Don't take it so hard. Surely to goodness, you don't want your father to be alone just now."

"Alone? He's not alone," she answered. "He has me and he has Sarah Jean. He's not alone." *Never mind what Mother said about Beau Videau.*

"You must not marry Charlie Videau," she had said. *What did that really mean? Oh, damn it all. I know what it means, don't I? Beau Videau is my father. Why can't I accept that? Damn it all …*

Amanda handed the letter to Miss Tilly.

Joseph Worsham is my father, she thought, *my real father. He always was … always will be … no matter what might've happened with Beau Videau and Mother.* And Amanda missed Joseph a great deal right now.

"It's not the same, love. God wants a beautiful man to have a beautiful woman to share—"

"He *had* a beautiful woman. My mother was the prettiest woman I ever did see."

"Aye. Your mother was bonnie."

Miss Tilly had a sad look on her face. A tear glistened on her cheek. Amanda looked down and began to read the letter a second time.

"Hey, what did your letter say, lass?" Colin shouted from in front of the barn. He left the wagon and started for the front porch. "I got one too, you know," he called, waving his letter over his head. "Say, I'm coming in to read it. Did your father say he'd be back anytime soon?"

"Oh, Colin. Joseph's found himself a new lady," said Miss Tilly as her husband ambled up the steps. Colin turned a rocking chair around so he could sit and face them. "You need to read your letter. There's a problem with that Semmes person. See what Joseph has to say about him in your letter right away. That one's a regular blackguard, he is."

Colin relaxed in the rocker.

While Colin read, Amanda let her thoughts race through the recent events. Her mother's untimely death had taken them all by surprise. There had been premonitions, right enough, but she'd never expected to lose her mother. And Joseph had always been good to every one of them. But now he was thinking of marrying another woman. He didn't say that exactly, but she knew it to be true.

Some people have to go through life without one parent or the other. Others lose both parents and have to make their way alone. But this family is held together by mutual respect and love, even when it's spread across the Atlantic from Cape Cod to England, as now.

Maybe she had been rash in her judgment of Joseph and this Patience woman. *Before Mother died, she had said very nearly the same things that Miss Tilly just said. The gist of it is, Father needs a woman to keep him strong and alive.*

Amanda decided not to try to prevent Joseph's plans in any way, but she didn't have to like the situation.

Suddenly she remembered something about the butterfly.

"Miss Tilly, doesn't a butterfly mean something—I mean, in the church?"

"You know, that's it. The butterfly is a Christian symbol to some people, sure enough. It means the body can be reborn, just as the Christ was given a new life. I have a butterfly pin that Colin sent away to England for several years ago. I'll show it to you sometime."

"I'd like that," Amanda said. "Maybe the butterfly was here to remind us of that part of God's love."

Amanda looked for the butterfly, but it was nowhere to be seen. At that moment, she had an eerie feeling about the butterfly, as though it had been, somehow, the spirit of her mother.

"No," she said out loud, "that's ridiculous. That woman named Patience is the 'Painted Lady,' if you ask me." She stood up and stretched.

"What's that, lass?" said Colin, who had finished reading his letter.

Miss Tilly yawned, stretching her shoulders and arms. "Tell us what was in your letter, Colin."

"That Semmes is a scoundrel," Colin replied. "From what Joseph said, the man was only trying to use him and his ships for smuggling and God knows what else. I've been given instructions to dismiss him straightaway."

"Did he say when he was coming back?" Miss Tilly asked.

"He said he wasn't going on to Charleston just now and would call for Amanda in a few weeks. Maybe they'll go to England and see about Sarah Jean."

"That's good," said Miss Tilly. "I think he'll be pleased with what Moses has done on his building project. The new cottage should be a very pleasant vacation place for your family, Amanda. When will it be finished, do you think?"

"Maybe by summer," Amanda replied. She strolled from the porch to the garden, looking for the butterfly, leaving Colin and Miss Tilly talking to each other about the letters.

She searched the garden for a few minutes and then decided to walk a bit. She left the garden and took a path that led around the house.

Chapter 50

Moses and Moss Moonie

Amanda Worsham
November 1828
Bermuda

A SHORT WALK LED TO the doorway where Moses and Sally lived. Moses was away working on the new cottage, so Amanda thought she would pay Sally a short visit. She could hear Sally singing as she approached the stone step that Moses had cut from limestone, and after knocking on the door, in a few moments Sally opened it.

"May I come in?"

"Why, yes'm, Miss Manda," Sally greeted, sounding genuinely happy to see her. "Please come in. I heard you got you a letter from yo' daddy. I heard Miss Tilly callin' for you 'while ago. What'd he say? Was it good news? God knows you could use some good news."

"He'll be coming back in a few weeks," Amanda said, stepping through the portal.

"I'm glad to hear that, Miss Manda. That'll do."

Sally positioned a straight-backed chair for Amanda, then sat on a handmade wooden bench and leaned her back against the wall.

"Sally, he's found himself a new woman," Amanda blurted.

"Lord a' mercy, chile."

"That's what his letter was about."

"You don't mean it."

Sally began rocking, as though she were seated in a rocking chair. Clasping her hands together in her lap, she shook her head from side to side and clicked her tongue against her teeth.

Amanda could see Sally was deeply concerned about the news, and she remembered the fear the night of the Grewno incident when Sally had tried repeatedly to revive Frances. She had seen Sally rock Sarah Jean that way, something Sally did when feeling anxious.

Love and caring for me and my family abounds in this sweet Negro slave, she thought. *More than any of us deserve.*

Amanda rose from the chair and sat beside Sally on the bench Moses surely must have made. The entire fitting was perfect; the whole thing had been put together with wooden pegs.

"Maybe I need to buy some furniture, some chairs, wardrobes, and things for you, Sally. I'm sorry I didn't think of it sooner than this."

Amanda was ashamed of herself for characterizing Sally as a slave, even in her private thoughts. Maybe that was literally a fact, but it was a situation she was determined to change as soon as she could decide the best way to do it.

"We don't need anything we don't already have, me and Moses," Sally assured Amanda. "We got chairs in the schoolroom upstairs, and we got chairs to sit down on at suppertime. Moses can make wardrobes for us and other things. We already talkin' 'bout just that. I reckon we going to be here a pretty long time 'fore Moses can finish this cabin and build another one t'boot."

As she listened, Amanda wondered if Moses could find the time to do anything for himself, what with all the other work he was doing right now. It could be, a few special items of furniture would make things easier for Sally, and Moses too.

Amanda looked around the meticulously clean room. Studying the baby crib on one side of the room, she felt sad when she thought of the love and effort Moses had put into its construction. But she was also glad he had done it. Maybe he should sell the baby crib now and put the money up for the time when he had his very own business.

"We all right," Sally tried to reassure her again. "Don't worry yo'self 'bout that anymore. I'm so happy just to be alive. We're learning how to read and do sums, and nobody thought we'd ever be in school. We don't need any more chairs. You been givin' us so much already. Thanks to you, we even got money put away. Maybe you don't know just how hard we pray to be free. We saving for that day."

Amanda wrapped her arms around Sally and hugged her. "I'm going to do what I said I was going to do."

"I reckon you is, chile."

They sat there for a moment; then Amanda stood. "Sally, do you remember seeing a butterfly in the garden anytime in the last few days?"

"No, I can't say I do."

"I saw one today. It came and tiptoed on Father's letter."

"Well, I declare—"

"It gave me a funny feeling because nobody'd seen it before and it seemed to disappear right after."

"Sometime' a butterfly live a long time 'fore the winter sets in. Sometime' the wind carries them away. Don't reckon they be anything funny 'bout seeing one, though, chile. What you mean?"

"It's the thing about a butterfly that a person's soul lives forever."

"You mean they be born again? I heard tell of that."

"Yes."

"But not a butterfly, chile."

"No, that butterfly landing on my letter may have been a message from God … about Father."

"What kind of message, chile? You got me feelin' funny now."

"That his life may be starting over … with a new woman."

"I see. What you got to do now is study 'bout somethin' else.

"I want to ask you some things about Moses. Is that all right?"

Sally sat forward and clasped her hands together in her lap. She had a big grin on her face.

"Well, of course, Miss Manda. I be pleased to talk to you 'bout anything. Moses is right dear to my heart, don't ya know."

Amanda crossed to the door and looked outside, then back to where Sally was sitting.

"Moses told me about when he was first born. He said he was found floating in a boat off somewhere in a swamp. Can you tell me any more about that?"

"Yes'm."

"Is it true?"

"That's the story they tell."

"You mean it's not true?"

"Not *exactly* true. We don't like to talk much 'bout it, but you axed me."

The word *axe* in Sally's answer gave her a start. She enjoyed listening to Moses and Sally talk. She would never say anything about pronunciation. That was the schoolteacher's responsibility. Moses's speech was inflected as she imagined Moss Moonie's to be. Sally's was a bit more polished, perhaps due to her more privileged upbringing. After all, Sally's mother and father had both been house servants at that plantation on Waccamaw Neck.

An expression of terror suddenly crossed Sally's features.

"What is it, Sally?"

Sally rose to her feet and grabbed Amanda's hands, a desperate look in her eyes.

"I know I can trust you, chile. Oh, I got to stop calling you that, you being our mistress now and everything. I know I has."

"What is it that's so bad? You're starting to frighten me."

Sally looked down and breathed a long sigh.

"What are you so afraid of?" Amanda said. "Look at me."

"Miss Manda, please tell me you don't want to know," she pleaded, directly into Amanda's eyes.

"Know what, Sally? What is it? No one can hurt you now, not here."

"It be somebody else I'm afraid for. Please, if I tell, you can't tell another living soul."

"I promise. I won't tell anybody. Really, I won't. Now, what is it?"

Sally squeezed Amanda's hands. "You know, it was ol' Moss Moonie found Moses, so the story goes."

"Yes."

"Well, she didn't find nobody in a boat."

"She didn't?"

Sally shook her head. "No. It was Moss Moonie made up that story so the law wouldn't come get her."

"Why would the law want her? She's a free woman of color, isn't she?"

"Yes'm, she is. But it was Moss Moonie Moses's mama was lookin' for when she ran away."

"Why?"

"To hide her. To help her run away, chile. Moss Moonie help lots of folks to run away. She hide 'em, give 'em somethin' to eat, and help 'em to find they way."

"That'd be something not just anybody should know about, all right. No wonder you didn't want to talk about it."

"If the law find out, they might kill Moss Moonie," Sally moaned.

"Helping a runaway slave, is that really a hanging offense?"

"Yes'm, sometimes it be. It don't matter what the law says, though. What matters is who find out. It be the law for the white folks we afraid of. We be afraid for Moss Moonie, don't you know?"

Amanda could sense the helplessness Sally felt. The basic rights most white people took for granted didn't apply to slaves. She shared the disgust so often expressed by her mother concerning slavery, glad she had started paying her two slaves wages. Maybe that helped somehow.

"Then Moses was born someplace else?" Amanda asked, getting back to the subject.

"No. Moses was born there in the swamp, right enough. And right then too. His mama found Moss Moonie just in time, if you know what I mean. Just in time. She sho' did."

"I see."

"Yes'm. A full moon was shinin', don't you know? An' his mama was just 'bout out of time. Poor li'l baby borned right there in the swamp."

"Mother told me I was born on a full moon. It was one of the last things she told me before she died."

"Yo' birthday comin' up right soon, isn't it?"

"January sixth."

"If yo' mama said it was so, I reckon it was so. 'Bout the moon, I mean."

"Do you know where Moses's mother is today?"

"No, ma'am, I don't. I guess she safe somewhere. Maybe someday we can find out. The Lord been good to Moses and Sally. Maybe He be good to her too."

"Maybe so."

Sally walked over to the clothes-hanging rack and started to put on her apron.

"Yes'm," she said, as she tied the apron strings. "Miss Manda, I was just about to go upstairs. I got housework to do now. Would you mind if we go upstairs pretty soon?"

Amanda shook her head, then after a moment said, "Sally, I think of you as a friend. Is that all right with you?"

Sally hugged Amanda and said with emotion in her voice, "Miss Manda, it's a joy to know you. To work for you … well, that's easy and gives me a righteous feelin'. An' I know you goin' give us our freedom someday. To be yo' friend … now, that's somethin' comes from the good Lord Himself. I be proud to be your friend. And when we be free, I think we goin' to adopt us a baby. I hear about it all the time. People need to give up they babies, don't you know?"

Well. That's a new thought. Adoption. And this sweet lady named Sally thought of it first. Of course. That would be just the thing for Moses and Sally to do. Amanda had a good feeling about that. *Do you have to be free to adopt a baby?* She had never thought about that before.

Chapter 51

The Ride to the Beach

Amanda Worsham
November 1828
Bermuda

AMANDA AND SALLY WALKED AROUND to the back door of Stuart Manor and went inside. Sally went upstairs to start her chores, and Amanda set out to find Colin. She wanted to go horseback riding. She found Colin still talking to Miss Tilly on the front porch.

"Well, lass," he said, getting up from his rocker. "I was beginning to wonder if I'd run you off."

"I wanted to talk with Sally and also to look for something. I didn't mean to be rude."

"Are you upset about your letter, love?" Miss Tilly asked. "Reckon I would be some, if I were you."

"In your letter, Mister Stuart, did my father say he would bring the lady named Patience to Bermuda with him?"

"Didn't mention that in my letter. He only mentioned business."

"You know," said Amanda, "I would like to ride one of your horses. Could I do that?"

"I reckon so. The horses really belong to your father now, Amanda. The gray one, the mare, would be the best. That one's a kind and gentle horse, not too spirited. I think a high-spirited lass like yourself shouldn't ride a high-spirited horse. It's better that way.

I'll tell you what. You go and put on your riding clothes, and I'll saddle her for you. What do you say to that?"

"Thank you, Mister Stuart. I'm certain Father would agree with your wisdom. Do you think it's safe to ride now? I want to ride to the beach."

"It has always been safe, lass. The only time it's not safe to be out is when the convicts are about. They've not been near here for a while. You be careful, and you'll be fine. I think your going for a ride would be just the thing for you. The beach isn't far, and you can be back before dark."

"You'll be away at tea time," Miss Tilly commented. "Maybe you should take a snack with you. I'll pack you something." She stood up and hugged Amanda. "I reckon things will work out, love. One thing, though, you be mindful about strangers, especially men. You're a bonnie lass like your mother, Amanda. Maybe we should go with you, Sally and I."

"No, Tilly," Colin objected. "She is almost grown-up now. Why, she's going on thirteen, I reckon."

"Yes, and Amanda has a burden on her mind. It's just …" Tilly paused for a moment. "Right this minute, we are her family."

Miss Tilly put an arm around Amanda's shoulders and gave her a hug.

"I think you're as smart as a young lady can get. You'll be safe. You won't take any chances. Old Lady Lou'll bring you back right enough. She's a smart one, she is, just like you. You go ahead. We'll be looking for you later to tell us about the countryside and what you see while you're out and about."

Amanda went upstairs to change her clothes. When she returned to the porch, Colin was standing by the front gate holding the gray mare's reins. She walked out to him and stood quietly for a few minutes, rubbing the mare's neck and getting to know her a bit.

"She's always been a good horse, this one," Colin said.

Just then, Miss Tilly brought out a small wicker basket. Colin tied it carefully to the pommel then helped Amanda climb into the sidesaddle, fashioned for a lady. It wasn't the most comfortable saddle she'd ever ridden on, but somehow it made her feel special.

"There's biscuits in the basket and a small flask of water," said Miss Tilly. "That should be sufficient, don't you think?"

"More than enough. I'll probably not be hungry, but it would be better to have it than not to. Thank you."

"You be careful with old Lady Lou, and she'll be good to you," said Colin, patting the horse on its rump.

Amanda reined left, brushed her hand across the mare's rump, clicked her tongue, gently kicked Lou's flanks, and they started off in a brisk walk. When Amanda waved to the Stuarts, they waved back.

The ride to Horseshoe Cove proved uneventful. Along the way, Amanda was reminded of the terrible events that had happened that fateful day, especially as she passed through the grove of tall cedar trees marking the place where Grewno had jumped in front of the horses.

Oh, why did Grewno have to do that? she thought. *By this time, the family would have been in Manchester, and Mother would still be alive. Surely to goodness, we would have left for England at the very next opportunity.*

Of that she was certain. Her mother had been ready to leave the very next day after their arrival, but Father had stopped to see about Uncle John and to see some of this beautiful island. The picnic had been planned as a carefree diversion.

Oh, if only that part could be redone, she thought.

When she reached the small bluff behind the cove, she reined in and dismounted to look for the way down to the pink sand and the water. It was then that she noticed the boy Harry Smith walking along the beach. She could see his red hair quite well, though he wore a hat and had his back to her. She didn't think he could see her.

Amanda mounted Lady Lou and rode until she came to the path leading to the beach. In a few minutes she'd come very close to him.

Chapter 52

Amanda's Picnic

Amanda Worsham
November 1828
Bermuda

WHEN HARRY SMITH HEARD THE horse, he spun around, a wide grin on his face. He seemed happy to see her.

"Oh, missy? Miss Amanda Worsham, isn't it?"

He had a veritable symphony of freckles across his nose and face.

"Mister Smith?" Amanda jumped down from the sidesaddle, holding tight to Lady Lou's reins.

"Please, call me Harry. You're Amanda from the beach party that day, aren't you? It was a picnic or something, wasn't it?"

"It was. I wondered about you, Harry Smith. How's your head? Lieutenant Hawkins told us you'd suffered a big knot on your head."

"Old Harry's doing just dandy, he is. I'm very sorry to hear about your mother, though, Amanda. One day Hawkins rode out to find me and tell me about her.

Harry pulled at his earlobe, studying his feet, and seemed in deep thought about something. Amanda was ready to ask what it was when he spoke up.

"I didn't get very close to your mother that day," he said. "But from what I saw, I know she was a beautiful lady. You favor her some."

Say, you're better-looking than I remember too. Maybe because of what happened the day I met you and the way I sort of put all that from my mind is the reason I don't recall those pretty eyes or the long eyelashes. Once I get past the freckles, I see you're more than just another farm boy. You went out of your way that day to warn us about the convict.

She liked him. He was cute. "It's a pretty day, isn't it?" Amanda said with a smile.

"Aye, that it is, missy. What brings you here? Just out for a ride?"

Amanda nodded. "Memories get heavy sometimes, I guess. What about yourself? Looking for a whale, are you?"

"Oh no, missy. Why, it'll be December before you know it. There's no whales out there on the reef this time of year—far as I know. Oftentimes I come here of a Saturday morning, though. I love to walk these beaches and listen to the sea breezes. Good for me thinking, it is."

"Mother pack you a lunch?"

"Aye. But it's long since gone. I've nothing to offer you, Amanda, just this bottle of water. That's all I've left."

"Well, here's a small lunch basket Miss Tilly packed for me. Let's see if there's enough for two." She pointed to the wicker basket Colin had tied to the pommel.

"Miss Tilly Stuart?"

"That's right. They've been taking care of me. We could sit in the shade up there somewhere, I think." She pointed to the bluff. "Too bad we can't have tea, though."

"Your father owns that Stuart property now, doesn't he?"

"Yes, Father bought it before he left for England."

"Is his business there?"

"Well, he has affairs in England to see about, but he went to bury Mother and Little Joe at the Worsham family estate near Manchester."

"When will he be back?"

"He came back last month, but now he's gone to Boston. He'll be back in a couple of months. I received a letter from him today."

"A letter. I never got a letter in me life. Saw one once, though. Me father wrote one to me mother, but that was awhile back."

"What would you say to a picnic? I'm sure we can find some shade up there—somewhere."

"I need to leave for home soon," Harry told her, sounding disappointed.

"Come on, Harry. We can both ride Lady Lou."

"I reckon we could. She's a fine horse. You wouldn't mind?"

Amanda thought of the warnings she had been given, by her mother and by Miss Tilly, about men … even boys. That all seemed remote and beside the point now. She liked this boy and felt he could be trusted, at least right now. She just knew.

"You behave, I won't mind," she said.

"Well, that'll be fun, missy. Let me give your horse a drink of water first. Wait a minute."

He took off his hat, poured a small amount of water into it from his bottle, and held it so Lady Lou could drink.

"Now there's a good girl, Lady Lou," he murmured.

When that was finished, he shook the water out and put the hat back on, then made a step with his hands, and helped Amanda to climb up. He stood there for a moment looking and rubbing Lady Lou's mane, as if sizing up both the horse and its rider.

"Whoa, missy. With your sidesaddle, there's no room for me. I really need the walk. I'm gonna walk. It's not that far, anyway."

Whoops! Should've known that. Too bad. No cute boy behind me with his arms around me today, Amanda thought. She kicked ever so slightly with her heels, and they were off.

"You see that bush there?" Harry Smith pointed to a bush she had admired on her first trip to the beach. She also had seen those bushes flowering around Charleston.

Not much in the way of blooms now, but a few year-round, according to Miss Tilly, she thought. *It's November, but blooms nonetheless. Could be the climate, I don't know.*

"That's called the South Sea Rose," he said. "You better watch your horse around that one. A horse will nibble whatever bush is near. That rose is poison. All of it—to you or me, or a horse unlucky enough to eat it. Makes them weak, it does. If a horse gets enough of it down, poor animal will sink to its knees and fall over dead."

Amanda kept Lady Lou well away from the bush.

"It's not a rose at all, but people call it that. When he was alive, me grandfather remembered when the plant was rare on this island. People brought it here."

In a few minutes, they found a shade tree. Harry scurried over and helped Amanda to slide from the mare to the sand.

The sand's not as pink here as it is on the beach, she thought. *The dry sand is different somehow.*

Amanda untied the wicker basket and opened it while Harry went looking for a good shady place for Lady Lou. Inside, she found three kinds of cookies and some fruit. She set the basket on the ground and looked for Harry. He had his back to her, tending to the mare.

Again, Amanda thought he was quite good-looking for his age. She wondered why she hadn't noticed before, that time when she first saw him on the beach. He must have changed in the five months or so since. She especially liked the way his trousers fit. He was thin but muscular and had a way about him too. Not cocky but sure of himself.

That awful day on the beach, when Harry had warned them about the escaped convict, she remembered he'd told Father what he would have done in his stead. He had said he wouldn't have gone off riding and left the ladies alone on the beach. That took some nerve. She had never seen anyone chastise her father before.

As Harry walked back to where she was standing, Amanda was glad he was with her.

A cool breeze blew landward from the beach, and she felt the chill of it. But chill or no, she knew she was safe with Harry Smith. She looked at him and wondered what it would be like to have him, just as her mother must have had Beau Videau so long ago.

Mother wasn't much older than me when she did that with him, she thought. *If she actually did, that is.*

Harry kicked a clod of dirt with his shoe, a worried look on his face.

"Missy," he said, still studying his feet, "I can't stay here very long with you just now and us alone and everything. It just wouldn't be the right thing to do. You know that, don't you?"

Amanda felt sorry for him and somewhat rejected at the same time.

I guess I knew that, she thought. *You're a good boy, Harry Smith.*

Probably most of all, she was glad that there wouldn't be any such event for her right now—that sex business her mother had experienced.

Amanda didn't dread sex. She was just not ready to be a mother. *There is enough for me to tend to right now.*

When they'd finished their short picnic, Harry held the reins for her to climb up to the saddle.

"Come here, Harry," she said, a note of happiness in her voice. "I want you to put your hands together for a footing to boost me up."

"Sure, missy."

Amanda readied herself to mount Lady Lou. As she did so, she suddenly had an impulse to lean forward and kiss him.

She did it. She kissed him on the cheek. "There," she said, laughing. "That's for being such a good boy."

Climbing into the saddle, she prepared to ride away. The cold breeze whipped her hair into disarray. She thought briefly about the butterfly. If the wind had, indeed, captured it, as Sally had said, she imagined it to be miles away at sea by now.

Harry smiled and raised his hand to wave goodbye. "Thank you, missy," he said, bemused.

Amanda started toward Stuart Manor. "Bye, Harry Smith," she called as she rode off.

Chapter 53

Yarmouth Harbor

Joseph Worsham
November 1828
From Boston to Cape Cod

THE DECK OF THE STEAMBOAT accommodated room for the coach and
a place to keep the horses. It was Friday afternoon, and the weather
was cold, the sky gray and overcast, and the wind made whitecaps
on the waves. But the passage across the bay from Boston had been
uneventful.

Before the steamboat departed from Boston, Patience gave the
captain his directions. The man showed a great deal of confidence.
He'd made this passage to Yarmouth Harbor with Patience on several
other occasions, and now he steered carefully past the bar off Sandy
Point toward a small private landing in Yarmouth Harbor, not far
from the settlements of Barnstable and Yarmouth.

Seems foolish to me, thought Joseph. *The steamboat has a shallow
draft. And it's high tide. The harbor must not be very deep here. Maybe
that's why the captain refused to signal a pilot before he entered the harbor. This captain is overconfident. He is too cavalier.*

The steamboat left Boston a little after midnight. With the
stopover for fuel and supplies in Plymouth, it had taken all morning and well into the afternoon to make the voyage, because of the
coach and the horses for the most part. One could arrange sailing

passage more convenient than that. Patience seemed obsessed with steamboats.

The water on this side of the cape was a cold, gray blue, and the waves smaller, gentler than on the Atlantic side. Joseph understood that. But as they began the last leg of the approach, the flags on the steamboat's short masts whipped so fiercely in the stiff breeze that Joseph thought a sailing vessel might have had a difficult time of it. The captain had told them the wind usually started up about three or four in the afternoon and settled down later.

When the crew finished securing the steamboat at the private slip, Lester and a few members of the crew freed the securing lines from the coach and rolled the vehicle off the boat deck onto the wooden dock. All the luggage, except their personal items, had been lashed in place on the coach for the passage.

Lester brought the horses out, one at a time, and led them off the steamboat.

The three travelers brought their small, last-minute things from the cabins to the coach and prepared to leave.

Thank goodness for this dock, thought Joseph.

After a time, the coach stood ready, and Lester drove it away from the dock and up the beach to a safer place.

Joseph opened the door of the coach and assisted Patience as she stepped up. He turned to wave to the crew of the steamboat as it backed away from the dock, began its turnaround, and started the return trip to Boston.

According to the captain's almanac, in two weeks the morning high tide would occur about noon. He would call for them again at this place then.

Joseph climbed into the coach and settled beside Patience.

Lester said something to the horses, and the animals began pulling the coach from the beach toward the road and their destination.

As the steamboat whistle blew a staccato signal that all was well, the paddle wheel began to turn in earnest. Joseph watched through the window until the coach reached the road and turned away so that he could no longer see it.

It was cold on the Cape, even if the wind was not as strong as it had been out on the bay, and it was quite cold inside the coach. Joseph and Patience covered their legs with lap blankets and huddled together for warmth.

The area near the landing was mostly marshlands. Patience had described the journey to the cottage as a trip through countryside of low, rolling hills, woods, pastures, bogs, and farmland. Through the window, Joseph could see a few large trees beside the road and some scrub pines.

The road, fairly well used, was bumpy. Along the way, Joseph noticed the hulk of a very large dead tree that had apparently been struck by lightning sometime in its past. He pulled the shade down to cover the window and shifted his attention to the inside of the coach. But just before the shade completely closed, a flash of lightning lit the dark sky. The image of the tree with its bare remaining limbs lingered for a moment, as if it were the vision of a horrible specter, beckoning and threatening, with upraised hands and outspread fingers.

As he perused the dark coach, a brief picture flashed in his mind of the dead tree's stark fierceness against the gray sky, an image he chose not to dwell upon. He didn't believe in omens, but that vision gave him a shiver, anyway.

It would take quite awhile to reach their destination, an estate cottage not far from a settlement known as Cotuit.

Lester brought the coach to a halt about halfway through the trip for a rest stop where he gave the horses an apple and a drink of water in a leather bucket. He offered apples and clean drinking water to his passengers as well. Afterward, he secured the horses and the coach and walked away from the road into the woods.

The wind died down to a dead calm. Taking an apple from Lester's basket, Joseph walked ahead of the horses along the road to give Patience her privacy.

After a short time, he heard Patience call his name. Tossing the apple core into the woods, he returned to the coach.

Plant an apple tree …

Lester stood by with clean water, soap, and towels for them to wash their face and hands. The rest stop had been a success. Joseph felt much better.

Soon, Lester lit the side lanterns, helped with last-minute tasks, climbed to his driving position, and brought the coach underway again. Joseph raised the shade and looked once again at the country-side as it passed by the coach window. Dusk had descended above the overcast sky. Here and there, the ground seemed covered with thin, wispy clouds of mist. Feeling sleepy, he wondered if the fog was his imagination. The view from the coach window reminded him of the moors in England. Again, Joseph pulled down the window shade.

Holding hands, he and Patience soon fell asleep as the horses pulled them along toward Cotuit.

When they finally arrived, Joseph found the cottage, as Patience called it, to be a three-story stone building set well back from the sea and dotted with numerous gardens and outbuildings. While still on the *Anne Bayliss* and before sailing toward Boston Harbor from Bermuda, Joseph and Captain Bob had studied the old *Carington Bowles* chart of New England and Cape Cod. On that chart Joseph had seen Oyster River Bay. Patience's cottage offered a good view of it.

The entire center area of the Cape was generally known as Barnstable, but the village of Barnstable was well north of the cot-tage. One could see Cotuit across the bay.

A lookout deck on the roof of the cottage provided a brass telescope, and Joseph reckoned one could see the Atlantic from up there and observe the ships as they passed by. The cottage was a very well-constructed, attractive structure. The same New York archi-tectural firm that Willard had commissioned to build his home in Philadelphia had designed and built the cottage.

A full staff lived in servants' quarters on the premises below stairs on the first level. The staff kept the property well managed, repaired, and ready for Patience whenever she chose to visit the Cape.

The estate keeper, Harold Grieves, lived in a small cottage with his wife, his two children, and his elderly father. He either ordered for delivery whatever supplies were needed or brought them to the estate. Joseph thought of his family estate near Manchester. The location was different, but the arrangement was the same.

At nearly ten o'clock, they were finally settled inside the cottage with their luggage. Patience showed Joseph to his room and left him there. Both were very tired and needed rest.

After selecting his attire for the following day, Joseph dressed for bed and soon after fell asleep.

He awoke the next morning with a feeling of joy after his restful, deep sleep—happy about being in Barnstable with Patience. And he liked this cottage. His room felt comfortably warm. The fire had burned low during the night and had almost gone out, but someone had come into his room very early in the morning and revived it.

Joseph also found that the clothes he'd selected the night before had been freshened, pressed, and hung ready for him to dress for the day. As he shaved and took care of his morning affairs, he looked about the room. It had a masculine decor and seemed comfortable enough, but it was not exactly to his liking. A hunt scene hung over the fireplace where he probably would have chosen a nautical painting. But that didn't matter much.

A pipe rack sat on the mantelpiece with an old pipe atop it. Beside it sat an empty tin for pipe tobacco. Joseph opened the tin to smell its fragrance. He didn't smoke, but he was curious about the various blends of pipe tobacco.

The fragrance …

He wondered where Traveler bought his scented pipe tobacco. And he wondered why Traveler never lit his pipe, preferring only to puff on the unlit tobacco. Oh, well, that didn't matter much, either. His gaze turned to the wall behind him to a door that led to the adjoining room.

He found the door locked.

Chapter 54

A Plot Laid in the Garden

Joseph Worsham
November 1828
Cape Cod

THE PREVIOUS EVENING, JOSEPH HEARD some staff members talking about Patience's arrival. Everyone seemed to think she might not return until spring, although he had heard she occasionally spent Thanksgiving at the cottage. According to what he'd overheard, that depended upon her mood and her needs.

A hubbub of activity arose quite early in the house. The business of bringing the cottage back to life had begun well before daybreak. Apparently, the whole staff was awake and on duty, lending the atmosphere an air of warmth and friendliness.

They enjoyed a spectacular morning sunrise, and after a good breakfast, Joseph and Patience went for a horseback ride to see the countryside. The grounds had been landscaped in a rustic but structured sort of way that blended well with this part of Cape Cod.

Behind the cottage lay a long, rambling bridal path. Patience rode beside Joseph in the fashion of a man—legs astride her horse. She seemed to be in deep thought, and he wondered what might be going on behind her serious expression.

Before they started, she had mentioned that the route would take the better part of a long, rambling hour to ride, but she hadn't said anything to him since they'd left the stables.

He estimated they were about halfway through the riding course when suddenly, she pulled up on the reins and jumped to the ground.

"Come here, Joseph. I want to talk to you for a minute."

Joseph halted his own mount and climbed down. "What is it?" he asked, more than curious to know why she'd so suddenly stopped.

The horses panted heavily in the morning air. Patience's horse pawed the sandy ground and bobbed its head nervously.

"In your room, did you notice the other door? The one that leads to the next room?"

"It's locked."

"You tried it?"

"Yes, this morning."

"That door leads to my room, Joseph."

"Oh, I didn't know."

"My late husband snored terribly. The room you occupied last night was his room. Did you know that?"

"I noticed the masculine decor, the faint odor of cigars."

"Yes. Well, I want to talk to you about the door, Joseph."

"Yes?"

"If you wanted to open it sometime, that would be all right. I mean, if you had a key, you could open the door and enter my room. I mean, if you wanted to."

She studied her horse's feet a moment, then turned to look Joseph straight in his eyes. "Don't want the servants to know about it," she said. "What I'm trying to say is, I really want to know you better, and there's so little time. I know I can trust you. At least, I think I can. I don't know just why I want to do this. But ..."

She opened her coat and drew a ribbon from around her neck. There was a key tied to it.

"Here," she said, a tremor in her voice. "I want you to have this. And no one must know. Don't *knock*. Someone might hear. There are so many servants about. Wait until the house is quiet, and come inside my room. If you want to, I mean."

She looked down at her riding boots, her face flushed and her shoulders trembling. "Oh dear," she said, "I hope I don't faint just now."

Joseph reached out and took the ribbon from her hand. He put his arms around her and kissed her. Long moments passed.

"Well," he said, "I think we needed that."

He hugged her for a moment, gently rocking her in his arms. When he smiled, she smiled back. Joseph put the ribbon and key in his pocket.

"Oh, I won't faint now," she said. "I don't want to miss anything that might happen from this point on."

"Indeed not. Nor do I."

"What shall we do for the remainder of the day, Joseph?" She squeezed his hand. "Does everyone call you Joseph?"

"Most do. My servants call me Mister Joe. Amanda calls me Father. Joe would be acceptable. I'll leave that up to you."

Suddenly her face wrinkled. She turned and bent to pick up a stick, then drew a circle on the ground.

"Joseph," she said after a moment, "you live sometimes in Charleston. You have an interest in a rice plantation. Do you own slaves?"

"I had two slaves until a few weeks ago. They now belong to my daughter Amanda. She is setting them free as soon as we can prepare them to fend for themselves. Schooling, that sort of thing."

"Any others?"

"No."

Patience dropped the stick and brushed her hands together to shake off the dust. "Good," she said. "That would be a problem. Could be Providence is taking care of matters for us. I know of many people who see nothing wrong with slavery. I am not one of them."

"It's an economic force in the world. I don't know what to say."

"That may be, but it is an institution whose time has passed."

"If you see it that way. Many believe the whole economic system of the South and the West Indies depends upon slavery. I've other business interests around that do a good deal better than the rice plantation on the Waccamaw. But I shouldn't wonder. Any business is only as good as the people who run it, the ones who do the work. I have done well by paying other workers a fair wage—others that are away from the plantation system."

"It is shameful to think of economic gain at the expense of a human being's suffering, Joseph. Best we not talk more about that, I think."

Joseph heartily agreed. He was changing his mind about slavery, anyway. The practice only caused problems in his life and hurt the people closest to him.

"Why don't we finish this ride and go back to the cottage?" she said. "There are business matters I must attend to, but I want you to meet Harold, my estate manager. He loves to hunt birds for his table and for mine when I'm here. Would you like to go hunting with Harold this afternoon? It would help to pass the day, and maybe you would enjoy it too. What do you say?"

"Sounds good to me. I'm a fair shot with a birding piece."

They rode toward the cottage in silence. Excited at the prospect of being with Patience during the night, he thought she was excited about it too.

Cape Cod is an interesting place, he thought, looking up at the sky as they rode toward the cottage. *It's turning into a very pretty day, and my whole life is changing.* He said a prayer that the change would be for the better.

During most of the afternoon, Joseph hunted birds on the cottage grounds with the estate manager, Harold Grieves. For most of the time, the two men kept themselves far away from the cottage. They shot a half dozen game birds before quitting for the day. Of these, Joseph accounted for two.

When he reached the cottage, Joseph went straight upstairs to his room, planning to change into his evening clothes.

Greta Berg, the second-floor chambermaid—a rather dour, middle-aged spinster who never seemed to need to smile—knocked at the door and called out his name. When he answered, Greta told him that Patience wanted to meet him at the summerhouse in fifteen minutes. She made a polite curtsy before leaving to return to her duties. She did not smile.

Joseph knew it would be cool in the summerhouse. It was more open to the elements than not, and it was very breezy today out there in the garden. Earlier, he had noticed that the landscape plants were beginning to take on the typical brown dead look of winter. The summerhouse wasn't a special place to entertain this time of year, but it was certainly private out there, and no one would overhear whatever was said. What did Patience want to tell him that was so secretive?

He dressed for warmth and left the cottage to walk to the garden. When he reached the summerhouse, he took a seat on a bench in the garden and waited for Patience.

In a few moments she arrived, taking a seat beside him.

"I want to tell you something, Joseph," she said. "It will be difficult for me to talk about this, but—"

She stopped suddenly and drew in her breath.

"Very well," he said, trying to comfort her. He folded his arms across his chest, rubbing his elbows with his fingertips. "What in heaven's name is it?"

Patience looked directly into his eyes. She was holding a handkerchief in her hand; the corner of it made a white flash in the edge of his vision. Seeing that flash against the blur of the dry, dead summer plants reminded him of a deer's tail bounding hurriedly across a lea of spent field peas.

"I am barren, Joseph," she said. "I cannot conceive."

Joseph said nothing. He continued to rub his elbows and only nodded his head. *Why is she telling me this?*

"That," she said, continuing, "was the big problem with my poor departed Willard, you see. I never really understood, though, what was bothering him … not fully, anyway. It wasn't until he started to drink so very much," she said, "and fool around with Jeannette, that the truth came out." She looked down at the handkerchief. "Jeannette," she said, slowly, "is a young French woman that managed our hothouses in Boston. Willard conceived a son with that woman … a child born out of wedlock. But it was his son,

268

nonetheless. Still," she said, again flipping the handkerchief, "I didn't understand, you see." She looked at Joseph. "He is so tiny … and has beautiful olive skin … like his French mother."

"You don't have to tell me about this," Joseph said, dropping his arms to his side.

"It just gets worse and worse," she said, ignoring him, a pained expression on her face. "Willard was so proud of the baby. He'd wanted a son all his life. He wanted a son, and I couldn't give it to him.

"Willard provided for the woman, Jeannette … for the child in his will," Patience said. "Now she lives in Paris with someone else, someone—a new lover, a new provider. And the boy …"

A brief, strange look suddenly crossed her face.

"Oh, he's such a good-looking lad. His name is Tim … Timothy Caldwell. He's fourteen now, in school in Philadelphia. Timothy wants to go to the military academy at West Point as soon as he graduates. I'll see to it, of course. He shall have everything he needs, just as though Willard were still alive."

She lowered her gaze, wrenching her hands together, clutching the handkerchief ever so tightly in one fist.

"I really admonished my poor Willard about his drinking, I fear. And I think I made his life difficult. He began to drink excessively after the child was born. And about the time I found out about it, he'd really become quite an alcoholic."

"And, Joseph," she said. "It was altogether by accident, I mean, that I found out about the child. I happened to find a copy of Willard's last will and testament with the secretary where he sometimes worked on his business ledgers."

She means the bureau, probably she means in *the bureau and not* with *it. Some quirk in her speech habits, perhaps.*

Patience continued, "It was during a time when he was drinking so heavily that I went through his papers, trying to find out what was wrong. And poor Willard was unconscious in his chair in a drunken stupor. It wasn't like him to be always drinking, you see. Drinking was something he'd taken up during the previous year. And he would drink until he'd pass out. Reckon I knew something was wrong, I just didn't know what it was until it was far too late. I never had a chance to discuss it with him after that.

"He went away for the weekend," she said, "and died while he was off drinking somewhere … of heart failure while he was with her, I think. Maybe he wanted to tell me, I don't know. I only know I feel that I failed him because I couldn't give him the son he so obviously wanted."

Joseph rubbed his hands together, then cleared his throat. *Why is she telling me such private things about herself and about Willard?*

"Well," he said, "I appreciate the difficulty you must have had in telling me about the boy, Patience. Shall we not worry about it anymore? Maybe from time to time something will need to be done to care for him. Perhaps I could talk to him, but right now I don't know about that. And anyway, what business is it of mine?"

Patience looked down at her hands.

"For now, why don't you and I plan to enjoy each other as much as possible and just not worry about that anymore?" he said.

She nodded in agreement. "I only wanted you to know, Joseph," she said, looking back into his eyes.

"God knows that situation was not your fault, Patience." He put his arms around her and hugged her for a long time. She kissed him and squeezed his hand.

Patience's expression soon changed to one of joy. "Come," she said, laughing. "Shall we retire to the parlor until dinner is served? I can hardly wait until tonight."

As they walked toward the cottage, it no longer seemed so cold or so windy in the garden. A joy, almost a dance, livened both their steps as they walked along.

Later in the evening, after the house fell silent, he unlocked the door to the adjoining bedroom, using the key Patience had given him earlier in the day. The key that had been tied to the ribbon she had pulled from between her breasts where she had been carrying it, perhaps all day.

She was waiting for him in the glow of the lamp shining on the bedside table. Beside it stood an open bottle of scotch whiskey.

"What ..." he said and paused.

"The whiskey will warm your soul, Joseph. I find I need it myself from time to time."

"But I distinctly heard you say, I thought you did not—"

"Drink spirits?" she said.

"Well, yes. What am I to think?"

"It is a ruse, Joseph, one of many. I find it useful to have a foundation of straight-laced rumors about me."

"And the talk of your husband drinking himself to death?"

"Well, Willard couldn't hold his liquor. That is so."

"But your coachman told me that he fears your wrath, should you smell whiskey on his breath."

"And rightly so. He is a good boy. He spreads that story well, perhaps because he truly believes it."

"Why would you do such a strange thing?"

"I will say no more, Joseph. Things are not always as they seem. Such things are for you to learn later. Have your nerves steadied now. There stands a glass." Patience pointed to the side table. "See to it. We've love's work to do here."

She's been drinking and doesn't want me to notice it—be bothered by the liquor on her breath, he thought. He poured himself about two fingers of scotch and drank it quickly as if it were medicine.

"You know, Patience," he said, as he leaned over to blow out the lamp. "If I were telling this story—if this were a play or a book, I mean—it would be what happens now that matters the most. Do you know what I mean?"

She laughed a robust and joyous laugh as she reached up to grab him and pull him down toward her.

They found each other in the darkness of her room and in the warmth of her bed, and their passion showed in the physical nature of their union.

* * * * *

Joseph climaxed deep inside her warm body as she clung savagely to him, holding him tightly against her with the full strength of her legs. She continued for a few moments longer before she, too, relaxed and released him.

For Joseph, the experience was extraordinary. There would be no guilt in the following days, guilt that he had not done the right thing by her during the completion of the act.

Maybe she had told him about her barrenness so that he wouldn't worry. Or she had told him about it because she simply wanted to talk about it. Whatever the reason, her confession had been most effective.

"What will happen now?" she asked, still breathless.

"I have some business to take care of in Boston. After that, I must return to my two little girls."

"Do you want me to go with you?"

"Maybe later, Patience. Now there is much to be done. Give me time to talk to my girls about us."

"Joseph." She reached over and squeezed his hand tightly.

"Yes, what is it?"

"I don't think I'm ready for this, either. I've thought for years I was happier not having to please anyone. I don't think it would be a good idea for me to get married again. Maybe I'll change my mind about that later, I don't know. Can we just think about it for a while?"

"Yes, sweetheart. Say, I was thinking, maybe we should go into some kind of business together."

"That would keep us in touch."

"I have enough money to do whatever is necessary."

"I don't need your money."

"I know."

Patience latched her door to the hallway from the inside and made Joseph do the same to his room door. It would be cold with no one to build up the fires in the two fireplaces during the night, but it was warm in her bed. They finished out the night in each other's arms, and the rest did him good.

The next day when they talked about it, Patience told Joseph she wanted to see him whenever possible and that she was certain that she wanted to form a business alliance with him. But she did not wish to marry him.

He agreed.

And so the beginning of Joseph's new shipping venture in the United States seemed solid.

Patience told him she had heard talk of a new way to ship goods overland, something to do with steam engines and iron rails, something called a railroad, something that required vast quantities of capital investment, land acquisition, and planning. But it seemed to be something that would be very important in the years to come. The only thing was, Patience made the statement that she really didn't trust steam power for transportation, but the speed of other transportation sometimes proved too slow, so she used steamboats regardless. It was a strange situation. Patience kept a running list of steamboat accidents. Far too many had occurred. Fire had always been a problem aboard passenger ships, but these newfangled steamboats carried the bloody fire along with them.

That did not especially bother Joseph.

It bothered Patience very much.

And I thought she liked steamboats. I just don't understand women.

Chapter 55

A Strangeness in Boston

Joseph Worsham
November 1828
Back in Boston

THE HORSES MADE A STACCATO sound on the cobblestone street as the carriage sped through the marketing section of Boston. The smell of the port, a pungent background aroma, underwrote everything else the senses detected. It was late in the afternoon, and Joseph was en route to the *Anne Bayliss*, observing the street activities through the coach window. A horse and rider hurried past the coach.

"Damn," he muttered. "Why whip a horse like that? Wherever that ruffian is going, he could spare his bloody horse and get there a bit later."

Lester drove the coach slowly around the corner.

Joseph slid over to the other coach window. *What? What was that?*

A flash in the sunlight as the coach turned—the image of a musket with a polished silver barrel dominated Joseph's senses. A shot rang out, and gun smoke filled the air as the musket fired. The lead ball barely missed him as it pierced the wooden window frame and buried itself in his luggage.

Who would do this? he thought. Then, as the coach rolled to a full stop, he saw the face of the man who had fired the shot.

Dear God. It's Grewno! But Grewno is in Australia. He must be.

Before Joseph had time to collect his thoughts, the man ran around the corner and vanished.

Did I actually see the man named Grewno?

* * * * *

"Should I chase after that man?" Lester huffed as he threw open the door to see about his passenger.

"Do you have the How Box up there with you, Lester?" Joseph asked.

"Yes, sir."

The How Box contained brandy, glasses, and clean linen kerchiefs. It was customary to carry such a locked box in a coach or stage should there be a medical emergency while traveling. Patience did not like alcohol for casual use, or so she said, but she and everyone else realized the need for the How Box.

"That scoundrel who shot at me is long gone by now. When the horses are secure, why don't you pour the two of us a brandy? By God, this is an emergency."

"Right away, sir."

Joseph examined the hole in his luggage. The ball had penetrated the brass hasp and lodged into a shoe. He decided not to tell anyone about this right now.

As Lester handed him a glass of brandy, Joseph warned, "Let's let Patience live without any of this knowledge."

Lester nodded in agreement. "I'll repair the window frame. She won't even know." He was shaking.

I'll make it right by the lad ... I will. But first I must make sense out of this.

Book 4

Amanda Prepares to Be on Her Own

Favour is deceitful and beauty *is* vain: *but* a woman *that* feareth the LORD, she shall be praised.

—Proverbs 31:30, KJV

Chapter 56

Gossip with Harry Smith

Amanda Worsham
November 1828
Bermuda

Now the sharp November breezes of Bermuda had turned calm. The afternoon sun cast soft shadows and bathed everything in an eerie, warm glow. It was like that sometimes in Bermuda and probably meant something important as far as the weather was concerned, if one understood such things.

Amanda did not. She sat in the parlor knitting, something she'd learned from Miss Tilly.

"Missy?"

Amanda heard someone by the front gate calling her.

It must be Harry Smith, she thought, looking to see who it was. *He's the only one who calls me by that name.*

"Oh, missy."

Sure enough, Harry Smith ambled through the gate toward the house, and Amanda met him on the porch. She was glad to see him, and he broke out in a big smile when he saw her.

"I've come to see if you need another hand to help with your cottage project, Missy."

"I think Moses or Mister Stuart would be the ones to answer that question, Harry."

"Isn't Moses your slave now? I mean, that's what I heard. And Colin Stuart is your father's overseer for the farm? Why, everyone's talking about it."

"Well, yes," she admitted, her smile fading. "It's true, Harry," she said. "Father left Colin Stuart in charge of things here, especially the cottage Moses is building."

"Where is he? Mister Stuart, I mean?"

"I think he went out to check something on the farm. Or maybe he's gone to visit Agnes. I see him walking away from there sometimes."

Harry wore an anxious, straight-lipped expression, looking at her through squinted eyes. "Yes, missy. And there's plenty of talk about that too."

"Whatever do you mean?" she said.

"Some say Agnes is a mite too lonely since her man died, and she *fills in* whenever she can."

Harry pushed his eyebrows up, an embarrassed blush on his cheeks. "With the man what's available," he said. "If you know what I mean …" He bit his lip. "Anyway, it's none of me business," he said.

Amanda knew what Harry meant. Oh yes, she had suspected for months something going on between Colin and Agnes.

But that sort of thing is better left unsaid, she thought. *Miss Tilly doesn't seem concerned about it, anyway. She certainly would know if there were any truths to that talk about Agnes. Childhood's end,* she thought. *Just as described in Ecclesiastes. So I'm pretty well all grown-up now. Is that it?*

Harry Smith began to smile, the blush fading.

Lord … the things people get themselves into, she thought. She saw very little humor in the situation. Maybe it was better to smile than not to, but that business was a hurtful thing … or it could be.

She could think of better ways to spend a Friday afternoon than worrying about Colin Stuart and Agnes Phillips. She certainly didn't want to talk about it anymore.

"Harry," she said, "I'll see to it you get a job if there's one to be had. Why don't you come inside to the parlor? We can visit for a spell. Let me see if I can find Miss Tilly."

"I'd love to stay, missy, but me mother will be looking for me about now. I've wasted too much time along the beach today. I should be headed back. Reckon it to be near three o'clock, don't you?"

"Very well then. Yes, it's about that time. You come by Monday morning, and we'll speak again about this. Be prepared to stay the day. Can you do that?"

"Aye, missy."

When Harry reached the gate, he turned to call over his shoulder. "Been thinking about you, I have. I never had such a pretty lass to kiss me before. No, I never did."

He's going to ask if he can come calling. *Maybe he wants to come back over to see me this Sunday.* He was very handsome. She almost hoped he would ask.

Harry waved once in a halfhearted manner and walked away. *He didn't ask.*

Amanda waved and watched as he headed toward the main road. *Well, maybe next time*, she thought, entering the house to find Miss Tilly. She was thinking about Agnes and Colin. *What a sad thing.*

She decided not to worry about it.

Chapter 57

Father Returns to Bermuda

Amanda Worsham
December 1828
Bermuda

"Land sakes, chile," Sally cried. "I do believe it's yo' daddy comin' down the road."

It was Sunday morning, and Amanda and Sally were upstairs in the front room.

"In that carriage yonder." Sally pointed beyond the open window toward the road. "Look, ain't that yo' daddy? Ain't that Mister Joe?"

Happiness flooded Amanda's heart. She had missed her father terribly during the months he had been gone. *It is Father.*

Oh, she was glad to see him! She ran down the stairs and out to the yard to meet him before he could sweep through the gate.

After bringing the carriage to a halt and alighting, Joseph picked her up, kissed her cheek, and squeezed her in a great bear hug.

"Amanda, it's so good to see you," he said as he set her down.

Colin came out of the house to take care of the carriage.

"Good to see you, lad," he greeted, reaching to shake Joseph's hand. "Really good to see you. Tilly will be glad too. Go on inside. I'll be along in a minute."

In the days that followed, Joseph checked into all the business details now part of Stuart Farm and told Amanda about Patience. The two of them sat on the porch and talked in the evenings.

Amanda sat quietly and listened. As her father talked, she thought of the things her mother had said, about Joseph and Beau Videau and the things about Charlie Videau. There would be time enough to worry about Charlie in the future. Now, the fascination and the love she felt for Joseph and the things he was telling her were most important.

Dear Lord, she thought, *Joseph Worsham is a good-looking man. But is he my father? Maybe not …*

Joseph spoke of the new business venture with Patience in the North, about the office soon to open in New York, and about the business with Traveler.

Who is this Traveler? she thought. *He certainly made an impression on Father. And Patience … well, that sure happened fast.*

Amanda pressed her fingers to her lips. *Damn such changes,* she thought.

Joseph told her more about the man called Traveler. Oddly, this Traveler person had hurried to catch Joseph on Cape Cod before the return trip to Boston. Traveler had arrived in a large, chartered steamboat and reported the news to Joseph that he was able start working as soon as need be.

Joseph told Amanda he had done all the necessary paperwork before leaving Boston to take care of the business about Traveler. He'd established a new branch of the family company now, one founded in New York, and he'd placed Traveler in charge of everything. Among other things, Traveler would oversee the building of six new sailing ships and the hiring of the necessary employees.

He also told Amanda that Traveler had agreed not to bother him with details and had agreed to being paid a percentage of the profits as well as his salary.

Amanda was curious but knew Joseph was always right about business. She certainly wasn't worried.

Except about Patience.

Lordy, what a name.

A letter came the next day from Aunt Meg. Sarah Jean simply didn't wish to return to the United States now or in the future, or so it seemed.

Joseph worked for two days writing a return letter. He agreed to leave Sarah Jean with Aunt Meg in England for the time being. Maybe that was the best thing for her. Sarah Jean still hadn't accepted Frances's death, and that was the problem.

In one of their late evening talks, Joseph told Amanda he thought Sarah Jean blamed him for Frances's illness and death.

If Frances hadn't been pregnant, she might not have died. Well, what a wicked thing to think, thought Amanda.

Later in the week, Joseph told Amanda he thought she should start her education in one of the American schools, of the sort that taught young women something other than the social arts. If she wanted to, of course. She knew Joseph expected her to be a business-person someday. He had told her so over the years. She would be the son he never had, whatever that meant.

She agreed to go to a school, and they settled upon the one run by the Moravian Church in Salem, North Carolina, called Salem College. Among other subjects, there she would have the opportunity to learn to speak German. Besides, Salem was close to Charleston, and that was where Amanda thought she wanted to live.

In the weeks before the two of them left for Charleston, several times Amanda was certain she'd seen Joseph either returning from Agnes's cottage or riding out that way.

Chapter 58

Real Schooling for a Young Lady

Amanda Worsham
August 1829
Salem, North Carolina

"Es tut mir leid." The young woman, gasping for breath in the warm, morning air, spoke to a group of girls who'd gathered beside the front door of the *Gemein Haus*. "Bitte—Studenten." She paused for a moment. "Wo ist Fräulein Worsham?" she asked with a decidedly *vee* sound on the *Worsham*. She leaned against the railing before continuing up the steps.

She had said something along the lines of, "Please, students, where is Mistress Worsham?"

Every one of the girls probably understood that much. She was speaking German that the girls were supposed to be learning. Maybe she'd rearranged the words a bit, Amanda wasn't sure.

At first no one answered. But after a moment, one student gestured toward the classroom.

"Sister Polly," she said, "Amanda's inside. She's in the embroidery class. Sie ist im Saal," she added, pointing toward the big room. The girl's expression revealed her pride at having answered the question *auf Deutsch*.

"You could say, 'Sie ist in der Saal.'" Sister Polly smiled in spite of her breathing difficulties. "But I get the gist of it. She is in the hall."

These girls were new to the German language, having recently come to the Salem girls' boarding school from various towns and plantations across the South.

As the sister and the girls approached, Amanda, who'd heard the exchange through the open door, felt as if she'd had a sudden revelation:

My fellow students don't "have" German, as they say. It takes a few moments for any one of them—for me—to translate something into English; it takes still longer to speak it. Some know French, as I do, mostly due to the efforts of each family's governess. But most of our group know some German: kennen, sprechen, *or whatever the proper word happens to be.*

Well, maybe German's not haphazard, exactly, but sometimes it seems so to me. The "polite form" or the informal—just what's wrong with "my" English words, anyway? Oh well …

The sister paused just inside the door. She said again, "Es tut mir leid …" She hesitated, again having difficulty breathing. "Fräulein Worsham?"

Amanda set aside her embroidery.

I hear you, Sister, she thought, sighing. Again, the vee *sound. It toots you what? But I must be careful not to mock the sisters. It just isn't the thing to do. Oh damn. Why doesn't she ever rest, anyway? She should take better care of herself—try to get well. I wish she would worry more about her own well-being instead of ours and maybe get better. Even so, I really love her.*

"What is it, Sister … Schwester?" Amanda corrected. She stood to face the young woman. "I'm sorry. What did you say? I have trouble with the German just now. I don't really have it, *Ich habe es nicht,* as you say."

She waited while the sister caught her breath. Amanda recalled the trip from Charleston to this Salem boarding school for girls. Sister Polly, very popular with the girls, was one of the first persons Amanda had met that day. Her thoughts racing, in an instant, she found herself traveling back in time.

* * * * *

In early spring, Joseph had brought Amanda to North Carolina via the family coach. The coach, which Joseph freighted by ship to Wilmington to make the trip to the Salem Academy much more comfortable, rattled along on the wandering farm and stagecoach roads. In her mind's eye, she saw once again the dogwood trees as they heralded the coming spring, their crinkled flowers scattering white splashes of color beneath leafless trees along the way, and she could hear the songbirds and the chattering of squirrels as the family coach approached Salem from the east.

Later, after making the arrangements, Joseph traveled on to Boston and maybe after that to England. Amanda didn't know where he was. She hadn't heard from him since he left. Those first days were a mixture of loneliness, shyness, and of confusion at having been left alone for the first time in her life. She knew no one in the school, but Sister Polly had befriended her easily. The days passed much easier because of the sister's kindness.

Sooner than she might have expected, the winter of 1829 and the spring of 1830 had passed. Now it was late summer, a time for quiet reflection, and school had started. Amanda had been away from her family and her responsibilities for over fourteen months, and she had discovered that she liked the arrangement. But there had been so many changes.

Moses and Sally stayed in Bermuda when Amanda and Joseph returned to Charleston. She felt a twinge of conscience about having left them to their own resources in Bermuda. Somehow, she felt remiss in their treatment.

But what would they do in Charleston? They're having a learning experience, too, she thought. *It's good for them to be away from that awful slavery in Charleston, especially with me in school.*

Amanda began studies here in business and other subjects that only young men studied elsewhere. The Moravians thought women should be educated, something God wanted them to do, and they liked to start the students at a young age. Amanda was going on seventeen now, but they had taken her, anyway. Joseph Worsham had seen to her training in the liberal arts through the efforts of several governesses, especially the last one, Mistress Kemble.

The Moravians certainly functioned against the norm. But for whatever reason, Amanda was glad for the opportunity to learn. She got along well with the single sisters, and she adapted well to her new life with them. She set about to learn as much as she could in the time that was available.

The months passed well.

* * * * *

Amanda smiled, turning her head to one side. She certainly was curious about this visit from Sister.

"Please speak to me in English," she said.

The frail, young sister with the plain but personable face paused before entering the room. She seemed to gather her strength as she lifted her skirts to come inside. She had been ill for some time with catarrh. All the students knew about it. Amanda thought Sister was breathing better now.

"You have a visitor, Mistress Worsham," Sister said in German, ignoring Amanda's request to speak only English. "Someone has come to see you. They are in the inspector's house. Your visitors are a fine lady and her son. That lad is so handsome. Why, he's downright pretty. You must come and see right away. Here is the lady's calling card."

Oh, will I ever learn German? thought Amanda. She reached out to take the card. "Ich kann nur ein wenig Deutsch," she said and smiled. "I can only speak a little." She thought for a moment and added, "Of the German. Thank you for understanding, Sister. Please, may we just speak English?"

"I know Deutsch is new to you, Amanda, *und du kannst* speak only a little now. But you'll get better with practice. You know, it's why we sprinkle it here and there in our conversations."

"Yes, certainly," Amanda replied. She looked at the card. In open, elegant scroll print, it proclaimed: "Patience Hannah Caldwell." She stood there for a moment, thinking. She recognized the perfumed scent that floated about the card. In an instant, she saw again the butterfly she now associated with that scent. *Patience.*

Yes, patience is in order now, she thought. *One must have patience. Apparently Joseph had.*

Sister Polly accompanied her to the inspector's house, reaching out to take Amanda's hand.

"Something good will come of this. I can feel it," she said. Sister was speaking English now.

Sister Polly waved goodbye and went back toward the *Gemein Haus.*

Amanda forced herself to think only of good things. She hummed a song to herself, the same little song Moses often sang when he was fretting over some problem—his way of dealing with something he really couldn't handle.

Dear Lord.

Chapter 59

Timothy Caldwell

Amanda Worsham
August 1829
Salem, North Carolina

A YOUNG MAN PACED NERVOUSLY back and forth, pausing now and again to look through the curtains at the walkways leading toward the inspector's house.

As he quickly pulled open the curtains to gain a better view, Amanda saw the young man for the first time. He was handsome, just as Sister had said. She determined immediately she simply must know this young man and soon, sensing he was someone she could easily learn to love.

So beautiful ... and he's here to see me, she thought. But why had she experienced no premonition of this?

Maybe this wasn't something bad.

The young man quickly pulled the curtain together.

He must have seen me looking at him, she thought, turning her gaze away. *What if he doesn't like me? Oh damn. It's better to do without such men.*

When Timothy Caldwell opened the door for her, Amanda walked into the room. The woman who must be Patience stood up, fanning herself delicately with a Chinese folding paper fan. Although she was not really pretty, in some ways she was quite attractive.

Patience filled her dress well. She possessed a certain air of respectability, and her mannerisms were those of a well-to-do woman. She kept her eyes on the young man as she fanned herself. She was wearing jewelry that flashed and sparkled in the rays of sunlight beaming through the curtains.

"Amanda," the woman said, "I am Patience Caldwell, and this is Timothy, my stepson."

Amanda executed a slight curtsy. "Happy to meet you both. I have heard a great deal about you—in particular, you, Patience."

Amanda smiled as her two guests exchanged greetings with her. And she listened as both said how pretty they thought she was. It was an awkward moment for her because this was the woman Joseph was sleeping with now, and also because she knew the lad to be the bastard son of Patience's dead husband.

She was beginning to develop a fondness for bastards, it seemed.

But why are these two here now? Father said Timothy attends a Pennsylvania boarding school.

"Amanda," said Patience, "I've hired a steamboat to carry my coach to and from Wilmington. It's a long, rough drive here from the sea. I fear steamboats, but the alternative is too forbidding. I shudder when I think of those corduroy back roads cross-country from Philadelphia to Wilmington."

"Yes, I know." Amanda didn't like the ride from Wilmington to Salem, either.

"But I want you to get to know Timothy now," Patience said, "while the two of you are unattached. He's in school, and there are only a few days before the new session begins again. This summer passed quickly. But summers always do."

"We must begin our return trip right away," Timothy offered. "There's not time to overnight at the tavern in town. Perhaps we could see you again when you are visiting the coast. In Charleston, perhaps?"

Timothy leaned forward and kissed her hand.

"My coachman, Lester," said Patience, "is expected in about fifteen minutes. He's worked out the business with the horses. I know the two of you would benefit from more time, but … well … this is all there is for now. Timothy, why don't you take Amanda outside for a few minutes?"

Amanda left for a walk with the beautiful young man and fell altogether in love with him before the coachman returned to carry him away. As she watched the coach disappear down the road, she knew she would marry that man someday.

Please, God, she thought, *let it be so.*

She was not quite the same little girl that the sister had been looking for earlier. Everything was altogether different now.

Chapter 60

Worsham House in Charleston
Sarah Jean Arrives

Amanda Worsham
June 1835
Charleston, South Carolina

An uneasy atmosphere had settled over Charleston. Amanda could sense it. She had moved into Worsham House in Charleston near White Point. Something bad was about to happen; she knew not what, but she believed her intuition about such things. Spring's so-called "sickly season" was almost upon them—bad air, that sort of thing. However, something other than bad air had sparked her sense of foreboding, the kind of business from which one could hardly protect oneself.

"Oh, I hope Timothy will come this year for a visit with Patience," Amanda said.

She was discussing things in general with Sally's cousin Arabella, a slave girl. Arabella belonged to Beau and often visited the Worsham family when Leonora was in town. She was Leonora's housemaid, and the Videaus had rented her out.

Leonora had not come to visit since Amanda moved back into Worsham House, but Arabella came often.

It had been several years since Amanda had completed her three-year study at the Salem girls' boarding school. She had received an adequate education there, and she'd especially displayed her proficiency at cross-stitch by designing her sampler—the Amanda Worsham sampler. Her sampler had been accepted, by the way. Amanda had been a good student.

She'd been put in charge of managing the family business in Charleston, and Joseph had gone away somewhere with Mother Patience, as Timothy called her. Amanda understood that she'd stepped into the shoes of the son Joseph had wanted all along and would never have now.

Her social life was rather skimpy, but no matter. After all, she did get letters regularly from Timothy, who was in his second year at West Point.

Amanda had turned twenty-one years old on her last birthday. According to the gossips, she was considered a spinster. But every time she had mentioned the subject of marriage in a letter, Timothy had either ignored it or replied in his own missives that he must finish school and make something of himself before committing himself to marriage.

"Oh, Miss Manda … Miss Manda," called Sam, the office boy.

Sam was a good lad Amanda had hired to run her errands. She'd given him instructions to come tell her immediately of any important news in the office.

There must be news.

She answered from the second-level porch. "What is it?" she called down to him.

"Oh, Miss Manda, you'll never guess what."

"Father's back." She hoped it was true. *Father just stays away*, she thought.

"No. It's your sister, Miss Manda. Miss Sarah Jean is on the *Anne Bayliss* inbound from New York. Isn't that good news? Captain Bob will be delayed in New York about a week and sent a message ahead by the Charleston and Savannah packet. You didn't know she was coming?"

"No, Sam. But it's good to know now. I'll probably just have enough time to get her room ready before the ship arrives."

"Is there anything else, Miss Manda?"

"No. But thank you."

Sam left, kicking pine cones along the street.

Good news, thought Amanda, wincing. *I've heard better news in my time.* She really had a strange feeling. She loved her sister, *but* …

* * * * *

When the *Anne Bayliss* arrived, Amanda welcomed her sister at the dock. But Sarah Jean gave her a cold and indifferent reception. Amanda felt she didn't know her anymore. At thirteen, Sarah Jean had an aura about her of someone twice that age.

One thing was certain: Sarah Jean had been formed in the image of Joseph's grandmother. She was the most strikingly attractive woman, and wherever she went, people turned their heads to watch her. Green eyes, long legs, and a long, graceful neck … these were the attributes that Sarah Jean possessed, along with her great-grandmother's golden hair for good measure. But something evil lurked inside Sarah Jean, something not quite tangible. It was there, nonetheless, and Amanda should have known it would be like this.

As the two climbed into Amanda's small carriage and Sarah Jean folded her parasol before sitting in the seat beside Amanda, suddenly Amanda knew what appalled her about her sister:

Sarah Jean is pure bitch.

"Well, love, have you found yourself a beau yet?" Sarah Jean said through a laugh. "Do the boys not like you, dear? I should think they certainly will like me."

Amanda shuddered when she thought of the local boys, Hollis Mackenzie in particular. Dogs after a bitch in heat came to mind. The two rode in silence.

* * * * *

Things didn't improve much after Sarah Jean had been in town for a month, either. She apparently had no morals, no judgment, and no common sense, and Amanda hated those things about her sister the most.

Chapter 61

Worsham House
At Sand Hills Plantation

Timothy Caldwell
July 1835
Georgetown, South Carolina

AT NOON THE TOWN CRIER dressed as an English gentleman from the about the 1600s stood in the town square and called out, "Oyez. Oyez. Oyez. People of Georgetown, it is the mail packet inbound for her renowned coastal run in the Carolinas … within the hour. Within the hour she will arrive—her first leg from Charleston. Our documents do not speak of her name. And tomorrow, the fourth of July, the year of our Lord 1835, she will return to Baltimore. You are well advised to purchase your tickets now for this glorious return trip to the North."

The crier repeated this message twice more. Soon the ship, with the help of men laboring at the rigging and with long mooring lines, snuggled up to the dock.

Timothy Caldwell strode down the gangplank, carrying a carpetbag, a quickness in his step. No person came forward to greet him.

"Well, how could they know I would be on this ship?" Timothy asked himself out loud.

He was thinking of Amanda and Mother Patience. At his earliest convenience, he caught the steamboat that traversed up and down the Waccamaw River. He was headed up river for the Sand Hills Plantation, about halfway along the steamship's run.

Again he arrived unannounced, so he walked the two miles or so to the main house. When he climbed up the steps, a green-eyed goddess came out to greet him.

"And who might you be, love?" she asked seductively. She was dressed in what Timothy reckoned to be a Paris summer dress, but her accent was decidedly British.

"Timothy Caldwell," he announced, dropping his bag. "I'm on break from West Point, to see Miss Amanda Worsham. Is she here? Is my mother here?"

"Timothy Caldwell, indeed. I have heard a great deal about you. Amanda can speak of no other person, it seems."

"And you … I haven't had the pleasure."

"I am Sarah Jean Worsham, Amanda's baby sister."

He immediately became excited, assessing her as she spoke to him, his eyes roving up and down her dress.

This really is a beautiful woman … No baby, this one, he thought.

She stood with her right leg forward and her foot, all the way up past her ankle, protruding beyond the hem of her skirt.

"And Miss Patience has gone to Savannah to shop and see about some business, love. Father has gone to Georgetown until tomorrow. There is no one here at the moment. We're alone with the house servants, Timothy. Won't you come inside?"

"Where is Amanda?" he asked warily.

"She's in Charleston tending to her Worsham house and her Worsham business."

The house servants served Timothy a late afternoon snack. Later, he and Sarah Jean went for a carriage ride across the plantation; she'd suggested a ride in the cool evening air. When they came upon a house used to store cotton—at least that's what Sarah Jean told him—she invited him inside. She told him how the planters upriver would send cotton downstream to be sold and how the Sand

Hills Plantation manager would purchase it and bring it here for storage until the price fared better.

They rested for a time, sitting on a bale of cotton. Sarah Jean's provocative manner made Timothy uneasy. He felt uncomfortable being alone with her and decided it was time to leave.

Suddenly, Sarah Jean screamed.

"What is it?" Timothy asked, alarmed. "Is there a snake? Are you hurt?"

"No, no!" she screamed, scrambling away from him. "Why did you rape me? I told you I wouldn't do that. You awful, wicked boy."

"What? Are you crazy? *Rape* you? Why, I never ..."

A slave barreled through the door, alerted by the commotion. "What is it, missy? This man hurt you?"

Then a white man came in ...

"What's going on here?" he demanded. "What's wrong, Miss Worsham?"

"That awful man raped me, Mister Bills." She pointed to Timothy.

A scuffle ensued, but Timothy escaped. In moments he was back in the carriage headed for the river. When he arrived at the wharf, he took a small fishing sailboat named *Everyman's Whimsy* and headed downstream, hoping to find his way to Georgetown and to safety.

"My god," he said out loud. "What's the matter with that girl? How do I defend myself against such a vile charge? What possible reason could she have had to accuse me of something like that?"

Amanda had told him in her last letter that Sarah Jean had only been in Carolina for a short time. He was surprised to see her here in All Saints' Parish. Suddenly he knew why she had done it. Probably for two reasons: she wanted to hurt Amanda, and she was pregnant when she arrived on the boat.

Maybe the baby was sired by some boy in England, he thought, *some man in New York, or someone on the ship she came over to America on.*

"Damn," he said.

Well, the steam packet would leave for Charleston and Savannah in the morning, and he would surely be on it. He could hide in Charleston in the army officers' quarters. Before he caught the packet, he spent a sleepless night on *Everyman's Whimsy*. Then in the morning, he paid the river steamboat captain to pull her back to the Worsham wharf.

He had no idea what he would do next.

* * * * *

"Joseph," Amanda said, "whatever do you mean, have I seen Timothy? Is he in Charleston?"

Joseph had just arrived and set his bag down in the foyer of Worsham House.

"Amanda, I wish you would call me something other than Joseph. You remind me of Frances too much as it is. And that's painful for me. You must know that. Besides, I must give you bad news. Shall we go into the parlor?"

"Bad news? Very well, Father."

In the parlor they sat on the couch, facing one another.

"So what's this bad news?"

"Amanda, Timothy Caldwell has been accused of raping your sister."

"Rape? I don't believe it. Did Sarah Jean say that?" *Well. It didn't take you long, did it, bitch? I don't believe a word of your story.*

"It's apparently true. The overseer, Mister Bills, was in the neighborhood and backs up part of her story, although he saw nothing."

"And where did this unlikely event, this absurdity, take place … and when?"

"At the Sand Hills cotton storage house."

"What was Timothy doing there? He was supposed to be en route to visit me."

"Sarah Jean says he came to Sand Hills asking for Mother Patience and never mentioned your name."

"Father …"

"I know. I don't believe it, either. And there is something else."

"Where is Sarah Jean now?"

"Well, that's it. She's here in Charleston, but she refused to come here to see you. I think her story is not the truth. I don't know just what happened that day, but when I asked the doctor to stop over, she refused an examination. Don't know what to think, I really don't."

I damn sure know what to think. "Where is Timothy now? What happened to him?"

"He's hiding in Charleston somewhere. I talked to the captain of the mail packet that brought him here."

"I must find him, Father. Timothy did nothing. I know he didn't. I can't even interest him in that way, myself. He wants to be self-sufficient. He will not even talk about marriage. He would never do such a thing. If that were his way, I would know. And you know that I would."

Joseph agreed.

"I must get to the bottom of this. Tell me, is Timothy wanted by the authorities?"

"No. Sarah Jean wouldn't file charges. I find that strange on top of everything else she says happened."

"But where is Sarah Jean now?"

"With Leonora Videau. Beau and Charlie are away."

Amanda was speechless.

Chapter 62

Sarah Jean Conveniently Loses Her Baby

Amanda Worsham
August 1835
Charleston, South Carolina

THE NEXT DAY, JOSEPH LEFT to meet Patience in Savannah. They would travel on to New Orleans on business, something about the steam railroads. Within a week, Sarah Jean visited La-La LaPorte, the ancient voodoo hag in Saint John's Parish, about her pregnancy. Sarah Jean came back without the baby. She had embraced a miscarriage of convenience.

In a fortnight, everyone in Charleston was talking about it. Hollis looked for Timothy and threatened to challenge him to a duel when he found him. These items of news came to Amanda through Arabella, who was living nearby.

On a hunch, Amanda sent Arabella to find out from La-La the truth about the miscarriage. There had, indeed, been one, but La-La thought the child was much older than Sarah Jean professed it to be. Sarah Jean had been pregnant for some time before she'd met Timothy. Arabella whispered to Amanda that the baby boy had black hair and looked "sho' 'nuff" Oriental.

Some poor man in England had fathered the child, Amanda concluded. His family must not have had enough money to suit Sarah Jean, of that she had no doubt whatsoever.

Chapter 63

A Visit to Videau Château

Amanda Worsham
September 1835
Charleston, South Carolina

IN SEPTEMBER, AMANDA THOUGHT IT about time she went out into the country to talk to Beau Videau, the sire, about that letter Frances sent to him from Bermuda—the letter Frances had told Amanda about before she died. As she drove the one-horse carriage into the shaded front yard of the old Videau homeplace, the magnificent fall colors of Charleston greeted her.

Was Beau Videau really her father and Charlie's father as well?

She tied the horse's reins to the white picket fence, then made her way through the gate and down the walkway to the porch.

When she rapped on the front door, the old housekeeper, Princess, answered her knock.

"Why, Miss Manda," she said, smiling. "Please come in." Princess's voice sounded almost like a person singing.

Princess took her wrap. "I'll tell misses you're here. They all away 'cept her."

Why isn't Beau here? Where is he? Amanda walked over to gaze out the window. She hadn't looked forward to this, but it really had to be done.

In a few minutes, Leonora Videau entered the parlor. Amanda never liked the stuffy woman very much. Oh, she was a Pinckney, all right, and an Allston too. She never let anyone forget that.

Beau Videau had always been physically close by when Frances was alive, at least it seemed that way to Amanda. Sometimes Beau traveled with Leonora, but she hadn't seen Beau or Leonora since Frances's death. They had signed the attendance book when they'd attended the belated small service held in her memory at the Methodist church in Charleston.

"How are you, child?" Leonora inquired pleasantly. "What brings you to Videau Château? Have you run out of places to go?" An air of haughtiness hung about her. "And tell me, what's this I hear about your Negroes? You just give them away?"

What the hell is she talking about? My Lord, thought Amanda. *What is the matter with this woman? Why is she so curt? She's never been especially rude, just difficult to like.*

"Please sit down, Amanda. You really shouldn't have thrown away that Negro boy, Moses. Why, I would like to have taken on a good yard boy myself."

Amanda didn't feel like sitting. She also didn't feel that Leonora's remarks deserved an answer. Instead, she stood by the window and faced the woman.

"Where is your husband? Could I talk to him for a few minutes?" Amanda simply ignored the question about her slaves. She had given them their freedom, and she didn't care who knew about it. But Leonora … well.

"What about, child? What do you want to talk to Beau about?"

"My mother told me before she died that she wrote a letter to him. She told me she had. Mother was quite ill at the time. I wonder what that letter said."

"There's no letter, I'm afraid. I'm always here, you know. I would know if there were ever a letter. I would know."

As Leonora spoke, Amanda suddenly understood Lenora's meaning: *the letter had come, and Leonora had destroyed it. Beau had not received the letter from Frances. He does not yet know he is my father. Well, damn.*

"Amanda, I'm certain you have the time and wherewithal to travel wherever you want," said Leonora nervously. "If you can just throw away your Negroes, you must have plenty of money. Beau's gone to Liverpool right now, and Charles is with him."

Lenora's words betrayed her fears. *She's afraid Beau would put me in his will if he knew*, thought Amanda. *Leonora read Mother's letter, and that's what's wrong. It must be true. Charlie Videau is my half brother. I just know it.*

Well, I must go, she thought. *I'm wasting my time here.*

Amanda excused herself and left.

Beau may be my father, but there's no love for me in this house. When he is gone, I will be discarded.

Chapter 64

Timothy's Affaire D'honneur

Timothy Caldwell
September 1835
Charleston, South Carolina

THE MORNING DAWNED SLOWLY OVER the wet and foreboding place called Washington Racetrack. Timothy thought it was curious these Carolinians held such fascination for both gambling and sport.

In many ways the remnants of British influence persisted, he thought.

Streaks of warm glow in the east and the call of roosters in the countryside heralded the coming of the day.

Timothy turned to view the array of torches burning in their stanchions. Supposedly, the smoke dismayed mosquitoes, but Timothy knew the truth: nothing dismayed the Carolina insect population. For this reason, heavy clothing remained in vogue, even in times of sticky heat, as now.

Two other men accompanied him. One was asleep in the back of a carriage, and the other, the track's night watchman, was sitting upright, as if he were stationed at his post. Both men, very drunk, snored loudly against the noise of horses and carriage wheels on the rocky roadway.

"Hail, Challenged One," called the driver of the first carriage. "It is almost the light of day, my friend," he said as he stepped down from the carriage. "I am to preside over this affair. Come, I must brief you concerning the rules."

A total of four young Charleston dandies dressed in black arrived in the two carriages. Each one wore a small, black mask—which merely covered the eyes—a thin disguise at best. With them came a fifth person: the tall, ugly, and very redheaded Hollis Mackenzie. He was quite drunk also and seemingly in no condition for a duel. He didn't get out of the carriage.

"Come. I would introduce you to this group. I am Sir Jack Ketch."

Sir Ketch was quite a dandy, if a rather thin and dour one. He pointed to a rotund figure of one of the young men dressed in black.

"This one is Sir Jeroboam," said Ketch.

The fat Jeroboam executed a slight curtsy, a ridiculous gesture.

"Jeroboam will serve as your second. You will find him to be both loyal and large."

The group of four men laughed.

Timothy saw no humor in any of this situation.

Ketch pointed to the second figure—a small, dark-skinned, handsome young man, a boy by outward appearances.

"Sir Namby-Pamby is this one's name, a person not wanting very much to be here."

Namby-Pamby managed a thin smile.

Ketch pointed to the fourth figure. "And here meet Sir Billycock. By any standards a gentleman, indeed."

Billycock only nodded his head.

"And as you may have guessed, each one of us are greeting you this morning with our respective *nom de guerre*, or pseudonym, as it were."

I should have anticipated this, Timothy thought. A cold chill along his spine forced him to shudder openly. "War Name," is what Ketch had said … Warrior Name, something like that.

Ketch seemed not to notice. Instead, he turned to the sleeping night watchman.

"That one, who may strangle on his own fluids at any moment, judging by the intensity of the snoring, is Sir Jackanapes—a rogue, if ever there was one. The other, Sir Judas Goat, for a fee, you understand, led the rogue to excessive drinking, I fear. Still, the situation suits our purposes well. This way no one can serve as a witness against the other, you see. No one outside this honorable dueling club knows the name of the others. We stand by that if need be. Should the loser of this affair become the deceased, no one will note the method of his demise. He will be left here along the track for the watchman to explain later this day. Poor Jackanapes. He really isn't one of ours, either. I just gave him a name to make him feel good."

They pulled Hollis from the carriage, forced him to his feet, and threw a bucket of icy water in his face.

"It is your time, Hollis," Ketch said. "You demanded this affair of honor … you know. To pontificate—we know the government in its benevolence passes laws to decree certain acts illegal. This duel is a perfect example. We harm no one of the general proletariat or masses, as it were."

"Is that all you do … fight duels?" Timothy asked.

"Goodness, no. Sometimes we enjoy a good cigar. Or we might help the needy—whether they want us to or not. The goal is to be anything but boorish."

Hollis stood, unassisted.

"Very well," Ketch said, pointing the way.

The six young men walked quickly to a wide place along the track.

"We adhere to the thirty-paces rule," said Ketch, as Hollis and Timothy were placed back-to-back. "I will say 'to begin.' When you hear those words, you are to step away from the other for a total of fifteen paces. I will count as you step. At the count of fifteen, you may turn and shoot. There will be but one chance. Now choose your weapons."

As the challenger, Hollis chose last.

"At this moment you may yield, or you may continue. The choice is yours."

Timothy said nothing.

Hollis only belched in the morning air.

That should startle the mosquitoes, Timothy thought. *Why did I get myself into this? What reasons have I to shoot this redheaded buffoon? What good can possibly come from this?*

"Very well," said Ketch. "To begin." Ketch began to count as Timothy stepped forth. "One … two … three …"

Timothy stepped smartly as if he wanted to look especially gallant, wondering whether either of them could really go through with this. Hollis had called him a son of a bitch and spat on Timothy. At that moment, Timothy wanted no trouble, especially with the bully Hollis. Timothy knew in his heart that he had been out of line to go alone with Sarah Jean into that cotton storage house. Everyone thought he had raped her there. Sarah Jean had told that story to the slave, to the overseer, and then later she probably told Amanda and everyone else. In his foolishness, he'd let them all think what they would. He had not done the deed of which she'd accused him, but Hollis was angry and rightly so—if it were true. Yet Hollis had no rights to Sarah Jean … not really.

They had posted no banns. Damn. Maybe they deserve each other, he thought. *The decent thing to do—at the very least—would be to let the family know ahead of the damn marriage. There seems to be a lack of common decency here, especially in Hollis.*

Timothy thought Hollis had jumped to defend Sarah Jean's honor to somehow become more acceptable to her. He was quite a homely lad.

"Nine … ten … eleven … twelve," Ketch counted.

Timothy continued to step proudly.

The racetrack grass sparkled with beads of dew as they caught the rays of morning sun. A dog barked in the distance.

"Thirteen … fourteen, and fifteen …"

Hollis and Timothy turned to face each other.

I will do the noble thing, thought Timothy. He raised his pistol, paused, fired into the air, then dropped his arm to his side and stood still. The echo of his shot reverberated in the stillness.

Hollis took great pains to aim squarely at Timothy. Wobbling on his feet, he stopped once to wipe his brow with his sleeve. After a few moments, he fired the pistol.

Timothy flinched and turned his head as the pistol fired. The lead ball whizzed by his nose, creasing his right cheekbone, right at the corner under his eye.

He'd survived.

Afterward, his second, the one known as Jeroboam, told him, "You are certainly the composed one, Sir Timothy. Indeed, you are, sir. Hollis was trying to kill you. He always does. That was the closest he has come to his mark. He doesn't like pretty boys. Carry your wound proudly. It is your mark of courage, your badge of pride. For a damn Yank, you're a rather good sport. Mind, now, if you place salt along that wound, it might scar a bit more."

Jeroboam turned to leave.

"The best, Sir Timothy," he said. "Oh, by the way, you are welcome in our club if it suits you. You've earned that privilege. Seek us, if you will, among the Knights of Retribution. An advertisement in the Charleston *Mercury* will find us, and we will find you. Remember, from this day forward, you are *Sir* Timothy."

Jeroboam reached into his vest pocket and handed Timothy a silver Saint Christopher medallion with the initials TWC engraved on one side.

"A memento for you. I hoped you would be alive to receive it. If not, well … I would have placed it in your pocket." He paused for a moment. "I know you're from West Point," he said pensively. "I give you the benefit of any doubt. Things are not always what they seem. You are a good man, Sir Timothy. May God bless you and be always with you.

"By the way, that little one, the one we call Sir Namby-Pamby … he belongs to a prominent family hereabouts, as do we all. But Namby's grandfather was a Revolutionary War hero … a French Huguenot. He admires you greatly. And you are Amanda Worsham's beau, are you not? Take care of her. I know I told you we stand by the notion we do not know each other. But, Sir Timothy, I believe you do know Sir Namby—or you will. And now *we* know you, don't we?" Jeroboam saluted and turned to join the rest.

Sir Namby-Pamby, thought Timothy. *From what I have heard, I think you are Charles Videau. But what does it matter?*

The group of five left in the two carriages. The others chatted among themselves, but Hollis remained silent as they left. In a moment, Timothy stood alone with the snorting drunkards and his horse. After a moment, he began to sob, his salty tears running easily along the pistol ball wound, causing it to smart sharply.

"I must leave this place," he spoke to the morning sunlight and to the two drunks.

Swinging into the saddle, he rode out of the Washington Racetrack, a different person from the one who'd come to fight the duel. Now he was *Sir* Timothy, whatever that meant. And he was on his way out of Charleston.

About sundown that same day, Sam, the office boy, came running toward Worsham House. When he arrived, he told how Timothy Caldwell was hiding in the army quarters.

"Mister Hollis done fought him in a duel, Miss Manda," Sam reported. "He was shot but not bad hurt, your Mister Timothy."

Amanda thanked Sam and left for the army quarters as soon as her carriage was ready.

Why did Timothy not come to see me? she wondered. *It is peculiar, that.*

She arrived too late. Timothy had already caught the northbound packet to Philadelphia.

Chapter 65

Marriage of Convenience

Amanda Worsham
Late September 1835
Charleston, South Carolina

ONCE SHE'D TOLD HIM SHE was pregnant with Hollis's child, Sarah Jean and Hollis were married soon after the duel. Nobody but Amanda and Hollis believed her story. When Joseph—after completing his preliminary business in Boston—returned to Charleston at the end of August, he promptly disinherited Sarah Jean and told her never to see him again. Then he and Mother Patience left.

If that wasn't enough, Amanda received a letter from Sally in Bermuda, saying Arabella was afraid Leonora Videau was about to put her slaves on the auction block because of a financial cutback. Arabella had actually sent a message in some fashion to Moses and Sally in Bermuda. Sally begged Amanda, *in excellent handwriting*, to please save Arabella from the slave auction. When Hollis heard of it, he demanded Leonora sell Arabella to him. Amanda objected, and Hollis threatened to shoot Arabella.

Does Hollis only know how to get drunk and shoot people? Amanda thought. *Well, he knows how to rape women, doesn't he?*

How could anything get worse?

In two months, Amanda received word that Timothy had run away from West Point. Immediately, Mother Patience had used the military and a Yankee detective firm to locate Timothy. She had also used her influence in Washington to obtain an army commission for him in the Florida territory.

Chapter 66

Lieutenant Caldwell

Timothy Caldwell
October 1835
South Florida

LIEUTENANT TIMOTHY CALDWELL RAN AS quietly as he could through the darkness, through the rough undergrowth, and along the weed-choked swamp trail. His wet leather boots, coat, hat, and bloused cotton pants protected him somewhat. Soon, it would be dawn, but for now, darkness still surrounded him. Certain he had seen something in the swamp off to his left, but peering into the deep shadows, he couldn't be certain what it was. Indians, Negroes, and Spaniards ... he couldn't be sure.

A sound startled him. He dropped to his knees in the weeds, then fell over flat on his back as the sergeant had taught him to do. That way, as it became light, he could see all round himself instead of just to the front ... improving his chances of surviving an ambush—something they hadn't covered at The Point: *Indian war tactics*. That was a business practiced by Francis Marion with his band of wild men, the ones who'd been so successful against the British Army. Many men had lived to tell about it, but that was a long time ago.

Timothy thought, briefly, that the military was mighty slow to catch on. He couldn't have learned Indian tactics at The Point even if he *had* finished. It was time some variation in "civilized" combat methods came about.

Learn by doing, isn't it?

The sergeant was a survivor, a man experienced in the ways of the Seminole, an Indian fighter. Whatever the sergeant said, Timothy determined to remember. Timothy wanted to be a survivor too.

The Seminole warriors had slaughtered many young men sent here by the army to "clean up" this Indian problem. But the Indians had made a mockery of the military's ways of fighting in the swamp. Timothy wondered how the soldiers with him were doing and where they had hidden. Well, they were on their own now.

As regulars, these soldiers comprised a small part of Company A, the United States Sixth Infantry, their job to ferret out and eliminate any Seminole people or property. Each man wore a hodgepodge of cotton and leather clothing, a uniform of sorts, each a different version. Some wore the summer uniform; some wore the winter; all of them ragged and dirty. The last few weeks had been spent slogging through bloody hell. But the sweat-soaked leather did give some protection against the mosquitoes.

The journey to the north had been more a trek through a hellish quagmire than an organized expedition. The odor of sweat-soured clothing clung to the soldiers as if it were a rude accompaniment, a backdrop, to the clouds of mosquitoes and other biting insects that hung everywhere, even in the darkness of the morning.

"Geez," came the hushed voice of young Jenkins, one of Timothy's men. "What'd we stumble into now?" Jenkins groaned. "What the hell are we doin' down in the weeds? I thought it was time for a smoke break. Geez." Jenkins paused, then groused, "And anyway, I could *piss* over a horse."

Muffled laughter rose from the men circled around Timothy.

"Quiet, men," the sergeant warned, speaking in a loud whisper. "Keep it down. There's no bloody horses about. But if the Indians are, they'll find you in the dark. You don't want me to have to send your balls home to your sweetie in a box, now, do you? Gaters will eat everything else."

"Why won't they eat ballocks?" a voice whispered. It was Geeter.

"Well, Geeter," the sergeant said, "troopers know gaters hate Yankee ballocks. Makes them real mad."

"How can you tell when a gater is mad, Sarge?" said Geeter.

"When he's got you by the ballocks, Geeter ... you'll know," said the sergeant.

More muffled, nervous laughter rippled through the night, then silence.

It's late and a long way to go before sundown, Timothy thought, trying to think of other things.

The magnolias would be in bloom now in Charleston. Thinking it might be safe, he rolled over onto his stomach. Dawn was breaking in the swamp. Creepy things could be felt and seen everywhere.

Timothy remembered the spring party Mother Patience had arranged for Amanda in Charleston. There had been magnolia blossoms cut and placed behind or under the corner chairs, and in the evening, the room filled with their sweet aroma. He'd been the guest of honor.

But here the thick, sticky, sweet smell of decaying things permeated the air—things that once had life. He hoped he wouldn't soon join them in their lifeless, decaying rest.

Maybe there really is no danger here. Ah, this is but a small diversion, he thought, *a journey through the swamp that undoubtedly will end well. Indeed, the trek upriver from the bay had gone well ... except for the snakes and insects. So far there only has been fear of the one and the nuisance of the other.*

The bay was named *La Baye du S. Esprit* on the century-old French *Carte*. The trek roughly paralleled the route of Hernando de Soto.

On that map ... was that French, Spanish, or Latin? he wondered.

It was almost unbelievable. Alligators, snakes, insects, panthers, and Seminole were everywhere. Something lurked out there. Timothy could feel it. And what about the rumor of Spanish ship crews taking on stores along the wild expanse of beaches? Rumors of their presence persisted. The Spanish didn't own this place anymore.

But it's so quiet. Timothy's thoughts rambled. He remembered breaking camp that morning just before dawn ...

The small company of soldiers had moved north from a point near Lake Hitchapuckcasy, or Hicpochee—whichever version one preferred of the Indian name for the small lake west of Lake Okeechobee.

That was one of the troubles with this godforsaken, mosquito-infested place: everyone had taken a shot at naming the territory around here. First, the Indians named the lake. Then the Spanish, the French, and the English tried to figure out what the Indians had said. All anybody had to do was ask the Seminole people, but nobody seemed to care what the Indians had to say. All anyone really wanted to do now was kill Indians.

The army called this whole area East Florida.

What did it matter, anyway? East. West. Who would ever want to live here?

Timothy looked straight up into the darkness and saw the flash of a shooting star streak across the sky. He made a wish. The beginning of a warm glow shone to his right. Sunrise was coming.

He wanted to be back with Amanda wherever she chose to be: Charleston, Manchester, Boston, New York. It didn't matter anymore about proving himself to her, that he could support her. He was sorry he had made such a fool of himself with Sarah Jean. Why he'd ever thought Sarah Jean was a goddess, he would never know.

Sarah Jean's as bad as I am. She'd accused me of raping her. Why had she done that? What did it mean?

Then Timothy thought about his birth mother, the beautiful French woman named Jeannette.

Jeannette abandoned me. Why had she done those things? What was her excuse to have behaved that way? Did it really make any difference? He thought not, but the sick, empty feeling inside wouldn't go away. *Wherever she is, she's probably lonely too. Ah well. If I ever get another chance to live my life the right way, Amanda will be all I will ever worry about.*

And Mother Patience, who had taken care of him but had refused to let him live with her. *She must be ashamed of me*, he thought.

But she had seen to it that he'd been offered a commission in the army fighting the Seminole in Florida.

Life is hard.

Suddenly, a commotion stirred behind him—gunfire.

His sergeant yelled, "Hold your fire. Hey … hold your fire. What the hell are you people doing? Don't shoot anymore. You're gonna hit your own men."

The guns fell silent.

"On your feet, men," screamed the sergeant again. "Snakes are here. They're everywhere! One just struck at me. And there's quicksand. Look to yourselves."

Timothy stood up. It was beginning to be light enough for him to see. More gunfire rang through the swamp, but he saw no Indians, only heard Spanish being spoken and a flurry of gunfire. During the volley, a projectile struck the ground at his right and ricocheted into his leather hat. He had been hit in the temple by a lead ball, probably by one of his own men.

He couldn't see. Beginning to feel weak in his knees, he fell forward on his face and saw stars, as if he were looking again at the now-sunrise-splashed sky. His consciousness faded to blackness.

He neither saw nor remembered any more after that.

Chapter 67

Wake Up, Lad

Timothy Caldwell
October 1835
South Florida

DARKNESS HAD DESCENDED BY THE time Timothy awoke.

God … my head hurts, he thought. Looking around in the darkness, he saw little and had no idea where he was. Suddenly he thought, *Who am I?*

Nothing. He didn't know *who* he was or *where* he was. The business of thinking was difficult. Awake, there were no dreams, no thoughts that meant anything to him, only confusion and pain. He rolled over on his side and fell back into nothingness.

Chapter 68

Very Well, I'm Awake, but Who Am I?

Timothy Caldwell
November 1835
South Florida

It was daylight when he again reached consciousness. Someone had tucked old rags about him, and furs covered him over. He was lying on a makeshift bed, a trench dug into the ground and filled with corn shucks for cushioning.

Corn shucks? he thought. He sat up, a severe pain in his groin greeting the sudden movement. *Nauseating*, he thought. *Oh, dear God ... that hurts.* He reached for his groin with both hands. Well. He sat there for a few minutes wondering what to do next.

An attractive woman with black hair shot with a streak of silver on one side and wearing animal skins lifted the deerskin flap that served as a door to the tentlike room and entered.

"Are you going to live, Beautiful One?" she asked, smiling. "By god, for a *gadjo* trooper, you're really something."

Nothing entered his mind in the way of a reply. Instead, he sat there with both hands rubbing his groin, rocking back and forth.

"You might as well just sit there and hold your balls. There's not much else you can do until that wound heals. Do you still not know who you are? I found this in your things. It's a Saint Christopher medal with the letters TWC engraved on it. That you, Trooper? TWC your name?"

He had no thought except for the pain.

"Do you like it here, love?" she asked.

"No."

"Why?"

"I don't know," he said. "What's your name?"

"Depends who you talk to."

"What do I call you?"

"Baba Lou."

"Who am I?" he said. "Baba Lou, do you know me? Why am I here? Where is this place?"

"We're in the middle of a swamp. Don't know the exact name. I just found this island some years back. The Seminole people leave me alone because I'm crazy."

"Crazy? What do you mean?"

"Bad medicine. They don't like my friends."

"Who are your friends?"

"Cat." She paused. "Cat ... Cat Ballocks."

A strange cough sounded outside. The deerskin flap parted, and a huge, coal-black panther stalked in, its muscles rippling fluidly along its body.

He felt no fear of the cat, but he wondered how he knew what this thing was, this panther. The panther purred in a rough and thunderous way.

"There are two of these," Baba Lou told him. "One black as Lucifer's shadow, the other albino. Brother and sister ... Cat is her *binak*. Her twin, as Gypsies say, but those two are opposites in every way."

"Albino?"

"All white, as white as snow ... but her eyes are pink."

"Albino ... white ... snow?"

"Yes, love. You really had a blow to your head, didn't you?"

He nodded but could summon no image with the thought. He took his hands from his groin and rubbed his forehead.

"Headache," he said, a puzzled look on his face.

"Yes. Say, Beautiful One, how about you get up and put these clothes on?"

"What clothes?"

"This is your uniform. I patched the hole in your trousers. I think someone poked you with a sword."

"Why would someone do that?"

"To see if you were dead."

"Did you find me like that?" he said.

"No. Some of my friends from Barcelona brought you here."

"Is this Spain?"

"Florida. My friends come two, three times a year. They get water, sometimes hunt for food, sometimes hunt for me."

"Who are they?"

"Sailors, marines, men off Spanish ships that stop here. You were lucky not to meet them in a fight. They took pity on you, love. You're the first really beautiful man I've seen who is not Gypsy, not from Spain or Cuba. They are the chosen ones, you know. Those Spaniards, God has given them the lime … the tropical West Indian fruit. You know what I mean?"

He stood up. His body was stiff, but the wound in his groin was the worst of it. He had no idea what she was talking about.

"The place they found you," she said. "That was the Spring of Life. It's an old Caribe Indian joke. So many snakes live there you really have to watch yourself, or maybe you die there. Snake bites you, you probably fall in a hole and drown—quicksand and all. Really funny, eh?" Her eyes sparkled. "Your friends, the men who were with you, bolted and left you for dead. My friends, the Seminole, go there for water and catch snakes for food. Maybe you stay away from that place from now on," she said, laughing. "Sorry that hurts. You get better … we'll see if that equipment works as good as it looks." Baba Lou pointed to his groin. "We know you're not Jewish. You've not been circumcised."

Suddenly he realized he was naked.

Cats, Spanish ships, soldiers … Rambling thoughts began to trouble him.

"Do I have a name?" he said.

"I'm certain you do. But for now, I'll just call you Trooper. If I were a man, I wouldn't care for someone calling me Beautiful One."

"Yes. Tell me," he said, "why do you live here in the swamp with a black panther named Cat? And what kind of name is Baba Lou? Are you from Spain?"

His thoughts were beginning to run together in sentences, but he still had no idea who he was.

"Baba Lou means 'Natural Wild Spirit.' The Spanish sailors call me that. The name came from an old Caribbean Indian legend."

Baba Lou paused for a moment. Then she smiled.

"Actually, one day I laughingly called my Spanish captain friend 'O Babo.' And the captain said, 'Why do you call me that?' Then I said, 'Because you remind me of my father. O Babo means "Pop" in the language of the Gypsy.'

"The captain said with a twinkle in his eye, 'Then I will call you Baba Lou. It means "wild and crazy bitch" in the language of the Caribe.' When he finished laughing he said, 'Baba, you're a pretty good friend for a sailor to find in his bunk.' At least I think that's what he said … he said it in Spanish." Baba Lou threw her head back and laughed loudly.

"You have no other name?" Trooper asked.

"Oh, I have a name. My name really is not important. I was born in Philadelphia. My family is Roma—Gypsies. But I gave all that up to come here."

"Why?"

"I like this place."

"And Cat? You like him too?"

"Cat and I tolerate each other. Gypsies as a rule don't trust cats. Cat's mother stood over there by that dead tree watching me for a while, then brought her two cubs to me some years ago … right before she died. She'd been shot through the stomach with a lead ball."

"Where's the white one?"

"She wanders. Stays away until she gets ready to come back. She'll come home soon now."

"What do you call her?"

"Hissy. She's an ill temper about her. And she reminds me of a ghost. She'll stand and watch you, then she'll twitch her tail around herself three times … as if she were crossing herself once … twice … thrice. It's really spooky."

That word brought a chill to him. Ghost? Hissy? He saw in his mind's eye a fierce white panther with pink glowing eyes hissing with a great show of ill temper.

"Does Hissy seem macabre to you … like a ghost?" he said.

"Not to me. But the Seminole are afraid of her."

"Swamp?" he said. "There are snakes here?"

"Cat eats them. Anything that crawls will probably be his dinner."

Trooper wondered if he would be next. "Why does Cat stay with you? Do you talk to him or something?"

"No. Cat was born with three testicles. He's not interested in mating. He stays with me and hunts this area for food. A strange family, that bunch of panthers. The mother trusted me to raise her young, one as black as old Coalie's ass, the other white as snow. But the mother panther had a proper color about her, a dirty ginger, almost burnt gold. She was pretty."

"What date is this?"

"It's November 1835. You've been unconscious nearly three weeks. I fed you, bathed you, and saw to your needs during that time. I even shaved you a time or two."

Embarrassed, he felt his dark skin turn a bright red.

"What about that scar on your cheekbone, Trooper? You don't know about that either, do you?"

"No."

Baba Lou crossed over to a shelf where three leather pouches hung and brought a small pinch of leaves and several sticks of bark to him.

"Here. Chew on this while you dress yourself. Your headache will get better."

He watched in amazement as she placed her hands on her head and removed her hair. "It's a wig, Trooper," she said. "I made it from my own hair. She shook it for a moment, as if it were a dust mop. Then she hung the wig on a pole. Her natural hair was close cropped and looked pretty much the same as the wig: black with a white streak on one side.

"Sure is hot," she said.

Baba grabbed a dress from her rack. To Trooper it was pretty, all white and grays … and black, a lot of black.

"This is my Gypsy dancing frock," she said, laughing. "How do you like the colors?"

"Colors?" he said. "All I see is black and white … and different shades of gray. It reminds me of a folk dress, I think …" He thought he knew whatever that was but found he did not.

"You don't see these colors? You must be color-blind, Trooper. To the Gypsy, color is everything … ask any *gadje*." She laughed and put the dress back. "There's a walking stick there by the door. When you're ready, come out. I've cooked stew. Soon you'll be able to travel. I want to take you to the village and see if there's a reward out for you. I think you belong to someone. Whoever that is must surely be missing you by now."

"Baba, what is a *gadje*?"

"Non-Gypsy … I don't believe you are Gypsy. Therefore, you are *gadje*."

Baba Lou left him alone in the tent room, and he began to consider how attractive she was to him.

At once many thoughts confronted him: lights, sights, sounds. And then, too, his mind filled with nothing. He had no idea who he was.

Troopers chewed the leaves and bark Baba Lou had given him and felt better having done so. Afterward, he went out to sup with Baba Lou. He found her squatting beside the fire. She'd already begun to eat.

Baba Lou gestured toward a tin cup and motioned for him to dip from the pot of stew.

"Te den, xa, te maren, denash!" she said. "'If they offer food … eat. If they beat you … run for your life.' It is an ancient Roma proverb of life on the road."

After serving himself, Trooper squatted beside her. The stew was good, but he was getting sleepy as he drank the broth from it. She handed him a spoon that she drew from a pouch she wore about her waist.

"The gnats are like spice to the food, Trooper. Good thing. We have so damned many of them."

When he finished, she told him it was time to sleep and sent him into the tent.

He fell asleep with little difficulty.

In the morning, Baba Lou was gone. Her wig was missing, so he walked outside to confirm it. Yes. She was gone. He didn't see the black devil cat, either. Therefore, thinking it was well nigh time to bathe himself, he stripped and folded his clothing, placing it carefully on a clean stone, then waded into the black water.

That was a mistake.

Immediately, a black serpent that had been sunning on a rotting log slid into the water and swam straight toward him.

God, he thought, *it must be a mamba or a cottonmouth. Those are the only snakes that will attack a person. How do I know that?* he wondered. Then, because he knew he couldn't escape from the serpent, he screamed. Before he had time to think of what else to do, two things happened:

First, Cat, the black panther, bounded toward the inky water from some hiding place in a tree, the bulk of its weight striking Trooper against his left hind shoulder, hurtling him into the rotting log face down. He saw stars but struggled to his feet, screamed, then jumped for the nearest tree and climbed toward safety.

Next, Cat darted from the scene with the black serpent clamped in its jaws.

A belated breakfast? Trooper thought, shuddering.

As he tightly held the tree limb, Trooper remembered his name. Timothy Willard Caldwell, the "TWC" engraved on his medal.

"Dear God," he said, out loud. "I owe my life to this group of social misfits. I am Timothy," he said. "But really, who am I?"

Memories came to him now in a cascade of images. As he slid down the tree, he heard laughter from the underbrush across the creek, the playful laughter of Seminole camp women who had ventured out of hiding for a better view of the proceedings.

Over the next two weeks, Timothy remembered meager, general things about life and everyday matters, but after that nothing remained beyond his name, Timothy Willard Caldwell.

And in the night, when Baba Lou cuddled with him, she told him of many things. Could be he would need to know such things. Secrets of the Seminole warriors, secrets of love in the night. He accepted all she told him. If knowledge brought success, his providence could only flourish as a Seminole … for now.

He learned of *Big Medicine*, of *Sweet Medicine*. He heard stories of *The Prophet* and other great shamans. He learned the method of time reckoning before a great battle. The Seminole leader passed around bundles of red sticks to each of the groups.

One stick thrown away—one day's passing. Why count the passing of days in that manner? It hurt his head to speculate. *Red Sticks? What the hell is a red stick?*

"Sure, the Seminole respect you as a warrior," Baba Lou said, her face resting on a pillow. She pushed herself up on her elbows. "I mean, soldiers in general. My people—the Seminole are my people now—respect the soldiers from up north as warriors … maybe not great warriors, or even good warriors, but warriors just the same. That entitles soldiers to be treated with esteem and caution, else they might crawl up to you at night with contempt and slit your throat … like a wild dog … or a white settler trying to steal their land.

"It's Great Spirit that sets men aside from the beast, Trooper," she said. "Of course, I like it when you sometimes act the part of a beast, Pretty One." She laughed. "At least I can tell you're thinking about sex.

"But Great Spirit speaks to men. Someone like the Prophet will hear and know what to speak to the rest about whatever is revealed. The fox waits for the rabbit. When the time is right, the fox catches the rabbit and eats it for dinner. But the Seminole, with cunning of Great Spirit, can wait and catch both fox and rabbit, if that be the hunter's plan. It is the hunter's choice. It is the way of Great Spirit. Survival is not a choice. No one has choice without the Great Spirit. And what will your choice be? Always listen, Trooper. The Spirit may speak to you. White men call Great Spirit God."

Trooper listened, only to wonder what her point was. He liked the way she smelled in the bed.

Chapter 69

No Conscience? No Shit

Timothy Caldwell
December 1835
South Florida

Some days Baba left Timothy alone. On those days he stayed in the campsite and tried to remember. His thoughts proved to be poor company.

A hawk circled overhead. *Very well,* he thought. *She tells me I'm a trooper. Is that military? Maybe someday I will know. For now this wild woman likes me, and I can live with that. Maybe the uniform she found me wearing belonged to someone else.*

He leaned forward until he could see his groin injury, probing it with his fingers. Perhaps it was time to try out his equipment. He seemed to know all about that sort of thing and experienced no problems having a part of himself stand firm in the night.

One item notably missing from his newfound awareness was his conscience. No voice inside spoke to him of virtue. But he was able to reckon time.

No conscience … no shit. What difference does that make?

He thought the month might be December.

Chapter 70

Oso Río Takes a Note to the Army: Rescue Timothy Caldwell

Timothy Caldwell and Colonel Ballard
December 1835
Fort King, Florida

Two weeks later, the army came to pick Timothy up. Baba Lou had sent a message to a nearby garrison for them to do so. She'd sent it by means of a runaway slave, a swamp trader and accepted-as-equal "Seminole" warrior she knew, a big man with nut-brown skin named Oso Río. Timothy had seen him once when the man had visited Baba. Easily seven feet tall … and heavy, his feathered turban seemed to float birdlike through the shadows and into the sunlight as he walked through the stand of hickory trees surrounding the camp. *Oso Río*, he thought. *I'm saved by a dark-skinned giant.*

* * * * *

Colonel Ballard, a representative of Washington's War Department, sat with crossed legs smoking his Cuban cigar and watching a handsome young officer brace to attention before the acting Fort King duty officer. The DO for today was Lieutenant Constantine Smith. Ballard and Smith had become friends.

The young man saluted Smith and said, "Lieutenant Timothy Caldwell reporting for duty, sir."

Smith returned the salute.

So this is the errant Florida lieutenant I'm to locate, thought Ballard, *the "special" young man named Timothy Caldwell. That simplifies my Fort King business. This Caldwell is known for having well-placed friends in Washington. Why, Caldwell, your "special" uniform is little more than rags. Special, indeed. The only special thing about errant officers such as you is a knack for staying in trouble … and for getting in the way.*

Ballard had received a dispatch now tucked inside his leather travel pouch about Caldwell that had come from Secretary of War Cass. Long ago, while still in Washington, Ballard had read the dispatch. In it, Cass had instructed Ballard directly to see to this man's assignment with the inspector general's staff. Ballard shook his head.

The IG. Now there's a muffin butt outfit, if ever there was one … a small group of men dedicated to the notion that a modern, well-trained army somehow had the obligation to "right" itself. There wasn't a bloody general in the lot. Inspectors general, my ass! The army ought to be worth more than any state's militia in that respect—as far as being right. But right itself? Why, the regular army is right enough. There's no need for any other "righting."

He'd taken limited action on the Cass dispatch and issued orders for Caldwell's commission reinstatement should he ever be found. Now, here at Fort King, stood young Caldwell—right across the room.

Ballard twitched, almost a shudder, against the heavy Florida humidity, then studied the floor.

Smith had his orders. Sure, Caldwell would have his commission reinstated. He'd probably be a line officer. But there would be no duty for him with the inspectors general. Ballard, on his own initiative, had changed that part. Young Caldwell was noted for his knowledge of the Seminole—in particular, Seminole fighting techniques. *Why, those savages won't wait like civilized gentlemen for battle*, he thought, *for their chance at glory. No. They waited prone behind trees, in tall grass, like snakes waiting for blundering fools to pass by.*

No, this Caldwell could serve the army better in the field. The army can use his knowledge.

After explaining about Secretary Cass and the War Department—in particular, someone's interest in Timothy Caldwell's progress in the military—Smith stopped speaking and looked away for a moment.

"Just what is it, Lieutenant?" he asked. "What is it you've learned? What kept you alive all these many weeks? It's my understanding you camped with the Seminole for a time. What can you tell us about them, eh? Anything useful?"

Ballard uncrossed his legs and rose to his feet. "I wish we had some bloody intelligence in this war," he said. "Traditionally, we know more about our enemy than he knows about us ... that is, until now. How can we win a war with these bastards? We know almost nothing about them. At ease, Lieutenant."

Timothy stood at ease, thinking that the army needed is its own *Big Medicine. And Ballard needed more Sweet Medicine at home.*

"What don't you know, sir?" he asked, facing Ballard.

"What we want," said Ballard, "is to round up all these aboriginal dingleberries and move them off by themselves, that's what. It would be easier, I think, to round up all the bloody alligators ... or snakes. Maybe what we need is the army equivalent of Saint Patrick, eh?"

"Ran all the snakes out of Ireland, didn't he?" Timothy commented.

"Aye."

Lieutenant Smith leaned back in his chair and frowned. "They're too damn smart to be rounded up, if you ask me. Seminole hide in the swamp, disappear for days at a time. They aren't afraid of us. They aren't afraid of snakes, either. I hear they eat them. And do you know how Seminole prepare for battle? They all drink a strong purgative. Yes, that's what. They call it black drink. Spend their time running to the woods. *Squirts—*"

Ballard interrupted him. "Caldwell, maybe you can help with this bit of information." He crossed his arms. "One of our informants told Wiley Thompson that the very next Seminole attack would be from Fort Brooke at Christmas with three red sticks. What the hell does that mean? Unless ... Thompson is the government agent, you know. Isn't that what these damn Seminoles are called anyway … Red Sticks? What kind of a bloody message is that? What do they take us for, anyway? Fools? The very idea."

Timothy faced Ballard. "I'm sorry, sir. Say that again, please."

Ballard took a step forward. "Does it mean that on Christmas Day we can expect an attack here at Fort King by three of these bloody Seminoles? Tomorrow's the Eve of Christmas in Washington. And by God … I suppose it is here as well."

Timothy knew almost at once what the message meant. "Sir, I beg to differ. That's not what the message says."

"Oh?" Ballard's, eyes flashed.

"Uh, no, sir. The attack will come three days after our Christmas celebration, sir."

"Very well, Caldwell … where? Here at the fort?" Lieutenant Smith said.

"The attack probably will come against a group moving between forts, sir. Maybe here or on the way to Fort King. Maybe somewhere else. It will be wherever the army is on that third day. What military detachment is moving?"

"Company B, Fourth Infantry under Major Francis Dade would have left Fort Brooke by now," Lieutenant Smith said with a smile on his face. "They'll be bringing all that damned equipment, heavily laden wagons, and everything else. And there are others too. Maybe a hundred men or more, all coming here to Fort King. I'll wager your group of three bloody, red-assed Indians will give them a wide berth. Think of it, man. All that noise, the animals, and the men cursing. Ah. That would be a sight now, wouldn't it, Colonel Ballard?"

"All due respect, sir," Timothy interrupted, "maybe you should dispatch a messenger—"

"Stand at attention, soldier," Smith ordered, his face red. "I don't like your damned intelligence. Three red sticks, is it? We'll see, won't we? I'll not commit any of our forces to a wild goose chase like that, surrah. Logistics is the game played here today. Anyway, that's why I am here, to moderate such trash as this. There's no way the

Indians can just have their way with us. If they decide to attack us here at the fort, it'll be over my dead body."

* * * * *

The white man's holiday came and passed. Two groups of three red sticks were counted out, one each by leaders of two Seminole fighting groups.

About eleven o'clock the morning of December 28, a massacre occurred along the hundred-mile-long sandy road leading from Fort Brooke to Fort King. One hundred eight soldiers led by Major Francis Dade were killed. Three Seminole died in the fighting; five others shed their blood on the sand—yet lived to fight another day. In time, this event would become known as The Dade Massacre.

Later the same day, after dinner, the great Seminole chief Osceola hid with a band of sixty warriors in the tall grass beside Fort King. Osceola undoubtedly had timed the event by counting his bundle of red sticks. The warriors remained hidden for two days awaiting time and opportunity; then, as soldiers came outside for exercise, Osceola fulfilled a portion of his destiny. He saw Wiley Thompson and Lieutenant Constantine Smith strolling nearby in quiet conversation along a path beside the grassy area. Osceola and his band of warriors surprised—and killed—both Thompson and Smith.

Chapter 71

Amanda's Private Talk with Patience
Timothy Is Missing in Action?

Amanda Worsham
December 1835
Charleston, South Carolina

ON A SATURDAY, NEAR THE end of December, Patience asked to have a private talk with Amanda.

Patience sat quite comfortably in the straight-backed chair with seat and back pads that Moses had made for Frances. But she was clearly nervous, Amanda knew, because the woman fidgeted with the buttons on her blouse and kept glancing out the window.

"The news of Timothy is not good." Patience reached for Amanda's arm. "The communiqué from the War Department said he's missing. Some awful battle in that swamp they call Florida."

"He may be alive," Amanda consoled, her eyes wide. "*I* think he is alive."

Patience shook her head. "Missing in that dreadful place means *dead*, I fear. In your mind, he may be safe, but time may dim your hope and dreams. But I have other things to tell you now. Shall we pray for our Timothy? We'll talk about him again when we have more information. Traveler will be in that Florida area March, next. He promised to check into this for me."

After a full minute, Patience continued, "I have something more important to tell to you than I ever thought I would reveal to anyone." Tears trickled down her cheeks. She took off her ruby and diamond ring and handed it to Amanda. "Here," she said. "This is yours. I want you to have it now. And, Amanda, there is a special brooch that goes with it, which I will give to you later. It's locked away with my secretary in Boston."

Amanda grimaced. "It is one of your most prized possessions," she protested. *But this ring—is it more important than Timothy?*

"It is proper to give someone you love something that you love yourself. If I didn't like it, it wouldn't mean as much to you now, would it?"

"No," she admitted. Amanda didn't know what to say. She was overwhelmed with the thought that Mother Patience loved her. "Whatever should I wear with this?" she asked, bewildered.

"Anything but a frown … anything at all. The full spectrum of colors in a rainbow will go with your eyes … and with that ring." Patience fell silent again, then looked up into Amanda's eyes and said, "I want to know what you plan to do with your life from this day forward. Do you have your heart set on anyone to marry … or will you spend the rest of your life alone?"

Amanda shook her head, clasping the ring tightly in her fist. *What was on Patience's mind?* A moment of silence passed as Amanda paced to the window then turned to face Patience.

When she put on the ring, she found it to be a little large for her slender finger. Amanda held her hand to the light and looked carefully at the ring. It boasted a cluster of diamonds and a heart made of rubies, the heart offset to one side.

What does that mean? It must have been especially made for Patience. Well, it is beautiful, but its design isn't exactly balanced.

"What will you do if something happens to Joseph?" Patience asked. "You are alone now, except for him, me, and maybe your people in Manchester. But your Aunt Meg must be in her late seventies. She's really too old to take care of herself. Could be you'll have to care for her soon, being that her husband died years ago."

"I don't know what to say, Patience. I have people to care for already. I, too, have responsibilities."

"You don't have those slaves anymore, do you?"

"No. I rewarded Moses and Sally with their freedom the year slavery was outlawed in the British Empire … in 1833. Emancipation came the first part of 1834. Moses and Sally are free in Charleston too. I filed the papers."

"Where are Moses and Sally?"

"In Bermuda. Moses is helping build ships in Saint George's. He loves to work with wood, and the shipyard loves his work. He and Sally should never have any trouble again. I certainly hope and pray they will not."

"Where would they be without you, Amanda?"

"That is a difficult question to answer." Amanda began to feel uneasy, but she kept her gaze directed into Patience's eyes.

"I had hoped to see you marry Timothy. But now he's gone."

"You said he was missing."

"Only God knows where he is or what happened to him. I'm afraid he's gone forever. The Timothy we knew perished in that god-forsaken place. There was an attack by rogue Spanish marines near a lake, near some little-known spring. And Timothy was severely injured. When the army rescue platoon arrived, they couldn't find Timothy. That place is riddled with snakes and quicksand." Patience broke down and began to sob, cradling her head in her hands. "I wanted him to marry. I wanted him to father a family of Caldwell children. The ones I never had with Willard. I'm barren, you see."

Amanda went to Patience and put her arms around her. "I don't think Timothy ever really wanted me, Mother Patience. He just ran away … ran away from West Point … ran away from me."

"I don't know about that," Patience objected. "But it doesn't matter. It doesn't change what I must tell you now. Nothing will change that. I've made up my mind."

"Why, Patience, whatever do you mean?"

Chapter 72

Patience's Will, Grace of God

Amanda Worsham
December 1835
Charleston, South Carolina

PATIENCE TOOK AMANDA'S HANDS INTO hers. "I have changed my will," she whispered. "If anything happens to me, you will inherit everything. Whatever I have."

"I don't need any more wealth, Patience. I really don't," Amanda objected. "Mother took care of that."

"That's the very reason I want you to have my wealth, too, Amanda. You'll not waste it or use it unwisely. I know you won't."

"What of Timothy? He may yet be found alive."

She ignored Amanda's statement. "I never wanted to leave it all to Timothy. I don't trust any man, especially with that much money. I've set up a trust fund in his name ... for him ... a million dollars. That's what I want him to have if he should ever return. If he's ... well, I'm assigning you to just see he gets it."

Patience squeezed Amanda's hand and took a deep breath. "I have obtained in Philadelphia what I believe to be good economic advice. For the better part of a year, I've been moving funds about in banks, mostly to London, some to Liverpool. It is all in my will. Be careful, Amanda. Politics in this country sometimes goes awry.

You and I must speak further of this, but for now, I am too tired … maybe soon?"

Amanda hugged Patience for a long time, feeling as if she had a mother again. *Maybe things will work out*, she thought.

"Amanda?"

"Yes?"

"In the Bible, you know, where Moses asked God about His name?"

"*I AM THAT I AM*"?

"Yes, that's what He said. More than it seems, I think."

"What, Mother Patience?"

"*I AM THAT I AM*. Don't you see? Like one of us saying, 'I laugh that I laugh' or 'I run that I run.'" Patience indicated the painting over the fireplace. "To the artist, shadows are everything," she explained. "Everything for the imitation of life. You stand in the glowing rays of God's grace … and it is the shadows you cast that set you apart from the rest. God will notice. I believe God said—"

Patience stopped speaking. She folded her kerchief, then looked again toward Amanda. "God said that He is life and … life is forever. God puts you here on earth for a time with but a wee bit of that life. A wee bit—but enough, to be sure. You must live, and you must love. Never waste a moment. Eternity is a long time to be someplace else with things here left undone.

Patience wiped a tear from Amanda's cheek. "You must love someone, Amanda," she said. "And you must love God. It's His longing that you do so. Life is precious. And you must ask Him for help. The Hebrew people were afraid of Him—afraid to call Him by any name. But you see, He did not really tell Moses what His name is— only that He is. You do not know His name—you cannot offend Him. At least not that way."

Patience rose from the chair and rubbed her hands together. "I've always wanted children," she said. "But I could not conceive. I pray your life will be different. God's gift to you is life, something but a part of His own. Your test is what you do with the life He gives you. Reach out to Him. Tell Him you love Him. More importantly, tell Him you need him."

"It's not what you have but what you do with what you have that counts," Amanda agreed. "Father always says that." Amanda knew that all the money and influence in the world cannot buy what only God can give. She thought of Sarah Jean and began crying again. *One child thrown away. At least the Worsham family still had the child of that last union, though the mother was dead.*

And Timothy, she thought. *Oh my. Could be he got away from Sarah Jean unscathed, clean. He'd really done nothing but act the idiot. Now maybe he's dead.* Amanda felt the urge to curse, but she kept it to herself.

"Almighty God talks to you, Amanda," Patience said. "Sure He does."

"I have never heard—"

"How else do you always *just know* what will happen?"

"You think that feeling of knowing is from God?"

"If you have Him in your heart, there is no room for any other spirit. Amanda, do you know that my late husband Willard was a cousin of John C. Calhoun?"

"No, I didn't know that."

"Well, he was. Calhoun's a fine-looking lad. Smart, but he's squandered God's gifts to him. He's a disgrace to the Caldwell family."

"Because of slavery?" *What has this story about Calhoun to do with anything? Rambling, that's what this is—nothing but rambling.*

"Yes," she said, "slavery. But he's right about states' rights and tariffs."

Amanda knew what Patience thought of slavery and slave states. Lengthy Calhoun speeches centered mostly around the support of slavery, slave states. Or of late, Calhoun had much to say about the Yankee Tariff.

But there are people who love to hear Calhoun speak. Beau Videau is one. Charlie Videau is another. States' rights are the latest song they sing in unison.

Patience interrupted her thoughts. "Amanda?"

"Yes?"

"Have you been to a picnic where Irishmen play those traditional games? Tug-of-war, stone throwing, pole tossing, hammer throwing—"

"I've seen Scots engage in those games, but Irish, you say?" *Here we go again.*

"In Boston a person can watch such as that. Firemen and the constabulary challenge one another."

"I once saw fire wagons race on Charleston city streets, Mother Patience. I found the spectacle dreadful. One wagon turned over. Horses lost footing on cobblestones, and they all fell. I can see the terror in those horses' eyes to this day and hear the men's screams. All Irishmen, I suppose. Did you know that a horse could scream?"

"Well, I didn't want to bring out such a memory, Amanda. I wanted only to make a point."

"Very well. Make the point."

"Yes. The tug-of-war … go back to that image for a moment."

"I see it in my mind's eye. Sweating bodies, Irishmen, the whole thing." *Whew. I really can almost smell it.*

"There's a never-ending contest of that sort in this country, Amanda."

"The Irish must be forever busy. Whatever do you mean, a contest? Are you saying there's a struggle between good and evil, something along those lines?"

"Not exactly. The contest is between states' rights and central authority."

"Federalists and—"

"No. Not that. Not political parties—that is not what I mean. Some sort of balance must be maintained, or the contest will end in freedom's destruction."

"Anarchy?"

"Worse. The reinstatement of feudalism."

"Mother Patience, can we please talk of other things?"

"If you like. But if we aren't forever mindful and take careful measures, the things I'm speaking of will pull this country apart. And most of all, God wants us to respect a human's life. Human life is human dignity, Amanda."

Patience fingered the cameo that she wore on her blouse, pausing a moment to catch her breath. "Irish play no part in this," she said. "I think I love them all. If only they would leave beer and whiskey alone."

"The South values its slaves," Amanda said. She thought Patience was trying to change the subject but clearly finding it hard to do.

"As property, not as human beings," said Patience after a moment of silence. "Amanda, have you read of runaway serfs?"

"Well, yes. The warlord or king would dispatch his ne'er-do-well court princes to escort the sheriff and fetch serfs who had run away. Is that what you mean?"

"Slavery isn't new, Amanda. One last image about the tug-of-war: the rope ... that rope really should be a chain, and each link ... each link another of our God-given human individual rights. It's our rights the struggle is about. Other people cannot necessarily assume your responsibilities. Some people are wicked. They kill all the ragtag and bobtail people they can't enslave. White settlers and the Seminole are an example of that situation. I don't know which is worse, enslaving people or killing them."

Dear God, Patience. Aren't we serious today?

"You know," Patience continued, "Andy Jackson is an acquaintance of mine. I'd hardly call the bastard friend, though. He helped the government kill a great many Indians, I think. And I guess he dreamed of building an empire for a time. But now he tells us the kindest thing we can do for our Indians is move them as far to the west as possible. Anyway, they do love to live isolated lives. Why should we just kill them? No white man will ever live out there in the western regions. We know that. It will always be a wild, uncharted area."

Amanda said nothing. She thought of the Lewis and Clark expedition.

"And speaking of Florida," said Patience, "do you know about Peggy Eaton?"

"The Peggy Eaton Affair back in 1831?" *Heavenly days ...*

"That's the one. Her maiden name was O'Neill ... a barmaid, I think. Not only was she disgraced, but her husband John Eaton,

Secretary of War under Andy Jackson, was forced to resign. Our friend Martin Van Buren resigned with him. None of that group favors Andy Jackson as president. Peggy Eaton disgraced all of Washington and especially John Eaton with her carnal inclinations. You know Andy Jackson married a woman not yet divorced? Bad luck, that." Patience frowned.

That Peggy Eaton business really was about states' rights, thought Amanda. *Jackson was against states' rights and John C. Calhoun was not—Jackson the statist, as it were. Moreover, wicked rumors linked Jackson to Aaron Burr ... rumors about forming a new "empire" with "emperor" Aaron Burr. Many Americans refused to believe the rumors. Burr was tried for treason but not convicted. Jackson wanted to distance himself from the whole affair. To counter the rumors, President Jackson opened the White House to each and all—especially to wild fur trappers and the like from Tennessee, men who chewed tobacco and spit into all the corners and fireplaces.*

Amanda thought about it. *John C. Calhoun is South Carolina, if one man is singled out for the job. His wife initiated the social upheaval centered on Peggy Eaton. The local news was stinging in its treatment when the story was current. And Calhoun really wanted to punish Jackson in some way. Jackson wanted strong central government and tariffs. South Carolina hated Jackson, along with his ideas. South Carolina hated tariffs also. And so did many others. It was as if faraway kings were in charge again—the same sort of thing that the Revolutionary War was fought over: faraway—too powerful—centralized government.*

Patience interrupted Amanda's thoughts. "I'm telling you this," she said, "because I hear Sarah Jean had her premarital carnal affair in England ... before she ever met our Timothy." Patience rubbed her cheek. "And I hear she forced a miscarriage."

"No doubt the rumor is true," Amanda sighed.

"Well, it happened in your precious Charleston, did it not? The only reasonable thing to come out of Washington's Peggy Eaton business was my friend Lewis Cass being appointed War Secretary in John Eaton's stead. Lewis obtained Timothy's commission. I spoke to him about it. But God help us, it may have been a terrible mistake.

John Eaton, by the way, is governor of the Florida Territory now. I almost forgot to mention that. Perhaps he can help us find Timothy."

Amanda smiled, wondering what to think of this news. She knew Patience received regular letters from friends in Washington.

"Amanda," said Patience, "recently Major Sylvester Churchill of the Florida Third Artillery was struck from his horse by a felled tree. He's the inspector general, you know. Our friend Lewis Cass will be in Europe soon, taking up his post as the new minister to France. Thank goodness. I've long ago arranged with Lewis for Timothy to be assigned to Churchill—if we ever find Timothy, that is. But Timothy can help Churchill with his duties mustering in new recruits and training them. I pray that if Timothy's alive, God never lets him resign his military commission. He's so lost on his own."

Chapter 73

Joseph's Hidden Past Is Hidden No More

Amanda Worsham
December 1835
Charleston, South Carolina

Patience paused for a moment to look out the window. "Amanda, have you read the Bard?"

"Well, yes. I have read many of his plays."

"*Antony and Cleopatra?*"

"Yes, several times. Miss Kemble, our governess in Charleston, loved it."

"Then you remember Messenger speaking to Mark Antony and saying, 'The nature of bad news infects the teller.'"

Amanda smiled. She remembered the line well. "Antony's answer," she said, "went something like this—first the messenger's line. Then Mark Antony's:

> Messenger: *The nature of bad news infects the teller.*
> Mark Antony: *When it concerns the fool or coward. On: Things that are past are done with me. 'Tis thus: Who tells me*

true, though in his tale lie death, I
hear him as he flatter'd.

Patience interrupted, "What do you think the messenger meant by that?"

"If the news is awful enough, then it harms the bearer, I suppose. Or maybe it means, please don't shoot the courier?" *Oh, the courier again, is it?*

"Yes. Sure, that's all well and good, but I have news to tell you concerning your father that may be better left unsaid. I simply don't know."

"I thought you were going to tell me something about Charlie Videau."

"What of Charlie Videau? Well, never mind. One thing at a time."

"Try me, Mother Patience. If you don't tell me about it, we may never know if it should be left unsaid." Amanda bit her lip. "Anyway, I have no premonition about it."

"But you see, because now I'm part of Joseph's future, he is part of my responsibility. The news taints me in its telling. It may be it's best not to know the future, Amanda. You would know, I think. But in this case, news of the past may simply hurt you."

"Go ahead."

"Not just yet."

Amanda shrugged her shoulders, a sick feeling welling up inside. This wasn't good. But she waited.

"It's the fault of rum," Patience said. "That's what I always thought. Rum's the root of it all."

"Father has no time for rum."

"My Willard did, God rest his soul. I blamed everybody, everything but myself. I was wrong, you see. Rum had nothing to do with it."

Amanda wondered what she meant.

Patience's hands shook. "Massachusetts upstart establishments make rum from molasses hauled out of the islands. Rum hauled by ships, Amanda. And you know, there was a time when I thought all the evils of the world came from rum … from demon rum, gin, sherry, and the like. It's the only real demon we routinely conjure up from hell, rum is."

"Demon rum?" Amanda saw mirth in this. Patience's strange ideas concerning rum seemed to fill this woman's every thought.

Patience nodded. "Yes. Only one demon per glass. That's what they say. Rum will not tolerate any other spirit. The navy uses rum worldwide to drive evil spirits from drinking water. And everyone knows it's the evil spirits that make us sick."

"Father hauls no rum. Nor does he use it. Why, I've never heard of that." All this talk of spirits was making her nervous.

"Evil ships' captains trade rum for slaves in Africa," Patience said. "The ships anchor at the beaches. The African chieftains meet the ships at the beach and trade hapless souls for rum. You know that's true, don't you?"

"Yes, I believe so."

"We all share in the guilt, you see. It's not the fault of the rum."

"I'm not sure I understand your point, Mother Patience. I mean, I do not use rum. I've freed my slaves. What guilt do I share?"

"Is it better, somehow, because African chieftains are involved?"

"Better than what?" Amanda asked. "Anyway, slavery trade is outlawed in the Empire. *Prior ownership* of slaves is lawful—right now, but not for long, I hope. We just spoke of that, didn't we?"

"What if ships filled their hold with slaves?" said Patience. "Hapless souls the crews caught themselves … caught somehow by trickery?"

"What difference would that make? I'll wager some were caught that way. Tell me about Father. I blame nothing on rum, Mother Patience … nothing." Amanda shifted her weight from foot to foot.

"Your father was born into wealth. That you know. But do you know he ran away from his safe harbor to seek his own fortune when still a young man?"

"No. That I did not know." *My Lord. What it this about?*

Patience twitched nervously and began to pant. She seemed to mix up her thoughts. "While in Liverpool, as a very young lad, your father spent his time lubricating the skids that led to the gates of hell with demon rum. He ran with the wrong crowd, as they say. He had the strength to tell me about it, and that's something in itself."

Patience was sweating through her blouse. Amanda suddenly could smell the mixture of Patience's perfume and body odor.

Does Father find that sexy or attractive?

"Traveler had already informed me of what our people knew, as he'd learned about it himself. That's Traveler's lot in life. Should anything, anybody, threaten our country in any way—well, that sort of thing's Traveler's business."

"Whatever do you mean? Father with the wrong crowd?" Amanda's eyes flashed with the news. *My father running about with ne'er-do-wells, with criminals? Nothing but a rum sot? Whatever will Patience tell me next?*

"He was involved with the selling of young white girls into slavery, Amanda—a practice called white slavery. Slavery by whatever name is an abomination in God's eyes and in mine. Joseph has since repented. He confronted the evil and the man in charge several years back, after your mother died, I believe. He made an arrangement, at that time, concerning trade in human goods … the selling of young women into prostitution in coastal cities in the States. Joseph did it to protect his family—you and your sister. Then it all went rather badly, and he told me about it. I contacted my friends in Washington, Traveler and the rest. With money and connections, plus the help of the British royalty, we destroyed the wicked business."

Amanda shuddered. "Father told you all of that?"

"Indeed, he did. If he hadn't, I wouldn't be here today about to go away with him. In his youth, Joseph was Sir Gay. When he first arrived in Boston, Traveler was looking for a Russian named Sergé, who was, to be sure, your father. That was a providential mistake. Joseph's traveling name was Sir Gay. Had Traveler recognized Joseph as the Sergé character at that moment, recognized him as the man suspected of running the white slavery ring, he might not have learned to trust your father. I might never have fallen in love with Joseph. Every person is entitled to make one terrible mistake. Your father made the same one twice. Mine was the way I treated young Timothy … the way I treated my Willard. So I made the same mistake twice. I'm trying, now, to rectify some of those mistakes. It's too late for Willard, but maybe it's not yet too late for Timothy—if he's alive. By the by, Amanda, if you really need help with something, Traveler's your man. I mean that sincerely. He's a *full commander* in the navy. And the navy assigned him to me—that is, to me as Ruby Heart. I pay all his expenses … and his salary." She made a sniffing sound, as if to punctuate everything she had said.

Amanda was speechless.

"The thing is, Amanda …" Patience rubbed her hands together. "The thing is, maybe it's like killing cockroaches."

"What?"

"When we cracked down on Sir Gay's London-based white slavery business, stepped on the cockroaches as it were, maybe more cockroaches lie hidden away still. By the way, Joseph asked me to have this talk with you. It's been driving him crazy. I dreaded telling you these things. But it's far better to have them behind us. I'm certain you agree."

Oh well, I'm certain God has forgiven poor Father. Can I do any less? She looked down in silence at the ring and its odd offset heart for a moment. "Patience, what does the design of this ring mean? I think it's simply too special. Odd. Spectacular." *We'll see if I can change the subject …*

Chapter 74

Ruby Heart
What the Hell Is That All About?

Amanda Worsham
December 1835
Charleston, South Carolina

"You certainly are *intuitive*, Amanda," Patience said. "Yes, the ring has meaning beyond style. It is for identification. In your own time, as you become *Ruby Heart*, you will understand. But I am too tired to talk about it now. There'll be another time. I'll tell you all about it. And about Ruby Heart." She hugged Amanda and left the room.

Ruby Heart—what the hell is that all about? Well, Mother Patience, thought Amanda, *I just don't know what to say.* She turned her hands palms up and raised them toward the ceiling.

"Do You really talk to me?" she asked God, looking at the wallpaper on the ceiling. "I wish You would speak louder."

As always, she heard no answer. But she did have an easy feeling about Timothy that seemed to grow stronger in her heart. *The news about Father?* It hurt to think those awful things of him. She loved him dearly. His stature had fallen somewhat in her eyes of late, however.

Oh, but what she suspected about her mother and Beau filled her thoughts. And the business about Charlie Videau—and many other things left unsaid. Secrets her mother never managed to tell before yellow fever took her to her Manchester grave. She'd only hinted at them, and that's what troubled her now.

Amanda cared little for rum, but gin with a quarter-lime suited her sometimes, with a little artisan well water and a pinch of salt … ice when you could get it … and a clump of rock candy.

What would Mother Patience think of that?

Chapter 75

Hollis Raped You?

Amanda Worsham
Mid-April 1836
Charleston, South Carolina

"Hollis raped you?" Just before the Ides of March, Arabella came crying to Amanda with a tale that Hollis had raped her and she thought she was pregnant. Amanda could not contain her anger. "What in the hell is the matter with Hollis? Is that all anybody does anymore—rape women?"

You spend a lifetime worrying, thinking that rape is the most awful thing that can happen to a girl—lady—and now Hollis provides a running tally of such. Damn!

What's next? she thought. *Hollis has a fit because I wanted to buy Arabella from Leonora. Now I know Hollis wanted the girl for his own household, all right. He wanted the girl for himself. Well, Sarah Jean would need some housekeeping help, but rape? That's really too much, even for Hollis. Hollis is crazy,* she thought in disgust. *He certainly needs to be taught a lesson. But so far there's no law that seems to care about such things. A Negro man on a white girl, yes. But a white man on a Negro girl is another story.*

The following seven months passed quietly.

Chapter 76

Sarah Jean Dies in Childbirth

Amanda Worsham
November 1836
Charleston, South Carolina

"Miss Manda ... Miss Manda!"
One late afternoon, Arabella's shrill voice found Amanda in the kitchen discussing the evening meal with Dora, the excellent new cook. Amanda was learning how to spice an apple pie. Amanda felt fortunate to have hired Dora, a free woman of color, as it was fashionable to say.

What's Arabella doing in town? Best to see about this.
Amanda hurried to the porch. The gray, rainy March morning seemed to hover all around her. She shivered as she straightened her apron, wondering briefly if it ever really snowed in Charleston. Maybe that was just a myth. It looked as if it might snow today, though.

"Oh, Miss Manda," Arabella cried as she ran up the walk, hands outstretched as if she were holding a great burden out in front of her. "You need to come quick. Miss Sarah's having her baby, an' she ain't doin' too good, no, she ain't." She began to cry.

"That child's not due for a fortnight, Arabella. Are you sure it's coming now?"

Arabella just nodded her head slowly.

There wasn't any use in pumping Arabella further. Amanda knew what the girl said was true. There'd been something awful about Sarah Jean's pregnancy all along. She'd purposefully miscarried the first baby. Now she was with child again, and there had been nothing but trouble.

"How did you get here from the farm, Arabella?"

"Ol' Hiram. He drove me in the mule wagon, he did. It's the trouble. Don't know what for to do, Miss Manda. Just don't know what. Ol' Moms Sooner sent me to fetch you, she did. Ol' Hiram, he say, 'Don't worry 'bout the mule, Arabella. Just jump up on the wagon,' or he say something like, 'At night, always take a lantern witcha to de outhouse.' Ain't no telling whatya fin' out dere.' He don't worry 'bout nothin', but I do, Miss Manda. I do."

Amanda thought briefly of the difficulties her mother had experienced, of the babies she'd lost. She missed Frances.

Best to get out to the farm and see about Sarah Jean, she thought.

She put her arm around Arabella, hating to see such anguish in the girl's face. Why should Arabella have to worry so about some white woman's baby problems? What responsibility was it of hers? She was seven months pregnant herself, which showed dramatically. She should be worrying about her own baby.

Amanda grimaced. *Damn this slavery, anyway. And damn Hollis Mackenzie.*

Arabella is Sally's cousin. If Hollis hadn't thrown such a fit, I could have bought Arabella when Sally asked me to, and Arabella would be free now. But Hollis said he would shoot her if I did that. Well, now we see where his superior guidance has led us.

"Ol' Mist' Hollis, he ain't goin' do nothin' right, I reckon."

"Where is he?"

"He's off drinking somewhere. You know how he is." Arabella looked at Amanda with heartache in her eyes.

Yes, Amanda knew how Hollis was—disgusting. She led Arabella inside, still hugging her.

"You go and tell Dora where I'm going. I'll see about Miss Sarah. Don't you worry anymore."

"Yes'm."

"And tell Dora I said to give you a bit of that apple pie when it's ready."

Arabella's face brightened a little. "I sho' will do that, Miss Manda."

Chapter 77

Amanda with a Baby to Raise
And Another as Well

Amanda Worsham
December 1836
Charleston, South Carolina

DURING THE RIDE ALONG THE sandy road that led to the farm, Amanda had time to compose herself and plan what she must do. The one-horse carriage was easy enough to drive, but she was afraid to hurry. Afraid to get there and afraid to delay. It was just awful about Sarah Jean.

If only she hadn't married that ne'er-do-well. Why in heaven's name does this family have to put up with so much? Money doesn't help a bit. If Sarah Jean had been the daughter of an overseer, Hollis never would have hung around. Sarah Jean had believed she was pregnant by that scoundrel. Now, that was a misadventure if ever there was one.

And poor, pregnant Arabella. Of course, that was Hollis's child too. Hollis had raped her. *Sick of Hollis*, she thought. *Aren't there any good men in the world?*

Sarah Jean had purchased farmland with money from her mother's estate. Hollis rebuilt an old double log cabin with a dogtrot midsection on the property and made it into their homeplace. The term *dogtrot* came about because dogs, possums, or any other critter could run freely on the open porch between the rooms. In addition, the cabin featured a wide front porch, and Hollis had covered the cabin itself with wood siding brought to Charleston from New England on Worsham ships.

When Amanda arrived at "Mackenzie Estate," as Hollis called it, she found a group of slaves standing in front of the main house. Moms Sooner, the old Negro midwife, was sitting in the yard in a rocking chair with a white baby wrapped in a torn blanket in her lap. The Mackenzie baby had come. Amanda knew it.

But what of Sarah Jean?

She had a sinking feeling. All at once, she knew Sarah Jean was dead.

And so she was. She had hemorrhaged to death. Something inside had burst when the baby came.

Amanda named the baby—a somewhat red-skinned baby with dark, curly hair—Joseph Worsham Mackenzie.

As time passed, Hollis refused to have anything to do with raising "Little Joe." And so Amanda took him to raise.

Damn Hollis Mackenzie. Amanda found herself repeating that phrase all too often as time wore on.

And later when things had finally settled down, Arabella had her baby, a precious little girl. She named the child Cassie May Johnson because Sally's people and Arabella's people were Johnsons.

It is a good name, Amanda thought, *a name Cassie May could go forth proudly into the world with.*

A child shouldn't be held accountable for the sins of the father. Arabella and Amanda both took upon themselves the role of mother for Cassie May and Little Joe, both fathered by Hollis Mackenzie. Amanda was dedicated to seeing that "her" children had the very best of everything—especially education.

Before Christmastide, Joseph and Patience came to call. They always traveled together; being together seemed to make them both happy. They probably never would marry because Patience just wouldn't. But no matter, Joseph seemed pleased with their arrangement. Joseph and Patience, with Traveler's help, were making even more money working as a team. The fact that they really didn't need any more wealth had nothing to do with their enthusiasm for business. Joseph had a knack for keen investment, no matter what the enterprise, no matter what the circumstances.

Chapter 78

The Old German Levee Road
Ride Out to Visit Moss Moonie

Amanda Worsham
Spring 1837
Georgetown, South Carolina

ON THE OLD WHARF NEAR Sand Hills Plantation, Amanda stood waiting for the steamboat. The morning wasn't especially cold or foreboding, but she felt a chill—not in the air, as the morning sky was clear. Rather something unidentifiable she simply felt inside. She pulled her shawl tight about her slim body.

"Now what, God?" she said quietly. "Now what?"

Joseph and Patience were coming back to All Saints' Parish from Charleston, where Patience had gone shopping for gifts to take on the return to Boston. She and Joseph would be leaving for home soon, but today, as Joseph had requested, they would tour the plantation on horseback. The three horses stood waiting alongside the wharf.

Amanda had come to Sand Hills the week before to help with family matters. Joseph had decided to sell his partial interest in the plantation to Beau Videau, and Amanda was happy about that.

At least Beau will take care of his people, his property. And Father will be free of all ties to slavery. Meanwhile, I will be working on Beau. He needs to leave the practice of slavery behind too.

358

She had heard the steamboat whistle as it left the landing down-stream. The boat would arrive soon. In a moment she saw it. She raised her arm to wave her scarf.

Joseph and Patience waved in return. All seemed well, yet Amanda couldn't shake feeling things somehow were amiss.

The steamboat pulled alongside the wharf, and soon the crew began to offload Sand Hills' cargo. Patience and Joseph disembarked.

Hugging Amanda, Patience said, "Touring the plantation will be too much for me, Amanda. If you and your father still want to ride today, please just go yourselves and take me to the house."

"All right. You rest, Patience," Joseph told her. "But I'm going. This is the last time I will survey this property. By next month it will belong to Beau."

In a few minutes they left for the plantation house where Patience would wait for Joseph and Amanda's return.

* * * * *

On the trail behind the Sand Hills Plantation, Amanda drew the reins up short until the horse stopped.

"Father, do you know the woman called Moss Moonie?"

Joseph reined in his horse beside her. "I do. Why do you ask?"

"How far is it to where she's living?"

"About a half hour. Do you want to go there? If we start right away, we can easily do that this afternoon. It's out across the old German levee road."

"I'd like that. I want to see her."

"Very well. Something to do with Moses, I'll wager."

"I want to talk to her about his mother."

"Well, let's get started."

Amanda's thoughts raced back in time ...

That night in Bermuda, right before I told him that I planned to give him and Sally their freedom, Moses told me about Moss Moonie having spots across her face. I remember his choice of words fascinated me. He said something like, "She's light in color, not red-boned, but she has black spots across her face. Folks say those spots be the mark of the

devil. An' they say pretty bad things 'bout what they don' understan'."
And then he added, *"People jus' don' know much 'bout spots, anyways."*
A profound comment, that.

The two rode in silence. When they reached the small log cabin, an old woman sitting in a rocking chair greeted them from the porch. The smell of wood burning permeated the air, and a pot of clothes boiled in the yard.

"Mist' Joe, it's good to see you," Moss Moonie said. "And I reckon you be Miss Manda. Good Lord, you look like yo' mama. Get yourselves down from them horses. I say you be pretty tired. Ride all the way from the Sand Hills, did you?" She walked out to meet them and reached for the horses' reins. "Love these creatures," she said. "God's own horses, they be. You be blest to have them. Most people who come see ol' Moss Moonie just walk." She turned to the open door. "Rooster," she called. "They be horses here to tend to. Come on out, boy."

"Yes'm," the voice answered from inside the cabin.

When Rooster came out onto the porch, Amanda surmised he was about ten years old. He was thin and tall, not at all like a rooster.

"Come rest your weary bones," said Moss Moonie, laughing. "Well, first you need see 'bout them necessaries, I reckon. It's out back." She pointed toward the outhouse. "That boy Rooster loves horses. He take good care of 'em. An' when you get back, we'll have some soap and water set out for you, by the water pump on the front porch."

Amanda glanced inside the open door of the cabin and saw a table inside with four chairs. She left to find the necessary.

Chapter 79

Ghost Panther

Amanda Worsham
Spring 1837
Georgetown, South Carolina

AMANDA WAS ABOUT TO SAY something when Moss Moonie began speaking.

"You know," Moss said, a strange look on her face. "They a ghost pant'er round here. Sometimes I see her. This spring she's got kits out there in that swamp. Well, she ain't no real ghost, don't you know? But she ain't the same ol' dirty buff color, either."

"You've seen her kittens?" Amanda asked.

"No. But I hear her coming round at night, sniffing this, licking that, pawing this, eating that—she messin' round jus' like a lost *hain't*. She stirrin' up things to feed her kits, don't you know?"

"Close by?" said Joseph.

"Close enough."

Good Lord, Amanda thought. *A ghost panther.* "Are you safe here ... I mean, by yourself?" she asked, her eyes wide.

"Yes'm. I don't do the devil's work, don't you know? I ain't alone. Got the Good Lord ... and I got Rooster."

Amanda shuddered. There was something dark about this, but she couldn't get a clear image of it.

"People come round here with women's trouble, don't you know?" Moss shook her head. Then she changed the subject. "Miss Manda," she said, "I hear you was borned in a caul. That true? You got the second sight, don't you? Can't pull the wool over yo' eyes!"

Amanda knew that Moss Moonie was referring to—those feelings she got now and again about things yet to come. It was about cold chills, and the sort of thing Amanda sensed right now. Moss Moonie obviously felt uncomfortable about discussing this devil business, as if she had already said too much as it was.

"You think she was born in a veil, a birth sack?" Joseph said, a stunned look on his face. "Is that what you mean … born in a *caul*?"

Moss nodded.

"She was," said Joseph. "But how did you know?"

"Maybe the Good Lord told me. Anyways I know … I know. I'll bet Miss Manda sees things the rest of us can't. She kin see what's comin', Mist' Joe. Somethin' might be good to know, an' maybe it be bad to know. But she don't see it all. Things happen she won't know 'bout. That's the way it is. Just axe her."

Amanda really had a strange notion about this. And she heard that word *axe* again, adding to her stress.

Joseph said nothing.

"Do you remember when Moses Ward was born?" Amanda interrupted, changing the subject. "He told me about some things surrounding his birth."

"Moses, he a good boy," said Moss. "Wasn't born with a caul, don't you know? But he got born, he sho' did. An' that's good."

"He's alive," said Amanda, her eyes squinting somewhat, "because you took the time to help his mother, and I know it. They're free, Moss Moonie. I gave Moses and Sally their freedom in Bermuda. He's a ship's carpenter now. He wants to know about his mother. Is she alive?"

"No. She died out there in that swamp." She pointed through the open doorway.

"But didn't she come to you for help?"

"She did. That girl come for to have that baby, don't you know? She left that baby out there floatin' in a boat, an' I find him. I sho' did."

"Why didn't you send her back to the plantation?" Joseph asked.

"I told her to go back. But she just ran away."

Amanda knew Moss Moonie was lying. Oh, Moses had been born here right enough, probably in the bed right there behind her. But Moss had helped Moses's mother to run away. Sally Ward had told her the truth about that story.

Amanda smiled.

"You see it. You know, don't you, Miss Manda?"

"Yes." Amanda was determined to get a clear picture of whatever Moss Moonie had said before, about doing the devil's work. "You were talking about the devil. Whatever do you mean?"

"When they come round with they woman's problems, I send them away."

"Women in trouble … women with child?" said Joseph.

Amanda drew a deep breath. She thought of Sarah Jean and the lost child she'd supposedly conceived by Timothy Caldwell.

Well, I know the baby wasn't Timothy's, don't I?

"Yes, sir, Mist' Joe. That's what I mean. That and a whole lot more. An' what good is what I do, anyway? The Good Lord makes it hard enough to get a baby. What if I do that business? What would happen to ol' Moss Moonie? Would anybody take care of Moss Moonie with the pant'er sniffing' round … or when the law come?"

"What's that got to do with anything?" said Amanda. "What do you mean?"

"Massa at a plantation think of a chile … his chile, any chile with a slave, to be his property, don't you know? Po' li'l baby don't have no chance. Some women don't want to help Massa out that way with a new slave. If Moss Moonie took a dead baby and threw it out in 'em woods, that ol' ghost pant'er probably find it … and take it to her young'uns. And the lot of 'em would have a taste for human folk, don't you know? What I gonna do 'bout that? She of the devil, anyway, that cat. What I'm gonna do with a dead baby?" Moss Moonie made a fist. "Maybe I throw it in that outhouse. A baby deserve more than that, don't you know? These old hands can't dig a proper grave. And God His Self don't want no devil's business like that round here."

She knew in her heart this woman was not one to put away babies. She rose from her chair and went to put her arms around the old woman with the spots across her face. She hugged her tight, then squeezed five twenty-dollar gold pieces into her big, rough hands.

A small fortune, she thought. "I know how you helped Moses into the world and his mother to find freedom," she whispered. "You never send anybody away. You just save babies and help people. I know it. Keep doing what you do, Moss Moonie. And God bless you."

Chapter 80

Timothy Is Innocent Rooster Saw It All

Amanda Worsham
Spring 1837
Georgetown, South Carolina

"Miss Manda," Moss Moonie implored, a tear in her voice. "I know you think that boy Timothy rape yo' sister, don't you?"

"That's what I heard."

"Well, he didn't. He sho' didn't. That boy Rooster was hiding out in the back o' that cotton house, don't you know? He see everything happen, which was nothin'."

Amanda drew in a deep breath. Could this be true? Was poor Timothy truly innocent of that charge, of that act? She'd known it in her heart all along. Rooster had simply been afraid to speak out against the master's daughter. Sarah Jean had lied. Amanda hugged Moss Moonie again and kissed her on the cheek.

"Mist' Joe," Moss called from the porch. "What 'bout this?" She paused. "Look out for a one-eyed, one-handed man wif a bomb," she said after a moment.

"One-handed bomb thrower?" said Joseph, laughing. "One-eyed? And why a bomb thrower?"

"That's right. An' then it be over."

Amanda saw no humor in any of this. Moss Moonie scared her. She thought of the man Semmes in Bermuda. He had an eye patch. But he had two arms. No, it couldn't be him.

"An' for you, Miss Manda, I got something over here." Moss beckoned her to the open window. "See that yonder growing in the corner of my garden? You all know what that is?"

"It's Carolina larkspur, isn't it?"

"I calls it *devil's apple*. It's the devil's own, it is."

"Own what?" Amanda said. "Yard herb?" *Damn. Some of this is funny.*

"You brew a tea from the leaves, or from the seeds, and you put some on the bed frame with a rag, don't you know?"

"Paint it on the bed frame? Whatever for?"

"All the bedbugs will die. Dat's what."

"We don't have bedbugs," Amanda protested. "Really we don't." *Well. Maybe a couple every now and then.* She glanced at Moss Moonie, who had a somewhat condescending look on her face.

Amanda made up her mind to always tell the truth when speaking with Moss Moonie.

She sees or senses the truth, anyway. Damn.

Chapter 81

The Pomander from Hell

Amanda Worsham
Spring 1837
Georgetown, South Carolina

"You need this, honey. Here, take this special pomander." Moss Moonie reached into her apron pocket. "I have it ready for you."

"You knew we were coming? I don't believe—"

Before Amanda could finish, Moss interrupted her. "You take this," she said. She opened her wrinkled hand to reveal a silver heart-shaped, intricately filigreed locket. It had an expensive engraved look about it.

"Some time back I fill it with seeds from that plant out yonder, don't you know? When the time comes and the devil comes calling, you brew that tea. Just dip this silver heart in a cup of boiling water. Let it steep, but not too long. You count, one Moss Moonie ... two Moss Moonies ... three Moss Moonies ... and when you get to seven Moss Moonies, right there you pull it out the hot water. It causes them to go mad—the one that drinks it, don't you know? An' you ken get away. Makes them see the Plat-eye. It won' kill. You can't kill ... the devil." Moss shook her head. "Nothin' can do that," she said.

Amanda hesitated, then asked, "I've heard Moses talk of Plat-eye. Just what is that?"

"They people in the swamp with cutoff heads, don't you know? An' they shrink 'em down, sew the eyes shut. In the swamp, you liable t' see anything … a swamp monster, a lost *hain't*, or the like. I never saw one. But we call 'em Plat-eye, don't you know?"

"Really. I just don't believe in such things. But this is a pretty pomander. Where did it come from?"

"It come from France, honey. It was my great-granny's back in the islands." She pointed to Amanda's own locket hanging around her neck on a gold chain. "That gold chain," she said. "That's what I need to fix this for you. Let me see it."

Amanda's fingers flew to her throat. "I bought it for the portrait locket. I plan to have a tiny image painted of the man I will marry and place it inside. If I ever find him, that is."

"They's plenty time 'fore that happens, don't you know? 'Bout a year, the way I sees it."

Amanda took the chain from around her neck and handed it to Moss Moonie. In a moment the silver heart pomander full of larkspur seeds lay safe around Amanda's neck. Doubts filled Amanda's mind. But there was persuasiveness in Moss Moonie's voice. Somehow it all made perfect sense. A silver pierced pomander heart hanging on a gold chain beside a gold locket. If one looked carefully and shook the heart, one could see and hear the seeds rattle inside … it was The Pomander from Hell, by Moss Moonie's decree. An amulet for the devil's own.

Amanda thought immediately of Hollis Mackenzie.

She and Joseph said goodbye to Moss Moonie and Rooster and walked out to the horses. In a moment, they were back on the sandy road headed toward the Plantation. Neither Joseph nor Amanda said a word for a long time.

Chapter 82

Ghosts ... Buckets ...
Piggins ... Sandcastles

Amanda Worsham
Spring 1837
Georgetown, South Carolina

ALONG THE WAY, JOSEPH AND Amanda saw many live oak trees
draped in Spanish moss, pine trees, and squirrels running along
branches stretched across the road. An occasional pecan tree
stood alone, a tribute to the old Austrian-German planter named
Buchheidt who raised this area from swampland and planted many
pecan trees.

The slaves referred to him as Ol' Marse Buck-hit. Master Bucket,
she thought. *Not very damn funny, that.*

They came upon streams to ford and shallow ponds to cross.
In these, Joseph would slow the horse until he found a crossing safe
from snakes and whatever else might lie in wait in the coolness of the
shaded water.

As they approached one particular place of shadows, this time
Amanda reached out and touched Joseph's arm, signaling to slow
his horse. Something about this place made her edgy, as if the devil
himself were waiting there ahead. But no bomb thrower appeared.
There was no one.

"Father," she said. After reining her horse to a standstill, Joseph followed suit.

"What is it? Do you need to rest?"

"No. Something up ahead … something waiting for us. There's a strangeness …"

And something else Amanda didn't like about this dark thicket lurked about, something not really obvious. All had been fine when they'd passed through here on the way to Moss Moonie's place, but now everything seemed different. The foreboding heightened as they lingered. Amanda felt the anguish and suffering of the slave gangs who had moved the earth to fill this swampy area and to build the levee road.

"Please wait, Father. I don't like this place one bit."

"Ghost panthers, indeed," Joseph mocked. "Bomb throwers? Ha! That woman should keep to rubbing warts off old ladies' noses and leave the fortune-telling to you."

He slid off the horse to his feet. Handing the reins to Amanda, he headed toward the thicket with two traveling pieces in his hands. He stopped to stick one into his trouser top, handle up—the other, he cocked—and started forward.

Amanda studied the levee road. Its simple appearance belied its difficulty abuilding. She grimaced when her thoughts touched upon the word *abuilding*. The word was in keeping with the low-class makeup of this so-called Low Country. Huge road gangs of slaves a half century ago had built this place. Now a smaller gang of slaves tended to the business of growing rice here. The day-to-day operation of the rice plantation was repugnant to her. Everyone in Charleston had a rice spoon, a heavy, solid, sterling silver implement used for serving rice. They served rice with everything: catfish, field peas, chicken, gravy, or disgusting servings of pig entrails they called "chit'lins."

She thought of the old German, the one the slaves called Marse Buck-hit. She formed a mental picture of him pouring the sand levees with an old bucket. And she remembered the small Bermuda bucket called a "piggin" and the sandcastle she had poured on the pink beach at Horseshoe Cove.

Buckets ... piggins ... sandcastles, she thought. *That's all this place is—just another damn sandcastle. This rice field doesn't provide a joyful business to help the South. It's a thing built upon human misery, a thing of sand. Without the slaves, it would quickly disappear.* Marse, *what a disgusting word.*

Amanda turned her attention to Joseph. She thought him a very handsome man, and maybe he was fearless, too, but that was something in her father she had never seen tested.

I haven't said anything to Father about Patience's story. Oh damn ... damn about his past before he met Mother, and damn it all, I don't think I ever will. Father must have his very own devils. I've thought that before, but what is it they say about letting sleeping devils lie, or is that sleeping dogs ...

Joseph reached the thicket. "I don't see anything out of the ordinary here," he said, looking back toward Amanda. "Must be a false alarm. No ghost panther."

At that moment, the wind changed, and the horses pricked their ears at a new scent. Both reared their heads and nervously pawed the ground, clearly sensing danger.

Joseph studied a live oak limb that stretched across the roadway. He stood still, as if frozen in place.

"Good Lord, Father. What is it?" Apparently he'd seen something only he could detect.

But what the hell is it?

Suddenly a loud roar rumbled ahead in the thicket. It started as a spitting hiss and ended with a terrible growl. It was a big cat; there was no doubt in her mind.

"Get out of there!" she screamed. "Father ... don't shoot ... run ... no ... don't run!" *Something is wrong,* she thought. "The cat's afraid of you," she said, in a more normal voice. "I don't think she'll hurt you. I think she only wants to get away."

The horses reared, making it difficult for Amanda to control her horse. Joseph's horse pulled its reins loose from her hand and ran down the levee road toward Moss Moonie's cabin. In a moment it was gone.

Then Amanda saw the cat, a large albino panther, as large as they come. No wonder people said it was a *ghost* panther. It had a frightful look about it.

Suddenly the big cat jumped down onto the road, behind Joseph, and swung its gaze toward Amanda.

The female panther, no doubt, the one Moss Moonie spoke of.

The cat twitched its tail about its body in sudden, staccato motions, as if she were counting: one ... two ... three. Then she turned and bounded away. All this time, Joseph had remained still as a stone.

"Amanda," screamed Joseph. "Dear God ... how did you know?"

"Second sight, I guess," she said.

Her horse had calmed now that the crisis was over. Joseph walked toward her with the traveling piece pointed at the ground. He had not fired.

Amanda turned her horse and rode up beside him. "Let's get on back to Sand Hills, Father. I want to rest now." *To say the damned least ...*

"Right."

Joseph paused for a minute, as if trying to regain his composure. "It will be a big load for your horse, Amanda, but we should ride double."

"Very well, Father. Did you see that ghost panther?"

"I saw it. I saw it. I surely did see it. Now let's get out of here."

Riding double was not difficult. Amanda was actually quite small. She smiled when she thought of the ghost panther. It wasn't that it was funny, but encountering it was the sort of thing a person might very well remember for a long time. She imagined the big cat to be with her kittens now, somewhere in the wilds of the swamp. She thought of Moss Moonie and Rooster. Then she remembered the Bermuda sandcastle Sarah Jean helped to build long ago. Sarah Jean had asked Joseph if a sand crab could move into a sandcastle and save it from the ravages of the sea. Amanda could see Beau Videau in her mind's eye with his right hand growing in size until he, too, became a sand crab.

Good enough for Hollis too, she thought, wincing. *Beau Videau might be my natural father. Sand fleas and shit,* she thought. *Billy goat lips be damned.*

Chapter 83

Bad Day … Good Day
A Killing in the Country

Amanda Worsham
August 1837
Charleston, South Carolina

In pink, Amanda devoted much of her time to driving out to the countryside and afterward writing a journal to record her adventures. She seriously thought that most of her adventures were over, her love life in particular.

It was an especially nice day. Amanda had gone shopping in town and then left for the countryside. She'd purchased some artist's materials and intended to try to sketch something in the country.

I've brought an old blanket to sit on if I spot something just waiting to be sketched, or maybe I'll just take a look around.

Oh, it hurt to think about Timothy Caldwell. She'd thought he would have been her husband someday. She really had believed Timothy would marry her. But the business with Sarah Jean had taken him away so easily. Then Sarah Jean married Hollis.

Amanda struggled with the memory of it. Meanwhile, she noticed several men working to repair an antique hand-cranked cotton gin. That design, one of the first, fascinated her because it reminded her of an overgrown music box. She found the people interesting that were standing around under a shed roof working, talking, and passing time, but as a subject for a sketch … well, she decided to drive on. Perhaps after a bit, she would find a scenic view.

After a time she came upon a vegetable farm, its fields awash with yellow crook-necked squash. Carts loaded with golden squash dotted the fields, and she found the scene lovely. She decided to try some sketching; she would paint with oils from her sketches later in her studio.

As she sat on an old blanket sketching, she thought of Timothy and Florida and Grewno and pirates. Sighing, she tried especially to put Timothy's memory out of her mind.

Putting the finishing touches on her third drawing, she heard two men in the distance talking to one another in German. She thought nothing of it. She found German comforting. It reminded her of her days at the Salem school for girls.

She turned to look at them. The white man was dressed in a black suit with frilly accessories—a dark-skinned dandy, as they say, —with moustache and stylish, pointed beard. The other, a young completely bald Negro, wore a brown velvet suit with a white lace blouse.

But what is that they are saying? She listened more closely. *It seems to be German but somehow not German—hard to catch the gist of it. But they are talking about me! There is something about that white man. I don't like him. Damn. I certainly wish I had more German under my belt. I should have paid more attention in school. Strange …*

She decided to pack up and leave. As Amanda drove her carriage away from the field, the two followed in a fancy brougham. She didn't think that she had ever seen the dandy or his driver before, but …

God. There's something about that dandy …

The brougham was fast overtaking her. She brought her quirt down smartly across the mare's rump, but still, the brougham gained on her.

At a place next to a freshly planted field of tobacco, the brougham overtook her. The bald-headed man grinned as he drove his two horses into the path of Amanda's mare, forcing the mare to falter and to abruptly stop, hooves rearing up into the morning sunshine.

Amanda screamed, tumbling forward over the front of her carriage. She landed, unhurt, in the ditch.

"What—" Amanda began, as the two men jumped from the brougham.

They caught her by her arms and pulled her into the tobacco field, catching Amanda completely unaware. Maybe her premonitions would not predict her own future.

"Let me go!" she screamed, to no avail. *I know this dark-skinned dandy!* her mind screamed suddenly.

"Grewno," she spit the name at him. *Where did he come from? What is he trying to do to me?*

She heard again his high, maniacal laugh. She saw the glove on his left hand … only on his left hand. Amanda knew the thumb beneath the glove wore the tattoo of a snake.

"Let me go, Grewno!" she screamed.

The two men paused at the edge of the woods and, unbelievably, released her. Terrified, Amanda remembered the horror of the first time she had seen this man.

What is he up to?

She tried to run, only to be caught by the bald-headed man before she could get away. When he slapped her and turned her to face him, she began to cry.

Holding a knife beneath her chin, the bald-headed man snarled, "Be still! I won't hurt you." Grewno had a pistol pointed at her back. "Why are you crying, little girl?" he mocked in a British accent. "Why are you so afraid?"

He spoke to the bald-headed man in that odd German. "Let her turn around," he said.

How could this man have escaped from the place down under? She couldn't remember its name. *It has been years since Grewno was transported. Maybe he'd learned his Cockney-British mixture there. But German? Where did he learn that?*

What could he intend to do with me now? she thought. *Rape? They said Grewno has lace on his drawers. It must be something else, not rape.*

She stared into Grewno's eyes. "Let me go, damn you. I'll pay you whatever you want, Grewno. You don't need me. You can't do anything with me."

"Pay me? You're going to pay me?" Grewno laughed. When he chuckled, his whole body shook. "It is I who will pay you. I recognized you near the field back there. I never thought I would see you again. You're the Worsham brat, aren't you? The one who fought me in the shadows on Bermuda. *Bruja … Witch.* I might have made it away from that place, but you drove into me with your horse. The damn Redcoats caught me. Shot me in the shoulder. I haven't had time to plan this out, but what will I do with you? Why, I'll have fun watching my man here play with you, I think. After that, who knows?" A wicked look rose in his eyes as he began again his maniacal laugh.

Amanda shut her eyes and began to pray. Suddenly, she heard shots fired, a volley of shots … five, maybe six. Then a swarm of lead balls, like the sound of hornets passed in front of her. She opened her eyes just as the storm of balls tore into Grewno's chest.

She knew he was dead when he started to fall. He had to be. She'd seen the devastation upon his chest.

He fell immediately to the ground, facedown in the young tobacco plants, his awful laugh silent forever. Dead also was his German speech, and Spanish and whatever other languages he spoke in his wickedness.

The bald-headed man began to run through the field toward the brougham, his arms flailing in the air, screaming unintelligibly as he ran.

Amanda looked in the direction of the shots, afraid more shots might be fired. She saw, instead, a group of five men climbing onto their horses, men neatly dressed, some with gray hair. But one tall man stood facing her across the field. He took off his hat and swept it in front of himself in an elaborate bow.

It's Traveler! He saved my life. God, I'm glad Father found that man.

The riders apprehended the bald-headed fellow quickly and put him in chains, then tossed him and Grewno's body in the brougham and drove away.

Traveler told Amanda moments later that the five men traveling with him were government agents and that they had been looking for these two for years. Grewno and his man were part of a conspiracy, a wild plan to walk into the capitol building in Washington with guns blazing in an attempt to bring the government to its knees. A similar event had taken place in England in 1820, in which the Cato Street Conspiracy, a group of Arthur Thistlewood's anarchist cohorts, had planned the murders of Prime Minister Lord Liverpool as well as other British cabinet ministers. Grewno had become part of what might be a worldwide conspiracy to foster anarchy in as many places as possible in order to render the world vulnerable to military coup.

Even as Traveler told Amanda of these things, she did not believe him. His tale sounded plausible, and yes, it made a good story, but she knew he was lying.

My heavenly days, man. Do you really expect me to believe such nonsense?

"You won't read about this in the papers, lass," Traveler said. "It would be an interesting feature article to be sure, but we can ill afford to have any of this gain notoriety just now. I'm certain you understand."

Of course. We don't want to give these rebellious souls around Charleston any new ideas. Especially by spreading a wild-eyed story like that.

Amanda decided to tell no one of this occurrence ... only to mention it to God in her prayers.

Chapter 84

Oso Río Rescues Timothy from Ambush

Timothy Caldwell
Christmas Day 1837
South Florida

THE TALL, ROUGH-LOOKING MAN MADE his way slowly through
the scattered undergrowth that covered the sandy place between
the marshy saw grass and the hardwood of the dry land near Lake
Okeechobee.

The pirates called him Oso Río—meaning "River Bear" in
Spanish—in deference to his great strength, fierceness, and butter-
nut-colored skin. In time, the Seminole people welcomed him, especially the women, and gave him the turban and feathers he wore.

Oso Río, a runaway slave out of Tombee Plantation on Saint
Helena Island off the Carolina coast, had determined long ago he
would never go back to the life of a slave. He fit well into Seminole
folklore where legends of men as tall as trees abounded. He was a
good man in a fight.

Even at noon, Oso Río cast a long shadow. Of course, it *was*
Christmas, and the sun was low in the Southern quadrant.

Later in the morning, a sizable band of soldiers commanded
by Colonel Zachary Taylor walked single file near Lake Okeechobee
through the woods. The young lieutenant, Timothy Caldwell, walked
among them. Some fanned themselves with their hats. Even in late

December, it was warm in Florida—especially if you were dressed in heavy woolen clothing. Others removed backpacks to drop them noisily beside the trail. Quiet they were not.

A flurry of gunfire suddenly filled the mists. The fiery eruptions came from all round—from shadowy groups of naked Seminole warriors, young men painted red and black, who hid in the tall grass until just the right moment. Death was far from the young soldiers' minds. Those Seminole warriors who crouched in the cover of trees and tall grass had other plans. In the dreadful moments that followed, many Blue Coats, as the Seminole called them, died in the furious battle.

Along with Oso Rio, another man accompanied the Seminole named Otulke-thloco … the one known as the Prophet. He had come from Georgia, gained some notoriety as a soothsayer, and had spoken to the warriors of many things. He told the warriors that his medicine would protect them. The men were fearless, though their number was a third that of the soldiers.

In the surprise volley, twenty-six Blue Coats died and over a hundred wounded. The battle seemed lost for the Blue Coats. The Seminole warriors came wielding knives and red war clubs until many of the troopers around Timothy lay dead—but Timothy was alive.

In the midst of the battle, Oso Río found a wounded Timothy cowering in the weeds, a soldier he recognized.

The huge figure that touched Timothy with a foot said, "Coon man, I'm a-gonna save yo' ass again. It ain't yo' time, man. It jes' ain't yo' time."

In the confusion of the battle, Oso Río hoisted him to his shoulders and carried him away.

Soon, the mounted volunteers, men from the well-regulated militias of Tennessee and Missouri, commenced a bayonet charge that saved the army from defeat, an event that provided mute testimony for sustaining a well-regulated militia.

The Seminole lost eleven men and had fourteen wounded. The Prophet lost some of his newfound credibility.

Oso Río left the cowardly trooper hiding up a tree as the noise of the conflict moved away into the afternoon. Soldiers who survived fled into the woods to seek comfort and safety. The rescued trooper was a small, dark-skinned white man the Seminole women called Raccoon. He was Baba Lou's friend.

In the silence of the evening, Oso Río returned, passing under a large live oak tree with Spanish moss hanging all round, a wet stream of fresh urine glistening on the trunk. Oso Río looked up into the dark branches of the tree. The smile on his face spoke of an inner sense of well-being, of a rich sense of humor. One laughed *with* Oso Río. No one laughed at him.

"Coon Man," Oso Río spoke softly, up the tree. "Time to come down. I'll take you to Miss Baba Lou. You notice I didn't call you Coon Soldier?' You ain't no fuckin' soldier, man."

Silence.

This live oak tree was named Old Woman of the Sandy Place in Seminole. He didn't speak their language yet. But he was learning. For now, he called the tree Nandi. It was his Zulu grandmother's name and had special meaning to him. In truth, he thought of the ancient oak tree as a woman. He remembered his Nandi and loved her still. He knew that as soon as the white men learned this "Nandi" was here, they would cut her down for her timbers.

Stupid white man, he thought. *You steal everything of value, rape the women, and destroy lives and property all along the way. What of the Cherokee, white man? What of the Cree? And what of the Seminole who came here long ago to avoid you? The word* Seminole *means "the greatest of warriors who want to live alone." Now the white man says the Seminole have to leave. But I can't go,* he thought. *What about me? What am I supposed to do, white man? Go back to Tombee?* It made him spit to think of it.

Better to deal with a badger. You hang your food cache up high, or the crafty old badger will find it. Then he'll piss on whatever food he can't eat at once, saving nothing for later, ruining it for any other. Only white men, they worse than a fuckin' badger.

Oso Río thought briefly of his mother. He missed her. But his father was one of the young white bucks that hung around the Tombee Plantation. He didn't know which one. How can you miss a man you never knew? It was great sport for the white boys to stop over and practice hump-ups with Cleo, the beautiful slave woman.

Cleo was his mother.

They all called her Cleo the Beautiful ... Cleo the Negress. She was tall, muscular, and very well taken care of, as were all of her girl children. Her boy children—well, that was a different matter. All were born into slavery. Strangely, no one minded if Cleo and her children were educated. "House Niggers," they called the girls.

Those white bucks, he thought, *they don't think of Cleo as a woman. They consider her a beautiful animal similar in many ways to a tame lioness. Cleo is a pleasure property.* When as a child, Oso Río had asked his Nandi why they did that, she just told him to hush.

His job had been to work in the gardens and in the yard, raking white sandy grounds with a broom he'd made from holly branches and honeysuckle vines taken from the woods, and to pull any nut grass that poked its head above the sand. He kept the yard bright and clean.

Whenever they held a party at the big house, he was the mosquito-chaser. He walked round the trees and bushes near the house at midday with a cane pole, shaking all the leaves. The startled mosquitoes would fly into the sunlight and maybe die of the shock. If he didn't catch them sleeping during the heat of the day, the mosquitoes would come out hungry at sundown, right in the middle of the party. So as a lanky youth, the white people called him Skeeter. Oso Río hated that name almost as much as he hated hearing his given name, Juno.

Maybe it wasn't so bad, the way they had treated him, but when he was well into the unbending teen years, they had used the whip across the back of the man Juno. Oso Río carried the scars on his back and the bitter memories. He'd run away from the plantation as soon as he was able. Much better to be with the Seminole who called him River Bear.

Yeah, man. I'm the fuckin' River Bear.

He wondered about Cleo, his mother. In his heart, he knew she was well. Thoughts of her didn't hurt much anymore.

"Heh-heh-heh," he laughed. "Look out, Coon Man."

Oso Río's Seminole friends called this one *Aroughcun*, "raccoon" in the Seminole language. He placed his wooden war club on the ground, needing both hands to climb the huge tree.

At about the twenty-foot level, in the midst of the leathery ever-green leaves and great, crooked limbs covered with hanging clusters of moss and mistletoe, he spotted the man.

"Damn," said Oso Río. "You sure got the right name, Coon Man." He laughed heartily, shaking the limb he stood on.

Silence.

"What's the matter wid-ju, anyway, man?" Oso Río grumbled impatiently. "Do I ha' to come an' get you?" He eased further out on the limb. "What the hell is yo' damn name, anyhow? Trooper? Baba Lou calls you Trooper, don't she?"

The small, cowering soldier suddenly charged Oso Río, sword flashing.

But as the sword swung in an arc toward him, Oso Río feinted left, the blade sweeping by with no effect.

The momentum knocked Trooper off balance, and the sword tumbled to the ground. He began swinging his arms, trying to gain enough balance to steady his footing on the large branch, but to no avail. He fell, striking each limb below as he toppled to the soft ground.

As Oso Río climbed down the tree, he could hear the man sobbing below in the weeds. The sobbing stopped before he reached the ground.

Oso Río reached the Seminole encampment carrying a bundle on his shoulders. The children ran out to greet him. He sent for Baba Lou, and when she arrived, he carefully placed the blanket roll at her feet. It moved. Oso Río pulled the blanket away and exposed the whimpering man they all called Raccoon.

"Very well done, Oso Río," she said. "I owe you for this. I can handle him now. Thank you."

Oso Río smiled, then vanished into the night.

✳ ✳ ✳ ✳ ✳

Later, in the darkness of her tent, Baba listened as her friend awoke and began to quietly sob.

"You found yourself, Trooper?" she said. "Last time I saw you, there were no tears, no judgment of right or wrong. What happened?"

"Baba? Is that you?" Trooper sat upright in the corn-shuck bed and wiped his cheeks of tears. "I remember it all, Baba," he said, trembling. "Now I remember the good and the bad. I used you. I'm so sorry for that. Really, I am."

"Now, don't you get all wobbly about this, Trooper. So you rolled me in the hay. What the hell? That's what I do for a living. That's why the Seminole tolerate me. They see me as a necessary friend. I trade for whatever I need. 'Course, I also sell herbs, potions, and such in the town." She moved to stand beside him. "You know, Trooper, they call you Raccoon." She laughed.

"Now, why would they do that? I don't have rings round my tail." He thought for a moment. "Or my eyes," he added, seemingly recovering somewhat.

"The women saw you when Cat saved you from the black snake. You screamed."

"So?"

"You squealed and ran up the tree like a raccoon."

"Oh? And nobody else would have?"

"Trooper, you get well and go back to your own kind. I don't think war is your calling. You need to go back to whoever really cares about you."

"That's just it. No one cares about me."

"Well, I don't know about that—a really handsome man like yourself. But you can't stay here. It's difficult enough for us to hide as it is."

The small, whimpering cries of a small baby awakening came from behind Baba.

"Yes, love," Baba cooed to the baby. "It is time for your meal, isn't it?"

Timothy Caldwell said nothing. Many thoughts filled his mind. This child, could it be his?

"Baba," he said.

She opened her blouse, placed a nipple in the child's mouth, and began to nurse in the darkness of the tent.

"Yes, Trooper?"

"Is that our … is that my child?"

"No, silly man. Do you think one time for you with me would do this? You sure do have some fine idea of yourself."

Timothy managed to stand. When he threw open the door flap of the tent, the light from the campfire flowed into the darkness of the tent. He could plainly see the naked baby, a boy.

My child … if I have a child, would be about two years old, he thought.

The baby's dark skin resembled the color of his own skin. Baba was Gypsy. It told him nothing. He reviewed the things she had told him, and fresh tears filled his eyes. This was all wrong. But so much of his life had always been wrong … so very wrong. He had to get away from this.

"When can I leave?" he said, swiping the tears away with his sleeve.

"No one is safe here, Trooper. I want you to leave with the morning light. I'll see to it."

Timothy dropped the door flap. He welcomed the darkness.

"How many children do you have?" he said.

"I have been with the Seminole for seven seasons now," she answered. "There are three children in the camp who are mine."

"I see."

"Three, counting this one," she added. "There would be more, if God were willing. The Seminole treasure their young. I nurse my children and sometimes nurse other camp women's children. Always it seems that I am either with child or lugging one around." Baba sighed. "I am a harlot," she said.

Timothy crawled back to the corn-shuck bed.

"I will see to your wound in a few minutes, Trooper. Looks as if a bullet creased your shoulder. I will also see you to your camp before noon tomorrow."

"Have you any children darker than mine?"

"You are convinced this child is yours?"

"Do you?"

"You mean with Oso Río, don't you?"

"Yes."

"If you saw the children, you would know."

The baby suckled contentedly. She did not comment further on the matter.

He had forgotten his wound. It seemed unimportant to him. In a few moments he fell asleep, thinking that no longer was his mind confused about what was right or what was wrong. The total experience thus far had cleansed him.

He momentarily awakened when Baba dressed his wound.

Chapter 85

Baba ... Dead?

Timothy Caldwell
January 1838
South Florida

IN THE MORNING, TIMOTHY LEFT the camp without escort and very much in a hurry. He wandered—lost in the woods and the swamp—for three days, without food or water, searching for the military's camp, a fort, a town, anything that offered safety. On the fourth morning he heard something moving heavily through the woods. He imagined a war party ... or a bear.

It was Oso Río. The deep bass of his laughter rumbled, nearly shaking the ground.

Timothy whimpered, "Why are you always there when I need you the most?"

"I been looking for you, man. It's time for us to leave this place."

Oso Río grabbed Timothy as if he were an abandoned back-pack, hefted him onto his shoulders, then trotted quickly through the darkness to a place of safety.

The huge man set Timothy down, then hunkered down to speak plainly to him.

"We always thought we would lose you, Coon Man," he said. "Miss Baba Lou knew you would never make it through a real war. But now that's all changed. Two days ago, she was killed in a raid against the village—against women and children while all the grown men were away. The troopers waited 'til they left, man. Cowards. That's what they be. Cowards and assholes."

"Baba … dead?" Timothy shook his head. "I saw her just the other day. I spent the night with her. She's fine."

"You saw her with the babies. I know, man," he said, tears running freely down his face. "I hate the white man, the troopers, every damn one. Really do. Sometimes I want to kill them all. But I know I could never do that. It's no good, man. Better to run away." Oso Río rose to his full height. "An' I don't really see you as a trooper, Coon Man.

"Osceola's gone … tricked by the Blue Coats … and under a white flag too. Do you know the Prophet told Osceola he'd have to die … have to be a martyr? That Seminole brave, Osceola, sat with his back to the wall and waited to die. He just waited, man—looking at the fuckin' wall. What the shit is they left for me? You and me, we got to go. Come with me, Coon Man."

Timothy followed as Oso Río started through the woods, his mind refusing to make sense of this.

What the hell does it all mean? He had trouble keeping up with Oso Río.

Chapter 86

We Got to Go, Man. We Got to Go!

Timothy Caldwell
January 1838
South Florida

THEY CAME TO A REST stop the better part of an hour later. Oso Río
sat on the ground, his knees up beside his face like a grasshopper, and
spoke quietly toward a bush.

"You two big boys kin come to me now," he said, huge arms
outstretched.

Two young naked boys crawled out of their hiding place, trying
not to appear afraid. But it wasn't working. Oso Río picked up the
darker, taller, of the two, then wrapped the child in a fur that he carried tucked inside his belt.

"This one's mine, Coon Man," he said. "I don't have no trouble
picking him out. He's so tall and everything. Heh-heh-heh."

"The other one ..." Timothy's fingers flew to his lips. "Is that
boy mine? Is he my son?"

"Yes. Miss Baba would never have given him up. But she's gone.
Somebody got to see about him, man. That's your job." He took a
second fur from his belt and handed it to Timothy. "He ain't got no
circles round his eyes, but that chile's the Coon Man's, all right. An'
that's you, ain't it?" Oso Río stood with his child cradled in his arms.
"The other boy is about two years old."

388

The boy stood, hugging Oso Río's leg.

"Miss Baba told me he's not Seminole. She named him Juan Carlos. Why Juan Carlos? Why not Timothy? Ain't that yo' name? Heh-heh-heh. Coon man, you really are something, you know it? I think Juan Carlos was her Spanish captain's name. Anyways, she liked dat name."

Timothy thought, as he watched the boy, that the face reminded him of his own face—the face he'd seen peering back at him from the looking glasses of his childhood. He reached for the child, but the boy pulled away. There was no love, no friendship in his eyes.

"You got to work on that, Coon Man. Come on now. We ain't got no more time. I saved yo' ass couple times, man. Now it's time you saved us all."

Timothy grabbed the boy and wrapped him in the fur. "What do we do now?" he said, carrying the boy in his arms.

Amazingly, both boys were quiet, as if they understood the peril.

"You know the Spaniards that Miss Baba had visits with from time to time?" Oso Río asked.

"The ones who ambushed my troopers awhile back?"

"It was the Spanish what saved you, man."

"What do you mean?"

"Miss Baba told me yo' people left you for dead. When the Spanish found you, they thought you was dead. They took you to Miss Baba, man."

"So?"

"They gonna be on the beach tomorrow morning. It' the first full moon of the New Year. The Spanish real punctual, man. That mean they be on time … if they go at all. Miss Baba told me all 'bout it. We got to talk to them, got to get them to take us when they leave—you, me and our two children. Miss Baba always say you look like a Spanish sailor. You're short and olive-skinned like they are … and like she was."

"I don't speak any Spanish."

"Neither did Miss Baba. But she got on with them, man. You just do it."

"Why do we have to run? Can't we remain here?"

"I can't go with the Seminole people. I'm a runaway slave, man. The white man got to have his pound of flesh from me. I can't go anywhere. My chile can't go neither. He ain't white. He ain't Seminole. He just like me, and everybody will know it. An' Miss Baba, she knew she couldn't go and leave her baby. Maybe we could've worked it out, but Miss Baba's dead now. You can't go with the Seminole either, man. I think they would kill you."

"What? Why can't I just take my child and go back to the fort? The military has no reason not to accept my son."

"Don't you know yet, man? You keep comin' out of these things alive. Sooner or later they gonna figure it out."

"Figure what out?"

"That you ain't much of a trooper, that's what. How many times kin you say you don't remember? An' you and me, we can't go nowhere but the place they call Mexico. Some folks call it New Spain. Whatever it is, man, dat's where we got to go. Anywhere but here."

"But I don't want a child," Timothy protested. "I'm not ready for that."

"As people want, ain't always what they gets," Oso Río said. *"Mahrime."*

"Mahrime? What is that? I don't know that word. But wait— maybe I do know it. It was Baba's word."

"Dat's one Miss Baba's words. You're right 'bout dat. *Mahrime* is Gipsy for 'it's all shit,' man. Least I think dat's what it means ... from the way her face looked when she said it, wrinkled and all dat—like she smelled somethin' real bad."

They started for the beach. On the way, they caught a horse that was running loose. Timothy rode with the two boys sitting in front of him, wrapped together with blankets. The boys kept quiet. It seemed to be their nature. But their eyes told a different story. Timothy shuddered at the hatred he saw for himself in the eyes of both boys.

Oso Río ran alongside the horse.

Chapter 87

Timothy, You Got to Save Us!

Timothy Caldwell
January 1838
South Florida

BEFORE SUNUP, OSO RÍO, TIMOTHY, and the two boys were in place on the beach. Oso Río untied the oversized pouch he carried at his waist and dumped the contents onto the sand. Against the whiteness of the sand, Timothy recognized Baba's wig and dress, the one she called her Gypsy dancing frock. Oso Río insisted he wear both to attract the Spanish. Timothy thought they must be a pitiful sight to anyone looking from a passing ship through a captain's glass.

"You got to save us, man. It's up to you now."

"How am I to save us?" Timothy asked, frustrated.

"I done told you, man. You look like a Spanish officer, all dark, short, and beautiful, like Miss Baba said. You get out on the beach and flag them down. With that wig, you kin pass for Miss Baba. When they come ashore, you talk them into taking us with them. That ship be here before sundown. I seen Miss Baba meet them before. Sometime' I try to go with her to protect her. I would hide in the woods behind her and leave her alone when they come."

"What am I going to say to the Spanish when they get here?"

"You got something for a white flag?"

"No."

"You got some white underpants?"

Timothy hesitated. "Yes."

"Pull them off, and we'll make us a flag. Get busy, Coon Man."

When the Spanish ship arrived, glints of glass from the rail reflected the sunlight, letting Timothy know the ship's officers were giving him an overall visual inspection with the telescope. Timothy cringed.

As a group of people, this beach party looks pretty odd. At once short and tall, burnt umber and white, adult and child. Fucking River Bear and a runaway soldier.

But he was certain his group appeared harmless to the Spanish who, after all, were just looking for some sport.

Before the sun set that day, Oso Río and his son were on their way to Mexico, working guests of the Spanish marines. The Spanish respected the memory of Baba Lou, having taken pleasure with her frequently. Communication was easy, thanks to a Catholic priest onboard, a Frenchman, who also spoke perfect English and Spanish.

But Timothy and his small boy stayed behind on the beach. Mercifully, items of men's clothing had been traded for the Gypsy dancing frock.

Jesus, thought Timothy, *what have I gotten myself into this time?*

Before the ship left, the crew donated a nanny goat. Timothy's son needed his milk to grow, and grow he would … if it were up to Timothy. Though he may not feel ready for fatherhood, he was weary of people not accepting the responsibility of their children. He thought briefly of Sarah Jean.

"They tell me your name is Juan Carlos, boy. That true?" Timothy asked his son.

Juan Carlos only whimpered. It wasn't certain he was Timothy's child, but odds were that was the case, at least in Timothy's mind. Timothy found only mistrust in the boy's eyes.

In a bit of unexpected good fortune, Timothy recaptured the horse that had carried them here from the lake. In the kit bag where he had left it, he found his uniform and changed clothing. This time, he was once again an army lieutenant. He thought that if God were willing, he would reclaim his life. Perhaps he also would try to become Sir Timothy. Maybe that would be important to him, maybe not. But Juan Carlos would be given his God-given chance. Of that, Timothy Caldwell was certain.

No child of mine will ever be without a father—or a mother, if I can arrange it. Those things are very important. He was thinking about his own mother and father.

"Damn," he said, right out loud.

Chapter 88

Ocean-Going Steamboat
Pulaskie to Philadelphia

Amanda Worsham
Spring 1838
Charleston, South Carolina

In late spring, Patience remained in Charleston with Joseph. Being the sickly season, maybe that wasn't the safest thing to do, but she had so many business items to take care of, so much to do about the Worsham family's problems. Joseph refused to move Sarah Jean's body to Manchester for burial near Frances. His daughter would rest in the private cemetery on the Mackenzie property, a bitterness reinforcement that served no good purpose for the family. For example, how was Aunt Meg to know, to understand?

When the time arrived at last to leave for Philadelphia, it was hot, stuffy, and the sea breeze offered little relief. Patience was having trouble breathing—a vapor, perhaps. Captain Bob was overdue with the *Anne Bayliss* from England, and Joseph was afraid to wait any longer for one of his ships to arrive. Captain Bob didn't want to sail one of Joseph's new ships registered under the United States flag. He loved the British Union Jack too much for that. His trip from Liverpool to Charleston transported a cargo of machinery for the fledgling textile industry in the Carolinas, an industry Joseph was certain would be important in the new world developing, a world of machines and steam power. He would see to it that such things came to pass.

Patience didn't like steamboats anymore, period. There had been several terrible accidents, explosions or fires, on steamboats, and many fine people had been lost. In October the year before, the *Home*, a coastal steamer belonging to James Allaire's Southern Steam Packet Company, had been lost off Cape Hatteras. James Allaire had been onboard, and Patience was especially mindful of the fact.

But Joseph had the last word. He booked passage for the two of them on the *Pulaskie*, out of Savannah. On the thirteenth of June 1838, the *Pulaskie* waited at the wharf in Charleston with 155 paying passengers onboard bound for Baltimore.

When it was time for the *Pulaskie* to leave, Amanda hugged Joseph, said goodbye, then turned to Mother Patience.

"Do you remember talking with me about terrible mistakes? What did you mean when you said 'We all share in the shame'?"

Patience studied Amanda for a moment before answering. "There's no shame in making a terrible mistake and then working with Almighty God to correct it, Amanda. The problem comes when people get the notion their pleasure, their convenience, counts more than another's life."

"Slavery?"

"You think about it. You and I speak often of prophecy, Amanda. If you study history, one thing is clear."

"And what is that?"

"If you could travel backward in time ... to any time you choose, there's one thing you could count on when you got there."

"One thing would be true you say? What would that be?"

"No matter the time ... no matter the place, you would arrive at a situation where mankind should be preparing for the next Great War. It's evil, you see, evil catching good people unaware. And that fills the pages of history books ... fills the Bible too, I must add. Have you read of the siege of Troy?"

"Ileum?"

"Well … yes … and Homer's *Iliad* tells of the whole pitiful mess. But the truth is, no matter how wealthy, no matter how self-righteous, if you aren't ready to meet military force head on, then you're likely to fall—be ground into the dust."

"A country, you mean?"

"An uppity country, you understand—obsessed with do-gooders—not paying enough attention to the military—young men willing to die to protect a way of life."

Amanda drew a sharp breath. *Uppity.* She could see Moses saying that in her mind's eye: *"An uppity nigger," he had said. Damn that awful word.*

"I'll not say more," said Patience. "We've happy plans to make, you and I. We must meet again soon and make such plans."

Amanda was still puzzled. *What exactly is the point? Time? Circumstance? God? Prophecy? War?* But one thing was certain: Amanda loved her newfound mother.

Patience placed a small folded note in Amanda's hand before turning away to leave. She said as she squeezed Amanda's hand, "Wait until I'm gone to read this. I love you."

Amanda stood on the Charleston wharf watching the *Pulaskie* pull away. There certainly was something about steamboats: they departed with impunity—and whenever it suited their crew. No need to wait for tides, or to wait for favorable winds. She felt a twinge of pain as she watched. She agreed with Patience. She didn't like steamboats, either.

But something else bothered her. The same old feeling of cold chills. But she had felt these things before, and sometimes it all worked out right. Maybe there was some difficulty here, some unpleasantness, and some danger. But she worked hard to suppress the feelings. She'd decided to pay less attention to them now that she was grown and not to annoy people with them.

Almighty God has better things to do than to talk with the likes of me, she thought.

Patience waved.

Amanda returned the wave; then she thought about the steamship *Home* and how *Home* had been lost at sea. She waved again, reaching up with her open hand, as though to touch Patience, who now bobbed so far across the open water. Amanda closed her hand, a gesture of futility. She could not reach her, but somehow heartfelt emotions bridged the distance between them. Patience knew that Amanda loved her, and that was comforting.

As she stood alone on the wharf, she began to feel better about things. She could do nothing more ... except read Patience's note. She pulled it from her pocket.

"Amanda darling," the note said. I can't say I trust steamboats. You and I must talk about the ring. If something happens to me, check with my secretary in Boston. There is a leather-bound ledger of notes, names, and addresses for you, and your copy of my will. Be careful.

"I received a message from the army just today, our Timothy has been found. But he was in a battle with the Seminole and has disappeared again. We should hope for the best and pray for young Timothy. We will speak of this as soon as we are able. I really don't know what to say. In the meantime, find Traveler. He may know about Timothy.

"God bless. I love you. Sincerely, Patience Hannah."

"Timothy lives! I must speak with Traveler about this," she spoke out loud. "What does everything else she said in the note mean?" Amanda asked the empty wharf. "And Mother Patience has no secretary."

She never mentioned a secretary, she thought. *Who could that be? Maybe I'll talk to Lester whenever I go to Boston. Patience loves me—a cryptic note at best. Goodness. Oh well, I will ask her about it when I visit Boston. Perhaps that will be soon.*

Chapter 89

Death Stalks the Pulaskie
Patience and Joseph Are Killed

Joseph Worsham
June 1838
At sea

JOSEPH SURVEYED THE PROMENADE DECK. It was well nigh time to escape the Carolina and Georgia sickly season, and there were people onboard bound for Newport and Saratoga who would pass the summer months in a pleasant climate. He and Patience strolled through the passageway that led to their cabin. When they reached it, he unlocked the door.

But what—who—was that in the passageway?

Someone darted out of sight, mumbling, "As it were … as it were."

Joseph realized at once it was the man called Semmes, the one-eyed solicitor he'd met in Bermuda. But what was Semmes doing on this steamship?

Grewno shows up, now Semmes. What the hell does it mean?

Joseph left Patience in the cabin and went to find the captain. On the way he saw Semmes again.

"I say, Semmes," Joseph called catching Semmes's attention, "what are you doing here … on this boat?"

Semmes paused when he heard Joseph's voice, but then he turned and scrambled up the stairs toward the deck. Joseph ran after him.

What the hell is he up to?

Outside, Semmes disappeared into the crowd of passengers enjoying the view of the Carolina coast from the port side of the deck. Joseph took off his jacket, held it across his left forearm, and moved carefully to the ship's rear, past the walking-beam steam engines. At once he saw Semmes running toward the rear of the deck, well behind the side paddle wheels.

Joseph called out, "Semmes ... Semmes. Wait, man! I want to talk to you."

As Semmes reached the railing, he turned toward Joseph, then looked briefly over his shoulder toward the Carolina coast.

Just a few more steps. Joseph ran, his breath bursting from his lungs.

Semmes pulled his gloved hand from his right sleeve.

The one-handed man. This was Moss Moonie's one-handed man!

Semmes reached for Joseph; the hooks in the glove attached to Joseph's coat. Semmes pulled away, leaving coat and gloved hand behind.

Joseph was stunned. *What?* Smoke rose from the gloved hand. *Bomb ... It's a bomb. Semmes is the one-eyed bomb thrower!* The thought seared itself into his mind.

Joseph instinctively pushed the jacket toward Semmes.

Semmes caught it, but before he could toss it over the rail, the bomb exploded, and Semmes fell overboard. Pieces of the burst bomb whistled through the air around Joseph. He heard a piece strike the boiler.

Stunned, Joseph wiped a thin spray of blood from his face with his sleeve. *I must find a crewman, any crewman*, he thought. When he did find one, the fiery last rays of the evening sunset made the *Pulaskie's* wake glisten with orange froth.

The captain wouldn't come about for Semmes's sake, but regardless, the watery place where Joseph saw Semmes fall into the sea was far away by that time. The crew knew nothing about the incident. And as the captain said, the coast of Carolina was really quite near, anyway. A person *could* make it swimming. Semmes must have known that—but a one-armed man? Or rather, one-handed—oh, well. Furthermore, no record existed of Semmes traveling onboard the *Pulaskie*.

The crew diligently searched the places where Joseph had sighted Semmes, to perhaps uncover any clue as to his business onboard. They found nothing.

The incident was the subject of curious conversation at dinner. None of the others had seen Semmes jump. But despite the occurrence, later in the evening, Joseph and Patience were quite happy and danced in the ballroom until very late.

Joseph held Patience closely throughout the last dance. She looked quite attractive in her evening dress. He decided she was one for whom it was well worth making allowances. Maybe she wouldn't marry him, but she had contributed immeasurably to Amanda's well-being and certainly to his.

When the song ended, Joseph led her to the cabin and to bed. He saw a bolt of lightning flashing across the sky through the porthole and thought briefly as he disrobed that it reminded him of the stark nakedness of that dead tree on Cape Cod.

In the bed, love and their need for each other took control, to make their union an altogether joyous occasion. They were together. They were joined, and they had their lives all planned.

* * * * *

Patience and Joseph drifted off to sleep. And when, later in the night, a great explosion rocked the *Pulaskie*, both were far away in their dreams. The huge, torn piece of what had been the starboard steam boiler carried away the promenade deck, part of their cabin, part of their bed, and the two lovers in each other's arms. The cold waters off the North Carolina coast covered the pieces that remained, for what fell into the darkness was torn and broken timbers and dreams.

It was the fourteenth of June, 1838.

Book 5

Amanda Is on Her Own

Deliver me, O my God, out of the hand of the wicked, out of the hand of the unrighteous and cruel man.

For thou *art* my hope, O Lord GOD: *thou art* my trust from my youth.

By thee have I been holden up from the womb: thou art he that took me out of my mother's bowels: my praise *shall be* continually of thee.

—Psalm 71:4–6, KJV

Chapter 90

"On Tea"
For the Queen's Birthday in 1663,
Politician and Poet, Edmund Waller

Seventeenth Century
England

> Venus her myrtle, Phoebus has her bays;
> Tea both excels, which she vouchsafes to praise.
> The best of Queens, and best of herbs, we owe
> To that bold nation, which the way did show
> To the fair region where the sun doth rise,
> Whose rich productions we so justly prize.
> The Muse's friend, tea does our fancy aid,
> Repress those vapors which the head invade,
> And keep the palace of the soul serene,
> Fit on her birthday to salute the Queen.

Chapter 91

God, Hollis, Get a New Word
Hollis, Drunk, Comes Calling

Amanda Worsham
May 1839
Charleston, South Carolina

"Niggerlover! Niggerlover!" Hollis shouted at the top of his voice in front of Worsham House. He was on horseback in the street beyond the gate with its arched latticework rose arbor. "Come out, you stupid, gutless niggerlover. Come out. You can't hide from me forever … you rotten bitch."

Hollis was becoming hoarse from shouting.

What does Hollis want now? thought Amanda. *The most despicable person I know.*

It was May. And in the four years since Sarah Jean's death, Hollis had been steadily drinking. Always surly, usually irrational, Hollis had also been steadily losing touch with whatever humanity he had possessed before Sarah Jean died.

Amanda quickly called Bridget O'Brien, a young Irish girl whose ticket to the United States Amanda had purchased as a Christmas gift. She sent her out the back of the house to run to the *Anne Bayliss* and fetch the captain.

Bridget, a very sweet person, had red hair and freckles. She also was proud and refused to join her Savannah family until she had worked out her passage. Amanda decided to tell her it was paid in full. She had grown to love Bridget in the months she had known her. Freeing slaves was one thing, but ending Bridget's servitude contract was quite another. Bridget would not have allowed Amanda to pay her passage to America without a six-year contract, as the girl was strong on courage, character, ability, and on doing what she thought *was the right thing.*

Well, Amanda, Amanda said to herself, *you can't save the whole damn world.*

Earlier in the day, Amanda had visited Captain Boyd and invited him to come over later in the evening with some of his crew for a home-cooked meal.

Now, she thought, *with Hollis screaming obscenities in the street, is the time for them to arrive, although it is not quite suppertime. They probably won't be here for a while yet.*

Amanda recalled Captain Bob's last visit to Charleston. He had arrived on the *Anne Bayliss* just in time for the Fourth of July celebration. Amanda had arranged for the factor to dispose of the mill machinery Joseph had ordered from Liverpool; then she invited Captain Bob and the first mate to the house for dinner. It was the first time she had met First Mate Boyd Hampton.

Soon afterward, Captain Bob Mathison returned to Bristol to retire with his beautiful wife, and Boyd Hampton had taken over as captain of the *Anne Bayliss.*

Amanda ventured out to the front porch. Hollis, reeling drunk, glared at her with hatred in his eyes. He goaded the horse with the heels of his boots and pushed his way through the gate, bending his head as he rode beneath the rose arbor.

Damn Hollis Mackenzie. "Hollis, now, what's wrong with you?" Amanda demanded. "Are you drunk out of your mind? Or just crazy out of your mind? Get out of the yard."

Amanda thought it ludicrous for Hollis to be calling anyone a filthy name like that, having raped Arabella and fathered her child. She refused even to think of that awful, hurtful *N*-word.

"Get your horse and yourself out of my front yard, Hollis," she repeated.

The horse began to nibble at the South Seas rose Amanda had planted by the front steps. The bush had grown tall and scraggly, since Moses wasn't around to tend to the yard, and it was in need of a good pruning. But Amanda remembered what Harry Smith had told her: "That rose is poisonous to a horse."

"Hollis," she warned, "you must stop your horse from eating my bush … this minute. That's a South Seas rose, and it'll kill him."

"There's no stinking rose'll kill my horse, Miss Manda."

He spoke the pet name the slaves all used for Amanda with a sneer, with disgust.

Amanda had freed all the slaves she ever had access to, and that undoubtedly was what riled Hollis. And after Sarah Jean's death, she had finally been able to buy Arabella and set her free. Hollis just couldn't stand that. Amanda knew how he felt, how the others felt—Beau Videau and all the rest included. She really didn't care, but their scorn was the reason she couldn't stand Charleston anymore. She couldn't even stand the South.

"You can't save the world," Father had told her in Bermuda years ago.

Oh, I miss Father.

"Hollis, just do as I say, will you?" she implored, tapping her foot.

Hollis leaned across the saddle to examine the bush. "Tha's not even a rose, Miss Manda," he said. "No manly horse'll eat a rose, anyway. That's stupid."

"Hollis, take your horse and leave while there's still time."

"Oh no, you don't, Miss Manda," he slurred, weaving from side to side in the saddle. "I've come to carry you away from all this. I know you really *want* me. You always have. That's why you were so mad at Sarah Jean when she married me. That's why you wanted my baby so much after Sarah Jean died. I know how you *really* feel."

Furious, she thought, *The nerve of the bastard, to say that to me now, after all I've been through.* "Who the hell would want you, Hollis?" she hollered. "I don't even think Sarah Jean did."

That was a *manipulation*—a mistake, if ever there was one.

"You get out of my yard right this minute," she said. "You hear me?"

"I'll go when I get damn good and ready. And you get that boy of mine dressed up to go too. And I'll take the nigger bitch's brat too."

"You crazy yellow dog. I don't want to go anywhere with you. I never heard such trash in all my life. And you're not going anywhere with any of my babies. All you ever do is drink and rape women. If I were a man, I ..."

Hollis dismounted, unsteady on his feet. He stumbled forward and grabbed Amanda, shoving her back up the steps toward the open door. The next moment found them in the foyer.

Chapter 92

Hollis Meets the "Pomander from Hell"

Amanda Worsham
May 1839
Charleston, South Carolina

"Arabella," shouted Amanda. "We have a guest. See if—"

Hollis slapped Amanda. "Shut up, bitch. You don't need no damn nigger to help you."

The slap smarted, giving her an attitude of coldness and intense determination.

The nerve of the bastard. "I was about to order tea, Hollis," she said, her voice was steady and cold, even as her body trembled. "You know I enjoy my tea. Come into the parlor, Hollis." When Arabella appeared, she added, "Arabella, fetch some hot water for me and my best tea set."

Hollis wobbled, refusing to go into the parlor and take a seat.

In no time, Arabella arrived with a tray and tea set, pot already filled with boiling water and two cups. She placed everything on the table beside the parlor door. Amanda pulled a straight-backed chair over and sat beside the table.

"Just a moment, Arabella." Amanda removed her gold chain with the gold locket and silver pierced heart. Removing the heart, she dropped it into the teapot. "I need some help. I feel a vapor coming on. Arabella, fetch the brandy. I need that too."

Hollis merely eyed her, saying nothing.

When Arabella returned with the brandy, Amanda poured tea into both cups. She counted the requisite seven Moss Moonies then pulled the cork from the bottle of brandy and poured some into her cup. She handed the brandy back to Arabella.

"Here," she said. "We don't need this anymore. Take it away. And that cup … I poured too much brandy in that one. I've changed my mind. Take that away too." Then she whispered, "And for God's sake, don't you drink any of it, you hear? Take the pomander out of the cup where he cannot see. Bring this cup back when you are finished, brandy and all. Do not pour it out. It's for Hollis—should put him on the floor where we can handle him. Do you understand? It has Moss Moonies potion …"

Amanda did not finish the statement. She only shook her head.

Arabella left the room with the tray and the brandy.

Hollis entered the parlor at that moment and leaned against the wall.

"Do you think I don't know what you're about, Miss Manda?" he said. "Do you think I'm stupid? I saw you put a huge lump of crystallized sugar in that pot. You think you are so smart. Got a sweet tooth, don't you?"

"Whatever do you mean?"

"Listen, bitch," Hollis said, trying to stand upright, "you're gonna have to fill in for your dead sister, that's what. That's what you really want, isn't it? You need to have me in the bed, don't you? Sure. You need that—"

"Hollis, you foulmouthed *crétin*—"

"Don't call me any of your family names, you bitch. What are you, French now?

"You should leave now. You really should."

"Bring that tea back, nigger—"

Arabella appeared in the doorway with the tray, the small teacup on it.

"Hollis, I poured that brandy for me. You've had quite enough, thank you."

"Well, you can relax," he said, teetering toward the table. "When I finish that brandy you poured for yourself, we're going to your bed. You'll see what it's like to be a Mackenzie woman. And it's about time."

He grabbed the cup and drank the hot liquid quickly. "Damn … crazy bitch," he mumbled.

Hollis burned his mouth, but that was the best of it. He'd just consumed the devil's own …

He cursed, rising in fury, and ran wide-eyed into the foyer wall.

Arabella rushed out of the kitchen holding a shotgun.

"You watch yo'self, Hollis Mackenzie. You ain't nothin' but white trash no way," she yelled, pointing the shotgun at him. "You ain't no better than all the Geechee white trash from here to Moncks Corner. Just listen to the way you talk. What you say?" The shotgun wavered, then locked on to Hollis. "What you say? Devil. I want to hear it. What you say, SOB. What you say—"

Hollis pulled a pistol from his belt. "Look out, nigger!" he yelled and fired.

Amanda dove for the floor. The ball whizzed by, clearing both Amanda and Arabella by a wide margin. Hollis ran through the front door to the yard and mounted his horse. The horse wheeled, tried to buck Hollis off, jumped the fence, and galloped down the road with Hollis holding on for dear life.

In a moment, they'd disappeared from sight.

Inside the foyer, Amanda hugged Arabella.

"If you know of someone with bedbugs, that tea will kill them … the bugs, I mean. Otherwise, be certain the remaining tea and the seeds in my pomander get poured down the necessary this night. That stuff is dangerous. God, what if it's fatal? Save me the pomander. I've enjoyed having it. Maybe I'll see Moss Moonie again soon."

She felt no remorse for having given Hollis the potion. Glancing outside, she saw that it was almost dark.

Chapter 93

Captain Boyd and Crew Arrive

Amanda Worsham
May 1839
Charleston, South Carolina

LATER, WHEN BRIDGET CAME BACK with the captain, a mob of men had congregated in the front yard, maybe most of the crew from two of her ships currently docked in the harbor. The captain pushed his way through and followed Bridget up the front steps.

"Lass," Captain Boyd said, huffing and puffing from the brisk walk. "What is it? Where's that crazy man? We came as soon as we could."

The last one to arrive, a huge red-haired man, stood in the gateway, so large that he filled the space encircled by the rose arbor. He had a checked scarf tied around his head and beads of sweat on his forehead, and a look of horror on his face. The men called him Tiny.

When Amanda came to the door, every man took off his hat. The expression on their faces showed extreme concern.

"Are you all right, Mistress Worsham?" asked the captain. "Are we too late to be of any help?"

"No, you're not too late," she assured him. "But he's gone. We're all well here. Hollis was drunk and threatened us with his gun. It's all my fault. I know it is. He came because of me ... because he wants me to go with him, to live with him, I suppose." She started to cry.

"But whatever it was, poor Arabella tried to protect us and came out with a shotgun. Oh, I don't know what to do. I just don't know. He left on a sick horse too."

"Which way did he go?" Boyd asked.

"Toward the farm, I think. That way." She pointed in the direction Hollis had taken.

Boyd stepped into the house. "Missy," he said, taking her shoulders in his hands, "tonight's a full moon. I'm going out toward that farm and see if I can catch him. If the horse's ill, maybe I can. What's wrong with the horse?"

"Hollis let it eat some of that bush beside the front steps."

"The *South Seas rose?*"

"Yes."

"See you in a bit, missy."

"Boyd, be careful. He has a gun."

"Well, if he's that drunk, he may not have reloaded. And anyway, see that big man standing there?" He pointed to the man in the gateway.

"Yes. That's Tiny," Amanda replied. "I know about him. He's your ship's carpenter. Why did he come? Why did so many men come?"

"Missy, when I told them the way Hollis raped poor Arabella, Tiny began to cry. When I told them of your sister Sarah Jean's dying while trying to birth Hollis' child, Tiny was furious. He went berserk. His mother had been raped, you know. Tiny's a bastard himself, doesn't know who his father is. His poor mother died birthing him.

"Tiny was raised by his old-maid aunt. She told him horror stories about things like that. He really has deep feelings about women and sex and having babies. He's afraid of women, anyway. But he's not afraid of any man, that's for sure. If we don't go after that lubber now, I'll never get old Tiny to leave here 'til he makes it right. Tiny thinks having a baby's the most awful experience a woman can go through. His old-maid aunt told him that, I think."

Amanda looked at Tiny, at how large the man really was, and thought having a baby so large—one that would grow into a man Tiny's size—might be a bad experience all in itself. Maybe that was what the old-maid aunt had meant. Amanda shook her head and took out a kerchief to wipe the tears from her cheeks.

The crowd left all at once, Tiny and Boyd in the lead.

Amanda was confident that her pomander had only caused additional confusion. After all, Moss Moonie had said, "You can't kill the devil."

Later in the evening, Boyd stopped by to tell Amanda they had caught Hollis about a mile from town. The horse was dead. Hollis had shot the poor thing when it stumbled and fell into the ditch. Hollis had vomited most of the way back to town.

When Amanda asked, Boyd told her that Hollis had volunteered to go to sea. Tiny had carried him to the ship. And with any luck, the *Anne Bayliss* would cross the Charleston bar with the tide. She was all packed with the Charleston goods for Liverpool and was ready for the return voyage.

"See you next trip," he said and left.

Amanda was happy to see Hollis go. She was sick of Hollis, and she knew Boyd wouldn't really hurt him. Maybe a sea voyage would do him some good. He might at least sober up.

Volunteered? She had a mental picture of Tiny seeing to it.

Tomorrow she would send someone to see about the dead horse.

A smart-looking young Welch farmer named Owain Heuews also arrived from Liverpool on one of the regular merchant vessels. He seemed intent upon making a success of himself in the Carolinas. Amanda liked him right away.

Owain, like many others, had saved his money until he could purchase the passage to America. He had arrived with very little in his pockets to sustain him in the New World, but he was a good and proud individual, and fairly well educated in business matters.

Amanda gave Owain a job as bookkeeper in the Charleston office. It would take him the better part of a year to save and prepare for the move north to Wilmington. He wanted to buy a farm somewhere in North Carolina.

Although Owain might have wanted to court Amanda, he did not. Was he timid, or was it because he was embarrassed at his station in life? Amanda wasn't certain, but she hoped it was a temporary situation that would change as he gained confidence in himself and his new life in the United States. When the time came, she made a job for him in Wilmington, though she had little in the way of office work for him to do, except the business of arranging for factors.

Amanda just *liked* Owain. She was very pleased whenever he came to her for advice, and he did so on several occasions. Before she thought much of it, 1840 had nearly passed. Already, summer had slipped into fall.

Chapter 94

Political Upheaval in Charleston

Amanda Worsham
Fall 1839
Charleston, South Carolina

CHARLESTON WAITED AS AN ELDERLY matriarch might wait: restrained, opinionated, and somewhat resistant to change … unless, of course, the change was the product of the fiery temperament and wit of the Southern plantation gentry. But as change soughed through the palmettos that year, the gentry bickered in the Charleston streets— at meetings, social events, church gatherings, sometimes standing in the street late into the night illuminated by lamplight and torchlight.

No new word came of Timothy Caldwell—nothing since the military communiqué Patience had received before her death.

Then in the fall of 1840, the South fast became a place of political abandonment, of political upheaval. Turmoil filled the streets of Charleston. Ideas tossed about became seething, writhing *creatures*— like cockroaches, worms, or snakes caught in the very fires of hell.

Liberty … equality … fraternity. These words were but toys in the hands of the young partisans of the South, not watchwords or a battle cry to freedom, as they had been to other generations and to France, our ally. Everywhere in Charleston, people argued politics, tariffs, a place called Texas and slavery … always states' rights and slavery. Abolitionists, pro slavers, revolutionaries, anarchists,

Federalists, loyalists, states' rights extremists, statists were all there—and others.

Religious and temperance fanatics, Whigs, pacifists, warmongers, atheists—Amanda heard them all on the Charleston street corners as she drove by in her carriage. They argued everything but Jacksonian Democrat ideas. People in Charleston tended to be single-minded on that subject. Any Jacksonian Democrat idea equaled political cholera. People in Charleston, for the most part, avoided the subject.

It was illegal for the gentry to smoke a pipe or cigar within the garden at White Point, near Worsham House, during posted hours, according to the city's ordinance. But a free man of color …

Well, if *any* man of color were caught smoking in such a manner, by law his punishment began at the guardhouse and could end with corporal punishment—according to the mayor's fancy.

Charleston's vigilante port authority, the South Carolina Association, enforced an infamous and now illegal requirement by federal law that any Negro sailor found onboard ship be jailed during his ship's time in port … jailed because of some whim of God (*black or white?*). But did Carolinians really *care?* Some Carolinians did. Amanda did.

Chapter 95

Hollis Is a British Navy Volunteer?

Amanda Worsham
Fall 1839
Charleston, South Carolina

IT WAS A TIME OF embarrassment for Amanda, so she stayed in her
house most days. But today found her on her way from the down-
town shops to the Mackenzie farm. She really thought the kind of
politics that manifested itself in Charleston extremely boring. She
tried to go at least once a week to see to the needs of the poorhouse
and also the yard slaves that she had freed and then hired to work at
their same jobs. These were any and all slaves that she could influence
her friends and neighbors to sell to her.

I really do not know what else to do, she thought. Because of her
actions, she had many such house and yard keepers around her. With
the influx of workers, there really wasn't much for Miss Bridget to do
after all, so Amanda decided to make Bridget her personal secretary.

Amanda spent some of the morning inquiring about the whereabouts of the new clipper ship Traveler had promised to bring.
Joseph had mentioned building such a ship before his death and had
arranged to name her the *Frances Courtney*. There had been no news
from Traveler, and it wasn't like him to be late to any appointment.

She'd received one bit of news, though. She found a letter via
ship's mail from Captain Boyd. It said that Hollis had been "vol-

unteered" into the British Navy. Apparently, he had made such a nuisance of himself at sea that he'd become unbearable, so Tiny convinced Hollis to become British. Tiny might have gone with him—just to continue his training on manners, but Tiny was much too large a man for the British Navy.

Well, Hollis dodged the bullet on that one, thought Amanda.

Chapter 96

Traveler Arrives with the Frances Courtney

Amanda Worsham
Fall 1839
Charleston, South Carolina

IN ANOTHER WEEK, AFTER FINAL checkouts were finished, the recently completed *Frances Courtney* made its maiden voyage and arrived in Charleston with Traveler onboard.

She is a beautiful ship, thought Amanda, *beautiful indeed. Her namesake, my beautiful mother, would have loved to see her drifting into the Charleston dock. Oh, well …*

When she caught up with him, Traveler said some good men were looking for Timothy. There were some leads … but thus far no Timothy.

Amanda decided to do her very best to forget about young Timothy.

It turned out that Traveler had made plans to ship Sea Island cotton to Liverpool. When Amanda told him perhaps they shouldn't, because she was having second thoughts about the entire affair, he said doing so was the least they could do since the poor slaves had worked all winter to remove the cottonseeds.

Beau's slaves. He wouldn't sell them to me.

"Economics and the humanities make poor bedfellows," he had said, shaking his head. "But it should be the very last such shipment. I think you agree, Miss Worsham."

"Yes, certainly, Traveler. And you may call me Amanda. I rather like the name."

"There's still the other shoe to take care of, Amanda," he said.

"*¿Por qué. Estos zapatas no hacen daño.*" She spoke in Spanish, knowing he would understand. "Why? These shoes don't hurt." Amanda was having a bit of fun with him. *Maybe he would change the subject now.* She had had a bad feeling about this conversation.

"The smuggler … Gill Fletcher will be after this ship now," Traveler answered, ignoring her.

"Whatever do you mean? Why?" *Damn!*

"Some of our men have been taken by them and killed. Gill Fletcher would like nothing better than to steal the new *Frances Courtney.* She can do thirteen knots or more. And they want to get even with your father, I think, because he stood directly in their way and refused to join them. Gill Fletcher isn't likely to forget."

"Isn't there anything we can do to protect the *Frances Courtney?*"

"Yes and no, Amanda. If they see you onboard, I'm thinking they will try to head us off with the steamship Fletcher keeps to the North. I would arrest the lot of them if I could. Damn it all! I need hard evidence. It's not that easy to spring a trap at sea."

"Father told me about Fletcher," she lied. Actually Patience had told her. Joseph Worsham had kept his peace on the subject. "I thought that was over long ago. Why now? Why harm me?"

"He's been waiting for his chance. Now, my operatives tell me, he wants to put *you* out of business and take this ship. And there's more."

Amanda shuddered.

Traveler was nervously working his fingers, worry clouding his eyes. Amanda found it an altogether disturbing gesture.

"I see Patience gave you the ring," he said, eyeing the ring's lovely heart-shaped setting.

Amanda held out her hand. "Yes. Isn't it beautiful?"

"Beautiful it is. But have you any idea what that ring means?"

"It means Patience loves me. She told me that before she died."

"Indeed, she does … or did, most certainly. But the ring holds a deeper meaning. One it's time you learn about."

"Very well," Amanda said, her curiosity piqued. "What does the ring mean?"

Chapter 97

So, Traveler, What Exactly Do You Do?

Amanda Worsham
Fall 1839
Charleston, South Carolina

"Patience's code name was '*le cœur de rubis*,'" Traveler explained, "a French phrase—*not a proper name*, you understand, or just *cœur de rubis*. I put it together for her after Patience chose Ruby Heart as her *nom de guerre*. Maybe it could be *le cœur d'rubis* It means, I believe, 'the ruby heart.' She asked me to say it in several of the Latin romance languages for her. You know, it is because of the seaports I visit that I pick up so many languages. I have a knack for it, I think. She wore it to identify herself to our operatives … to strangers who would be our friends, as it were, *especially* to the French. They were told in advance of the ring, of its offset heart, and the ring identified her as the one they sought. If that phrase is incorrect—*they* should likewise be incorrect, or something like that, *feigned*, because they have been instructed in that way. Amanda, should that be 'had been instructed'? I speak these languages, but I don't really know *each one's grammar*. But you can hear that in my speech, can't you?"

"But why would Mother Patience need a code name?" *And why so much damned confusion! The offset part especially is weird.* She said nothing about his amazing talent.

"Patience loved this country. Our country. She took us off budget with our plans. She had the wherewithal—and the knowledge—to make *my* business possible."

"What *is* your business, Traveler? Why are you … what you are?"

"My business changes almost with the tides. I do whatever must be done to keep us free, to keep us strong. I'm a poet errant, Amanda. Not the knight errant, but more the Sancho Panza. I believe you *know* him, don't you?"

Off budget—the government's budget?

Amanda ignored the reference to Don Quixote. She had observed times when Traveler changed the subject rather than provide a direct answer. Somehow she must convey the sense of urgency she felt—to keep the ideas flowing in her head.

"What of the military? Isn't that the military's job?" *What was the heart of rubies? What did it mean?*

"Certainly the military has that responsibility," Traveler agreed. "Patience knew all the important military leaders, their civilian counterparts. Her money, her friends, her clear mind made the military strong enough to hold its own in this world. Otherwise, well, I just don't know. As to why I am here …"

Traveler fisted his hands.

"When she was alive, Patience reached out to people. She helped us. Maybe she still does. You have the ring … *her* ring. I'll wager she made you privy to everything that was her *persona*. What you lacked, she has probably given to you now in her will. Else, why would she have given you the ring, Amanda? Now you are *cœur de rubis*. Or perhaps you're simply Ruby Heart—as if that *nom de guerre* were your actual name. That would be your choice. But if you change the name, you obviously must change the ring. Do you understand?"

Amanda nodded. Suddenly, in her mind's eye, she saw the problem clearly.

"May God protect us from the deeds men do in the name of good," she said.

"Did Herodotus write that?" Traveler asked. "He was always speculating that the jealous gods will strike down too much success—especially prideful success."

"My Aunt Meg said it. Well, Herodotus might have done so first. Something about a dying soldier, wounds covered with … *flies*. Not to disturb them because the flies were *satiated*. I don't know. It's a general comment on history, don't you think? Life is very dear."

Amanda thought quietly for a moment. Had Almighty God struck down a prideful, successful Joseph in that fashion? No. However, she knew … she *knew* that Joseph most certainly had been happy. Content, so to speak, and at peace with God the night he died.

"Aunt Meg may have been thinking about the awful snubbing most Anglicans gave Methodists during the eighteenth century. But, Traveler, I wonder about the things you do, the things you take upon yourself, in the name of freedom, as you say."

"I see where you're going, Amanda."

"Well?" Amanda was adamant. "What of the meddling possibilities in this ruby heart business?"

She waited for Traveler's response.

Traveler took his time, taking out his pipe from a vest pocket, placing it in his mouth with the bowl upside down, and puffing nervously—of course, not bothering to light it. He presented a strange sight, but somehow the gesture fit his other mannerisms.

Finally, he answered, "It's not what we do, Amanda—as in *good works*. Whatever happens to our country dictates our actions. Freedom always comes at a high price and will almost always cause pain for somebody. Case in point—Grewno. There really wasn't time to consider his feelings—only time to act. And act we did. Was that good? I think not. Not good, but *necessary*. Do you see the difference? Eliminating vermin like Grewno is what we *have* to do."

He didn't wait for an answer. He put his pipe away and smiled.

"And the bald-headed man we put in irons that day when Grewno died suddenly? It turns out, he wasn't wanted for anything."

"Did you turn him loose?"

"Yes."

"Where? In Charleston?"

"No. We took his chains off in Baltimore."

"Baltimore? Why Baltimore?"

"Why not? We love Baltimore. Ah, to be young and free in Baltimore."

"And bald-headed too, I suppose. Is he one of your men?"

"You surprise me, Amanda. Everyone cannot work for us. He's just a small-time thief from Statia. He speaks Dutch. You know … Saint Eustatius … one of the Leeward Islands."

Amanda somehow wasn't surprised. "I thought they spoke some form of German or German words that I never learned."

"Dutch."

"Do you know Herodotus is the consummate suspense builder?" Traveler asked.

Amanda shook her head. She almost felt in a vicarious manner the relief Traveler displayed in his change of mood. She understood he would not discuss his business further at this time. Maybe if she took up the mantle of *cœur de rubis*, he would someday.

"Herodotus conditions countless generations to receive the definitive historical comment," he said.

"Yes?" *What does Traveler have in mind?* she thought.

"And he never makes it," he answered.

"Patience reached out to help you?" Amanda could change the subject too. Traveler's humor escaped her.

"Yes, certainly. And she reached out to poor Lester. Then lastly, she reached out to your father."

"I see."

That was a blatant lie, and it had come from Amanda's mouth. She most certainly did *not* see how this puzzle fit together. Why had Mother Patience given her this ring before that fateful trip? Had she known in some prophetic way she would die in an explosion? And the business of the great wealth Patience had left Amanda in her will. Was it simply a gift of love? Or was it something more? Amanda could no longer be certain. She'd wondered at the time if Patience had been just trying to mend a bridge between them—because of Joseph … and because of the loss of her mother. Patience's gesture had seemed to be simply an offering of an inheritance, something she had not really believed would ever come to pass.

But it had.

"Traveler, I understand you are a free agent. What, exactly, is that?"

"My mother came here as a white slave. She was, of course, not free. She brought me into the world, and I am lucky for that. Prostitutes often undergo abortions each month. I am free because she wanted me to be free. I resist any kind of oath ... or the kind of swearing that involves contracts. Don't you see? That's the very thing our 'heart' group wants to curtail. People bind themselves to a cause, and then they have to see it through—no matter what."

"Centralized government–type things?"

"Aye. All of us—our group—each one wants to be here, not because an oath binds us. No oath can guarantee that kind of loyalty, anyway."

"I see your point. But I still don't really understand what it all means."

"We have reason to believe a bomb was planted onboard the *Pulaskie*. At least, there's a very good chance someone did something nefarious to cause the explosion."

"I haven't heard anything about a bomb, Traveler, really." *Well*, she thought once again, *he really knows how to change the subject—a master at it.*

"We interviewed the survivors. At this point, your guess is as good as mine about what happened exactly. But I know these people, the ones we suspect of doing this evil thing. They don't quit easily. They like to accomplish their goals."

"Traveler, the ruffian named Fletcher will not get the *Frances Courtney.* I will not allow that to happen. What would you have me do?"

"Leave for Liverpool when the ship is loaded with cotton. Leave precisely at seven in the evening this Friday, next. Just be onboard, you and your party. I'll take care of the rest."

"Very well. I'll pack my things. Are you certain you can protect us? What if they decide to plant a bomb on this ship?"

"I think we have everything under control. You've seen the guards, haven't you?"

"Your marines? I saw them marching together, marching but not in uniform. They seemed to be escorting a person wearing a wide-brimmed hat with a gunnysack pulled down over the hat and face. They were playing soldier, weren't they? And punishing some poor soul."

Traveler didn't say more for a long moment. Then he smiled and said, "They do look like marines, don't they? Some were marines in the old navy. You must have seen something that you misinterpreted. My men have practiced no marching activities. They are quite busy as it is. A detailed escort for some criminal onboard this ship? Amanda, I don't think so. And I really believe you'll be safe on this ship."

"Father told me I could trust you. And I owe you my life, anyway."

"No matter."

"Oh yes, it matters. My family will be with me. I'll be traveling with Arabella and the two children, Little Joe and Cassie May. They will travel with me from now on. I don't know for sure about Bridget, but she might want to go as well. I can't talk her into leaving until she thinks she is no longer indebted to me."

"Whatever you decide to do about your family will be fine, Amanda."

"When shall we be onboard?"

"Start loading post haste."

"Why the hurry?" she asked.

"We are being watched. I want Fletcher and his gang to know you're onboard. And bring that little flag of yours, the one with the red-and-white checker design. That was a sign of wealth a hundred years ago, I believe. It looks pink at a distance and will really get him riled up."

"You know about that?"

"Your father told me. Something left over from colonial Virginia."

Pink. That word was all it took to break Amanda's thoughts away from the present and send them back in time to Bermuda. *Pink sand. Pink memories.* She knew what Traveler meant. The flag's colors did run together when viewed from a distance. But that was not the point. It was *her* flag. One of the things left to her by her Father. Amanda remembered …

＊ ＊ ＊ ＊ ＊

In Bermuda, Frances had perished, victim of the prevailing fever, or yellow jack fever. Then Joseph had left Amanda alone in Bermuda with the Stuart family and the two slaves, Moses and Sally, while he escorted Frances's body and the unborn baby to Manchester.

It was a time of abrupt loneliness, of starting anew. Then when Joseph returned, he brought the news that Sarah Jean would remain in Manchester with the Courtney family. And he'd presented Amanda *some years ago* with the pink flag that Traveler was referring to right now.

Years ago Joseph had commissioned a flag maker in Charleston to make it for her because he knew Amanda loved the red-and-white check that colonial Virginians had treasured as symbols of wealth. Such cloths as those were labor-intensive to make, what with the fabric being handwoven from cotton colored with berries. The resulting checkered cloth made smart table napkins, or *serviettes*, as they probably would have called them, before the Americans cast off anything in their vernacular that sounded even remotely British. The flag especially pleased Amanda because Joseph specified the fringe and the letter *A* sewn on the flag were to be Kelly green, for she thought the combination quite smart.

When Amanda accompanied Joseph on long ocean voyages, she was permitted, even encouraged, to fly her pennant from the ship's maintop.

To Amanda, her flag signified that she *had arrived*. When she first saw it, she wondered if she would ever grow to be as tall as it was long. It was a rather large flag, with a split tail—a first-class pennant. At any rate, she flew it with pride. The flag and ship were hers. Indeed, all the company ships were hers—plus the responsibility for managing the shipping business.

But pink? Well, maybe. Many have seen my flag, she thought, *but maybe you're the first one to call it pink. I'm presupposed to see the red checks I know are there—so I don't see pink. Perhaps Traveler is color-blind. She knew some men were.*

With that, her thoughts returned to the present.

Chapter 98

A Trap Sprung at Sea

Amanda Worsham
October 1839
Charleston, South Carolina and at sea

As THE *FRANCES COURTNEY* PULLED away from the port of Charleston, Amanda thought about the flag. It was hardly a call to arms, but as Traveler told her to do, she'd made sure it gently flapped in the breeze on the foretop. Her flag …

The sea gusts were light, but the *Frances Courtney* ran easily through the harbor, sails only partially unfurled. Some billowed in the breeze; some did not. Traveler told her that her new ship's captain, a man from Connecticut, had said that the sails would be filled once they reached the open sea. There was too much chance of getting into trouble in the harbor under full sail.

Amanda had not yet met this captain. Traveler had hired him in New York during the ship's final stages of construction.

Captain Tom Beale—and don't you forget it—probably had some good years left in his career. He had an excellent record to date, according to Traveler. Amanda should have spent some one-on-one time with him, and she would have, except Beale had asked for emergency shore leave as soon as the *Frances Courtney* docked in order to make arrangements for a severely ill elderly aunt who lived in Kingstree, South Carolina, not too far away.

He'd returned just as the crew was preparing the *Frances Courtney* to sail.

My mercy, she thought, *I must take care of that problem—and soon. No good not knowing one's captains in this business.*

After the *Frances Courtney* crossed the Charleston bar and headed out toward the blue water, the sails began to fill and the sunset faded to full dark. The new ropes creaked, the sails rustled crisply, and the waves slapped the bow. The moonrise was hours away, but on the sea, the froth atop each wave glowed with lumines-cence. Small, glowing things gave off their faint mint-green light as the water around them was disturbed.

"Two men to every watch," she heard the captain say. "Four eyes to search out our bearing," or something to that effect.

Amanda surveyed the bright running lanterns and wondered if because of them the ship was too much of a target in the darkness. Traveler approached from behind her.

"Are you certain I shouldn't be afraid?" she asked him, turning as he reached her side.

"To be scared is a natural thing. But the truth is, we're not the only parties to this trap, Amanda."

"Fletcher?"

"No. Somewhere … There …" he pointed into the darkness, "is the fifty-gun frigate *Lafayette*, a strong, new ship. Gunners of the old school."

Amanda searched the sea beyond Traveler's outstretched arm. There … yes! She could make out the ghostly, ethereal faint-green froth of a ship's bow cutting through the sea.

"She's running quiet without lights," Traveler said.

Amanda caught a whiff of what she knew was the smell of a man-of-war: dried urine, filthy bodies, and the like. How anybody could live onboard one of those things was beyond her ability to reckon. She thought of Hollis.

"There," said Traveler, "she's passing us. Now, watch this."

He pointed to the port side of the *Frances Courtney*'s head. A rocket hissed furiously into the darkness and burst far overhead in a red, white, and blue star shell.

"Won't Fletcher's crew see that?" Amanda asked.

"Indeed. I am counting on it."

"They'll think we're celebrating. That we're crazy, or something."

"Exactly. Navy rockets. We aim them safely with tubes."

Amanda saw cinders fly in the darkness. "Steamboat!" both her ship lookouts yelled, almost in unison.

Well, that's working just fine. Now …

"Ahoy the ship." The voice came from aboard the steamboat. "Stand by for grappling irons and boarding."

A cannon fired. The shot went across their bow.

"They've taken the bait, Amanda." Traveler turned sharply to the sailor standing by. "Tell your captain to switch to aerial bomb shells, now. It's time to signal the *Lafayette*."

"Aye, sir." The sailor hustled to deliver his message.

The following events were memorable, but Amanda could hardly watch, knowing that people were being killed, and that somehow, she was involved.

The *Lafayette* came out of the darkness, and a voice, reminiscent to Amanda of the town crier in Bermuda, demanded that the crew of the steamboat surrender immediately. Then, when the steamboat opened fire, the *Lafayette* fired a broadside into it. Fletcher could be heard screaming and cursing as the steamboat sank.

"*Adiós*, you bloody devil," Traveler called.

There were no survivors.

"You won't read about that in the papers, either," Traveler added, pointing into the darkness. "There goes the other shoe."

When the battle ended, Amanda and Traveler found a moment to talk.

"Traveler, tell me about yourself. Father said you are a freelance government man. I still don't understand. What does that mean?"

"Free agent. What I do is off budget, as they say. No part of Congress—no part of the government, for that matter—will admit financing what I do. They will act as if they either don't know about it or won't speak of it, *even at gunpoint*."

"How are you paid?"

"There have been some arrangements made. I told you about *cœur de rubis*."

"Patience? I always pictured her as a butterfly."

"Butterfly? Butterfly, my foot. If she were that, it would be some Saracen-pounded bone-and-steel butterfly. Patience was one tough lady."

"Well, I never knew *cœur de rubis*, only Mother Patience."

"Miss Patience carried us a long way down the road. But until your father came along, hers was a limited effort."

"Oh? What did Father do?"

"He set our group up in business with him and paid us a commission on what we earned for his company. The arrangement was worldwide in scope."

"Did you do well?"

"At two and a half percent, my part, I now have over a quarter million dollars in the New York banks."

"Father did that well?"

"Yes."

"I had no idea."

"Not only that, but your father inadvertently financed a great deal of what we did—especially the international trips." Traveler paused. "And activities that we couldn't otherwise have engaged in. A retirement fund has been set up for one and all."

"I am happy for that. But you're suddenly frowning. What is the bad part?"

"I lost some good operatives. Robin Pierce, Charles Haskins …"

"What of Mary Haverty? Father told me about her."

"She's alive and well in Boston—a very sweet Jewish lady. And smart as a whip—I think I'll go and propose to her the first thing when I get there," he chuckled.

In the background of her thoughts, Amanda heard the ship's master say, "Now you can put the topgallants and the royals on her, mister." She reckoned that would mean more sails, more speed. At that moment, she decided to do whatever it took to find Timothy Caldwell and try to start over.

"Traveler?"

"What is it, Amanda? You need to know something more?"

"This may surprise you, but I know about Father's white slavery business—about Grewno and the rest."

"You didn't believe my story about Grewno, did you?"

"It was a reasonable story, but it wasn't the truth, now, was it?"

She felt a twinge in her heart, the kind of pain Traveler must feel now too. After all, she was discussing white slavery. Traveler's mother had actually been a white slave.

Traveler sighed. "No, it wasn't."

"Is that threat to the Worsham family really over now?"

"Amanda, I honestly believe that it is."

"This business of *cœur de rubis*. Is that a conspiracy—Patience and the heart of a ruby conspiracy? Something like that?"

"No. Our efforts are focused only as a guarantee, a kind of insurance policy that freedom will survive, not only in our country—the most wonderful example of freedom—but in the world. But ours is a job that will never be finished, I fear."

"Are you certain there is no conspiracy?"

"Aye."

"Traveler?"

"Yes."

"What is it about you and language? You speak so many—"

"I have a gift, Amanda. It has to do with God's curse."

"What? God's curse? Whatever do you mean?"

"The Tower of Babel. God said, *I will confound your language.* Yes?"

Amanda answered, quoting the scripture: "It is Genesis 11:9.

> Therefore is the name of it called Babel; because the LORD did there confound the language of all the earth: and from thence did the LORD scatter them abroad upon the face of all the earth.

"I suppose God did mean that. He certainly did exactly that. And here we are. People, some people, even a hundred miles apart, unable to communicate."

France and Germany, she thought. *England and France, for that matter. The exception is that to communicate one must work for it, study, learn the languages, that sort of thing ... as I have.*

"He also grants the gift of language to certain of us. Grewno was one, though he misused it, I suppose. Many disappoint Almighty God. The other curses, some of them, have to do with mankind's having to work for a living instead of simply enjoying the luxury of naïveté."

"The Garden of Eden, the Tree of Knowledge, do you mean?"

"Indeed."

"Traveler, your gift seems to me to be pretty praiseworthy. You speak the languages I can speak—or *have,* from *study,* as the Germans say—fairly well."

"Some tell me I have a *Bourgeois* middle-class accent. If I stay somewhere for a few weeks, Paris, Rome, Rio, for example, then I become more proficient. It's a gift, as I said, but not a perfect one. One must work if one seeks perfection. Of that, I am certain. And that applies to all things. A thing worth doing at all is worth doing well. Probably your mother always said that? Well, maybe not. But mine certainly did."

And you certainly took her words to heart, didn't you?

Chapter 99

To Know for Certain about Beau at Last

Amanda Worsham (Flashback)
August 1839
While still in Charleston, South Carolina

"AMANDA. HEY, AMANDA."

Beau Videau's familiar voice came from the front steps. He was shouting, and Charlie Videau joined in with him.

"Amanda. Are you home, Amanda? Please be home—"

Amanda swung open the front door. She greeted the two with a big smile and hug.

Well, I wondered where you two were. She was about to say so ...

Charlie spoke before she could. "Amanda. I am your brother. Can you believe it?"

"Yes, my child," said Beau, laughing. "Charlie and I just returned from England. We visited your Aunt Meg in Manchester, and she told us about a letter your mother sent to her by ship's mail long ago. Apparently, the copy Frances sent to me got lost somewhere. I will have to see about that. I will, indeed."

Amanda's heart was beating so fast that she simply stopped listening. She could not speak. She looked at the two, her father and her brother, and knew that somehow, and with God's help, everything in her life was about to change.

Chapter 100

Timothy at Last

Amanda Worsham
October 1839
At sea

"ALL THIS TALK OF CURSES. Isn't it about time for God's rainbow?"

Amanda looked toward the skyline. The moon had risen well into the sky, and she could almost see the waves, no longer luminescent, but capped with faintly green, frothy wave tops. Of course, she saw no other ship. Instead, she looked in her mind's eye to her memories, her hopes of finding Timothy, and her dreams of somehow having stable family life—maybe children of her own.

What if Timothy couldn't be found? What if he'd been killed this time?

Would she ever find another young beau? She was getting older, and she had become the brunt of Charleston's gossip—old maid, indeed. The idea of spinsterhood scared her, although outwardly she tried to show her indifference to the whole affair.

Why, she had even gone so far as writing to Miss Tilly in Bermuda to find out about Harry Smith. The news surprised her. He had moved in with that British lieutenant—the one who'd helped them in Bermuda. Amanda had thought the lieutenant was cute. So, apparently, had Harry Smith. What was his name? Hawkins? Anyhow, it was that British lieutenant who had gone on half pay from the king's service to settle in Bermuda to live with Harry Smith. They were learning to be farmers.

And of Owain Heuews, Amanda learned he'd married a North Carolina girl and become a farmer now too. His bride's father was a land-poor farm gentleman. Owain was probably destined to inherent those farm holdings someday.

Well, she thought, *that turned out fairly well for old Owain.*

And Charlie Videau? Well, one doesn't fall in love with one's brother now, does one?

"Goodness," she said, thinking of Traveler's statement concerning her safety—in front of the now-defunct white slavery business. "It'll be a long, long while before I forget any of this—"

Traveler interrupted her. "Still one item more to reveal to you," he said.

"What? I have no prophetic feelings. You have a surprise? What is it?"

He signaled to a man waiting in the darkness, one of the "marines." Even by ship's lamplight, Amanda saw the twinkle in Traveler's eyes.

Amanda refused to take part in Traveler's game, whatever it might be. Instead, she began to plan how she would find Timothy. She would hire a steamboat. Yes, that was it … a steamboat. Traveler would come along with her, and the search would undoubtedly take them to Florida. Traveler could bring his marines. They all would be safe.

"Traveler?" she said.

"Yes?"

"Why did Mother Patience give me the ring and everything else, as you say? Did she know about the bomb on the *Pulaskie?*"

"Certainly not. She only knew of the risks involved. There had been threats against your father. She told me, told all of us, that you could handle this job in time. She simply wanted to be with Joseph."

"There's no other reason?"

"None that I know of. Well, there is one." He smiled.

"That she loved me?"

"Yes."

And what of the courier Amanda had looked for through the years? In an instant of whimsical fantasy, she imagined herself queen and the courier awaiting her pleasure. Then she saw herself as a great stage actress with "Demon King" standing in the wings. He would enter her stage singing and dancing. For a moment, she dreamed she might even see the archangel Gabriel. He always showed up at the most important of times. He would tell her God's curses had been lifted long ago.

Perhaps my courier has been shot. If not, perhaps I shall shoot him myself.

Finally, in a moment of quiet reflection, Amanda no longer felt qualified to have a premonition. *What really would it mean to know the future?* She guessed that her Timothy could more than fill her dreams in that regard and scored the rest to a young girl's overactive imagination. *What good are dreams, anyway? If only I could find Timothy.*

A commotion on the stairway leading from the cabins below deck drew their attention. Presently, a small shadow of a man climbed out of the stairway.

It was Timothy Caldwell.

"We found him in Florida," said Traveler. "Do you know we—you—have people in Florida working in live-oaking? Well, you do. Live oak timbers make ships like Old Ironsides, the Constitution. Anyway, they found Timothy wandering around in the swamp accompanied by a horse, a nanny goat, and a child. I don't think he needs to be in the army anymore. But he will tell you about all of that. I'm sorry. I lied to you. We did escort him aboard. We have the child also. Your Bridget is with him right now."

Stunned, Amanda barely managed to say, "I don't believe it. What's next?"

Her thoughts began to spin. She remembered something that, like as not, she might have considered to be the most important life event to her.

Not anymore, however. Beau is, indeed, my father. Will wonders never cease?

The memory of that fact sparkled in her mind's eye. *God has blessed me again*, she thought. *First two fantastic mothers, then two fantastic fathers, and now Timothy. Thank you, Father God.*

She felt no sadness about Joseph. She just loved him …

And she fainted … for the first time in her life.

Chapter 101

God's Rainbow
Timothy, Onboard the
Frances Courtney

Amanda Worsham
October 1839
At sea

AMANDA AWOKE FROM HER FAINTING spell with a start. Traveler was slapping her wrists, trying to rouse her.

"Where is he ... where is *my* Timothy?" she mumbled. There was a blanket draped over her legs. "Good grief, man, what happened? Did I faint?"

"Indeed, you did," Traveler answered, rocking back to his knees. "I was afraid it was something more. But now you're awake. All is well with the world, it seems. We put young Timothy in the small cabin next to yours. He is fine, I think he is only very tired. Too much excitement, maybe.

* * * * *

Worried about him, Amanda headed for Timothy's cabin. She woke him when she knocked at the door.

It is strange, she thought. *A few days ago, I never wanted to think of poor Timothy again. And for a time, I thought he was dead. Now there is little else on my mind. But what can I do? I can't ask him to marry me.*

As Timothy shook the sleep from his eyes, she took his hands and studied his dear face for several long moments.

God, she thought, *Timothy, you are such a beautiful human being. And I thought Father was the best there ever was. But you are the best. Decidedly shorter and darker, but far more handsome.*

Timothy was still dressed in the clothes he wore when Amanda first saw him stumble out of the staircase from below decks.

"Amanda," he said, "I feel I never really knew you before …"

Emotion filled his eyes, and several tears fell to his cheeks. He stopped speaking for a moment, looking deeply into her eyes.

"Amanda, I never understood my feelings, either."

Amanda blotted his tears away with her kerchief. "Come with me, Timothy Caldwell," she said.

She pulled him into the corridor and led him to the front of the ship. They stood there in the darkness, arms entwined, for several minutes, saying nothing, a cool mist bathing their faces. Both felt a calm that oftentimes one only experiences on the bow of a sailing ship running *with the wind.*

Almost as a prayer, Amanda began thinking deeply about her Timothy.

With God's help, we will meet the future He's spread out before us. All we must do is this: we must work together, aligned with God's plan. Two hearts melded as one are stronger for this task than one alone could ever be. And aligning with God is the only way I can go. I must somehow take Timothy with me. But only Timothy can manage that.

Amanda held her ruby and diamond ring, the ring that Patience had given her, up to the light of a nearby lantern.

"You see the red and the white here on this ring? All that is left to complete the setting is the blue … the blue of the sea, the navy blue. They represent the colors in the flag that flies above the stern of the *Frances Courtney.* Mother was English, but I am certain she would understand. It's the flag they call Old Glory, you know."

"But, Amanda," Timothy said, "don't you care about the British Union Jack? That was your father's flag, wasn't it? Those colors are on that flag too. Red … white … blue … these colors all look gray to me. The truth is, Amanda, I am color-blind. But Mother Patience and Traveler told me you have lavender-blue eyes."

Amanda looked beyond the rail into the darkness. "Yes," she replied, "I have Mother to thank for that too."

Color-blind … what else about you don't I know? He has no notion of what lavender-blue means.

Then she pointed to the North Star. "You see that star just beyond the tip of the Big Dipper? That's a white star. Surely you can see that."

"Yes."

"That's where my destiny lies. There … in the North. In years past, part of my family left the Virginia colony to escape the Revolutionary War. 'No taxation without representation.' That slogan became the colonists' call to arms.

"The other part of my family, the French part, fought the British in Charleston. You see, I have only just learned that Beau Videau is my real father. I am a Videau. And some men in his family, my family, died in Charleston in the first war with England. We fought that stupid second war with England along those same lines, a small rogue nation pitted against strong Mother England. In a sense, it was states' rights all the same.

"The truth is, Americans just don't like being governed under a strong central authority. And now the South is balking bitterly against punitive tariffs legislated against them. It's states' rights, you see. They'll fight for states' rights. I think they really don't give a damn about anything else." *War … war … war. Joseph even told me his Uncle Matt died at Trafalgar with Lord Nelson.*

"But, Amanda," Timothy interjected, "there's no war coming."

"Oh yes, there is. I can see the first skirmish coming within a decade or so. There's no way the South will give up its states' rights. No way, indeed. And all the fuss about slavery, slave states, and free states. That situation is only symptomatic of the real problem. The South considers there would be secession decision, whether to own slaves legally or no, as their sovereign states' right. Something they signed on to when they signed the Constitution in the first place. It's a matter of principle, you see. Some want strong, central government. Others want to see more power given to the individual states."

"You really believe there will be a war?"

"There's little anyone can do to stop it, I fear. There's talk of South Carolina's secession from the Union. The things they've fought over in Congress for years—things like slavery, tariffs, tax nullification, the division of Virginia into two states and the like will be well settled by the North in about a fortnight following any secession.

"The Carolinas, and the other states that might break away, won't be there to vote against whatever law the North desires.

"But I digress." *No need to trouble poor Timothy with all of this. I really should let him speak, but ...*

"And slavery?" she continued, back again on her bandwagon. "England is patrolling the sea-lanes with its warships. They have outlawed slavery ... slavers bringing people in chains from Africa in slave ships. Only smugglers and pirates carry slaves now. Since few new slaves are arriving from Africa, the value of slaves on hand has increased.

"But England bought off her plantation slave owners in 1834—so much capital, they offered something like twenty million pounds sterling, I believe, to the plantation owners *en masse* for the slaves that were freed. And now the American South will expect similar treatment from the American North, don't you see? There were problems with that arrangement for England, indeed, and for a long time."

The "best-laid schemes o' mice an' men gang aft a-gley" to quote Robert Burns, she thought. *The best-laid plans of mice and men often go awry.*

God. That old Scot's dialect is heavy—worse even than German or Dutch.

"South Carolina is watching the Republic of Texas, which is being courted for statehood as we speak. Texas is the bride-to-be, as it were. First Texas manipulates for annexation, then she withdraws the offer. Having done that, Texas enjoys a good negotiation position for her future attempt at annexation. The thinking is that South Carolina, and any separated group of Southern states, would be courted in the Texas fashion following secession. It's all greed—greed and arrogance. Listen, I'm no monument to historical knowledge—"

"I know nothing of Texas's annexation," Timothy said. "But I've heard talk of a fort called the Alamo. The Seminole speak of it in wonder, at the bravery, at the Big Medicine—enough to fight to the death, the foolishness, and the Sweet Medicine to stand in one place and wait for the inevitable."

"Medicine? The Alamo, you say?" Amanda said with a start. "South Carolina needs the kind of healing that comes with more time on one's knees and through careful reflection and soul searching. South Carolina doesn't need any Alamos and fights to the death. It would be far easier to work within the politics of the thing. And I hate politics," she added.

"Politics bores me, Amanda. Enough of this troubling talk. Let's change to a lighter topic. Are you going on to Liverpool now?"

"Yes, I am." *Whew! Thanks for changing the subject.* "Most of the money I have is there. After Liverpool, we will return to New York. But there's enough money in the banks in Philadelphia to begin to prepare for the war. Railroads or railways, steel mills, textile mills. Things Father would have had his hand in if he were here."

"And you'll be doing these things all by yourself?"

"I've a four-year-old boy and girl to raise. I'll do whatever I must."

"Twins? Are they yours?"

"No, they were fathered by Hollis Mackenzie. They're brother and sister, right enough, but not twins, and no, they aren't mine. Cassie Mae Johnson's mother was a slave girl named Arabella. Joseph Worsham Mackenzie is my sister Sarah Jean's child. Hollis sired both at about the same week. I'm raising them, and I love both dearly. My children will not be punished because of Hollis Mackenzie's sins. But I certainly do have my hands full."

Timothy fell silent.

"There is a storm brewing," Amanda said. "In many ways, it will be a fury the likes of which this country has not yet seen. People will be afraid England will get involved, but I know better. Slavery is hated there as much as I hate it here—*by some, anyway.* England needs the South's cotton, but cotton can be grown elsewhere."

"You were born in Charleston, weren't you?" Timothy asked.

"Yes, I am an American, but my ancestors were British and French. Now, especially at this time, I must remain and help the United States. I will never forsake the United States or England. Somehow, in my heart, they are the same. Just how that will play out, only God knows."

Amanda turned to stroll slowly toward the front of the ship, away from the lanterns, away from the light. Timothy followed her into the darkness.

"To bring war to this country over states' rights, well, slavery is the most despicable thing I can imagine. There is no way the South can break away from the North and form a separate country. Why, that would result in two countries too weak to survive any other powerful country's interference."

When Amanda reached the forward railing, she turned to grasp Timothy's hands.

"The coming tempest will rain death and destruction on those who are foolish enough to unleash it," she said. "Just as it says in the Bible. When that happens, I want to be far to the North and safe in a house built upon a rock. Maybe I'll be able to help this country survive. God never intended for His people to be sold into bondage, and that certainly includes the Negroes."

Amanda closed her eyes, seeing in her mind's eye the shadowy image of what was coming.

"The plantation system of the South is built upon a sandy place, Timothy. The wealth, the years of gathering, the way of life for those who suck their pleasure from the misery of others will soon dissolve, as surely as a sandcastle dissolves in a rising tide."

"I love America, too, Amanda. What can I do to help you?"

"Traveler tells me you had a child with you when you were found. Tell me about that."

Timothy looked off into the distance. "There was a Gypsy woman, a friend of the Seminole people, who took care of me when

I was wounded, when I didn't know who I was. I slept with her. She had my child. His name is Juan Carlos. He is three years old."

"A Caldwell then."

"What do you mean?"

"He's a Caldwell, Willard Caldwell's grandson."

"I suppose he is … I never thought about that."

"Could be there's much you never thought about, Timothy."

Chapter 102

Timothy Proposes Marriage

Amanda Worsham
October 1839
At sea

NEAR WHERE THE LIFEBOATS STOOD lashed in place awaiting steadfastly their time, should it ever come, of panicked seamen and frantic fingers, the two lovers paused. For now, all was quiet save the whistling of the wind through the ship's rigging.

Two bells—the ship's bell sounded quickly, decisively. One hour into the midwatch.

"It's after midnight, Timothy. Those bells ... I believe it's one a.m.," Amanda said, yawning playfully. "Time to put you to bed."

"But what should I do, Amanda?" Timothy leaned against the railing. "I mean about my life, about young Juan Carlos and everything else."

Come on, Timothy. Snap out of it. "I should think that would be obvious."

"Go back to West Point and finish?"

"With a child?"

"I could make arrangements ... if I had the money. My life is such a mess."

"No, Timothy, your life is fine ... just fine. But there is something that only you can do."

448

"What? Anything."

"*Marry* me. But first you simply must find yourself." *Oh, my dear! Find yourself!*

There will be time in the weeks to come to find out about the army and Timothy's military responsibilities. I said it … marry me!

"Now. No, tomorrow!"

Timothy looked away for a moment, then took her into his arms. "I thought I'd lost everything, Amanda. I thought I'd lost you. I remember a shooting star I saw once in the swamps of Florida and the wish I made."

"What was the wish, Timothy?"

"That if I ever had the chance again, I would never let you go."

"Is that a *yes*?"

"Please marry me, Amanda. I don't want to go the rest of the way without you. There was a time when I felt the only way I could marry you was if I could support you. I've given up on that notion. I've absolutely nothing to offer you but myself … and a stepson named Juan Carlos."

"I'll take it," she said, laughing. "And, Timothy." She twirled about, making her dress swell out at the hem, petticoats all showing. "Oh, do I have a surprise for you," she said, thinking of the million dollars or so waiting in the bank for Timothy that Mother Patience had willed to him.

"Traveler," she called out into the darkness instead of mentioning Timothy's wealth.

A voice answered from the darkness, "The commander's gone below, ma'am." It was the same "marine" from before. He was still on watch.

"Go wake Traveler, and tell him to find a cabin for this man. He is my betrothed as of tonight."

"Aye, ma'am. He's not sleeping but awaiting your betrothal announcement. I think he knew it was coming."

Overhead, a shooting star streaked across the night sky, and they both saw it.

"Make a wish, Timothy," said Amanda, laughing.

"I already did."

"I'll bet I know what your wish was."

Timothy joined in her laughter.

There was no way the premonition, however realistic, of a coming war could dampen their joy and love. Timothy must have gotten his second wind, she thought, as he danced a jig around her when Traveler came to show him to his cabin.

She had whispered to him, "Give me maybe thirty minutes to get ready, then come quietly to my cabin. There'll be no latch on the door."

* * * * *

Timothy left her cabin early the next morning, saying he wished to talk to the captain … something about the ship's heading. Amanda thought it an example of the little boy she envisioned inside Timothy wanting to come out and play ships, captains, and the like.

She stayed behind to talk with Arabella and Bridget. The twin bunk, something very much like a sleigh bed, needed attention. The bedclothes, sheets, blankets were in disarray. When Bridget shook the covers to tidy up, two sets of undergarments—one Amanda's, one Timothy's—fell to the cabin floor. The three young ladies looked at each other and giggled, realizing what it meant.

"It's about time," Arabella and Bridget said as they left to fetch clean linens.

About time, indeed, thought Amanda.

Her family responsibilities, her entourage, had grown to three children, a fiancé, and two gentle female employees.

It was about time. It was also about circumstance and human frailty.

She would raise her children under the United States flag.

What would the future bring? The answer will just have to wait until another day, she thought.

Chapter 103

Amanda Sees Her Prayers Answered

Amanda Worsham
October 1839
At sea

AMANDA RAISED THE LID OF the wooden trunk covered with water-proof painted canvas that stood at the foot of her bed. Surprised, she found that Bridget had packed the kaleidoscope Joseph had brought back from Manchester years before when he'd returned to Bermuda after burying Frances. It was positioned carefully to one side of the top tray.

What is this? she thought. *Providence?*

She picked it up to study it for a moment, turning it over in her hands. Pointing it toward the brightly lit ship's window, she could see the colors inside, all blues, blue white, and clear crystal. She remembered Joseph's fascination with the Courtney lavender-blue eyes.

That was it.

Suddenly Amanda knew why the thing had saddened her so long ago. There were no warm colors in it. There wasn't even a green-colored stone inside the custom-made device. The blue, white, and clear stones were at once beautiful and sad, emitting a coldness that only a child who had just lost her mother could feel.

Well, she thought, *I'll fix this. I'll send it along to the toy maker or jeweler whenever I can. It simply must have warm colors inside to break the light into the fanciful and beautiful warm designs. It could be pieces of Bavarian crystal or rare stones—whatever. Shards of ordinary glass in proper colors could lend perspective to the viewer as well as could the finest of jewels.*

Her children must view life in the best way possible, if only through a kaleidoscope.

Alone in her cabin, she glanced up at the beautiful vaulted ceiling, crafted of a dark and resinous hardwood with inlaid marquetry along the sides. Closing her eyes, she imagined the ceiling was the wide expanse of stars one could see from the ship's forward deck in the middle of the Atlantic at midnight. She could see the Great Bear constellation that Captain Bob had said he used as a sort of calendar. And there were others—star groups that moved across the sky and marked the passing of the months, the seasons. She saw a shooting star in her mind's eye. She missed Captain Bob and wished him well in retirement, "half pay" as he called it. She vowed to inquire about him.

She spoke softly as if she were talking to God. "Heavenly Father," she said, her eyes tightly closed, "Almighty I AM THAT I AM. I think maybe You and I have some work to do. Slavery simply must be stopped. You'll help … that's true, isn't it? I think maybe the name I AM THAT I AM might imply the same message as does the word *PATIENCE.*"

When she opened her eyes, she began her new life. For one thing, she must find Patience's secretary. She had to find out about this ring—*cœur de rubis, ruby heart—Patience had given her. What did it mean? And the brooch she mentioned. How about that?*

She quite suddenly remembered that Mother Patience had an odd way of speaking about her writing bureau.

She called it her secretary and would say something like, "You'll find those letters over with my secretary."

So. Maybe the mystery was becoming clearer. But whatever that piece of furniture in Mother Patience's Boston townhouse held, it would just have to wait for another time.

Amanda experienced the first glimmer of insight into this Ruby Heart business. Mother Patience had taken it upon herself to try to change the future … to try to change the government. And the truth was, she had grown tired of it and longed to pass the mantle along to someone.

That someone is me, thought Amanda.

And whenever the changeover came about—if, indeed, it ever did—Ruby Heart's new persona would be working toward an end to slavery. People such as Moss Moonie and others who risked everything to help runaways escape to freedom needed help. They needed confederation, leadership, and resources.

Maybe they need me. Patience often spoke of the new "railroads." Well, the Underground Railroad will need, and will receive, my help. Indeed.

She thought of her mother. *Frances would certainly be proud. And I think she would approve of what I am doing as well. "Waste not want not," she'd said from time to time about money. So I will be frugal with her money, with Father's money, with Patience's money. Whew …*

Now, she thought, *I must choose my wedding dress from the items Bridget packed for me. Of course, we had no idea I would be married on this trip. Who did?*

She looked upward as if she were looking through the ceiling of the cabin, as though the ceiling were transparent.

Oh yes, You knew, didn't You, Almighty God?

In her mind's eye, she could see the entire expanse of night sky.

Almighty God gave her no answer, but she was not troubled by that. She felt a warm sensation inside, in her very being, and she had only peace in her heart.

* * * * *

Bridget surprised Amanda with a Celtic wedding dress that belonged to herself—her *hope chest* wedding dress. She had brought the simple, but beautiful, light-blue garment along … just in case one of them, Bridget or Amanda, would need it someday. Amanda was but a tad smaller than Bridget, so it needed only a few alterations. Perhaps Bridget had had a premonition of her very own.

Timothy, still in the army, wore his military uniform. Bridget was the maid of honour, as it is said in Ireland. Bridget not only provided the Celtic blue wedding dress, but she had a Celtic porcelain horseshoe, a Claddagh ring, two Irish wedding bells, and a short piece of red, green, black, and gold-plaited rope—something especially for the Irish, Celtic knot. She showed the two lovers how to clasp their hands, one above the other, with the rope to form the four-handed Celtic knot. Amanda had Frances Courtney's engagement ring and wedding band in her jewelry chest. But she felt it was important to humor Bridget, so she wore the Celtic wedding band. What was it, *Claddagh*, or something like that? Miss Bridget was a treasured friend. Amanda would keep the Celtic things always.

Goodness, thought Amanda, *my life surely is something.*

Traveler was the best man and vowed to repair Timothy's military career. He, and perhaps now Amanda, had all the right connections in Washington. Time would tell.

About noon Amanda was ready, and the ship's captain was happy to "marry" the two lovers. It turned out that Traveler, as always, had planned for this event well. Captain Tom Beale was also an ordained Methodist minister—a man who had given up the cloth for a seafaring life.

"By golly," Captain Tom Beale said, "there's a first time for everything: first time for you two to get married and the first time I ever performed such a ceremony at sea. Maybe I'm a bit rusty. We'll see."

The ceremony he performed was short but biblical in nature. When he had finished, he paused for a moment and said, "I now pronounce you man and wife.

"Now, Lieutenant, please kiss the bride. And may God bless you both, and bless you with *fair winds and following seas*—which means, in your life's journey, may you have the very best weather conditions, and may you always go with the tide."

Amanda added, "And give us children," to the captain's blessing.

She paused, admiring her husband. Then she danced in a circle with Timothy.

Afterward, she turned to Captain Tom and said, "Now, take us on to Bermuda. We need a short stay-over there. I've business to take care of before we go on to Liverpool. I hope you are agreeable, short notice and everything."

"Yes, ma'am. Traveler has already briefed me about the special nature of this trip."

"Special, indeed," she responded to a round of applause from her entourage: Traveler and most of her crew who'd all gathered around.

Amanda's new life had begun. There was "Irish" dancing with every one and all, the same as if it were Saint Patrick's Day.

Miss Bridget informed them that according to Irish tradition, "If in October you do marry, love will come but riches tarry. At least it is a Tuesday," she said, laughing, "and wealth will follow."

All clear in front of Irish Celtic mores and traditions, thought Amanda, smiling. *I really do love Miss Bridget.*

And I have seen my prayers answered.

Epilogue

Moses Gets the Last Word

Let us hear the conclusion of the whole matter: Fear God, and keep his commandments: for this is the whole *duty* of man.
—Ecclesiastes 12:13, KJV

Chapter 104

The End of the Beginning
Moses, Reminiscing, Watches
the Flirt Sail Away

Moses's ward
October 1839
Bermuda

ON THE STONY RISE BESIDE Saint George's harbor in Bermuda, Moses stood watching the robust hundred-forty-ton sailing ship *Flirt* clear the last reef far out on the azure sea. Bright canvas sails filled with the morning breeze as she picked up speed. She was true to her namesake, as she seemed to lean and slip upon the waves, dancing, rejoicing, as she raced for Atlantic blue water.

Moses and Sally were visiting friends who lived nearby in a white, stepped-roof pink house, one of many new and colorful Bermuda cottages. Sure, Moses helped Francis Peniston build the *Flirt*. Crafted mostly of Bermuda cedar, the *Flirt* was a wonderful ship. Moses was master class in his shipbuilding skills and very much in demand. Builders of the new Bermuda Clippers valued Moses's skills.

Now the *Flirt* was beginning her maiden voyage, and Moses was pleased with his handiwork. For wherever the winds took the beautiful *Flirt*, squeezed between the close fit of her cedar boards would be oil from his fingers, the sweat of his brow, and tears of joy from his cheeks.

Moses always worked hard. It was no secret that sometimes warm tears graced his labors. Freedom was a wonderful blessing, and the past seven years had been especially pleasant. In 1836, James Athill, a freeman of color and a successful shipbuilder, finished *London Packet*, a particularly beautiful brigantine. In 1837, it was the hundred thirty-one-ton schooner, *Agnes*. Each was a special accomplishment for Bermuda's freemen of color. When the *Agnes* danced her turn upon the waves and her sails filled for the maiden voyage, Moses had laughed out gleefully.

"Well, Miss *Agnes*, you got all the linens out blowing in the breeze today."

Now it was *Flirt* that was free, and so was Moses. He had been freed, along with his wife in 1834, the year of emancipation in the British Empire. But Moses knew that Miss Manda really freed them much earlier than that. She'd freed them when Miss Frances died, in 1826, and they had the freeholder papers to prove it. And to go with his papers, he had a Certificate of Good Character from the vestry of Saint George's. He felt in his heart that he was, indeed, somebody.

I know, he thought. *Miss Manda always said it was so. But it's different, somehow, when you earn it. Heh-heh-heh. Not too long ago I would have said "earns it," don't you know?*

Moses and Sally adopted six children of color. It was a wonderful new juncture in their lives. Again, tears of delight ran over his cheeks. His heart would go with the *Flirt*—as would his prayers—wherever she would go. Moses lived now in Bermuda with his beloved Sally and their adopted children. He watched until the *Flirt* dipped below the glass horizon, then turned, and started the long walk home.

"Almighty God, I sure do love You," he said, a big smile on his face. Moses's education could clearly be heard in his voice these days.

And You know what, Lord? I love Miss Amanda too. I sure do. I can't wait until I see her again. And I hope and pray that it's very soon.

"She's on the way, old son, she's on the way ... "

Moses just knew ... didn't hear.

Epilogue

And All the Rest Is Vanity

About the Author

The author, William Hite, was born in the 1930s in the beautiful, subtropical state of South Carolina where much of his novel, *Sandcastles, Tall Ships, and Vanities* takes place. He is the eldest brother to his sister, Mary Elizabeth, and his brother, Edgar, born to William Hite Sr. and Mary Worsham Hite. William used his mother's maiden name as the surname of his main character, Amanda Worsham, in honor of his mother. Mary Worsham Hite was a long-standing member of the Daughters of the American Revolution. The Hite family attended church regularly and instilled Christian values in their home. After graduating from Marion High School, William graduated from the University of Texas in El Paso before enlisting in the United States Army. William has been married to his longtime love, Patty Jo, and they each brought four children to their marriage for a combined family of eight children, fourteen grandchildren, and four great-grandchildren. They enjoy traveling together and spending time with their families. William enjoys reading, writing, and playing the guitar.